THE ULTIMATE CONSPIRACY

Europe's top political figures are the targets of a master assassin.

A former secret agent is called in to lead the investigation.

And soon, the whole world will feel the shockwaves of a deadly campaign beyond terrorism . . .

Brutal. Chilling. Explosive. Edgar Award nominee Roland Cutler presents his most suspenseful thriller—a devastating journey into the world of modern espionage and high-powered intrigue . . .

TO KILL A KING

Praise for Roland Cutler's thrillers:

"Powerful . . . suspenseful . . . bizarre and chilling!"
—*West Coast Review of Books*

"Political intrigue . . . corruption and treachery!"
—*Publishers Weekly*

TO KILL A KING

ROLAND CUTLER

BERKLEY BOOKS, NEW YORK

TO KILL A KING

A Berkley Book/published by arrangement with
the author

PRINTING HISTORY
Berkley edition/December 1987

All rights reserved.
Copyright © 1987 by Roland Cutler.
This book may not be reproduced in whole or in part,
by mimeograph or any other means, without permission.
For information address: The Berkley Publishing Group,
200 Madison Avenue, New York, N.Y. 10016.

ISBN: 0-425-10412-5

A BERKLEY BOOK® TM 757,375
Berkley Books are published by The Berkley Publishing Group,
200 Madison Avenue, New York, NY 10016.
The name "BERKLEY" and the "B" logo are trademarks
belonging to Berkley Publishing Corporation.

PRINTED IN THE UNITED STATES OF AMERICA
10 9 8 7 6 5 4 3 2 1

To my wife Ruth,
who climbed all the
mountains with me.

PARIS

It began with something small and insignificant, like the first whisper that destroys a career. But it provided them with an insight. Before Paris, there had been only a suspicion, a loose linkage of facts that could have spilled in any direction. Paris gave them an imprint, as clear and definable as a signature chiseled into stone. Now only the quarry remained a question. There was no longer any doubt about the hunter.

1

Ahmed knew he was being hunted.

The whisper spread its undercurrent of terror through the bazaars and street markets of St. Oeun, like the filthy water that washed its gutters. They were searching for him, slender men with swarthy faces, dark Arab faces like his own. They would deliver his death.

It was unclear exactly who had made the decision, in what dark room hands had been raised and the question settled. The geniuses at the Special Bureau knew only that the exact hour of the boy's death had been established long before, carefully penciled into the empty pages of the executioners' date book.

"Ahmed, be afraid," voices warned. He heard it whispered in all the shops and cafés, heard it everywhere that dismal morning, even from the terrified lips of his mother, who had roughly shaken him out of bed. But Ahmed never truly believed the danger, not until the very end when even the faces in the bazaars closed against him like steel shutters. Yet the terror was there, its imprint clearly stenciled on the features of his handsome face. Lines drawn with the tension that marked his final hours.

Everyone agreed Ahmed was a clever boy and should have known better. Especially after a month of photographing the Russian, a month of careful maneuvering that peeled away all the secret layers of Kirov's existence and should have signaled a danger of its own. But in spite of his ability with a camera, Ahmed was still a boy in many ways and believed himself invulnerable. He never truly understood that his murder was a distinct possibility. Not until those final terrifying moments was there any comprehension on his part that he was as much a target as the quarry he stalked.

So he did not flee but continued on his normal rounds, his only precaution the small Belgian automatic hidden beneath the dashboard of his expensive Italian car. He left the two dismal rooms he shared with his mother and three younger brothers and went to the café on the Rue Belliard. There he sipped a syrupy Turkish coffee and joined the other voices disputing in Arabic the merits of various teams contending for the World Cup. He paid a visit to his pudgy tailor where an expensive velour jacket was being carefully remodeled to the current fashion. He drove in to see Ali, the Moroccan mechanic he trusted to look after his Lancia. He was living in a world of perfect disbelief.

Yet there was ample reason for Ahmed to know why he was being hunted. This became evident later, when the dark emissaries of the Special Bureau completed their meticulous investigation. The whisper of his betrayal was now a fact. Ahmed had seen terror in the eyes of those he trusted and knew. But even these warnings were ignored, the way he often ignored other pressing, but often unpleasant, matters that crowded in upon the more pleasurable aspects of his life. It was a trait his mother often berated him for, a trait that chiseled deep lines of worry into her already troubled brow.

Had he lived, Ahmed might have changed; after all, he was only twenty-three. But the cynics at the Special Bureau doubted that. Still, they were grateful for his death, for it provided them with an important link, although that was only verifiable much later on. " 'Yea, and a child shall lead them,' " someone in the Bureau commented wryly, and in a way, that was Ahmed's final legacy.

In truth, Ahmed dreamed of escape. But where could he go? He had entered France illegally. He had no valid passport. To purchase a decent forgery in these days of careful border inspections would take more money than he had, money he could obtain only after he had completed his assignment and finished photographing the Russian. He had to hold out until then. And so until that moment arrived, Ahmed took refuge in fantasy and dreamed about the boots.

His heart ached for those boots. He had been dreaming of them for weeks. He had seen them displayed in a fashionable shop on the Rue Rivoli and hungered to possess them. By afternoon, when the car was ready, he had made the decision to buy them. Besides, he was safe on the Rue Rivoli. Within the shop's plate-glass and chromium glitter, he could relax the persistent knot of worry.

The boots became his opiate. In them he would defy his murderers. In truth, they were gorgeous boots, irresistible boots, with pointed toes encased in silver and floral designs embossed in genuine crocodile skin. The boots brought dreams of Los Angeles and New York, places in which he would find refuge and achieve a final glory.

Ahmed paid for the boots in cash, which took the starch out of the salespeople and even got Ahmed the attention of the snobbish manager, who forced his own crocodile smile when Ahmed left the shop. Cash was how he got paid for photographing the Russian, and cash was how he liked to pay, spooling off the dollars he especially loved from an eighteen-carat-gold money clip he had purchased at an open-air stand on the Rue des Rosiers.

But this was not the flea market. The establishment on the Rue Rivoli catered to rock stars and oil sheikhs, which the manager undoubtedly thought he was. It gave Ahmed special pleasure to lean back against the velour upholstery and watch the shop girls scurrying on his behalf, bringing boxes of tasseled loafers for his inspection. They were pretty girls with well-shaped legs and small, tight bottoms who responded to the flirtatious glances he darted from beneath long, dark eyelashes. Ahmed was vain about his good looks, a fact he confirmed by repeated glances in the highly polished mirrors that completed the shop's ostentatious decor.

He stretched, wriggling his toes and yawning with pretended boredom, as he studied his meticulously polished nails. He caught a glimpse of his handsome face in one of the wall mirrors and unconsciously patted the mass of curly black locks above his dark, dramatically curving eyebrows.

"Monsieur?"

One of the salesgirls was standing in front of him, eyebrows raised expectantly. Ahmed brought his gaze toward the cordovan loafers encased in their cardboard box like identical sleeping Pharaohs. He studied the gleaming leather for an instant, then shook his head in the negative. The girl smiled a regret. The glance she shot him was filled with limitless possibilities. Ahmed returned her smile. He seldom missed with women.

Ahmed had learned much in the three years he had lived in Paris. Money erased all distinctions, even the dark color of his skin and the Semitic profile most Frenchmen despised. Because of the Russian, money was flowing his way again. He had just suffered through a short, dry period primarily caused by his having to lie low during one of the repeated flare-ups that broke out between rival factions of Fatah, the

TO KILL A KING

Palestinian umbrella organization that counted him as a member and now sought his death.

Ahmed had never placed his loyalty permanently. Only a fool did that. Ahmed considered himself a soldier of fortune. Over the years he had been employed by one or another of the rival groups that made up the PLO, switching allegiances as easily as he switched clothing styles. At the moment he favored the Syrian brand of resistance over Arafat's bungling leadership. But who could tell how long that might last? Situations changed. In order to survive, a man must change with them; so his credo went. It was a credo he espoused nightly to his mother and three younger brothers, all of whom depended upon his agility in maneuvering between the various rivalries for their support. But now there was no allegiance he could count on. No power offered its arm of protection to the helpless boys he would leave behind.

His mother, of course, had been pleased at his new assignment. She considered it a step up. It had taken him safely away from the internecine warfare conducted by his onetime allies and found employment for his considerable talents as a photographer, which she hoped one day he would safely become. After all, it was a family occupation, she often boasted. Ahmed's father had owned a small photography studio in Nablus before they fled to Tyre, where Ahmed had grown up and where he had learned his trade before the Israeli invasion forced his family's move to Paris.

So Ahmed took the pictures. Secretly, of course. The Russian knew nothing so far. He was predictable and unsuspecting. But then Ahmed had played the game well and knew all the intricate maneuvers of deception. His victims usually suspected nothing, not until they turned on their car radios and were blown into dust that only an angel of Allah could recover.

But in the last few days Ahmed had begun to realize his prey was about to slip away. The Russian was making arrangements for travel. Ahmed had reported his observations and had been told to keep on, as if nothing had happened.

He would follow the Russian to Cannes. Of that Ahmed had no doubt. After all, the Russian was in the motion picture business, wasn't he? At least, that was his cover. And that was where all the motion picture types went at that time of year. He would be safe in Cannes, and the thought instilled a special moment of comfort.

The thought of half-naked starlets displaying themselves around the edges of an ice-blue pool had inflamed Ahmed's imagination. After all, he was young and good-looking. His clothes came from the best shops. His custom-fitted shirts were made of pure silk and embroidered with his initials. He owned a Rolex and a pair of Gucci loafers. What more could they ask for?

"And if they do not send you to Cannes, what then?" his mother admonished, waving a handful of unpaid bills in front of his face. "Who will pay these?" Well, he was no fool. He had been careful to prepare a second set of negatives and knew where he could get a good price for them. Ahmed had learned long ago that if someone was willing to pay a price for something, there was always someone else who would also pay. He sensed that the Russian would be worth a great deal.

Ahmed never saw the man who ran him. He took orders from a telephone voice. He was contacted by phone and in turn made his reports from various pay phones around the city. The voice on the other end gave his instructions, and Ahmed followed them. He left the pictures in specified places and picked up an envelope filled with cash. The arrangement suited him. He had little curiosity about knowing more. People with the gift of curiosity often wound up dead. Now his own life would depend upon it.

Ahmed left the shop two inches taller, elevated on the cantilevered heels of his new purchase. He walked around the block twice, checking the mirrors in the shop windows he passed for signs that he was being followed. But there was no one. He checked his watch. He had two hours before his next photo opportunity, as he liked to term them. The Russian took his midweek meals in a bistro on the Left Bank, just off the Boul Miche. Ahmed had plenty of time to visit the Bois.

He ducked into a *confiserie* and used the telephone. The woman he called was a Nordic blonde named Adrianne with blue eyes and platinum hair. She cruised the Bois in a white Porsche, making contacts with her customers over her car telephone, a purchase Ahmed planned to make with his next big installment. The combination of lust and technology always turned him on. But now he needed her in a different way. She would hide him for a few nights, of that he was sure. For money she would do anything.

Adrianne answered on the second ring. She was free until

TO KILL A KING

eight. They made an arrangement for six-thirty, which gave him a half hour to navigate the evening traffic.

The Lancia cruised through the now darkening boulevards. It had turned colder. Ahmed kept the top up. The car was already too recognizable. He should have turned it in for something less conspicuous, but he could not bear being parted from it. Besides, once he was on the road to Cannes, it would no longer matter. He would be safe.

Streetlights splintered the dusk with carbon arc brilliance, guiding him into the Etoile, now a tangle of traffic, then down the Avenue Foch and into the Bois itself. At this hour there was a quickening in the air that matched the quickening of his pulse. In spite of the menace he felt around him, the thought of Adrianne always made his blood boil. She was especially gifted at her profession, and he never minded paying the premium she asked for the services he demanded. He was enchanted by her sleek, impersonal manner. For him it epitomized the glamorous life he craved.

Ahmed turned into the park. He usually met Adrianne near Longchamps. The racetrack would be deserted, and there were plenty of places to be alone and undisturbed. He heard a sharp beep, and Adrianne's white Porsche slipped into the lane in front of him. He realized she must have been watching for him. He eased the car into the higher gear to follow her, catching a glimpse of her silvery mane in his headlights.

They sped back and forth along the serpentine curves. Ahmed liked the feel of the powerful engine. He was erect now, excited, craving sex and speed in equal doses. And Adrianne drove like a Valkyrie.

The Porsche slowed down. Ahmed put his foot on the brake and eased the Lancia into a lower gear and followed her between a dark plantation of trees into an unlit cul-de-sac he did not remember using before. Conifers loomed on either side, weaving their naked branches into a dark canopy overhead. Crystals of drizzle were collecting on the windshield. The Porsche slowed to a stop. The passenger door snapped open, inviting him. Ahmed braked and got out, slamming his door shut behind him, loving the rich sound of expensive metal. He walked toward the Porsche slowly, a splendor in his new boots.

He had started to slip inside the Porsche when the door crashed shut and the car roared away, screeching around his own car and back into the darkness of the road beyond, leaving only a blur of motion on his startled retina.

Stupefied, Ahmed took an involuntary step forward and stopped, eyes fixed on the dark figures slipping toward him through the trees.

It took a moment before the images took on shape and dimension, then meaning. Fear prompted him instinctively, moving him back toward the shelter of his car, to the gun hidden inside. But the men around him moved swiftly, professionally, cutting off his retreat, leaving no place for him to run. No place to escape.

He dodged around the car toward the trees. But his legs would not move. The boots weighed like iron. He cursed them now. They were stiff and inflexible, impossible to run in. They had become his doom.

Ahmed heard a tiny cry, like a terrified cat, realizing an instant later that it came from his own constricted throat. By then it was too late. The men were around him. He caught the sheen of light on their agile features, mirror images of his own.

Hands gripped his shoulders and forced him to his knees. His arms were twisted back painfully. Their eyes glittered with hatred. Their words were an assault on his ears, a harsh flow of Arabic.

Betrayer. Traitorous dog. Cursed of Allah.

A hand gripped his hair and twisted his head toward the weapon now raised in front of his face. Ahmed saw the dagger of light shimmering on wet steel, watched in fascination as the barrel turned toward him, swollen at the end with a fitted silencer. Then the immensity, the horror, of what they were about to do was torn from his lips in a cry of disbelief.

The shot and his scream came together, dying away quickly, deadened by the mist and the whispering shimmer of falling rain.

2

Rosensweig faced his fate.

Thirty feet ahead, the body lay in a patch of melting snow, arms twisted unnaturally, like the wings of a bird tortured by children. A white sports car badly in need of a wash stood alongside the victim, set off from the surrounding area by a border of string and red tags that flapped in the wind like the beating of summer wash.

A gathering of Sûreté professionals stood in a circle around the dead boy, stamping frozen feet against the icy ground. Rosensweig was a small man, huddled within a heavy overcoat, smaller than the men who parted to make a place for him with polite, but scornful, faces. They averted their eyes as Rosensweig came toward them on his uneven gait, pitching his sound leg ahead of the artificial one like a trawler towing a wreck. The leg had been lost in a war that was still undeclared, part of an operation no one remembered, its history contained in a still secret file now yellow and moldering with age.

Rosensweig shuddered as the wind speared his back. The morning was rank with drizzle. The sky hung like a sheet of filthy metal above the bare trees of the Bois. Fleets of discarded newsprint blew across muddy latitudes separating still shuttered pavilions that would open in early spring to serve nannies with bawling infants and tourists festooned with cameras. Now they were silent, mute witnesses to a winter that would not vacate, a spring that refused to warm. The sound of an occasional vehicle growled along the distant serpentine curves, struggling to beat the morning traffic into the central city.

Rosensweig barely nodded to the men around him. His face was an icon, silent and expressionless, a cold blueprint of suspicion. His small, tight mouth was flanked by deep shell pockets of scar tissue that marked either cheek. Only his eyes conversed, sweeping the terrain with the harsh, indelible accuracy of his unforgiving gaze.

Information was passed to him, whispered from chilled lips like confessions through a grating. The Arab had been shot through the left eye. Yet, even disfigured, he was still a pretty boy, blessed with an aquiline sensuality and glossy black locks. He was outfitted in the usual cheap flash, but the boots were a museum piece, American and expensive. And all the usual decor was intact. Heavy gold links clasped his wrist and looped like a sleeping serpent around the boy's delicate dark brown throat.

Rosensweig had glanced through the victim's file on the way down. The boy had been a bit of a whore, part of a small army of mercenaries who earned a sometimes lucrative living, providing dubious services to a slew of revolutions in exile. Paris was infested with the type.

Laughter splintered the silence, echoing like cannon shots across the barren ground. Rosensweig raised a drooping eyelid. The two men in sweat suits who had stumbled over the body during their customary morning jog were sharing coffee and a joke with two uniformed flics outside a distant police van that housed a mobile lab.

Rosensweig dug his fists into the worn material of his pockets. He had forgotten his gloves and scarf, in spite of the admonition of his housekeeper, or perhaps because of it. Madame Dessage was a harsh, reproving woman, but she was invariably correct. A chillness coiled around his chest and he coughed. She often called him perverse. Perhaps there was something perverse in his being there while other men his age were nestled beneath goose down, their backs up against warm female flesh. His own wife had been taken long ago. Her memory was an agony, securely bolted behind a door he never opened.

Official forms were produced, and Rosensweig scribbled his signature. The gesture itself was a benediction, relieving the Sûreté of any further responsibility. For better or worse, the bitter gift of jurisdiction was now his own.

Relief stitched itself through the faces around him, along with the bitter edge of spite. The spite he was used to. After all, he was a Jew first and a Frenchman only on sufferance. The present situation was his by right of inheritance.

The Sûreté viewed the spate of terrorist bombings and executions presently convulsing Paris as a visitation descending on France like a plague, threatening to undermine her people's confidence in their hereditary institutions. Plain and simple, it was a situation resulting from the refusal of that gang of stubborn kikes presently in power in Jerusalem and their imbecile belief that some parched acreage beyond the Jordan was theirs by right of biblical genealogy.

That situation was as distasteful to the Sûreté as the current regime, which had conjured men like Rosensweig out of exile and granted them its current favor. And yet the old fox was not fooled. Politics had nothing to do with it. Rosensweig knew the Sûreté was only too glad to turn the matter away. Political crimes were a bottomless swamp.

The motive for the Arab's killing resided in some impenetrable muck not of their comprehension—or of anyone else's for that matter. The boy had betrayed some loyalty or carried out some betrayal. It mattered little which. There would be no solution. His execution would concern no one but the mother who would grieve for him, believing all the grand stories he had painted about the next big deal that would provide stability, a shop, a living for boys younger and still innocent, who would quickly grow to provide Rosensweig with even more files. More *merde* to wade through.

Rosensweig gave them a receipt for the boy, and they handed him the Russian.

He materialized in a handful of pictures they had discovered beneath the spare tire in the car's trunk. Viewing them caused surprise to flicker like a tic in the old man's face. That in itself was a minor miracle, for it was a face that had experienced more than its share of the century's horrors.

The photos came together with a 35mm camera and a telephoto lens found hidden in the jackboot. The boy, it seemed, had a talent. There were about a dozen photographs, all mat enlargements, lovely snaps, clear and well lit. They caught their subject in the casual poses of someone unaware that he is being lensed.

Rosensweig pursed his lips to keep from saying the Russian's name aloud, reserving it as a private satisfaction. The young men around him would not have known it in any case. The Russian's celebrity existed in another age; only its remembrance was still preserved, like some rare butterfly, in Rosensweig's unforgiving memory.

He huddled over the grainy images like pages in the Talmud, forgetting the chill and the damp in his shoes, his attention focused on the handsome face staring out at him, a face older than the last time he had seen it. The mane of black hair now sported glimmers of gray, like bright rails of silver against the night. But the body had kept its tone, looking younger and trimmer than its forty-seven years. There was still a hint of flamboyance in the expensive tailoring, still a zest in the eyes. And sadness too. Far more than he remembered.

Rosensweig's tight lips dented sardonically as he viewed the Russian's arched eyebrows and artificial smile. It was an actor's face, all mirrors and sleight of hand. Nine years before, the Russian had belonged to a Moscow directive. Now he belonged to no one, not unless one counted Joyce, and of course, Joyce would have to be counted—that much was certain.

In a special sense the Russian belonged to Joyce the way Rosensweig belonged to the faces that stared out at him from their silver frames in the darkness of his apartment, their ashes scattered from chimneys in Treblinka and Sobibor. Joyce had tracked the Russian, marked him, netted him, and brought him over. The Russian owed his life to the bargain Joyce had made with the KGB. But Joyce was presently in Washington, shepherding the dying embers of his power. And Rosensweig had a dead Arab on his hands and a trunkful of pictures. And no language with which to create a meaning.

Rosensweig shuffled the pictures, edging them together into a neat pile in his hands. He turned and, without uttering a word, limped back to his Citroën, oblivious to the smirks of the Sûreté. He sought the embrace of the sedan's warm cushions as the car sped him through the mist-enshrouded boulevards of the awakening city.

The Russian was a commodity Rosensweig had not dealt with for a very long time. He tried to pry his mind away, to focus on the slew of matters waiting to fill his morning. But the Russian formed a persistent and annoying piece of geography that could not be avoided or removed.

Had Kirov been reactivated somehow . . . would they? Now, after all this time?

Like his lost leg, the image of the Russian would not disappear. It remained with him for the next few days, vandalizing his nervous system with nagging evidence of its existence. It became an invisible annoyance, a thorn that would not go away, a menace that might yet destroy them all.

3

If Rosensweig bore a silent burden of worry, he was not alone. It was a season for anxiety, sparked by events within the next seventy-two hours that temporarily erased the Russian from his brooding consciousness.

The first occurred in Rome, where a popular government minister was shot at point-blank range as he entered the Tiber-side apartment of his mistress, a well-known film star. The assassination shocked the government and became an arena for parlimentary recriminations.

Within twenty-four hours the former mayor of West Berlin and the leader of his party, the second largest in Germany, was blown to pieces along with his expensive Mercedes in the concrete bunker of an underground parking lot beneath the quiet streets of Bonn. The mayor was an immensely popular figure whose expressive features were familiar to millions. Shock, grief, and mourning followed, along with worldwide expressions of sympathy.

Less than a day later the kidnapping and execution of the Spanish ambassador to the Netherlands occurred, and his mutilated body was unceremoniously delivered to the Spanish embassy in the rear of a laundry truck, gory with blood and entrails.

The media went into a frenzy. The public was stunned. Several terrorist groups rushed to claim these killings, which at first seemed unrelated. Yet newspaper stories in all three European capitals indicated a suspicious link between the victims. All three were allegedly involved in forms of political maneuvering whose purpose was the installation of intermediate-range ballistic missiles on European soil. The editorials, later taken up by various media throughout the continent, conjectured that a new and deadly phase had begun in the opposition to nuclear proliferation.

The editorials wondered if the anti-proliferation movement, which had been peaceful up until then, was now entering the arena of terror. This question was given further support by a series of incidents directed against various NATO facilities: blown pipelines; incinerated storage areas; vandalized missile sites. More questions followed. But very few answers.

These stories were of course denied by the various governments involved. Other reasons for the deaths were put forth. A Mafia investigation, in the case of the Italian. Basque independence for the Spanish scenario. The German situation was confused, since the mayor had ostensibly supported the Greens, who were against the installation of the American missiles.

In any case, the various intelligence agencies involved were taken by surprise by the expertise of the terrorist operations. More disturbing was the depth of penetration the assassins had been able to achieve, in spite of the security measures employed to protect all three targets. It indicated the development of a whole new phase in the terrorist war, and that was reason enough for convening the inevitable security conference to which Rosensweig trudged like a dutiful husband called upon to perform on the night of an unwelcome anniversary.

The delegates met in Frankfurt, collecting in the small, steeply banked auditorium of a concrete structure, its anonymous fifties-style architecture now glaringly outdated.

The British came out in force, as did the Germans. The Italians had the next largest contingent, a well-tailored company who preened like impresarios after their recent success against the Red Brigades.

There was the usual mingling in the marble-floored lobby, after which the intelligence overlords filed inside, clumped by nationality and moated by gaps of empty seats. Only Joyce had been omitted, a signal of his current fall from grace. No one mentioned his absence, though his presence still inhabited the hall like some wayward spirit at a séance.

His absence made the old hands uneasy. With Joyce, they knew where they stood. He would have waded them through the official party line, given them the correct perspective. There were no miscalculations with Joyce. He played for the deeper view. A long-distance hauler, that was Joyce. Not one of your quick-change artists, tap-dancing for survival in the political vaudeville of changing administrations. Joyce was the absent quotient, and without him, many felt they were adrift on new seas, without sails or compass. And instead of Joyce, they got Stepinak.

The conference was chaired by a tall, magisterial Dutchman, but it was Stepinak who ran things. He was a bulky product of Slavic inbreeding, with watery blue eyes and impressive flesh, who illustrated his points with the aid of various electronic displays. And that, quite apart from everything else, was enough of a reason to want Joyce returned.

Joyce was not a computer man. Neither was he one of those frenzied holdouts still pounding away in some obscure attic on an old Remington. But he did oppose the almost fundamentalist devotion to machine analysis now pervading the corridors at Langley, and perhaps in that opposition lay the reason for his exile. There was a good deal of conjecture back and forth on the subject, but old hands, Rosensweig among them, knew that the reason for Joyce's exile lay in quite another direction.

Joyce was a threat to the new order of things. A damaging embarrassment and a thorn in the side of the new masters. Death to the seekers of unpopular truth was now the order of the day, and so old Joyce had to go. In the old Frenchman's colorful parlance, Joyce had become Galileo before the cardinals, his martyrdom divinely ordained.

So instead of Joyce, they got the ponderous Stepinak and the rest of his three-ring circus, consisting of enormous color blowups, detailed graphs, statistical diagrams, and piles of photocopied material, suitably bound in spiral plastic with color-coded sections. These were handed around by a trio of pretty females, dressed identically in three-piece pin-striped business suits, whose smiles were as perfect as they were impersonal.

Stepinak opened with a classical gambit.

"Gentlemen," he began in a colorless monotone. His tiny blue eyes seemed lost in his white doll's head, which seemed to roll across his shoulders without the support of a neck. "As you know, we are presently engaged in a final, desperate battle for the hearts and the minds of the people of Europe. A battle none of our governments can allow the Soviets to win."

Feet were shuffled. A throat was cleared.

"We are waging a war over missile sites and the future of the NATO alliance." He continued. "Not since the worst days of the Cold War have we faced such a threat. A threat made more critical by the presently wavering loyalties of the European population beneath the continuing bombardment of terrorist assault. The situation is now approaching crisis proportions."

Stepinak leaned forward, his voice filling with the self-righteous urgency of a witness before a congressional committee.

"For a while our counterattack had been successful, as many of your efforts attest too. But even as infiltrated and compromised as they are, many terrorist organizations have remained active in spite of continuous and aggressive efforts to stamp them out. They have, in fact, survived—and added a new and even more dangerous twist to their activities."

He paused and scanned the room from right to left with the precision of a television camera.

"Afraid to trust their own operatives because of the fear of defections and betrayal within their ranks, the leadership of these organizations have turned elsewhere for help. We have just witnessed evidence of this new form of aid, more dangerous, better organized, and more murderously effective than anything we have encountered before."

There was a general murmur of agreement when he paused, especially from the Germans. The British were silent, the Italians fidgety.

Rosensweig could not argue with Stepinak's analysis of renewed terrorist activity in Italy, or the German Red Army Faction, formerly known as the Beider-Meinhoff Gang. This activity had now spread into Belgium and north into Scandinavia. Before an opinion could crystallize, they were assaulted with rapid-fire images, controlled, Rosensweig realized, from a small device concealed in Stepinak's massive, but shapeless, fist.

Rosensweig, with Gallic skepticism for things technical, was less impressed than the three Germans who sat in the row below, making marveling little *ah*s each time the huge displays lit up in dazzling color.

Atrocities assaulted them. Aircraft wreckage. Derailed trains. Air-terminal bombings, followed by detailed photographic blowups of the recent assassinations.

Rosensweig half expected music, but the presentation was silent but for the names and dates of each incident and a rapid-fire analysis of the means employed to achieve the destruction. There was much crossing of legs and a general shuffling of shoe leather before the American spoke again. This time his reedy voice was amplified through a loudspeaker.

"These recent operations, though ascribed to various terrorist groups throughout Europe, have, in fact, not been carried out by these groups at all—or, for that matter, any of the organizations familiar to us. We have evidence of a new terrorist entity. An organization we have termed The Nucleus."

There were skeptical noises from the floor. But Stepinak ignored them, forging ahead like a ship against the waves.

"The Nucleus operates with complete independence, even from the organizations that initially set it in motion. Existing free of the usual forms of infiltration or identification by any of our intelligence services."

There was a general murmur at this development. Surprise certainly, but also some doubt.

Rosensweig squirmed in his seat, not sure how to react to the announcement. The information had an effect greater than its content. Rosensweig realized it was also a form of control, a reassertion of authority by the Washington viceroys Stepinak represented.

"The Nucleus," Stepinak continued, "is guided by a mysterious hand, motivated, we believe, by a general hatred of the West yet not specifically bound to any particular ideology. Equally dangerous is the uncertainty it has created. We do not yet understand its ultimate object or the purpose for its existence. We know only that it is capable of the highest level of terrorist operations we have yet encountered."

Stepinak glanced around, allowing the impact of his words to settle, before he signaled and the screen behind him filled with highlights of passages in the notebooks they had been given, outlining the similarities in the recent terrorist operations and minimizing their differences.

The argument, even Rosensweig had to admit, was a persuasive one. It relied on two main points, the first being the extraordinary level of intelligence possessed by the terrorists and not encountered with such consistency by any of the organizations they had combated before.

The second was an extremely detailed and overly technical laboratory analysis of the type and kind of explosive devices used. The bombs were consistent in their degree of sophistication and destructiveness. "A new industry standard," someone had murmured in an English boarding-school accent.

Voices broke in after that. Most voiced disagreement. And that was natural, for it was a time of uncouplings, shifting faiths, and changing loyalties within the alliance. There was a feeling of being bludgeoned, manipulated, of not being told everything that was known. All the old suspicions had returned.

Rosensweig's eye was assaulted more than once by a sardonic glance from General Bruno. Bruno had an imposing head and a powerful jaw. His bald pate shone as if waxed. He possessed expressive features that would have made a perfect Roman bust or an advertisement for Fascist virility. Bruno had a subtle sense of humor and a style to match. Bruno, too, was an old ally of the invisible Joyce.

Rosensweig and Bruno went back into the sands of antiquity, their relationship cemented by a series of unofficial and sometimes felonious activities on each other's behalf. The latest concerned a certain synagogue bombing that resulted in the death of an old woman and two ten-year-old kids. A tragedy as affecting as it was brutal.

The terrorists had been careless, almost arrogant in their escape, leaving a clear trail to an apartment block in Milan. They were apprehended almost immediately. But even before the French authorities could arrive, the terrorists had been discreetly loaded aboard a private jet winging them to sanctuary in Libya.

Whether sound diplomacy or clever oil policy, it was not justice. But just then, justice was a short-selling commodity.

In a strange twist of destiny, the aircraft transporting the terrorists exploded in mid-flight after pausing to refuel in Palermo. The following morning, a mysterious package arrived at Rosensweig's apartment. It bore an Italian postmark but without a card or return address and contained a single item. A child's toy airplane with a broken wing.

Bruno, like the other old campaigners, remained silent behind their smiles. They knew their presence was merely decor, frosting on the torte. They were not playing but being played. The endgame was already in progress.

As for the less experienced—notably, the junior Italians—the idea that such an organization could exist without the knowledge of their respective intelligence services was not easily believed or accepted. There was a certain diminished pride, a cancer of confusion that splintered their self-confidence.

After that a certain weariness settled itself upon the more experienced shoulders. To combat such a threat would require the kind of strategy, coordination, and flexibility the alliance was famous for begrudging, rather than providing to its members.

There was another equally irritating factor: that an American intelligence organization should have scored such an obvious coup on their home ground was a major cause of pique. Especially when certain secret understandings concerning jurisdiction might well have been violated. Not to mention the total lack of information pooling.

After all, in spite of the cleverly bound mass of photocopies they had been provided with, there was nothing concrete. No names. No dates. No photographs. But then, that was a well-known characteristic of the agency in question, which had always been both contemptuous and notoriously suspicious of its European allies.

There were the usual closing remarks. The meeting was turned over to the Dutchman, who suggested their breaking up into regional committees for further discussion. Stepinak transferred his clumsy bulk to the floor, where he huddled with several dark-suited aides, then hurried off through a side exit, leaving the delegates to pick their way toward their various committee locations, guided by the same smiling female totems.

There was a heated discussion afterward in which Rosensweig himself took part, but his viewpoint cast a speculative doubt on the conclusions drawn. It was not especially popular with a faction eager to support the American contention. Also in opposition were those whose governments just then found it more expedient to accept some courtship from Moscow.

Most delegates kept their own counsel, but a seed of suspicion had been planted, and if that was its only purpose, then the conference had accomplished a great deal. There was the usual failure to agree on any but the most customary and standard security procedures.

In the following weeks, efforts were redoubled even in the most skeptical capitals. Ministers were suffocated in their movements by grim contingents of bodyguards, creating little pockets of anxiety wherever they appeared. Greater efforts were made to penetrate each of the enclaves of opposition. But that, of course, was exactly what the enemy expected. As usual, a new war was being fought with the tactics of the last. Only Joyce seemed to understand that, but Joyce was presently a general without an army.

Most were blissfully unaware that they had already been outmaneuvered by an enemy they could not name. An enemy who had offered them not a battle but a feint, and whose purpose was far deadlier than their imagination could predict.

4

The stewardess gave each passenger a funny little nickname. It was one of the games they played, trying to ease the boredom during the long hours across the Atlantic. But Joyce was not an easy candidate. There was no comical way to caricature a man with one arm.

Joyce was a stocky man, full-chested and imposing, with a full head of white hair, worn close-cropped. He looked taller than a man of average height. Perhaps it was due to his square-set boxer's stance, which gave him a look that was at once blunt and decisive. He had once been described as looking like an old fortress set out on a crag, distant and difficult to reach, protected by tricky currents, its technology outdated and no longer good for much but the back of tourist postcards but somehow still formidable, a thing to ponder. It took a second glance to determine that the sleeve, tucked so carefully into the outside pocket of his suit jacket, had no substance.

There was a certain charm about the man. The flight attendants recognized that at once. There was humor in his expression, in the wry, level gaze that framed you out of a face that was so seamed and lined, it could have been lifted wholesale from a Newfoundland cliff. Not a face, a bowsprit, someone had once labeled it. The paint worn off from going head to head against the northern seas. A face that was all splinters and cracks, clefts and jagged unfinished edges, with bright blue eyes peeping out from bushy, overhanging brows. The image of a battler or a survivor, both of which he undeniably was.

He dressed simply, favoring black single-breasted suits and plain white shirts graced with a dark blue tie. He even wore a hat on occasion—a stained brown fedora, a relic of a distant age—worn at a jaunty angle when the weather was threatening. Otherwise he went bareheaded, walking briskly with a kind of forward angle that gave you the impression a bit of brick wall had come loose and was heading your way. There were people from Washington to Tel Aviv who had foolishly collided with that wall. The experience was not a pleasant one. Few wished to have it repeated.

For most of the flight Joyce sat edged against the window in an empty row in business class, smoking cigarettes without filters that he puffed rather than inhaled, held in a pincer between his first two fingers, tucking it into the hand as if he were protecting the glow from the wind or the gaze of unfriendly eyes. It was less an affectation than a habit retained from his childhood on the hard streets of South Boston. A parish priest with the build of a longshoreman noticed that the boy, though undersized for his age, had a certain talent with his fists, a talent that should not be neglected. A scar or two from his days as a club fighter still showed whenever Joyce winced or placed a worried notch in his forehead.

At first the flight attendants laughed at this little mannerism with the cigarette and took turns imitating it between duties. One by one the whole crew went in turns to have a look. They found themselves passing him more frequently than the other passengers, sharing little comments and jokes—affection, finally. But exactly why it was offered they would not have been able to say.

They continued looking for things to bring, offering him sweets and the like, which he at first refused, then accepted, revealing a weakness for Swiss chocolate, which they smuggled into him from first-class.

Later, when the film began and they saw he had no interest in such distractions, they invited him back to their serving station and let him in on their little imitation, a laugh he good-naturedly shared with them.

Each flight attendant in turn refilled his coffee cup and felt compelled to confide intimate stuff about husbands and lovers they would have denied ever confiding to a complete stranger. But those regrets would come later. In the meantime they poured out their little secrets, and Joyce, for his part, showed no slackening of interest, for he had an instinct for listening.

Actually they could not be blamed for their little indiscretions. People often had the same feeling about Joyce. They believed that what flowed out of them in his presence would remain locked somewhere deep inside. Part of that came naturally, a measure of the priest's genes he carried. Part was training and long experience. The rest, no one could say, for Joyce had worn many masks in his time, changing his outward appearance with the ease of an Indian god. Some described him as devious, having layers within layers; others saw only the plain bluff face and believed it immutable. But these were the simple and the foolish, who truly believed in the forgiving heart of God. Joyce trusted only in his anger.

"Sorry, dear, but we're about to land. Please fasten your seat belt."

Joyce opened his eyes and grunted a response to the look of professional concern directed at him by the flight attendant. Twisting in his seat, he found the ends of the straps and fastened them across his lap. Then he glanced around the compartment, which was beginning to rouse itself out of mid-flight lethargy. Attendants bustled back and forth, making little pilgrimages to collect pillows and headsets. Joyce had not bothered with his, which was still sealed in its plastic jacket. He had returned from the galley a half hour before and must have dozed for quite a while, but he did not remember dreaming.

Joyce occupied the block of seats right behind first-class, usually reserved for business travelers. It was only half filled, and the two seats beside him were empty, allowing him to lower the armrests and stretch his legs across them.

He took a sip from the glass of Scotch on his traytable, feeling the effects of sleep recede. It had been an easy thing for the two-man surveillance team that got on with him in New York to keep track of his movements, but they were clumsy hacks, and Joyce barely included them in his gaze. He had learned to accept the pairs of invisible eyes that monitored him throughout the day. They were there in the morning when he left for the ten-story concrete module that imprisoned his days. They sat with him in the caterpillar crawl of suburban traffic and were a comforting gaze across the well of airspace dividing the identical slabs of his Virginia condominium.

Joyce had nursed a double Scotch across the Atlantic, resisting the urge to consume more. He needed to be clear-headed tomorrow, then realized tomorrow had already arrived. The rectangles across the aisle were collecting the soft gray light of an English dawn. He would have just enough time to get to his hotel before the agency car would come to collect him. Another example of brilliant scheduling. Thirty years in government service should have conditioned him to every sort of inefficiency, but somehow it never did. He often cursed himself for possessing a kind of credulity that believed men would perform their functions and that prayers would be answered, when he, of all men, knew better.

Joyce exhaled slowly, allowing the emotion to drift away, trying not to anticipate the unpleasantness he knew awaited in ambush. But he was unable to prevent a sour current of distaste from curdling through him.

A smiling attendant approached expectantly. But Joyce refused her offer of a boiled towel and turned instead to gaze into the comfort of darkness beyond the double-paned glass beside him. The darkness was God's, not his, but he was tired of the competition. How much of his life had been squandered in a different kind of darkness, as both hunter and prey? Now he was neither, but the men who summoned him had long memories. Joyce had been their master too long, and now they were his. The era when he could control their actions was long over, leaving a special vacuum of weariness. There had been too many assaults to repel. He had descended into the labyrinth too often.

The next few hours would tell their own tale, but he found it impossible to deceive himself. After being leashed for almost a decade, his enemies were rummaging for influence like ravenous boars. His own agency had helped keep a grip on that leash, reason enough for their hatred. Joyce knew what to expect. But he had lost his appetite for turf struggles, for power brokered for its own sake. Too much of his life had been spent prowling the shadowed corridors—first in the Far East, after Korea. Then Europe, during the Berlin airlift. Africa after that, then the Middle East, where he had sacrificed a limb, an artifact from some long-buried operation. Finally coming to Imperial Washington in the years of the Pax Americana. Strange fate for a man who had once applied to a Jesuit seminary.

Why had he not gone through with that? he wondered. It would have fulfilled his family's deepest wish, taking up the chalice as his line had done for generations. He had actually gone through the prelims, taking up residence with the brothers in a grim, gray-faced monastery on the Hudson. That had lasted for a term or two. But he had dropped out and still failed to answer the question that had dodged him for almost thirty years.

So while other men had chosen family, love, conventional

fulfillment, he had lived on a different edge, paying the price finally in the inevitable coin of loneliness, especially after Mary's death. And suddenly Mary's wasted face appeared in his memory, staring up at him from the hospital pillows, causing a tightening in his diaphragm.

It had been how long now? Seventeen years or so, he supposed. Seventeen years he had been a widower. Not technically, of course, since he and Mary had never married. Why hadn't they? he wondered. But that was another question without an answer.

Mary had been his what?—his mistress, he supposed. His sisters would have used that word in a whisper. Poor woman, they would have said, placing the blame for her shame squarely upon his shoulders without knowing that it was Mary herself who had refused his ring and his proposals. She preferred their arrangement, her own place and their weekend liaisons. Bringing her own bottle of Scotch and the cartons of cigarettes that eventually killed her.

She had been through three wars and God only knew how many men before he had met her. But none of that ever seemed to bother him. He pictured her in bed beside him. Her tiny, sharp, pointed breasts and slender hips, the pout of her vag, as she liked referring to it. Always giving it a little pat before letting him administer to it. Christ, why had her dying cost him so much?

A shrink might have helped ease the agony. But belief in that had come too late, if at all. Now he was too far gone. He had been sealed by his own ambitions. Licked, stamped, and posted.

Joyce sighed, fighting away the demons with another sip of the acrid liquor. The landscape of his face was reflected back to him in the glimmering panel, exaggerating the crags and hollows of his cheeks and the long, unbroken angle of his stubborn jaw. It was a profile some ancient sculptor would have appreciated. A throwback to some stoic Roman legionnaire following Aurelius into the Rhenish forests to plug the barbarian tide. Another lesson in futility.

Joyce sighed and adjusted his watch. One day, perhaps two at the most, then he would be flying back home. If the two-bedroom flat forty-five minutes from downtown Washington could be considered a home. Yet it was there he trudged each night to face the silent interior with its immaculate maid-kept neatness and the dismal hum of the refrigerator. A monk's cell with all the conveniences.

He reached for his glass and took a deep, warming slug. The taste brought its special measure of comfort. There had been a bit too much of that lately, some voice of conscience recorded. He stared at the amber fluid, feeling himself drifting toward its glow like some inevitable beacon. Not that he had ever really abstained, but the peril was present now, reflecting a deeper hunger he did not know how to name or satisfy. So he fought the urge to put down another and consumed a piece of chocolate instead. It was his little indulgence now, his last defense. Like an old woman with a Pekinese, clutching its warmth against the inevitable.

With professional heartiness the captain's voice announced they had arrived fifteen minutes ahead of schedule. Joyce raised his glass toward the men watching him. It provided an empty celebration.

5

The house he was escorted to was a handsome Edwardian relic, refurbished to house the European headquarters of an international conglomerate, as the shining brass plate outside advertised. It came equipped with the standard uniform of respectability, down to a carefully tended bank of tulips warming its cozy facade. No one would suspect the kernel of deceit walled in its core.

The drive circled to embrace the house and protect its visitors from the danger of a casual glance. Joyce shrugged himself out of the luxurious automobile that had picked him up at his hotel, before either of the two company thugs seated in front could tear open the door for him. He strode through a quickly opening entryway into a small wood-paneled vestry where he was faced by a fingerprint scanner that resembled an oversize baseball mitt. Unlike the Roman gargoyle that bit off the hands of liars, the machine had no sense of mythology. It merely whirred like a damaged electric fan and returned Joyce's hand intact. He was buzzed into a narrow corridor where he became the meal for the gaping mouth of a shining, metal-walled elevator.

Muzak accompanied Joyce into the underworld. The door opened on a choice of directions, but a strip of plastic girdling the sterile halls lit up in a pretty pink neon hue to direct him through the labyrinth to his goal, a gleaming stainless-steel door marked with a panel of security slots. Joyce reached for the plastic card he had been given and fed it into the uppermost slot. The door acceded noiselessly, welcoming him into the fluorescent glare.

A swivel chair waited, upholstered in black leather. It defended one end of a long lacquer counter, also mirrored in black. Joyce was alone in the large room except for the squat figure of Peter Stepinak overflowing his own narrow plastic chair.

Stepinak sat less at the table than in a cockpit surrounded by two swivel-necked terminals and various sets of keyboards, phones, and blinking plastic buttons. Global management directed by computer chip.

Joyce received no greeting.

Stepinak was a mute effigy, affecting to ignore him. His face frozen in the smile of a cheap Buddha. But even silent, Stepinak bristled with emanations, giving off an aura of sour radio waves. Physically he resembled a circus bear someone had stuffed into a three-piece suit. He overflowed the space that sought to girdle him, contradicting its sleek, streamlined efficiency with his sloppy bulk.

Joyce inventoried Stepinak's massive paunch, the plump, lineless hands now mashing computer keys like some demented pianist. His neck was as thick as a roll of blood sausage, vised in a white band of collar above which his badly proportioned head lolled, like a broken doll's. Sprays of wispy, colorless hair were plastered crossways across his bald dome like a headset. His face had all the distinction of a lump of clay worked over by an untalented child. It was inset with watery blue eyes, as lacking in depth as the terminal he faced. The red mouth was a narrow gash of spite.

Joyce waited out Stepinak's rudeness with bemused patience. This was not their first encounter.

During Joyce's years in Southeast Asia, Stepinak had been the paymaster to the warlords of the Shan Army. He had supervised shipments of raw opium out of the Golden Triangle on Air America transports, pipelining the coarse brown bricks directly to Corsican processing plants in the Mediterranean for distribution on the sidewalks of American cities. There had been legions of Stepinak's then, cynical robots schooled in the big-buck theory of geopolitics, trying to leverage Stone Age tribal cultures into battling a twentieth-century tidal wave of Marxist holy wars.

Joyce had been one of the heretics, a skeptic within the temple. His situation reports had been contradicted and overruled. He did not believe in theories about dominoes. Nor did he believe in the viability of native Vietnamese forces, in a country whose infrastructure was managed by a Chinese immigrant population interested only in financial exploitation.

But Saigon had been abandoned, and Joyce had survived to oversee those who had tried to destroy him. Stepinak, too, had survived, weathering the guerrilla warfare directed against his agency. There were still assignments for men like Stepinak, even in those soft post-Vietnam years. And because he could not be dispensed with, Stepinak and his ilk burrowed deep, waiting and watching, accumulating a kind of negative power that he used with all the cunning of his peasant forebears. He was not a pretty enemy. In the clutch, he was tenacious and deadly, never quitting until he had succeeded in bringing his enemy to ground. Taking perverse joy in hanging, skinning, and dressing his kill.

A disk whirred, and the charade came to an end. "Let's get to it, okay?" Stepinak directed. Joyce did not miss the fine edge of contempt to his voice, which alternated between a high-pitched whine and a hoarse bass growl. Stepinak's lack of cordiality was not a pleasant omen. Not when the orb of power rested in his shapeless little fist.

Sausagelike fingers scrubbed at the keyboard. Lights dimmed and images composed themselves on the terminal screen in front of Joyce. He leaned back, wondering exactly how many scenes like this he had witnessed. How many surveillances and the clasp of hands sealing a betrayal. He felt himself sliding toward something dismal and fought the sourness in his gut, narrowing his eyes as the scene resolved.

A crowded street corner in a middle European city. Movements of passersby as the camera zooms in on a short, squat figure in a raincoat and matching hat. Faces blur past, obscuring the target until his face appears sharply focused, frozen and enlarged.

Stepinak's coarse voice echoed in the room. "His name is Bunin. Nicholas Illyich Bunin. Recognize him?"

Bunin . . . Joyce knew Bunin. A middle-management KGB hack. Joyce tried to shake off the shadows. He had seen all of this before. He was cold suddenly, aware of being transported to his personal sphere of purgatory. The screen lost Bunin's oily countenance and filled with bytes of data.

Bunin, Nicholas Illyich. Born Moscow 1928. Rank: Major, KGB. Middle-ranking liaison to KGB directive region 6. Reports directly to Technical Bureau KGB, Central Moscow. Believed to act as outside auditor and control for middle-level operatives throughout regional directive.

"Okay," Stepinak interjected. "Here's where it gets interesting."

Lettering dissolves into Bunin's tiny black pupils, squeezed by pockets of fat. Action unfreezes around him. Bunin pushes his way toward the entrance of a small Konditorei. He enters, moving to a table in the rear, taking a seat opposite a figure seated with his back to the camera. Bunin makes conversation. The other responds, shrugs, pauses for language that cannot be heard, gestures with his right hand. A waiter passes, obscuring the two. An attractive brunette stops to question the waiter, then steps out of the frame. Bunin is now alone at the table, spooning the other's unfinished portion of pastry onto his own plate with a look of sly satisfaction. The camera swings wildly, trying to pick up his companion. Catches a shoulder, almost loses him, snatches at his head and shoulders as he turns full face to the lens. Freeze frame.

"Recognize him?"

Joyce was silent. The man frozen in the terminal was Victor Kirov.

"Kirov. Victor Kirov, or Victor Sorge as he now titles himself. He's passing himself off as a Romanian these days. In the film business, if that's a business—or didn't you know?"

"No. Not really," Joyce responded quietly.

"I'm surprised. You made him, didn't you?"

"I was present at his defection," Joyce said in a flat, dry voice.

"Act two coming up." Stepinak squeaked jovially.

Paris. Night. The same jerky hand-held camera moves in tightly on the front of a bistro. Through the dirty plate-glass window several people can be seen seated at a table. One of them is Victor. There are two people with him. One is swarthy, slick-haired, and bearded. Corsican, perhaps. The other is a pretty brunette. Parisian. The three are in the midst of negotiating something. The image blurs to a halt. Shoots into reverse. Backing out, the camera focuses on a white sports car across the street. A young Arab sits behind the wheel, holding a camera in his hand. Freeze frame.

"His name is Ahmed Bazou. He was a Palestinian national. Incidentally, the guy with Victor is a major dealer in heroin futures. The pussy is a French actress. The name is not worth remembering. Only the tits. Your buddy Victor's living well these days. Okay. Act three, coming up."

A café in a quarter near the Place de la Bastille. The Arab hurries inside and uses the telephone. His face is tight, serious. The call lasts only a few seconds. Hanging up, he leaves the café, crossing the street to a public phone. He makes another call. Freeze frame.

Stepinak began a dry commentary. "Not well trained, our

Arab friend, and that's his problem. Not much in the imagination department. Alternates between these three phones, always the same three. Dials different numbers, always to public phones in different quarters of the city. But always the same voice on the other end." Stepinak touches a button. A voice is filtered over the audio.

Joyce leaned forward, picking up the first clicks of transmission, then the muffled, static-covered drone of voices speaking a kind of verbal shorthand that lasted only seconds.

"We ran it through all the analyzers, then matched it with analysis from six other intelligence services, including the Mossad. The voice belongs to Roger Francis Killian. No mistake."

Roger Killian . . . Christ.

"You want me to run a bio?" Stepinak uttered sarcastically.

Joyce shook his head. He carried his own.

Killian's name had produced an involuntary sensation, as if someone had sharply struck a reflex point. Joyce had first heard Killian's name during a high-level briefing in Rome. The briefing had been conducted by Italian intelligence after the leaders of the Red Brigade had been apprehended and had begun to talk. Before then, Killian's existence had been a rumor, a suspicion, but never a fact.

Joyce remembered the reactions on the faces of the senior intelligence officers when they learned they were dealing with a fanatical revolutionary who controlled a small group of assassins responsible for many of the major kidnappings and political murders of the last decade. Not one of them had any suspicion of Killian's existence. And with good reason. Killian's group never numbered more than half a dozen, always operating outside the organizations contracting him. That method insured total secrecy and complete surprise. Killian operated free of the usual informants and infiltrators who tipped so many terrorist operations.

According to the informants, Killian's contacts were always at the highest level. Since most terrorist organizations keep their action units totally separate from each other, even insiders never actually know who is responsible for which operation. That was why Killian's existence could remain a secret for so long.

Killian's menace rested in the combination of professionalism and fanaticism that drove him. Money was never a motivator, except as a tool to accomplish his immediate goal. He

TO KILL A KING

made no profit from his activities and turned back the money he did not use. In that, Killian was a cleric still. Like Joyce, he had given up one church, only to construct another.

Killian identified himself with various radical causes. In Central and South America, he had organized workers into armed resistance groups. Arrested by the Brazilian police, he was brutally tortured and sentenced to death. He was removed from his cell each night, a pistol shoved into his mouth and the trigger pulled. His release was a form of miracle arranged at the intercession of the Vatican.

Killian dropped out of sight after that. He formally renounced his vows and began training in Cuba as a paramilitary specialist. His history became vague after that. There was some evidence that he led guerrilla fighters in Peru and Bolivia during the early seventies. In the early eighties he switched his field of activity to Europe, acting as a liaison and arms supplier to various urban terrorists. After that he dropped out of sight, until the Red Brigade confessions established his new persona.

The screen went blank. Stepinak swiveled toward Joyce, expressing all the warmth of a Chinese gate lion. "Okay, Mr. Senior Consultant. We got Bunin to Kirov to Killian. Now, what the fuck does it mean?"

Joyce leaned back, forming cathedrals with the fingers he brought to his lips. His face was blank, his eyes dark points of tragedy.

"Surprised to see your boy Kirov keeping such heavy company?" Stepinak taunted.

Yes. Joyce was surprised. Seeing Victor had shaken him. But his expression remained impassive. "Don't tell me you haven't figured an angle? And I thought you were the best we had, Herr Professor Joyce."

Joyce forced a smile. The room was suddenly oppressive. He jerked out of the chair and began a casual stroll around the table, to Stepinak's obvious annoyance. The massive figure pedaled his own chair around with brushing motions of his tiny loafer-clad feet.

"Kirov involved in something like this, after all this time," Joyce mused aloud. "Possible, yes. But probable?" Joyce allowed the question to dangle.

"You tell me. You were his Father Confessor, weren't you?"

"Hardly." Joyce drawled casually, drawing a finger along

the top of a dust-covered console. "Just an old fraternity brother."

"Cut the bullshit, okay?" Stepinak growled. "You brought this Kirov, or Sorge, or whatever he calls himself, out. You saved his ass. Without you he'd have a KGB bullet up his ass. He's been bumming around Europe now for almost ten years, sticking his hot little fingers into every nasty little hole there is. You name it, he's done it."

Stepinak reached down and drew a file from beneath his desk. He slid it along the polished table toward Joyce.

"Take a look. Your buddy's run the gamut. From smuggling diamonds to pedaling stolen technology. You know him better than anyone. So you tell me: Why the connection to Killian? And why now?"

"Why not now?" Joyce stated firmly. "He doesn't ask our permission for his timetable. Figure out where the financing is coming from, then we'll have an idea of the target."

Stepinak's eyes narrowed spitefully. "I don't need you to tell me that. We think Killian heads up a terrorist organization we call The Nucleus. We're talking about the most lethal group of assassins operating in the world today. Killian gets his mandate from the top. Someone makes a deposit in a bank somewhere and he goes to work. He makes an earthquake and we sit around waiting for the aftershock. Only, now we've got your boy, Victor. He's the link we never had before. So what's his angle? What's he in it for?"

"I'll need time to figure that out."

"You don't have any," Stepinak snapped.

"Paris is a big place to hide."

"Paris. Bullshit! Fuck the French, they're all assholes. They'll screw us any chance they get, even if it meant tipping Killian that we were on to him. They even find out we've got a man on the streets and they'll start yellin' bloody murder. Paris is the best hideout the son of a bitch has got."

"All right," Joyce said evenly. "Then let's start with the linkage. How did you manage to make Kirov?"

"Routine. We were spot-checking Bunin on the odd chance we'd pick up some new mark he was working over."

Joyce knew the technique. Stepinak would have Bunin shadowed on the possibility of stumbling onto a KGB investigation, hoping to snare some operative with his hand in the till. They would then approach the agent, offering to provide an alternative to the man's dilemma. An old snare but neatly effective.

"In any case, we got Kirov on film and checked him out. It looked interesting, so we started some secondary surveillance on everyone he's been in regular contact with. You haven't been keeping tabs lately, have you?"

"No. Not lately."

These days, what Joyce knew about Victor filtered down the pipeline from old contacts who looked in on the Russian every now and again as a favor. The news was sporadic, and sometimes he heard nothing for half a year or more. His last real inquiry was over two years ago. Victor had just started in the film business then and seemed to be doing well. But that was how it always began.

"We want everything you've got on Kirov," Stepinak barked aggressively, his eyes dark points of malice.

"It's all in the reports," Joyce said wearily.

"Reports, bullshit. Those reports don't tell us anything. We want all the numbers painted in. That's why you've been loaned out to us."

"I want some sleep," Joyce said, turning toward Stepinak.

Irritation flashed across Stepinak's face; his lips twitched. "Before you sleep, think about this. Our analysis thinks your boy Kirov came over, not as a defector but as a plant. He fools the parties-that-be into believing he's clean. He is allowed to roam free over here, on our side of the grazing. But he burrows deep, waiting for us to sleep. And when they're sure we think he's as innocent as a baby's ass, they slide him back into service. Bunin runs Kirov. Kirov runs Killian."

"You believe that?"

"Who cares what I believe? It's what Washington believes." Stepinak finished with a scowl. "Killian is the most dangerous terrorist in the world today. We don't know where or when he's going to hit next. But it will be big, I guarantee you that. A regular tidal wave."

Which placed his skin neatly hanging on the line, Joyce mused, with a tight little smile. How cleverly it all fit together. Bunin to Kirov to Killian, with Joyce thrown in for good measure. Brought over, not to aid in any investigation but to preside at his own demise. It was good, very good. He had to hand Stepinak that. Getting all the birds with a single low-budget stone.

"Yes. Washington would think that," Joyce finally echoed, fingering the file in front of him.

Stepinak's lips twitched to form some remark, but he thought better of it and said only that Joyce would be picked up at seven.

"And once we start, you can forget sleep for a good long time. We'll run the flab out of your brain," he said, finishing spitefully, then picked up a phone and mumbled something Joyce had no interest in hearing. A moment later the steel door slid open, and a thug in gray pinstripes came to escort him out. Joyce slipped the file under his arm and called a good night, but Stepinak had already turned his back.

6

He was running between the darkly clumped trunks, racing past the bloated shapes sprawled in the tall grass. They were Indians, half starved and ragged, killed by swarthy men in green fatigues who were now hunting him. He could hear them filtering through the trees behind him, stolid, relentless. No matter how fast he ran, they were there, steps behind. The forest thinned, then slipped away. A dog ran toward him across the open ground, a starving dog with a dead infant clutched in its jaws. He ran faster. But the explosion caught him before he could reach the cover ahead. It broke close to his ear like a burst paper bag. Something clubbed him between the shoulder blades. He fell. Tumbling downslope toward the feasting animal . . . toward his awaiting death—

Killian woke in a dead sweat, shivering.

The room was dark, filled with stubborn shadows that resisted the gradual penetration of light. An electric heater glowed in one corner but was insufficient to prevent the chill from penetrating the insulation of Irish wool that covered his lean, almost skeletal torso. The chill ached deep, gnawing at old wounds and fissures of muscle that would never heal. Pain throbbed in the places where his torturers had applied their skills, etching him with a sawtooth of agony.

He coughed, clearing phlegm from his throat, tossed off the blanket, and rose from the daybed. Killian skirted the shabby furniture of the sitting room and went to the window, staring dully at a bleak winter sky above the jumble of metal chimneys and steeply angled roofs. Church bells were pealing somewhere in the distance. He hated this view with its absence of anything green and living, as he hated this cold city with its officious bustle and self-satisfied bourgeois complacency. But its very size and impersonality provided him with the anonymity he needed to operate in. For that he was grateful.

Killian cracked the knuckles of his large hands and caught

a glimpse of himself in the mirror that hung on the far wall. Zinc had worn through in several spots but did nothing to obscure the gaunt figure that returned his gaze. He had touched up his hair so he no longer resembled the bleached bones of some outdated relic. But his cheeks were sunken pits, the parched skin lined and creased. Imprisonment had scraped the color from his face and pleated his skin with a fine mesh of lines like a worn textile. His jailers knew various ways to kill, and worse. How to force the hair on a man's head to go gray and make him offer up his mother and sisters if that was required. The memory of those years belonged to another age, and the distant bells reminded him that it was an equal age since he had last served Mass.

Strange how each morning that thought still found its way to his head, leaving him with a gnawing emptiness like an unfilled tooth. His family, what was left of it, still thought of him as a priest, still called him Father and sought his blessing. He could not shake that illusion out of them, nor make them understand that he was now a man who performed a different kind of rite, a different and far more effective ritual of blood.

But destiny had fashioned an ironic twist. Having once been a cleric, he still had access to certain unique advantages. It placed him in direct contact with nuns and priests who had left the Church. Among these exiles there existed a kind of unofficial network that crossed borders and stretched throughout Europe and indeed around the globe. Connected by a bond, rare in the modern world, they provided Killian with contacts, safe houses, and even the use of a courier system whose messengers never quite understood the real nature of the messages they carried. No amount of money could ever purchase such accommodating efficiency. Nor could it buy the same kind of secrecy. The members of this network provided each other with shelter, financial assistance, and a special kind of devotion. Having once taken Holy Orders, they were bound by a special kind of oath that made them far more trustworthy than even the most fanatical members of Killian's own organization. Of course, none of these ex-clerics even remotely suspected what occupied Killian in the months between visits. Most were still so unworldly, they would not have been able to add up the simplest of clues. As naïve as they often were in political matters, only in their company did Killian feel even remotely safe.

The house he presently inhabited was owned by a former nun he playfully referred to as Sister Celeste. She was a good-natured woman in her late thirties, thick-waisted and plain, with a matronly bosom and prematurely graying hair, who smiled at his use of her former name.

Killian used her house often, arriving after midnight to avoid being noticed by the neighbors and hiding his aging maroon Volvo in her garage. He remained indoors, out of sight of any possible notice, and usually left in the dark, hours before dawn. Perhaps fatigue was making him careless in the regularity of his visits, but he trusted the sister or at least had no reason to doubt her tolerant acceptance of his ways. She knew him as a kind of unofficial fund-raiser for the Liberation Theologians of Latin America, whose position in the official church was anathema. After taking her into his confidence, she accepted his need for secrecy. She believed he was an agent for various religious groups, helping to supply weapons for the urban guerrillas of Latin America, whose revolutions were sanctioned by the new theology.

Sister Celeste was unusually intelligent, which caused him some moments of hesitation. But she offered her services to his cause without question. He had come to trust her. He used her on important courier operations and at night shared her bed. But that had taken time and patience to accomplish. Like the other sisters he depended on, Sister Celeste secretly thirsted to make up for years wasted in cloistered seclusion. She needed an affection he well knew how to arouse. To bind her to him with emotional bonds of steel.

Necessity forced him to make love to these women, an act he found personally repugnant but one dictated by a desperate need to survive. With distaste he remembered long nights spent in disordered beds, fumbling to satisfy an urge better left neglected. But such contact welded them to him. They performed his wishes without question, their eyes brimming with adoration. These women formed his private sisterhood, strategically located throughout the continent, places where he could crawl for sanctuary—hidden nests, unknown and unsuspected.

"Les journeaux, Madame."

The voice of the delivery boy echoed through the door. Killian heard the slap of newspapers strike the dirty floor outside, then the careless timpani-like sounds of the boy's heavy shoes as they clattered down the front stairs. Bringing the daily papers was a chore Sister Celeste tipped generously for. But the little bastard was irreverent about the time he got the newspapers there.

He heard the sister shuffle to the door and the several words of conversation she exchanged with the boy before he heard the door gently close. A moment afterward there was a knock at his door.

Killian crossed the room and opened the door. Sister Celeste faced him holding a half dozen British dailies.

"These just came," she said in heavily accented English, which she insisted they speak. Killian would have just as well conversed in French. He was fluent in several languages, his accent virtually perfect in each. But Sister Celeste wanted to improve her own. He reached out to take them and, for the first time, read something in her eyes he had never seen before.

"What's wrong?" he asked.

She shook her head. "Nothing. I am unwell, that is all."

He nodded sympathetically. Since his arrival they had slept in separate rooms, which did not displease him. He reached out to touch her shoulder and felt her tremble.

"I am sorry," he said softly, forcing a kind of tenderness into his voice. She nodded but did not look at him.

"You will want lunch soon?" she asked, her eyes downcast.

"Whenever," Killian said vaguely.

"It will be ready whenever you wish."

Celeste turned to go. Killian watched her heavy body moving across the dark passageway toward the kitchen before he closed the door and carried the papers over to the littered table where he cleared a space and began feverishly scanning the front pages.

Most contained the usual hysterical parrot screeches of the gutter press. Something ghastly in the Middle East. Unemployment up. The stench of a scandal in some Ministry or other. Then he found what he was looking for.

SECRET RENDEZVOUS. MINISTER COMPROMISED!

The headline proclaimed a steamy rendezvous at an Italian resort. Killian bent closer, eyes focused like a stalking wolf. The minister had been photographed in a compromising position with a young woman.

Killian's mouth puckered, combining interest and disgust. He turned to the facing pages of the couple disporting themselves, staring at the newsprint image of the paunchy middle-aged politician and a half-naked girl.

Killian's mouth tightened, forcing down the surge of excitement he felt deep in his gut. It had come, as he knew it would. They had presented this opportunity to him as a gift.

Killian allowed himself to absorb each picture, before he stepped to a nearby table and unlocked his briefcase. Inside was a thin manila folder, filled with a half dozen newspaper clippings.

Carefully he arranged space on the table and laid the newspaper beside the other headlines.

PARTY SECRETARY AND LOVER IN TRYST!

UNION LEADER BATTLES BOOZE AND BOUNCERS!

NUDE PLAYGROUND FOR LIBERALS!

All told similar stories of British politicians caught unaware. Each story was reported by the same paper in the same crude journalistic style. Each announced itself as an exclusive. Yet there was no way to identify the photographer or reporter, beyond the idiotic title the newspaper had given him.

SUPER SCOOP!

The words impressed themselves with a mixture of pleasure and distaste. At first he had wondered if they were dealing with one man or many. That was what intrigued him. If it was one man, then how did he gain such immediate access? How did he know where each story would be happening and when?

But it was one man; Killian knew that with instinctive certainty. He had operated in similar circumstances too often not to sense the risk taken, the cunning and stealth involved. Now he had been proven correct in his beliefs. It was one man. Acting alone. Unstoppable.

Killian had been tracking these stories for some time, timing their appearance for a measure of predictability. What had begun merely as a surmise had now crystallized into an actuality. Somehow this Super Scoop had found access into the innermost reaches of Her Majesty's Government. A way to predict movement, pierce the previously impregnable net of government security.

Killian's belly tightened with a strange feeling of excitement. It had taken time and patience, but now he knew who this Super Scoop actually was. Unwittingly he had provided Killian with the prescription for an assassination.

A noise in the other room startled him. It sounded like the

clatter of metal on the wooden floor. Instinct flagged a warning. Killian felt for the weapon he kept strapped to his calf. He moved stealthily toward the door, easing the knob until it opened a crack.

Sister Celeste stood in the room beyond, the room he used for a bedroom. She was kneeling beside his bed in the process of picking something up. His valise had been pulled out from beneath the bed; the lid was open. Sister Celeste was staring at his automatic pistol. He realized instantly that she had been going through his things. Three silent steps took him into the room and brought him to her side.

Sister Celeste turned and looked up, startled to see him. But there was no fear in her eyes. A kind of defiance was stamped on the soft features of her homely face. She rose and held out her hand; the weapon rested in the palm. Snub-nosed. Lethal.

"Is this yours?" she asked quietly, as though she were speaking to one of her parochial-school charges.

Killian nodded.

"This too?" She held out his silencer.

Again he nodded.

"And these?" She held the stubs of his airline tickets.

This time he made no acknowledgment.

"These prove you were in Bonn when the mayor was killed. You were in Rome and Amsterdam when those men were killed. And these." She held newspaper clippings in her hand. They reported the bombing of a military air base near Wiesbaden. Another showed machine-gun bullets sprayed in a U.S. military supermarket.

"You were there when all of these incidents happened."

The accusation was clear. Killian was stone-faced. He had been wrong not to trust his first instincts about Celeste. He had been careless, a vice he would have to make atonement for.

"Were you part of this horror? Did you help kill these men?" She searched his face for an answer. What she read in his eyes confirmed what she had until then only dared suspect. He could see the knowledge was bitter, a form of betrayal.

"I trusted you," she whispered. "I loved you."

"How did you find out?" he asked in a hoarse tone.

"I don't know when I began to suspect. But you always seemed to arrive on the heels of some disaster. By accident,

TO KILL A KING

cleaning your room, I discovered a road map. You had marked your route. Each city was the scene of some terrorist incident. I watched you burn the map and other papers. I knew something was wrong. When you sent me on errands, I began to examine the packages you asked me to deliver. They contained money and explosives, didn't they?"

Killian said nothing. His eyes had become points of cold steel. "Who else knows?" Killian uttered softly.

"No one," she answered. "Only me. Why did you do it?"

"God's will," he answered.

"Pray with me, my brother," she whispered, going to her knees on the threadbare carpet.

Killian slipped to her side, his head bowed. She bowed her own. She placed her hands over his. The words were said silently, a prayer for forgiveness. When she was finished, she crossed herself and prepared to rise, her fleshy hand reaching to grasp the arm of the chair beside her.

Killian's arm moved so quickly, the nun was almost unaware of the movement. She never saw the lean sliver of steel, sharp as a razor. Nor did she feel the long blade of the Peruvian skinning knife carving through the layers of fat protecting her belly, cleaving between her heavy, shapeless breasts and penetrating the muscle of her heart. The knife was tipped with curare. The heart was paralyzed within seconds. The blow was a mercy, no more painful than a dentist's injection, and over so quickly that his victim's brain did not have time to record the outrage until life was no longer a possibility.

Killian's fingers gripped her shoulder and twisted her torso away, so the thick stream of blood spouted away from the trunk and onto the carpet nearby. He heard the silent gasp as her eyes bulged. He allowed her body to slide easily and noiselessly to the floor.

He tidied up afterward, working methodically, leaving no trace of his sojourn. The nun clothed herself in routine. Shopping on Tuesday, bank on Wednesday. She would not be missed until later in the week. By then Killian would be far from there, his track lost within an intricate maze of deception.

7

The hotel was located in Hamstead and specialized in what the travel magazines like to term typical Victorian charm. There were the usual chintz curtains and brass tack-room gear, together with a noisy pub on the main floor.

Joyce's bed-sitter looked out over the heath. Each window framed its own landscaped image. He had climbed to it along a dark stairway after the car dropped him in front. The small entry was silent. Not even the bored and turbaned Sikh desk clerk was around. But Joyce had the bitter confidence that Stepinak's team was positioned to keep an eye on him.

He took a light meal in the pub, then returned to his room for a bath. The day was warm, almost sultry. He left the windows open, wondering if he would be able to sleep. He seldom could after a long flight. Only when he was immersed in the large porcelain tub resting on the feet of four imperial lions and had a double malt Scotch securely riveted in his slippery fist did he allow himself to digest the morning's assault of facts and images.

Seeing Victor had unnerved him. Under any set of facts, his own responsibility to the Russian had ended almost nine years before, when he had debriefed and released him with a new identity and enough money to begin another life. But there was something more. There had always been something more. A factor that remained after all the requirements of their professional relationship were no longer relevant.

"You've given birth to me, my friend. In dubious conception," Victor used to wisecrack. And in some peculiar way, perhaps he had.

They had first encountered each other in the dark silence of a Finnish forest. Victor had flown to Helsinki from Leningrad, the trip arranged to appear as a purely routine flight after an equally routine briefing session with the chief of Victor's Moscow directive. It became the first stage of Victor's defection.

TO KILL A KING

Joyce remembered his first impression of Victor. The handsome face, more alive and compelling than the photographs he had studied, a face suffused with ambition. Confident, almost arrogant. Yet redeemed by something else, something masked and lurking just below the surface. It was a quality Joyce detected only gradually. He sensed a vulnerability, a hunger for contact—even love, perhaps—combined with a fear of the very thing it desired.

At the beginning Joyce had mocked his amateur foray into psychoanalysis. But there was something valid in what he had detected. Time had shaped it into truth.

Victor's case had been difficult, crossing service lines and delineations of influence. The ice was thin, and Joyce had to skate gently. Victor was a specialist, talented and inventive. Not an ideologue, no. Joyce had read that fairly early on. Victor liked to live well, perhaps too well. He had too great an appetite for things Western, an almost insatiable hunger for pretty women and sleek cars, and that, after all, was what gave his game away.

Moscow had given Victor special status with free-lance jurisdiction over the northern area of the NATO command. He was allowed to operate outside the normal KGB channels and conventional structure of bureaucracy. Victor had snared several top-level Scandinavian technocrats before Joyce even had an inkling. There was a certain, almost Oriental, finesse in the manner of his operations. A Japanese precision to his methods, analyzing his quarry in the subtlest psychological terms that went beyond the usual grabbag of greed and lust. And Joyce was fascinated.

Victor operated on his victims' sense of guilt, delving for the soft spot of anguish that turned superficial loyalties against themselves. Perhaps Victor had the same fractured core within himself and sought a like vulnerability in those he stalked. Whatever it was, it had taken all of Joyce's craft as a hunter to bring him to ground. Victor was elusive and wary, protecting himself with layers of satellite armor, but in the end it was his own side that actually betrayed him.

Victor's ambition had become a threat to those who ran him. He played the game too recklessly, too arrogantly, for the plodders who used his success first to advance themselves, then played him off as a disposable pawn in one of their endless power struggles. And on that rock Joyce had built his church.

But it was a close thing. By the time Joyce had been brought, Victor had already compromised one of the alliance's most sensitive operations. But through some mysterious understanding, even at the moment of his greatest triumph, Victor sensed the precariousness of his position and held back from turning over the documentation he had gathered, feeding his superiors only odd bits of trivia instead.

Joyce sensed the desperation of a man caught in the middle, but he had been forced to act more intemperately than he wanted. The timing was not precise, the ground far from prepared. Joyce did not yet have enough to bolt his case to. One false move and cover would have been blown for an entire network. There was too much risk, but Victor was hanging by a thread that could snap at any moment. So he made a gambler's play. All or nothing on a single toss of the dice.

Victor had been sleeping with the wife of a Danish officer, a member of the NATO General Staff with full access to all the secrets of the Northern Defense Command. Joyce recalled the terror on her face when he interrupted her casual shopping trip that chilly morning in mid-September.

She had taken the ferry from Copenhagen and was waiting for Victor on the terrace of a picturesque inn outside Malmo, composed and elegant in a black leather coat, an attractive older woman with lean, aristocratic lines anxiously awaiting her lover. Joyce became a nasty intrusion, rude to the point of obscenity. But he had to penetrate her armor. In the end, he left her trembling and frightened, soiled by the knowledge of her betrayal.

He had to deal with the loathing in the woman's eyes. But his act had produced Victor, his feelings ruffled, his superior insularity broken. And he arrived on schedule. And that became Joyce's first and perhaps only victory. For in Victor's defeat also lay his own.

The debriefing was scheduled to last thirty days. Not the kind of timetable Joyce wanted. The agency wanted revelations, vital information. A headline a day, complete with fanfare and fireworks. And afterward, the informant to be disposed of like a dirty paper towel. His new masters failed to understand the relationship that had to be developed, the need for trust and eventual bonding. Their informant was a free-floating planet whose roots had been severed, perhaps irreparably. They never took into account what his future needs would be, shuffling him off to "baby-sitters." Men who had reached a dead end in their careers and were marking time until retirement. The new men at the top never took into account that the process could work both ways. That defector and debriefer were locked in a special relationship, cemented by a special kind of trust and even affection.

So the forest became a sanctuary, dark and cool. They had a hunting cabin all to themselves, on loan from a Finnish security service. The cabin was blond and as varnished as a pair of skis. It faced a glassy blue lake bordered by a shimmering ring of white birch and capped by the endless blue of the northern summer. It was an idyllic setting suited for lovers, snapshots, and memories. Instead it served to incubate Victor's betrayal.

"Our honeymoon cottage," Victor joked. And in a way it was.

They occupied separate rooms, sharing the living quarters in common. A small security force occupied another cabin on the other side of the lake; otherwise, they were alone.

An agenda was agreed upon, with two intensive sessions each day. One in the morning, the other just before dinner.

Victor insisted on his own copies of the tapes they made. Joyce gave in to that demand. It was to be the first in a whole series of capitulations.

Victor also insisted on keeping his weapon, claiming he did not trust the Finns. It was a small thing and Joyce permitted it, just as he permitted Victor's pre-dawn circling of the lake. "Jogging," Victor remarked cynically. "Just like you Americans."

But joggers did not carry 9mm automatics. Nor did they fear a bullet in the back of the ear. So each morning, just before the sky brightened, Victor made one of his annoying little jaunts, which was irritating to the Finns since it implied less than confidence in their presence. But it was something Joyce allowed. It eased his subject's nerves.

It was not an easy interrogation. Victor was stubborn, exacting. He demanded some form of payment for each new level of information. Joyce remained patient. The vein was particularly rich. Victor had been privy to many operations. He'd exacted his own form of survival insurance with bits of evidence collected against a high level of KGB officials. So it became a game of poker, of bluff and counter-bluff. Chips tossed into the pot and cards endlessly reshuffled.

Victor had none of the usual characteristics of the classic defector. Joyce was used to the opening stages of elation and supreme self-confidence, followed by rounds of aggrandizement and boasting, followed in turn by self-pity and the defector's feeling of being aggrieved.

Victor had shown none of these symptoms. He had no remorse. He was free of the usual bitterness about his motherland, expressing no doubt, no moral indecision. He was also free of the gradually emerging symptoms of depression most defectors wallowed in. If anything, Victor seemed to have defected long before the final act that actually brought him over.

Victor was suspicious at first, resentful. He bargained endlessly, trusted no one. He demanded a numbered Swiss account. Proof of deposits. Assurances against reprisal that Joyce could not really guarantee. And finally, protection from the processes of Joyce's own bureaucracy.

"I want none of your second-rate resettlers, isn't that what you call them? I have no ambitions to own a green card or to be housed somewhere in Des Moines, working in a car wash. No thank you. I will plod on my own, if you please."

Joyce smiled but held firm, until he got what he wanted. Yet in the end he had given Victor everything. All of it. But why?

Joyce had his reasons. Victor was a major catch, that much was obvious. Joyce had provided as generously before, when the defector ranked as high. But no, not as generously. Never as much. He could not deceive himself about that. He had never extended himself so far, so drastically, playing off valuable chips when there was no appreciable result beyond insuring Victor's life.

Unless you counted it as payment in exchange for his own. But that was to come.

Of course, Joyce liked the Russian. That counted as a factor. He had admitted that to himself early on. There was something innocent beneath the cynicism that you sensed and responded to. In spite of himself, Joyce even felt a kind of parental involvement in the prospect of Victor's future existence. Father Joyce and his prodigal son, Victor liked to joke.

Then there was the Alexi factor. Alexi was Victor's son.

His only child and heir. Was it the knowledge that Victor had a child, someone he obviously loved, that moved Joyce's sympathies, or was it something else subtler and even more elusive?

Joyce only knew the boy from Victor's snapshots. He remembered a handsome youth with an appealing face, a boy who was now dying of leukemia in some provincial Russian hospital. But they had not known that at the time, neither of them. So that, by itself, could have been the reason for his caring.

So the give-and-take continued. And the Finns observed through binoculars from their hidden blinds, watching the volatile Russian and the stolid American. The Father and the Son, they dubbed the duet. But for Victor they had another name. Cocking their fingers in Victor's direction, they nicknamed him the Holy Ghost.

Victor was a dead man once he left Joyce's charmed circle of protection. The Finns knew it. Joyce knew it. Only Victor seemed completely unaware, plotting his future with a maddening sense of unreality. Weighing one possibility against another. One day it was a villa on the Riviera. The next a town house in Paris. Or had the whole thing been a sham, a game played for his own amusement and to see how far he could go with the sympathetic American?

"I will become a country squire," Victor stated one evening while glancing through a copy of *English Country Life* that had somehow been placed in the cabin, along with some Finn's idea of entertaining English reading matter.

"A country squire, yes," he continued gleefully, his imagination churning with the idea. "With an ascot and riding britches. Why not? I'll purchase an estate and spend my life hunting foxes while you keep the bears from hunting me."

Victor laughed uproariously, and Joyce could not help joining in.

It was not entirely a one-way street. Victor was curious about Joyce, questioning him about his past and his beginnings on the streets of Dorchester. His career as a club fighter. Dwelling on his family's expectations of his becoming a priest.

"They should not be so disappointed," Victor stated. "You have a talent for inducing confession." And Joyce was forced to admit that truth.

Joyce made little forays into Victor's ideological beliefs, a game that never ceased to amuse him.

"I prefer a discussion of dialectics to take place between a woman's legs. Does that provide you with an insight into the deepest level of my socialist soul?"

But Joyce never really knew if Victor really had one. He sensed other dimensions, deeper layers that Victor kept well protected. Just as he kept his own secrets in spite of their intimacy, their lovers' walks, as Victor termed them, taken each twilight around the lake. But a soul? That was a different matter.

These friendly interrogations were followed by long sessions that flowed into the small hours of the morning, when weariness lowered the guard a little, and bits and pieces of the puzzle that was Victor revealed themselves like clues to some vast archaeological dig.

"You know, once in Moscow I thought of selling out. I had it all then. Two cars. A Moscow apartment. A country *dacha*. A collection of rock recordings worth a fortune. A special school for Alexi. A pretty mistress. I said, what the hell, I'm living like a capitalist, why not go the whole distance? Why not try it out on the other side? What's to hold me? Patriotism? Love for the socialist motherland? But, you see, my mother was dead. And my father, who was KGB and had filled his quotas so admirably and sent so many to rot their lives away in the Lubianka, he was the single most hated object of my childhood."

He was stretched out on the couch, drinking *slivovitz*, one arm behind his head.

"So what then—loyalty, perhaps? But to whom? My superiors, who would sell me in a second to increase the vodka supply at their luxurious *dachas?* My wife, my darling Irena, and her little afternoon infidelities with any member of the cinema industry who tosses her a crumb of recognition? My mistress, then? Another whore, so much more tiresome than my wife. When she fucked someone, she was unable to resist the compulsion to confess. Such tears. Such scenes. Such weariness, you cannot imagine. Ending, of course, with her renewed dedication to my insatiable lust."

He laughed and took a long drink of the clear liquid whose taste reminded Joyce of melted acrylic.

"So loyalty to what? To whom? The great Russian people? One has to get beyond that somehow. Is life any different on the other side—are the people, except for their accents? And this so-called freedom of yours, which is really the power to spend as much as you want. And, of course, your precious civil liberties, which are primarily taken advantage of only by your criminal class. Your average citizen doesn't even vote, does he? So much does he care for his precious Constitution."

Victor looked to Joyce for agreement but received none. Joyce's face had become a mask.

"What the hell, I said," Victor continued. "It's only the money separating us, isn't it? That's it, you see. The freedom of the press. I've read your press and watched your television, God help your masses. Such banality. Such distortion. Such care to avoid scandal for fear of frightening the advertisers.

"Life is as precarious for you as for us. The age forces us to conform to it, not the other way around. Oh, yes, we will have some lunatics who try to bend us to their fanatical ideologies. Then life swallows them and we return to all the normal agonies. One day we will all realize that and the whole sham will fall to pieces in our hands like an old newspaper one finds in an attic. So for me there is nothing but the money and the pleasure it will buy, in the few moments we have before the shades come down."

"And your son?" Joyce asked softly.

Victor became silent, his face framing a look Joyce had never seen before. A look of pain and concentration.

"'I will take care of Alexi,'" Victor said, forcing an air of assurance. "I will get the boy out . . . somehow."

He lapsed into silence, holding his glass close to his chest, gazing somewhere inward. Joyce remained silent. So the boy meant something. Then there was more to Victor than the cynical rendition of greed, or had that, too, just been part of the charade, an attempt to touch Joyce's secret and sentimental heart?

The KGB came for Victor on an overcast morning three days before the end of their stay.

The two of them had been eating breakfast, or rather Joyce had. Victor came out of his room a little earlier than usual. He declined coffee and set out on his daily jaunt. Normally it took half an hour. When the clock edged toward fifty minutes, a wrinkle of concern appeared in Joyce's forehead.

Five more minutes or so passed. The kettle began whistling. Joyce heard a footstep and rose to pour the usual cup of tea with three cubes of sugar that Victor preferred.

Turning, he glimpsed a shape reflected in the glass of the tiny porch beyond the door of the kitchen. He reached for the kettle when the notion struck him that the image in the glass was giving off a shimmering blue reflection. Victor's running suit was black.

Joyce dropped just as the man came through the door, both hands wrapped around a submachine gun. The spray of bullets shattered the glass panes of the kitchen cabinets above his head, blowing the still whistling kettle across the countertop.

Victor's automatic fired twice, an obscene spitting sound that toppled the man into the room and sent him crashing across the kitchen table, shattering plates and creating a wave of linen cloth that spilled jam, butter, and rolls onto the wooden floor.

Victor dodged across the room and dragged the assassin from the table to the floor, pulling him onto his back and staring into the glazed expression of death.

"Remember those Finnish friends of yours? The ones you swore would protect us? They are bleeding their guts out across the lake," he uttered contemptuously.

Victor kicked the Russian's weapon over to Joyce. Then he moved to the porch and, keeping low, peered through the open door.

"We've got to try for the car. But be careful. There are more of them out there in the trees."

Joyce hefted the weapon, balancing it against his hip. It would not be especially easy to fire with only one hand, but he had practiced with a similar weapon on an FBI range in Washington just for the hell of it, one weekend the previous summer.

Glass shattered, and Joyce wheeled the nozzle toward the front door. Kicked open, the door shot back. Joyce leaned into the crook of the counter, steadying the weapon along the Formica surface and squeezing off a short burst.

The KGB man spun into the room, like a quarterback on a sneak, arms wrapped around his weapon. He fell on his face for short yardage.

Joyce turned and his gaze met Victor's.

"Now."

Victor shot through the rear door, dodging in a zigzag

TO KILL A KING

down the slope toward the green Opel station wagon parked two hundred yards away, through the woods.

Joyce trained the barrel on the trees beyond, wondering just how many there were and if his life would end here, alongside the lake, which was not a bad place for it. His mind filled with a line from Tolstoy. How could they kill him, whom everyone loved? And he wondered how many in his century had uttered the same perplexed thought the instant before their lives were snatched away?

He was moving with Victor along the rear of the house, then across a narrow interval of shielding brush to the shed containing neatly stacked piles of firewood.

Beyond the shed, wood had been piled in shoulder-high clumps, like a line of barricades marching toward the trees. Using them as cover, they inched along, Victor first, automatic held in front of him, Joyce a step behind, breathing hard and holding the submachine gun against the outside of his leg.

It was unusually quiet. The lake was a glassy sheet of substance reflecting a sky occluded by scudding clouds. It was windy and suddenly colder, but Joyce was not aware of the chill. Only of the trees ahead, silent verticals of black.

Victor slipped between the trunks and signaled for Joyce to follow. They moved from tree to tree, Victor first, then Joyce, each covering the other as he crossed the open spaces of ground.

Perhaps it was then, in that endless, erratic dance taking them from tree to tree, when the fear was greatest, that Joyce was gripped by a special feeling of connection between himself and the Russian. They were no longer defector and interrogator. Their roles had become interchangeable. Joyce knew in his guts he did not want the Russian to die.

Bullets tore a swatch from the tree trunk above his head.

Joyce dropped to one knee and struggled to swing the barrel toward the fire. Victor was on his belly in the soft grass, the automatic held in both hands.

Shapes darted stealthily between the black verticals, coming in low, straight ahead, and on both sides.

The vibration shuddered through him as the submachine gun sputtered.

The shapes became men and were torn backward, a magazine image ripped in half.

"Go on!" Victor shouted. Joyce pushed to his feet, moving as quickly as he could, bent in a low crouch. He tripped over a huddled shape beside a fallen log without seeing him but regained his footing and stumbled on, impelled by his own forward motion.

There was a blur of green through the tree trunks. Joyce homed directly for it, turning to kneel behind the rear fender and covering Victor as he came through the trees.

Victor made it to the car and disappeared inside. The engine sputtered into life.

The door on his side flew open. Joyce jumped inside and pulled the door shut.

"They're waiting for us to come down the road," Victor said. "They send two to flush us out, then herd us into an ambush."

Victor cut the wheel hard over. They skidded off the track into the brush to avoid the dirt road that skirted the lake. They headed directly into the trees.

That was when the firing began.

Bullets tore bark from the slender plantation of pine embracing the cabin. They sped between the graceful black verticals rising to form a spiny thatch of needles sixty feet above the ground.

Joyce clambered over the front seat, lowering himself until he was on his knees, the nozzle of the submachine gun resting on the top of the rear seat. Victor pressed a button, and the glass half of the station wagon's rear door was lowered, opening a field of fire.

Shapes appeared, running behind the car, following them into the forest, appearing in shafts of filtering sunlight, then disappearing into velvet shadows.

The car kicked and spun, skidding in and out between the tree trunks, hitting some and jarring Joyce off-balance. He got off several bursts but didn't think he hit anything. His ears were filled with a painful roaring.

They came out lower down, along the road that looped around the lake. Victor propelled the Opel along the narrow band of asphalt that pierced the dark stands of fir. The trees thinned, falling away to meadow on one side, then on both.

Joyce half expected a car to follow, but none did. They reached the village on the far side of the lake, holing up in a tiny house until Finnish intelligence arrived to blanket the area. The KGB had disappeared, taking their dead with them. The three Finns guarding the cabin had all been murdered.

They did not return to the cabin, spending the remainder of their time allotment in a small house outside Helsinki, guarded by a cohort of grim-faced security men.

Joyce wondered why Victor had returned to the cabin after finding the security men slain. Their arrangements had been locked into place. He had all the papers and assurances he had bargained for. He could have claimed the money in his numbered account and disappeared within the concentric folds of a dozen false identities that had been prepared for him. Joyce never pushed for a reason. Victor offered only one.

"You didn't have to come back. Why did you?"

"But you are my benefactor," Victor said with an enigmatic smile. "I couldn't just let them have you. Where would I get my spending money?"

But that was not the reason, could not have been. And both of them knew it.

In the end, Joyce had drawn an impregnable circle of protection around the Russian, using factors perhaps better employed, diminishing his own power in the process. Overseeing his quarry's safety long past the need, doing that still. Deluding himself that he was parent to a wayward prodigal. Believing Victor to be the son he had always wanted but never had. Believing he had created some kind of sanctification for himself in the process. Ironically his destiny had been fulfilled. He had become a good shepherd, after all. Pastor to a parish of one.

Victor had become his flock.

Joyce lay back against the porcelain, clearing Victor's image from his mind, trying to make sense out of what Stepinak had shown him. For the moment he would discount the possibility that Victor's defection was a KGB maneuver. Victor was a defector, and pressure on defectors was standard procedure, even if it was in violation of the deals he had made. But Victor was no ordinary defector. He had been a valued, even talented, agent, resourceful and clever. He knew all the standard ploys and had even invented some. No matter how desperate he became, Joyce could not believe Victor had allowed himself to become trapped in an association with anyone as volatile and dangerous as Roger Killian. Not the Victor he had once known. But men change. Circumstances bend them, even the strongest.

Joyce rose, dripping, and got into his terry-cloth robe. He lit a cigarette and stood at the window staring out over the heath, shadowed and verdant with the pungent green of early spring. Then he returned to the table on which he had placed Victor's file.

A brief was being prepared. Evidence was being gathered. An indictment as much against Victor as against Joyce himself and the dying influence he represented. But Joyce did not delude himself. Questions had been raised that demanded answers. Not only for Stepinak but also for himself. Had their whole relationship been a sham? Was Victor running Killian and being run by Bunin, as unlikely as that seemed?

He had to find answers.

It was not Victor but the Killian factor that frightened him most. It presented a danger that could not be rationalized or dismissed. As much as he feared for Victor, the Russian still possessed skills that could insure his survival, provided he still wanted to survive.

And what of his own survival? Was that being tested as well?

Joyce lay down on the bed and lit another cigarette. He had marked Victor, compromised him and brought him out, severing bonds of loyalty, family, and country, bonds that could never be reconnected. But he had failed to provide another country, a different loyalty, another kind of bond. What he had offered Victor would never be enough. Just as it had never been enough for him.

Joyce got up and returned to the window, his eyes fixed on a landscape that offered beauty but no refuge.

The car returned for him at seven. The driver conferred with the Sikh, who dialed Joyce's room. There was no response. The driver went up and knocked on the door. No one answered. The surveillance team burst in several minutes later, but the rooms were empty. The file was gone. Joyce had stepped into the night and disappeared.

8

For Trager it was a hunter's dread, the fear of the professional who might miss his kill.

Trager's dark figure darted cautiously between the olive trees, keeping low, moving along the edge of a culvert that broke into an irregular series of steps crumbling toward the rocky beach below. From where he was, he could see the coast of the island pointing toward a misty headland and the oxidized bronze of the Turkish coast across the narrow channel.

Easy ducks, slow and easy . . . count the beats. That's a good lad. . . .

Trager filled his lungs as he ran, trying to ease the tension, concentrating on the heft and swing of his athletic body. But he was encased in a sweaty muck that ran down his face and soaked the entire back of his serge coveralls. He wore a leather jacket over khaki mechanics' coveralls he had purchased in an East End surplus emporium. A canvas bag was slung over one shoulder, banging uncomfortably across his lower back. He was curly-haired, good-looking, and conscious of it—too conscious of it, some of his lady friends thought. But Trager never let their opinions affect him. They existed to be used and then discarded, like partners in an endless dance.

Trager felt his cheeks burning, less from the exercise than from the hot Mediterranean sun. His fair skin was freckled and blotched from overexposure. That came from trying to cram a tan into the business. He knew better and cursed softly, as the slope drew him down faster than he wanted to go.

Shit!

Trager skidded to a halt at the edge of the olive grove, pausing where the flinty soil dropped sharply to a rutted track edging around the slope like a ragged belt. Silvery leaves provided some shade as the sun climbed toward noon. Below, neat plots of cultivation sprouted between the rough stone walls of a tiny village with red-tiled roofs that spilled toward a brilliant sapphire sea. Reaching past the houses, a low stone wall slung a protective arm around a tiny cove that was no more than a spit of choppy water. Anchored there, fishing boats bobbed and ducked on the ripples like a gym full of fighters.

Opposite the village was a small white hotel—more an inn, really—which squatted at the top of the rise above the beach. It faced forty feet of gleaming white hull riding at anchor beneath two soaring masts. The beach itself was empty except for a rubber dinghy and two blazing orange towels. Reclining on one of them was a naked woman.

Trager was not surprised. He had been awaiting her arrival for the past two days, watching the sea from his perch atop the wall of a crumbling farmhouse that spied on the inlet. The fishing boat that brought him from Mykonos would return to pick him up that evening. By then he would have what he came for.

Low walls of jagged stone traveled in irregular tracks around the slope, providing Trager with the cover he needed. The inhabitants of the island never came out during the midday siesta. Only the visitors at the hotel would be sunbathing at this hour. Mad dogs and Englishmen. They were the target he sought.

Off you go, boyo . . . off to see the Wizard . . .

It took all of fifteen minutes for Trager to circle the village and pass the cove. He had timed that to within seconds. Dark heads bobbed in the water alongside the sloop. He heard the splash of a swimmer as he dived over the side. Trager felt the desire to plunge in with him and feel the chill water against his burning skin, fierce and lovely.

The wall Trager followed made an abrupt turn, leaving a space of uneven ground for him to cross without cover. It was the only place from which he could be seen by the swimmers below. The woman's back stared at him, her head turned seaward. He glanced at the groove of her spine and the deeper one between her buttocks. She was coated with oil and gleamed in the sunlight like a pretty bronze statuette.

Trager felt his stomach knot. Sweat trickled beneath his armpits. But nothing moved in the landscape below. Nor was there any sign of movement at the hotel. Umbrellas above the half dozen tables flapped unsteadily as the breeze combed through them. All the windows were shuttered against the brilliant, almost painful, sun. Trager heard another splash.

TO KILL A KING

He sucked breath and crossed the open area with an indifferent stride, then disappeared behind the wall that crossed behind the hotel and ran almost to the water's edge.

He froze. Waiting. Seconds crawled spiderlike across the black face of his watch. Then silence.

He had not been seen.

Trager dropped to the ground. Stones had been removed in the wall, creating a dazzling window of light. Trager slipped the bag off his shoulder and closed his hand around the cool metal inside. He had already calculated the distance and made all the necessary adjustments. All he had to do now was wait.

The woman turned over, rising on her elbows to stare at the male figure splashing toward her with an easy stroke. Droplets of oil slid down between her breasts toward the dark pit of her navel. A sliver of white skin coiled around her naked hips, accenting long legs that were crossed at the ankles.

Trager felt a tightening between his legs. God, she was lovely. The ground beneath him undulated with the warmth of a woman. He was getting a hard-on. He tightened his lips, biting back the giggle he felt bubbling inside. A hard-on, can you imagine? What a wonder is man. A bloody freaking wonder, that's what.

He closed his fingers around the handle of the pistol grip. The Prince was coming out of the water.

Spray streamed from the royal body as the Prince tiptoed over the stones and lowered himself to the towel beside the woman. Trager tensed and brought the sight to his eye. The angle was perfect. He could make out every detail of their bodies: the glinting line of sweat under the woman's shaved armpits; the thickening bulge growing beneath the almost transparent material of the Prince's narrow black bikini.

Trager sucked breath, watching the Prince's hand reach toward the swaying, uptilted nipples. He focused the image in the cross hairs of his sight and snaked his finger around the trigger. The mechanism was specially made. There would be no sound. Not even a click to mar the perfection of his kill.

SUPER SCOOP STRIKES AGAIN!

Trager stood against a plate-glass store front beneath a cold drizzle, watching a turbulent eddy form around the news kiosk opposite, stalling the wash of commuters streaming toward the Piccadilly tube stop. The headline disappeared, snatched by eager hands.

Trager could not suppress a smile. The other headlines were as flat as deflated inner tubes. He had scored big this time, and the thought brought its own kind of pleasure.

After developing the negatives, he had actually debated about setting up an auction and offering them to the highest bidder, but he knew the losers would only have diluted the impact by rushing to fabricate covering stories of their own. After almost seven years in the trade, Trager was wise to all the dirty tactics of Fleet Street.

He had been clever offering it to McNabb first. The cagey old Scot almost leapt off his swivel chair when he opened the envelope Trager handed him and saw the prints. The old bastard tried to act as nonchalant as if he had been offered coverage on some nuns' picnic. Still, there had been barely a quibble when Trager named his price. McNabb had paid up without a grumble. And why the hell not? Trager was the smartest paparazzo in London—Europe, for that matter. This was his fourth big score. Trager could still hear McNabb bellowing, "You lucky son of a bitch! How in hell did you pull it off?"

Mac still didn't understand that luck had nothing to do with it. Nor did any of the other ass-wipes he had shared grog with in the pubs around Fleet Street. They had no idea he had the power to do it again and again, any fucking time he wanted.

A woman passerby jerked her head around, startled by Trager's unconscious grin.

He turned up the collar of his new cashmere topcoat against the rain that had started to fall and stepped into the bustle. He had purchased the coat at Harrod's. That should impress the little blond bird who worked in a Kings Road boutique near his studio. He wanted to catch her before her shop closed.

The thought of her shapely legs and tight little bottom propelled him toward the taxi stand with special urgency. His mind had not stopped playing back the image of the girl on the beach, the deep indentation of her navel, and the savory triangle beneath. Bloody sweet delight.

He pulled open the cab's door and shouted the address to the driver, injecting himself into the dark interior, settling himself against the cushions as the vehicle groused into the evening gloom. He had invested enough time and money in the coy little bitch. She had better come across tonight. But the way his luck was running, Trager was damned confident she would. There was no way under heaven he could possibly lose.

He never noticed the blue BMW that slipped in and out of the lane behind his cab, nor would Trager have been affected by it if he had. It was not new enough or swell enough to magnetize his attention. Nor would he have been concerned about its presence outside his studio later that evening while he was so fortuitously occupied with the resilient flesh of his cozy little blonde, who, as predicted, was wise enough to offer him her physical bounty after he had spent so lavishly.

Trager was flying too high to allow minor coincidences to disturb him. And that was just as well. For he would have attributed them to the jealousy of his fellow paparazzi who often tailed a compatriot in the hopes of latching on to his good fortune. And so, the tiny nicks on the metal of his lock that might have suggested a forced entry to the more wary went unnoticed. As did the occasional face that looked slightly familiar but which he could not place. None of these details signaled a warning, nor disturbed the euphoria of the moment. They remained only dimly perceived shadows at the outer reaches of his consciousness, minor blemishes upon the perfect beauty of his rainbow.

9

The festival was always the same. A perfect little bourgeois pigsty, agrunt with the feeding sounds of greed.

The town was also fouled with traffic, as it was that noon. Vehicles swarmed like frantic insects along the wide boulevards and clogged the narrow side streets. Taxis and limos hovered around the entrance of the large hotels like flies over feces. Horns blared and drivers cursed. Victor tried to remain calm as he edged his rented Jag into the snarl outside the Carleton, whose white and ornately Victorian facade he somehow found offensive.

Impossible.

Victor cursed and shifted into park. He eased himself out from behind the wheel and strode toward the entrance, tossing his keys to the harried valet who came out of the elaborate doorway. Victor ignored the man's exasperated protest and strode inside.

The afternoon had turned sultry. Victor was perspiring in his white double-breasted suit. Inside the rococo interior he recognized an Italian distributor, a Czech director, and the marketing consultant to a major American studio. He had spoken to the Italian and the Czech earlier in the week, but neither saw fit to toss him a bone of recognition. Perhaps business was too generous a way to describe their encounters. Victor had pitched and they had listened. So far neither had returned his calls.

Victor pasted an expression and brushed by, sinking inside his plastic smile. He had been trying to drum up interest in a score of projects, with no success so far. The festival was in its dying days. Time was already edged against him. He had to return to Paris with at least an option. A deal memo. *Anything*.

With a dark stab of desperation he headed toward the concierge.

There was a stir at the elevators. A woman emerged encased in gauze, naked breasts bobbing like anchored buoys.

Photographers closed around her. Lenses whirred and snapped, making the sounds of gorging hyenas. The woman's semi-clad body brought a flood of images from the previous night. Victor had spent the evening tangled in the damp sheets of a hotel suite belonging to an aging Swedish actress who was desperate for a comeback. Her ardor had been as mechanical as his own, inspired as much by the role he had offered as his pretended worship of her reconstructed body and silicone-inflated breasts. What they had exchanged was not love but desperation.

Of course, they had performed all the usual expected maneuvers. They were professionals, after all. But in the end, the comfort each so desperately sought from the other had become impossible. In the morning, each remained capsuled in a gritty silence.

Victor continued past the sordid exhibition outside the elevators without turning his head.

The concierge's calculating gaze absorbed Victor without emotion. An imperceptible movement of his fat little fingers sent an assistant scurrying to search the cliff of tiny nests behind him. Victor's stomach clenched as he prayed. There had to be something. Anything.

The boy returned with two messages. Victor felt an instant of elation as the concierge's hand opened like the jaws of a lamprey, snapping up the folded bill Victor deposited in his moist palm.

Victor was not a guest at the hotel, but a sizable gratuity insured that the world believed he was. Calls for him were forwarded to a line that was forever busy. Messages were then recorded at the desk. With round-the-clock screenings, parties, and meetings, no one suspected anything out of the ordinary. Victor was actually installed in a tiny hotel on an unfashionable street behind a market, whose Czech owner provided discretion and a discount.

Victor stepped away from the desk and took a seat in a quiet corner of the lobby, waving away an approaching waiter. A glance confirmed that neither was the one he expected. With a sinking feeling he scanned the bits of paper. The first was from someone named Vincent Roberts, a name he did not recognize. The second caused his eyes to darken. He rose and went to the phone.

An attractive woman stabbed an appreciative glance in his direction. She stood in the center of a jabbering cluster of badly dressed Brazilians, flaunting designer labels. Victor held her eye an instant longer than was necessary before turning toward the phones. Except for the actress, he had not been with a woman since driving down from Paris almost two weeks before, and the woman's dark eyes and glistening lips caused a reciprocal itch. But he ground out the urge like a trashed cigarette.

Control, Petrushka. That's an angel. Just a little while longer . . .

Victor was just over six feet and could still pass for forty in spite of the wear. His dossier, on file in the warehouse of a Moscow directive, made a point of stating he was attractive to women. The accompanying photograph offered proof. There was something magnetic about his blue eyes and expressive Slavic features. The devil's gift, his mother liked to joke. He had long ago learned its price.

Victor took a seat inside the wood-paneled booth, opened the messages, and dialed. A man answered almost at once, speaking English with an accent that suggested expensive prep schools and middle-Atlantic comfort.

"Vincent Roberts?"

"Speaking."

"Victor Sorge here. You left a message at my hotel."

"Right. Glad you called. I saw *Dark Current* in New York and wanted to get together with you for a drink. I represent Michelle Duran."

Victor groped for recognition but came up blank. "I'm sorry, but I don't seem to know the name."

"You will," Roberts said confidently, and Victor imagined a corporate salesman type. Blow-dried hair and forgettable features.

"Michelle's been working in Canada for the last couple of years. She's here promoting a picture for the Canadian Film Board. *Northern Adventure*. Have you seen it?"

Victor remembered noticing the film listed for viewing at some obscure hour of the morning. "No, I'm afraid I haven't," he said regretfully.

"It's screening tonight. I didn't know if you had the time or if we should get together first."

Victor did some juggling, resketching the possibilities he had outlined for that evening. "I do have some time later, say about seven. At my hotel?"

"Sounds great," Roberts responded in the same positive

tone Victor already found annoying. "What exactly did you want to discuss?" Victor asked, almost as an afterthought.

"Why don't we wait until we sit down in person," Roberts answered. "I think you'll find it interesting."

"All right. I like surprises."

"This is going to be one of the more exciting ones. See you then."

Victor hung up, not altogether puzzled by the call and imagining the usual predictable angles. News that he was casting was common knowledge. The agent probably wanted inclusion in the package. With a tightening stomach he opened the second message and dialed the number it contained.

10

Bunin awaited Victor in the far corner of a tree-lined square filled with a ragged collection of boys kicking around a soccer ball. Twilight brushed smudges of shadow across the uneven ground, blurring the shapes of whitewashed buildings embracing the open space. Bunin had chosen well. The narrow streets were filled with homebound workers, many of whom stopped to watch the game or cluster in one of the several cafés that ringed the square, before turning into their own streets. Few would notice two strangers exchanging casual conversation on the merit of play.

Victor had taken a cab to the working-class quarter, far from the glitter of the festival. He had exchanged his white suit for a zippered jacket and dark pants, adding dark glasses and loafers. Before approaching Bunin's squat, solitary figure, he stopped at a small café to purchase a blue package of Gauloises. Then he strolled to where Bunin was watching the frenetic skirmish, his pupils shifting like oiled dots as they followed the black-and-white ball that spun back and forth across the uneven stones.

Bunin's red lips twitched in disgust as the missile veered off before reaching its goal. Victor remembered Bunin's passion for the game, as if the stolid mass of Bunin could feel passion for anything.

In spite of the warm weather, Bunin wore a coat and hat made of the same waterproof material. Beneath the dirty brim, his sallow skin looked jaundiced in the half-light. Bunin's nose was varicosed with a fine mesh of capillaries. The reek of brandy clung to him like cheap cologne. It recalled Victor's earliest impression of their relationship.

Bunin had been Victor's first case officer after his discharge from training school. Victor had been posted to Bernau, where Bunin had taken a liking to him and demonstrated his techniques for unmasking potential defection in the sensitive defense project Victor had been assigned to protect. Bunin had been a good teacher. Naturally, a scandal would have shaken the top of the tree, as Bunin liked to say, showing his teeth in a yellow smile.

So Bunin, like the good dog he is, lifts his leg and waters the trunk each day. And at night the tree shakes down its fruit. And that way, Petrushka, the system takes care of its own.

So they sought elsewhere to fulfill their quotas of the disloyal, quotas needed to justify the existence of the security apparatus, and without which it would cease to exist.

Bunin taught Victor the necessary facts of life. We exist to ferret out the enemies of socialism, therefore those enemies must exist. And if not . . . Bunin grinned. Like the Jews, we would have to invent them.

Bunin was as tenacious and cunning as a Siberian wolf, snaring the foolish and the indiscreet, manufacturing treason where none existed, pocketing the possessions of those arrested. Buying and selling on the illegal markets. And generous when he had to be. And soon Victor was able to purchase his first fast car and a collection of jazz recordings. Billie Holiday and Miles Davis, which he listened to each evening, accompanied by a bottle of peppermint-flavored vodka, slipping into reveries of grandeur in which his rise in the Party apparatus was both quick and filled with glory. But then Victor had always been ambitious.

Even in the early days in Odessa where he had been shipped by his father after his mother's death. He had been weaned in a luxurious and artificial Moscow setting provided by his mother's artistic connections. Life in the provinces was stultifying; a gray, monotonous existence. Socialist realism in spades. A life of slide rules and production quotas, which he despised.

In his last year at the technical academy where he was preparing for a career as a chemical engineer, he fell in love with a slender girl named Zorina. She had green eyes and honey-colored hair wrapped in a chignon. He was eighteen and devoured mystical poetry. They walked together, dreaming of a life abroad. Paris. Los Angeles. New York. She wanted to become an actress. She would be sent on tour and then defect. She admitted this without shame, knowing Victor would never repeat what she confided to him. To realize her dream she would have to be admitted to the Film Academy in Leningrad. There were few places, and one needed high party connections she did not have.

As the date of graduation approached, she became more desperate. Victor had already been accepted into the Academy for Advanced Studies. He would be living in Moscow. One day, when he arrived at her door for their usual walk to school, he was told she was ill. She did not appear the following day or the day after. A week passed. Victor grew desperate. He went to her house, insisting on seeing her.

Her mother admitted him, weeping in shame for her lies. Zorina was no longer living at home. She had left without a word to anyone. There was no letter for him. Not even a farewell. Victor was heartbroken. Then a friend whispered something. Another friend echoed the whisper. Victor was angry, then disbelieving. Finally he was forced to accept the truth.

All the while they walked together, holding hands, exchanging chaste kisses, he touching her breasts outside her coat, no more, Zorina was having an affair with her drama teacher, one Gregoriev, a man some thirty years her senior. He pictured them screwing on the dusty couch in his clutter of an office. Zorina on her knees with the old man's swollen cock between her pretty, wet lips, laboring to bring him off. Victor grew ill on the image, the thought that it was the same mouth he had kissed and tongued, the act he had hungered for in each of his nightly fantasies.

It turned out Gregoriev had introduced Zorina to a high party official who often showed an interest in protégées of the drama teacher. The interest manifested itself in small private parties, during which the young ingenues were expected to show their talents by reciting passages from Chekov in the nude on a small stage in the teacher's studio. This was followed by notorious drinking bouts that turned into grotesque orgies. All of this was well known in upper Party circles and eventually led to the official's downfall, but not before he secured for Zorina a place in the Film Academy. Victor realized he had been a fool, an innocent. But he had learned early on that the system did indeed reward ambition.

Bunin was an alcoholic. Victor often joined him in his less serious bouts. Afterward they would pile into Victor's new car. Victor drove like a demon on the deserted rural highways. Risking his neck became a form of penance, easing his burden of self-loathing and providing its own tortured means of forgiveness. Yet in spite of his feelings of guilt for what he

TO KILL A KING

was doing, he loved the money and the feeling of power. But that was before he was required to kill.

Time never erased the Czech's face. It remained in his memory as stark and white as the shell of an egg. It had been raining that night. The street was dreary. Walls of damp brick rose on either side, looking like a thousand others in East Berlin, all part of the nondescript wasteland beyond the cement wall dividing the city.

Bunin had run the operation. But Victor had pulled the trigger. It would look good on his record, Bunin insisted. A first step toward promotion. And Victor had always been ambitious, hadn't he?

He remembered walking toward the target, like a bridegroom toward his intended, remembering hearing snatches of Mendelssohn's Wedding March. Idiotic, of course. And equally unexplainable.

He had paced out the distance, rehearsing exactly when he would draw his weapon, when he would fire. Strangely enough, it had gone exactly as planned. Only the sound of the weapon startled him, tearing him out of his trance. The Czech's face fell away in front of him like a cardboard prop. He turned away, then forced himself to stare at the dark, huddled shape on the wet sidewalk that had once been a living creature, the arms and legs bent like a swastika.

A moment later Victor heard someone call his name, and he froze, half expecting to see the face of God. Instead it was the grinning face of Bunin, peering out from the rear of the car that had arrived to speed him away. He remembered the dark pattern of windows on either side of the claustrophobic brick walls, dark and empty sockets, staring like the mute eyes of the blind.

"Allez, allez! Vite!"

The boys' shouts brought him to the present. Victor shoved both hands into the pockets of his jacket and assumed a casual stance, eyeing the spinning football a moment before he spoke. "Is it Alexi?"

"The boy is holding his own," Bunin answered in his harshly accented French. "Fool, pass!" Bunin shouted, matching his outrage to the shouts around them, as one of the players missed a chance to score. "It's Vasnikov," he continued in the same breath, turning to follow the play downfield. "As usual, he wants more money."

Victor exhaled slowly. The demand was not unexpected. Vasnikov was his son's physician. His skills were formidable, only exceeded by his greed.

"He's mad, of course," Bunin hissed. "But what do you expect? The exchange rate is favorable. Even in Kiev they know that, my friend. I had to fight for francs. He wanted dollars."

"And what if I can't raise any more?"

Bunin shrugged. "Do I have to spell it out for you?"

No. Victor knew exactly what it meant. His son's bone-marrow transplants would be halted. The boy would be transferred to a People's Hospital. There his chances of surviving the leukemia would drop to one in a hundred, or worse, with a defector for a father. An instant later the thought crossed his mind that the money was actually for Bunin.

Like most KGB of his rank, Bunin was rapacious, out to gouge as much as he could. Victor had no illusions about that. But Bunin absorbed risk every time they met, every time he passed Victor's payment to the medical staff of the small hospital outside Kiev reserved for high Party officials and special research cases, as his son Alexi had been designated. This was not the same as smuggling caviar or vodka. If Bunin were caught, not even his KGB rank would save him.

"How much?" Victor queried.

"Five thousand," Bunin said with a shrug. "Look, I tried to make them see reason, but Vasnikov is frightened. He's always whining about some new investigation. Imagine! I asked him, how many commissars' sons have you dried out? How many drug addicts with generals for fathers? Let them investigate that. The bastard said, 'A general is a general. Your case is different.'"

Victor was silent. Vasnikov was right, of course. His case was different. Nine years before, he had been scraping for smuggled dollars exactly like Bunin. He had been a hot little property then, running KGB networks through Belgium and Scandinavia. Supporting a luxurious Leningrad apartment, his own brand-new Zhiguli sedan, and an actress in Moscow. Pretty Victor, soaring like Icarus, on his magical wings of wax, living his frenzied delusion of pleasure and success; a simpleton unaware that he had become the pawn in an intricate game of power, until the sun licked his wings and he came tumbling into the world.

The American agent who brought him over had given him

life instead of the usual false identity and the endless fear of a bullet. But Victor felt there were times a bullet might have been a blessing. Moments like the one he was facing now, knowing his son was fifteen hundred miles beyond his help. He did not delude himself. He was an expatriate with six passports and no country. His mistake had been leaving the boy with Irena, his ex-wife. The error had been fatal. Irena was a bitch, even if she was the boy's mother. She had been willing to let Alexi go, but she had whined, demanding money, some kind of security, when he had none to offer. By the time he got the money together, the boy was already too ill to travel. He should have taken Alexi with him. He had never forgiven himself for that. It was a constant reproach. Images of the boy haunted his dreaming, growing more resonant as time ate up more of his life. It had become a silent ache, like a small stone in his heart.

"All right"—Victor exhaled deliberately—"but I'll need some more time."

"I'll be in Paris on the nineteenth of next month. I'll contact you. And don't worry, the boy will be fine. Pass! Damn you!" Bunin exploded, turning to follow the whirling missile downfield.

Victor stepped away, moving laterally between the trees, leaving Bunin's squat figure a blur in the descending darkness.

11

The faces of three American motion picture stars hung above the Majestic's vast terrace, blown up like Stalinist posters.

Victor secured a corner table and ordered a glass of champagne. The meeting with Bunin caused Victor to miss the reception given earlier by a major independent.

A good portion of the international film industry had streamed across the terrace throughout the afternoon. Victor had done what he could with the overflow, shaking hands, posturing like a clown. Winding up huddled around a tiny table in an out-of-the-way café with two avaricious Lebanese who represented a theater chain in Singapore.

They had bargained in three languages and finally shaken hands on the delivery of a five-picture package he was distributing, all the work of unknown Hungarian directors. Their assurances gave him the only real plus he had garnered in almost ten days. But it was barely enough. The festival would end the day after tomorrow, and Victor would return to Paris with nothing to show the syndicate of Corsicans that backed him. He needed to raise enough capital to keep his film operation going and somehow find enough to satisfy Bunin. Something concrete had to materialize.

He looked up and noticed the woman, and his heart jumped. *Zorina*. But, of course, it wasn't. A moment later he realized she was heading directly for his table.

She wore a white jumpsuit of parachute material and a wide leather belt. Her hair was black, coiled in a thick knot that emphasized the perfect sculpture of her small, dark head. She carried herself with a fluid movement that caused heads to turn, lured by the movement of her supple body outlined within the flowing silk. A table full of Arabs glanced around sharply, peering at her behind dark glasses.

Later Victor would find himself returning to that first image, trying to separate the reality of that moment from the compulsion she would become. Now he saw only her eyes and the strange speech that flowed from them. Calm and self-assured one moment, the next revealing a dark, vulnerable need. It was a need Victor recognized. A hunger very much like his own, and he was stirred deep in the recesses of his sentimental Russian heart. *Oh, how well they played you, Petrushka. Played you and reeled you in.*

Victor found himself on his feet with her hand in his, conscious of the darting glances that made them the focus of attention and the smile that had frozen itself to his lips.

Roberts came up a step behind her and made the introductions. The American wore a raw silk jacket and a silk shirt of pastel blue. He had the self-assurance and good looks of a male magazine ad. A face anonymous in its perfection. Victor noticed he did not wear socks.

They arranged themselves around the table, and as a waiter poured champagne they made the usual small talk about how impossible the traffic and the crowds were and how terrible the films were that year, or rather Victor and Roberts did. Michelle said nothing. She toyed with her glass as they chatted, raising her eyes to glance from one to the other with a darting, quicksilver gaze.

He found himself returning the examination. Her eyes, he realized, protruded slightly and had a slight Oriental cast. Her cheekbones were prominent, a photographer's joy. But her upper lip did not quite match the lower, marring the first impression of perfection. There was also a noticeable irregularity in the line of her jaw, giving one side of her face more prominence than the other. But in spite of it, or perhaps because of it, she was remarkably beautiful.

She was aware of his observation but did not seem uncomfortable because of it. Their eyes met and held. It was Victor who pulled away first.

He almost missed Roberts's casual comment concerning *Island of Glass* and *Dark Current*. Apparently Michelle had seen both films. Victor had produced the first, acting as distributor of the second. Still, he bowed a gracious thank-you and wondered where she had viewed them.

"Montreal, actually," she said with a smile. It took Victor a moment to place the intonation. It was the speech of Swiss boarding schools. An accent without a language.

It turned out they were less impressed with the fate of Victor's films than with the career of Lorraine Dessage, the young Parisian actress who had starred in them. Roberts took it for granted that Victor had been the cause, though that would have reversed the truth. Lorraine's career was pure alchemy, the product of a liaison with a German electronics manufacturer who had backed the promotion of both mediocre efforts. Victor did not contradict the impression. Nor did he rise to the bait when Roberts said they thought he could do the same for Michelle.

"You see," Roberts continued with his salesman's enthusiasm, "at the moment there is considerable interest in Michelle's career."

"What kind of interest?" Victor asked, aware that Michelle's eyes had not left his. Earlier in his existence her attention might have flattered him. Now he was used to the ploys of ambitious actresses.

"I'm not at liberty to disclose the details. But the people behind us believe Michelle is going to be a very big star, Mr. Sorge. When you see her picture tonight, you'll see why. What she needs is special handling. Total commitment and belief."

"So I gather," Victor commented dryly. "But that kind of commitment takes a great deal of money."

"Fortunately that's not a problem," Roberts emphasized. "What we're looking for is the right kind of individual. Someone with the background, experience, and savvy to realize her potential and be willing to devote a major effort to building Michelle's career. We think you're the kind of man who could provide the service we need."

"That's very flattering," Victor managed. "But you see, I do have other involvements."

"We realize that. We wouldn't expect you to give up everything. Not right away. But I assure you, Mr. Sorge, the remuneration will make it worthwhile," Roberts concluded, stressing the last word.

Victor smiled and took a sip from the columnar glass. The lure was a pretty one. But he had been through conversations like this before, only to see them come to nothing in the end.

"We don't want you to decide anything, not without seeing Michelle on film. We want you to become a believer before you commit to anything."

"A believer," Victor said, trying to keep the bitterness out of his smile. He had been that once. "Of course. But I don't suppose I'm the only name in contention?"

"No," Roberts answered. "But the field has been pretty

well narrowed. I can assure you of that. If you like, I'll send a car to take you to the screening. It's at two-thirty this morning. I realize it's inconvenient."

"Part of the game," Victor said with a smile, wondering exactly which one it was they were playing.

It was four-thirty when Victor emerged from the theater. The boulevards were deserted except for a scattering of movie people returning from late screenings. The town never slept during the festival. Even at this hour he could have found some kind of amusement, had he so desired. Instead he found his car and cruised the quai, letting his eye trace the silhouettes of motor yachts and sailboats bobbing on a jeweler's current of hammered silver.

He did not think much of the effort, a *cinema verité* treatment of life in a provincial Canadian town. Michelle had a featured role, but the feelings she aroused made him forget the rest of the film. She had barely said a word during their meeting that evening, nor did she have many lines in the film, but the director had been aware of her ability to communicate profound emotions without speech. It was a quality as rare as it was provocative. She was good, damned good.

So what's bothering you, Petrushka? But he did not know.

Victor had returned to his own hotel after their meeting to shower and nap before the alarm woke him at one A.M. He had closed his eyes but was unable to sleep. Their conversation replayed itself in his mind, until he rose, went to his briefcase, and dug out the distribution grosses on both pictures.

Roberts had mentioned seeing *Dark Current* in New York, but the film had never opened there. The lie was clumsy, but then lies were habitual with theatrical agents, and he put it down to that. Michelle, too, had professed seeing both films in Montreal, yet only *Dark Current* had ever played there.

What's the matter, Petrushka? Is the scenario just a little bit too familiar? Does it smell like rotting fish?

Victor slowed to a stop along the quai, staring at a scroll of jittery moonlight dancing on the jet-black sea, his mind filled with conflicting voices.

Perhaps it was the timing. A beneficence coming as it did, when it did, just when he needed it so badly. Yet he could not deny its probability. Such things were an everyday occurrence in this insane industry.

Then what was wrong?

First you want to believe, and that is the greatest danger of all. Let me inform you, dear, innocent Victor. Before you is a hook, baited and dangling in front of your gaping mouth. A miracle, for those innocent enough and stupid enough to believe in such things. And the girl. A bit too enticing, no? Impossible for a man like you to resist. They've done their homework, dear boy. Competent, whoever is behind it. A professional. Knows just where you're weakest. Honey, those of you in the trade like to call it. The snare within the petals.

How many similar snares had he woven? How many men had he caught in the same way . . . and women? The KGB had used his looks and charm exactly as someone was using hers. He did not judge her. He had been as much a whore, edging up the ladder until he could use others the same way he had been used. Now, in some peculiar twist of destiny, the same technique was being used on him.

For an instant he thought of bolting, giving up the film company, the Paris apartment—all of it—and disappearing again, submerging somewhere and starting over as he had done so many times before. But the image of Alexi flooded his mind.

He had to go on, as much for the boy's sake as for his own. There was precious little left of his life except for that. But what could they possibly want from him? What did he have that was worth offering? He struggled to find a hope, to wash away the doubts and force his heart to believe. It was luck, all this, happening just when he needed it most . . . pure luck, you see.

Christ, Victor, aren't you entitled to a little luck for a change? Isn't everyone? But the dark voices would not go away. *Since when have you ever had luck, Victor, or hope?*

No, he had only the bitter rind of his ambition and the certainty of the condemned. Knowing that even if it was a trap, he was as powerless to resist the lure as any of his own victims.

12

Joyce slipped across the channel on the boat-train to Ostend. He was an anonymous figure in a short raincoat standing alone against the taffrail, watching the cliffs of white chalk disappear into a polluted mist. He blended into a rowdy crowd of young Brits on a one-day spree, out to swill duty-free booze and have a joyous fistfight with the Belgian constabulary waiting in riot gear on the other side of the landing barrier.

A roaring drunken phalanx broke the police line when the boat pulled in, sweeping all before it, including the passport inspectors, and Joyce trickled off with the other passengers, making his way, unnoticed, into the pelting Belgian drizzle.

He consumed a filling *carbonade* in a tiny bistro beside the main station that catered to train employees, then spent the better part of an hour in a post office telephone booth. Some of the numbers he dialed were in special codes, routed through various government circuits to the personal lines of ministries in Bonn, Vienna, and elsewhere. Others were to private individuals who answered in a variety of languages but expressed no surprise at hearing the familiar voice and quickly jotted the specific requests he made. Of the men he spoke to, some held high office; others were exiles behind desks, outsiders who no longer secured the favor of their governments but still possessed a conditional access to the inner chambers of power.

Others had seemingly severed all connections with the intelligence services that had once employed them, living by their wits or on pensions or on the secret hoards they had squirreled away. Many were burnout cases on the mend but hungering for harness still, who would smile or shrug at a wife or lover, prepared to disappear without a question. They formed part of Joyce's personal wealth, a network of employable delinquents, skilled in arts that sent the less fortunate to prison. A shadow army awaiting a role, recruited from those who held a stronger allegiance to each other than to the transitory interests of their own parochial governments.

From Ostend, Joyce took the night train to Paris, remaining in the dining car until it closed, making detailed notes on a yellow pad, placed alongside the file he had taken from Stepinak. Consuming quantities of Swiss chocolate he had purchased on the boat, duty-free. Staying awake as the express doggedly clattered across the industrial flatlands of northern France.

To those he shared his compartment with, he appeared a stolid father figure in tortoiseshell frames, benign and smiling, absorbed in his sheets of notepaper, which he managed remarkably well with one hand. He was a comfort to fall asleep beside.

The drizzle followed him to Paris, where there were other calls to make. After which he spent the balance of the morning purchasing a cheap vinyl valise and two changes of clothing, cotton underwear, a dozen pairs of identical black socks, and some antiquated shaving gear, including a tablet of unperfumed soap, a bristle brush, a plain porcelain mug, a safety razor and blades. He tested his new equipment in the restroom at the Gare du Nord, emerging in the anonymity of a dark blue suit, white shirt, black shoes, and tie. To the casual eye he was just another weary prole with an attaché case, trudging off for another day of labor in the hive.

The balance of that day was spent in little pilgrimages, visiting various parts of the city whose sensibility Joyce knew like an old lover. But there was a whole new feel to be gotten, a new texture to be sensed. His guidebook was Stepinak's purloined file. It was not a reconnaissance in the exact sense of the word, more of a glance around to get the image right.

He did not neglect himself. He stopped at a *confiserie* on the Rue Vignon, where he replenished his dwindling stock of sweets. Afterward he treated himself to a nourishing workers' meal in a noisy bistro in the Rue de Saints Peres, a steaming pot-au-feu and a half bottle of red wine, followed by a sweet lemon sorbet and a warm glass of Armagnac.

By nightfall he was picked up along a particularly nasty stretch of the Boulevard Clichy, by two men in a black Renault with whom he exchanged a cheerless silence. They drove him to an underpass beneath the peripheral highway that girdled the city. There he transferred to a maroon Citröen, in which Rosensweig sat planted behind the wheel.

Between the two men there was no greeting and less love. They shared only the memory of their last encounter. But a line of credit had not been fully exhausted. On balance, there was more owed to Joyce than debited to him. Like the blood tie of kinship, it created both attachment and resentment in equal measure.

In a special sense, they were a sort of kin. Joyce had always felt that, united both by the profession they followed and the physical sacrifice each had made in its pursuit, and though each had never recognized the other's handicap, neither referring to it by word or gesture, it created an invisible bond.

They made almost two complete circuits of the periphery. During the first tour it was Joyce who did most of the talking, summarizing what had transpired in the dark cavern of Stepinak's lair. He told the tale in a dry, emotionless tone, calculated to lull the man beside him into a forgiving mood.

Rosensweig was silent during the telling, betraying all the emotion of an icon as he guided the wheel in both gloved hands, his face pinched against the glare of headlights from the opposing lane. But he absorbed what Joyce had to say. Like Joyce, he had a talent for listening.

As Joyce glanced out at the bleak industrial waste that passed for scenery, he could see the old man's eyes begin to narrow, betraying his apparent disinterest. That was when he played his trump card.

"Did you know Killian was in Paris?"

And that engrossing tidbit, laid like an offering on the altar of their long relationship, restored grace between them.

There was a strategy of surveillance to hammer out. A sensible schematic, flexible but not too ambitious. Not entirely narrow and efficient enough to retain the necessary degree of secrecy.

"And where are we to get the personnel for such an operation?" the old Frenchman asked testily. "I have nothing!" Thus the bargaining began.

In the end, it was settled so that Joyce would provide the directives, static watchers, and follower teams, while Rosensweig constructed an umbrella of protection and the secondary logistics so necessary to their game of deception.

"And the cash?" Rosensweig uttered, with a sharp upward glance. "They keep me fed with scraps from the table."

Financing created the usual agony. Joyce was proposing a major operation, one Rosenswieg's bureau would have no official knowledge of, except, of course, the tiny, select handful the old man currently trusted. The Frenchman was kept on tight financial restraints by the powers that ruled over him. The money would come from funds Joyce had at his disposal, as both men knew all along. But Joyce maintained his poker face and continued the game for the sake of the old man's pride.

The cash would come from certain numbered accounts unknown to the auditors of Joyce's department, little caches of currency salted away in special numbered accounts that existed for just such a contingency. And if the funding fell short, as the Frenchman had faith it would? Well, there were reserves of goodwill existing in several quarters he could call on. Money was not a major worry, Joyce reassured him.

"For no one but God and America," Rosensweig muttered, with an envious cluck of disapproval.

They swung off the highway, threading their way toward central Paris, making a series of stops along the route Joyce had earlier diagrammed, stopping first at a silent lane behind the Boulevard Montparnasse, a street that seemed inhabited by half the hairdressers in France, where Victor worked in a complex of tiny offices. They moved on to the Rue Bonaparte, twisting its narrow way toward the Seine, where Victor occupied a fashionable apartment designed from combining two artists' lofts.

It was after midnight when the maroon Citröen drew to a halt before a walled residence in Passy, on a street that was filigreed with dark branches and moonlit cobblestones in front of handsome, walled residences with wormwood doors.

The old Frenchman hobbled inside a steeply gabled three-story Norman imitation, leaving Joyce to contemplate the comfortable suburban surroundings. In ten minutes Rosensweig returned carrying a large manila envelope that he laid on the seat between them, gesturing for Joyce to take a look inside.

Joyce felt the glossy finish on the photos before he held them in his hands. He viewed the portraits of Victor in the dim yellow ceiling light the Frenchman turned on for him.

"An Arab boy, too, then. A kind of jack-of-all-lowlife courier for our Fatah friends. Strictly low-level, but with a talent, as you can see. Someone put a bullet through his head. We don't think there was a Palestinian connection. At least none we could find. But your friend Victor fished in some murky waters. Someone else had an interest in him? Your friend obviously interested someone."

Joyce nodded. That much was obvious. But the Arab was connected to Killian. What need was there for Killian's surveillance of Victor, unless he wanted some kind of insurance? Unless he suspected Victor was playing another kind of game. Joyce allowed the images of Victor to absorb him, fighting off all the inevitable questions. It was Rosensweig who broke the silence.

"So then, are we hunting him or saving him?" the old man said with a sardonic grin. But as to that, Joyce could not yet fashion an answer.

It was after two when Joyce found his way to bed, weary and aching in his bones. His new home was a tiny studio in a modern, nondescript twelve-story slab located in Passy. It came furnished, compliments of Rosensweig. But the phone had a scrambler, and there was a separate way out through a subterranean garage, should he ever need it. There was a TV and a view of more modern slabs across the air shaft.

Joyce showered and flopped down on the couch with a glass of brandy he poured from a labelless bottle he found in a cupboard. He awoke with the glass still in his hand, the liquor tilted at a dangerous angle. The windows were filled with gray, the room was filled with chill, and the phone was jangling.

He scrambled the receiver to his ear and uttered a hoarse, "Hello."

"You have a peculiar way of bringing me luck," Rosensweig said on the other end. "We found him."

"Found Victor?"

"No, not Victor . . . Roger Killian."

13

Even in death she had a lovely face, had Sister Celeste. Her murderer had thoughtfully wrapped her in insulating layers of plastic that delayed her physical decay and made viewing her body far more pleasant than it normally would have been.

Joyce inspected the small but tidy house she occupied in a dismal industrial suburb, wandering from room to room while Rosensweig held a hurried conference with several detectives from the Sûreté.

Rosensweig was right about his luck. They had been extraordinarily fortunate. The nun would not have been discovered except for an accident. There had been some leakage in a nearby chemical plant, and the police had ordered a temporary evacuation of the neighborhood. But their luck did not end there. The house itself was almost completely free of fingerprints, and those remaining belonged to the slain nun. Robbery had been ruled out as a motive, which baffled the Sûreté, until a sweep of the area produced a newsboy responsible for delivering the ex-nun's papers—foreign papers, no less—which immediately touched off the suspicion of something political.

Questioned further, the boy revealed that not only was he hired to deliver the papers, but also to take them away. Miraculously he had been particularly lax that week and led the police to a considerable pile of newsprint, wrapped and ready for burning. The papers were carefully dusted and yielded several perfect print samples. One of these belonged to Roger Killian. When the police computer indicated a special code, Rosensweig was immediately notified, a scant hour and a half from the time he had dropped Joyce off at his new digs.

Rosensweig broke off the conversation and hurried to Joyce's side. He spoke in an excited whisper.

"She drove a car in for servicing within two weeks of her death. The car was not hers, a Volvo. About eight years old.

Four-door, maroon. The car was not in her garage, not parked anywhere around the house. I think it is fair to assume it was Killian's."

"Even if it is, he's got a head start."

"True. But look how carefully he wrapped her up. He must have thought she would not be found for some time. The neighbors say she was very regular in her habits. She shopped once a week, on a Tuesday. That gives him almost five days before anyone would have questioned where she was."

"All right." Joyce nodded. "Even if you're right and the car belongs to him, how long will he hold on to the car, assuming he hasn't dumped it already?"

Rosensweig shrugged. "It's not much, I admit. But it's all we have."

"Has this information gone out?" Joyce questioned.

"Only if I choose to release it," Rosensweig said quietly. "But that would compromise your friend Victor, would it not? I mean, should we manage to locate Killian, they would scoop him up, wouldn't they?"

"Locating Killian would be an accomplishment."

Rosensweig grunted. "You think it best to wait?"

"No. I think we should send out trackers. We might get lucky again. But my trackers, not yours. If we catch him, the credit goes to your bureau."

Rosensweig nodded. It was a bargain at any price.

So Joyce spread wide his nets.

His fisherman were a hastily assembled team, made up of experienced expatriates from behind the Iron Curtain who had once been part of espionage networks within their own countries and were now retired in the West. Two Czechs, a scattering of Hungarians, the rest Poles.

Joyce made contact by phone, offered each what little he had, and sent them off without the identity of their quarry but with the admonition that they were to track only, not to apprehend. These were old hands, and he could trust them to obey. Contact was kept through a Paris switchboard run by a team of Rosensweig's inner elite.

Rosensweig already had men in place at the airports, but Joyce knew his quarry was far too wary to go there. Airport security was at a high level of vigilance just then. Killian would want maximum flexibility of travel, which eliminated buses and trains and meant he would stick to the roads. But just as a precaution, he had Rosensweig dispatch teams to check those modes of transport while his own men scoured the web of highways that converged upon Paris. It would be hard work and he had a dim view of its success, but there was always the possibility Killian, meticulous as he was, would commit another error. And so he dispatched his forces, motley though they were, and with them sent a prayer traveling on a fragile wisp of hope. As for Joyce himself, he also had a rendezvous to keep, and curiously enough, it, too, was in Germany.

14

Killian greeted Munich with the indifference of an old campaigner.

He had taken two days to reach the city, traveling the secondary roads from Brussels into Germany on his gray march south. He made a decision to get rid of the car as soon as he was outside Paris, but he hesitated about how best to obtain another. Barring something unforeseen, he had almost a week before the nun was discovered. He kept his radio tuned to the local police band, but there were no reports of a maroon Volvo, nor was anyone who fit his description ordered to be apprehended. So he risked holding on to the car. Obtaining another was a gamble that came with considerable risk. Having to steal one was reserved as a last resort. European cars all had origin stickers. Their license plates were marked with their town and region, thus easy for the police to trace. Besides, it was a dependable car, a car he liked. He had been forced to give up most things he loved, and the car was a small but essential comfort. Perhaps he was just getting old and sentimental.

He broke his journey in Düsseldorf, called upon one of his sisters, and got dinner and bed for the night. She was a lonely, talkative creature, and he was forced to listen to her mindless chatter until well after midnight.

In Munich he took up residence with Brother Hans, a blond, wispy-bearded, acne-cheeked celibate who had left the monastery sometime within the year. Killian provided the brother with reassuring counseling and in return received a low-level courier who asked few questions and believed what he did benefited the souls of other lost and wandering prelates. Poor booby. Yet Killian was thankful for the young man. A wiser, more experienced hand also came with a risk. The longer one played the game, the greater the danger of misstep, betrayal, and exposure.

The little lost brother also came with an inconspicuous residence in the old city, providing Killian with easy access to the tourist-choked streets surrounding the Hofbrau in which he became just another anonymous face. He waited two full days before making contact, hours spent in close and careful observation of a ski shop on the Theresienstrasse, scouring for the telltale insignia of some intelligence service. A listening outpost. Following cars or street-strolling units. But there were no signs of these, just a stream of interested buyers and the procedures of casual commerce.

When he was satisfied, Killian sent the little brother in as the go-between, watching through the plate-glass window as the monkish candidate navigated the displays and spoke to the medium-sized blonde at the counter. She listened politely as he mentioned the items he wanted; her eyes flitted to the window for an instant, then regained their professional distance as she stepped into the stockroom. A moment later a man appeared, bearded and smiling, his hands filled with knitwear.

To their neighbors, Helga and Dietrik seemed an ordinary couple. They were in their middle thirties, outgoing and athletic, fond of sports and vacations. They lived in Schwabing, just off the Leopoldstrasse, a neighborhood renowned for its artistic pretensions. It was a home for wanderers, actors, singers, and the like, where people did not pry nor think it odd when their neighbors whisked off for a weekend without explanation, or sheltered a casual houseguest for a day or two for either sex or hospitality; it mattered little.

Dietrik was dark-haired, sported a beard and shaggy locks. His face was pocked and somewhat swarthy. He was muscular and vain of his build. Helga was smaller, blond, and well knit, very typically German. Helga's father had been in the SS. He still attended rallies and reunions, where he sang the good old songs and vented the good old hates, without benefit of any intrusive conscience. Helga's mother had divorced her father when Helga was nine. As she grew up, the realization of what men like her father had been capable of became first an unbearable burden, then something she had to atone for. She believed him to be part of a monstrous unrepentant establishment that could not be reformed, only destroyed. So she became one of its destroyers, an adept pupil of those who made bombs and connected them to automobile starters and retired overweight Molochs of the German economic miracle to their condominiums in paradise a bit earlier than expected.

TO KILL A KING

Dietrik postured, pontificated, and swaggered. But he had the kind of reckless daring that was often useful when bracketed by more prudent supervision. It was Helga who kept him on an even keel. Dietrik was good, but Helga was better. She was utterly reliable. She would kill on command, even sacrifice herself if she had to, and Killian understood this and kept it as a rare gift to be used only on the most sacred mission. It was a gift he was about to make use of.

Half an hour after Brother Hans left the ski shop, Helga picked up Killian on a side street off the Ludwigstrasse. They drove out to the Kuntshause, once a Nazi showplace, complete with impressive neoclassical columns. On the trip out, Killian outlined a tentative timetable he would fill in later. Helga absorbed everything with typical tight-lipped intensity.

"Dietrik is not to know anything. Only that I want him to stand by. Is that understood?"

Helga nodded.

"Our target is more important than any of the others so far. But we will not have time to prepare the same way we did before. We will have to remain ready to move at a moment's notice. We will improvise if we have to when we get there."

"I understand."

"You must also understand that the targets themselves believe speed and secrecy of movement is their best security. Normally they would be correct. This time they will be wrong. We have found a way to anticipate their movements. We will arrive at their destination at precisely the same moment they do. The normal security precautions generally taken for people of their importance will not have been taken. They will rely on a token security force. That is where our advantage lies."

Helga's expression did not change as she made a turn and they drove away from the Fascist arena.

"There is another thing. One of the targets is a woman. That sometimes presents a problem, but I have to count on it not being a problem for you."

Helga turned toward him for the first time, and her large blue eyes fixed on him like a dutiful child's.

"It will not be."

15

Joyce made his entrance into Germany on a rain-swept twilight, brandishing his Canadian passport to a border-control team that waved him through without a second glance. His back ached slightly from the all-day march across France, but he swung south toward the A5 to Frankfurt as the rain dissolved into a cold and starry night.

He had quit Paris before dawn, leaving the neatly kept studio in a grimly anonymous apartment block Rosensweig had provided for his use. He tidied up the tiny kitchen after washing the few dishes he had used during his two-day sojourn. During that time he had ironed out the technicalities over transport and a slew of other details, all essential to his operation but made more difficult by the typical French penchant for providing bureaucratic obstacles to every situation.

The car was a metallic-gray four-door Mercedes, not new but guaranteed to provide him with the proper blend of comfort and respectability appropriate to German genes. A locked pocket beneath the dash contained a cache of passports and dollars. Whatever else he needed would be provided along the way.

At Heidelberg he swung onto the 27, continuing his southward leg to Stuttgart, refusing the constant offer of food and lodging proffered by each road sign. He arrived in the bleak hours before dawn, taking up residence in a nondescript hotel near the center of town with a public garage next door.

If Joyce dreamed, he was unaware of it. He fell into a soundless void and awoke to the snorting of traffic and an awakened city brilliant under a clear and cloudless sky. Joyce had a special fondness for southern Germany. He lost himself for a while, investigating the shopping streets, enjoying a sense of refreshment beneath a warming sun that deeply shadowed the loden green of the steep valley walls enclosing the town.

Late afternoon found him on the A6 speeding toward Ulm. He turned off before he reached the city's environs and followed a convoy of double-hitched trailers south. He turned off the secondary road and descended the narrow medieval lanes into the postcard charm of Swabish Hall. The town straddled the Neckar River, which churned in a dirty gray foam between its ancient stone embankments.

Joyce found Voss and Heckler waiting for him at a corner table in the dining room of the Drei Konig. The hotel's dining room was bustling with early diners. Both men stood at his arrival, and he shook each proffered hand with professional solemnity.

Voss was the senior of the two by a decade but looked younger. He was gifted with an actor's face and an affable manner. He was all smiles and *gemutlichtkeit,* bustling on about what Joyce would eat and drink. Heckler was waspish and sour, with a funereal face and manner. He was meticulously attired in a dark business suit that contrasted sharply with Voss's leather jacket and white crew-neck sweater, an outfit that gave him the air of a successful submarine commander. Voss handled the field assignments, while Heckler specialized in research. They were a casting director's dream.

There was some comforting small talk and a crisply done schnitzel to dissect before they ordered pastry and coffee, accompanied by a bottle of Jagerschnappes. Using a copy of the file Joyce had purloined, Heckler had begun a biography of Victor's sojourn in Germany. He ran down the facts quickly in a meticulous accountant's manner, devoid of expression or sympathy.

"Subject establishes himself in Copenhagen after his defection, pursuing no particular aim except that of pleasure. There he drives a playboy's Porsche and lives in the duplex apartment of a hotel catering to the whims of Kuwati princelings. He vacations in a series of resorts from Elat to Southern Spain, traveling first-class, always accompanied by a different woman. Each of them beautiful, vain, and expensive. His liaisons lasted no more than six months, during which time he added other members to his ménage. Questions?"

Joyce assured him there were none so far.

Heckler cleared his throat and rushed on. "Subject attempts to organize one business or another. A formula race-car syndicate, several real-estate ventures. One or two paid off, the others ended inconclusively. In three years the account settled on Victor was depleted. Questions?"

Joyce shook his head. "You're doing marvelously. Please continue."

Heckler's voice droned on. But the facts descended into bitterness. Victor's contacts with Russia were minimal. Letters were sent through normal channels to his wife in Kiev. He received few replys. Irena was bitter, in need of money, and casting around for other lovers. His son seemed well, though the boy found some difficulty in adjusting to school. Victor did not seem particularly affected. But that was to come.

After that the record went spotty. Victor left Denmark on what looked like another of his innumerable pleasure trips. Reservations had been made at a hotel on the Riviera, but Victor never appeared. A French contact team wired for instructions, but a decision had been made to suspend surveillance. Almost nine months later Victor went to ground in southern Germany. He took up residence first in Munich, moving to Stuttgart a year later, where he remained continuously for almost four years. That was where Heckler proceeded to arrange the pieces.

Joyce listened sympathetically as Heckler expounded, while Voss looked on with bemused tolerance. Though he was aware of much of what Heckler was saying, Joyce never interrupted, accepting the information as if he were hearing it for the first time. He listened intently as Heckler described the new Victor, living the sober, circumspect life-style of a Bavarian businessman. Each quarter he offered a pretty set of books to the scrupulous tax authorities in the name of Karl Ecker Associates SA.

It was a success story of sorts. To his associates, Karl Ecker was a refugee from the wrong side of the Berlin Wall. He had escaped just before things got really tight and made it big in Berlin before coming to Stuttgart. Victor, alias Karl Ecker, was well liked. Even respected, Heckler assured them. During the whole time he resided in the town there wasn't a murmur, not even a hint of scandal.

In actuality, Karl Ecker Associates SA was a cleverly worked-up front for industrial espionage, decked out to look like one of a hundred consulting firms specializing in computer technology. It was a neat little operation. Victor ran a team of specialists, using former technicians of various Bonn intelligence services, pipelining his product to a London-based cartel that distributed it to a score of industrial giants, both European and Japanese.

Note in the Stepinak file, here: Was Victor selling both ways, and had the product flowed to the East as well? But there was no hard evidence to corroborate that assumption. Not as yet. Joyce needed more.

Heckler unfolded a pair of steel-rimmed glasses and began quoting from a small leather-bound notebook he placed between his coffee cup and brandy glass, listing a series of bank accounts in various pseudonyms that Victor had employed and which he was presently researching. There was an extensive list of deposits and withdrawals that could be enumerated, but Joyce waved them aside. His duty done, Heckler sat back, his eyes as blank as a doll's.

Voss picked up the narrative from there. He had made contact with one of Victor's former operatives. The man was now a partner in an electronics firm in Karlsrue who feared for his pension. Voss had manipulated the pressure points, and the contact had become extremely cooperative, outlining as much as he knew of Victor's operation, its personnel, and its inner workings. Joyce listened with equal rapture as Voss fondly related a colorful series of anecdotes about Victor's exploits in the microchip wars. Some were amusing, some less so, all were worth repeating, but none produced a change in Heckler's mournful expression.

There had been a woman, of course. Her name was Heidi Stull. She fit the usual pattern of Victor's conquests: attractive, young, a secretary when Victor discovered her, then his mistress. Later Victor found her employment as a private secretary to a leading executive with the region's largest microchip distributor. There she prospered, spending lunch hours with her boss over crystal and silver in expensive little out-of-the-way restaurants where they could hold hands and gaze into each other's eyes without being disturbed. She put in hours of dedicated overtime, reclining on a comfortable leather couch with her long, shapely legs wrapped around her employer's pudgy torso, absorbing his whimpers of passion. When she became disturbed over this lack of respect for her dignity as a woman and threatened to quit, her employer ensconced her in a pretty little flat with a new Mercedes sports coupe in the garage. So she became his official mistress and, of course, Victor's pipeline into the company's complex technology. In the tradition of all happy endings, darling Heidi wound up as the executive's new young bride, Voss finished with a lascivious grin.

Darling *kleiner* Heidi, as Voss liked to call her, was presently inhabiting a fairy-tale setting outside Uberlingen, just a short hop down the A19. And *ja*, darling little Heidi was available for an interview. *Naturlicht,* she was more than a little annoyed at this unexpected violation of her privacy and the intrusion into her colorful and interesting past. They could be there by eight if they left without a second cup, or did Herr Joyce prefer remaining overnight in this darling *gemutlicht* hotel?

Heckler bid them a mournful farewell in the parking lot outside. Voss then took control of the Mercedes, propelling the sedan at maniacal speed along the autobahn. Delight illuminated the Bavarian's features as he dispersed slower traffic into inferior lanes. Voss had a tour guide's loquacity and kept up a running commentary on the rolling Swabish scenery, while Joyce nodded in appreciation as the picturesque villages rolled by.

They reached Lake Constance at seven, racing the sightseeing boats back to the red-tiled roofs of the town over which floated a formation of onion-domed steeples. Voss made a stop at the Hotel Hecht. He suggested Joyce take a lager inside while he went to call darling Heidi.

Three quarters of an hour later Joyce followed a whitejacketed waiter onto the terrace of a pavilion beside the placid steel-blue lake. A scattering of diners were entertained by an overdressed trio playing a Telemann sonata. It was there that he met darling little Heidi.

Voss made the introductions quickly, referring to Joyce as Herr Schmidt. Voss slipped away, and Joyce ordered a glass of Bodensee and caressed his tablemate with a reassuring gaze. Her eyes remained fixed on his empty sleeve and were filled with malice, while her fingers playing nervously with a cigarette and an expensive gold lighter.

She wore bangs cut straight across the forehead, while the rest of her hair fell helmetlike in two plaits on either side of her angular face. Joyce had no doubt of her ability to attract men. Her skin was lightly tanned, offering a golden allure. She was dressed in a stylishly cut leather coat, buttoned close to the neck, setting off a classic cherub's mouth and pale blue eyes, a typical and forgettable cover image for any one of a hundred chic magazines.

Joyce chose soft tones of conciliation, delivered with the smoothness of an old trouper enacting a role for which he is beloved in the provinces. He reassured her that they wanted nothing from her, nothing that she did not choose to give, would not give freely and of her own accord.

"Ich kann Sie nicht verstehen," she blurted angrily. *"Was wollen Sie denn?"*

But of course she didn't know what he wanted, Joyce soothed. What they wanted was information, nothing more. Some reminiscences from those faraway days when she was young, and the world foolish, and she hungry for its possession.

Here Joyce interjected that he meant all that he said figuratively, that she may have acted without thinking, and perhaps— perhaps, mind you—have accidentally taken some work home from the office though the company forbade that practice. He said all this in the kindly tone of a father who knows his child has done something wrong but is ready to forgive. If only the child will confess her wrong, then all will be sunshine and light.

"Ich habe nichte zu verbergen," she repeated resentfully and with more emotion. But her eyes shifted nervously. Her fingers broke a cigarette, which she trashed in the glass ashtray, replacing it with another held unlit in her nervous fingers. *"Ich habe nichte verbrochben."*

No, you did nothing wrong. Joyce nodded with understanding. And regret, for Victor was someone they all loved deeply. And indeed his look of regret and sorrow deepened, especially when he produced a small sheet of paper from his inside pocket that had been a parting gift from Heckler and laid it on the table between them.

It was a list of deposits to an account in a Frankfurt bank, deposits that totaled a great deal more than could possibly be made on a secretary's allotment, no matter how generous her employer. And these deposits, made in that far-off foolish time, had been withdrawn before they could be brought to the dubious attention of the tax authorities. More the pity, should they ever take an interest in the person who made them. Joyce smiled the smile of a priest before a purgative confession.

And the play, which had been familiar, if a little dull, up to that time, suddenly took on new life. Dialogue was improvised. New grounds of expression were explored. There were tears, of course, so necessary to any melodrama.

"I loved him," she said in heavily accented English.

But hadn't they all? Joyce said reassuringly.

"Whatever he wanted, I would do," she said in a hushed tone, and finally, inevitably, she had.

There were more tears, of course. And in the end, dawn finally broke. New insight streamed through. And applause for a performance well done.

The applause was supplied by Voss, who played back the conversation Joyce had so carefully taped for transcription. Frau Voss was a first-class stenographer who dutifully served them coffee on her best Meissen service the following morning and whose neatly typed notes accompanied Joyce's breakfast, a wholesome if too filling pan *kugel*, followed by the inevitable Swiss chocolates that were his addiction.

An encore was demanded and freely given that next afternoon on a tourist-filled steamer between Uberlingen and Lindau, to all appearances an affectionate conversation between father and daughter. Joyce did not make the return trip but left his darling Heidi at Meersburg and was picked up by Voss on just the other side of the quai.

While they waited for the second transcription to be typed, Joyce sipped another lager, indulging in beer and chocolate, basking in a spring sun that did not truly warm but gave the promise that somewhere the ice was at last beginning to break.

16

At Innsbruck there was no obliging host, and Killian was forced to find shelter in an inexpensive pension on a crooked street near the town center, with views of snow-covered peaks that ringed the town. He took the lift up the mountain, getting off at the first level and strolling past the crowded restaurant with its view of distant peaks shrouded by rags of torn gray cloud.

He remained on the mountain for two hours, during which time he strolled a series of trails shaded by overhanging conifers. On one of these he encountered Stepan.

The boy trudged on ahead. He was a young Croatian in his middle twenties and was carrying a backpack and camping gear. He was sandy-haired and handsome, with broad shoulders and an athlete's manner. Killian struggled to keep up in the thin, crisp air. When the boy stopped, Killian passed him and continued on ahead to a narrow overlook, waiting for Stepan to catch up.

Killian spoke for several minutes; his delivery was brief but intense. Stepan took the plastic envelope Killian handed him. It contained a substantial sum in Swiss francs, two passports in different names, and several telephone numbers written on a notepad. Killian insisted the boy memorize the numbers and then burn them. There was also a map, penciled in red, indicating the location of certain hostels where Killian expected the young man to be and the dates on which he expected him to be there.

They parted as casually as they had met. Killian took the lift back down to the city below, where he strolled with apparent aimlessness for several hours. At a busy outdoor café Killian was approached by a tall Italian whose blond locks dangled to his shoulders.

Vittorio had a Florentine face, stamped with the softly modeled features of an old master. He wore close-fitting motorcycle leathers. Killian indicated the table was taken, and the Italian moved away.

Two hours later Killian's maroon Volvo was on the road north to Garmisch. He pulled off the road at the first rest station and left the car with the attendant, instructing him to fill the tank. Killian stepped over to the side of the repair area where the same Italian in motorcycle leathers was making adjustments to his machine.

Their conversation was casual and concerned the merits of Japanese over German cycles. It lasted the same duration as the conversation Killian had had earlier on the mountain. The Italian also received a plastic envelope, left lying on the ground after Killian bent to examine the carburetor. The envelope contained dollars and a road map, carefully outlined in blue. Neither man betrayed any special emotion, and to the casual eye it seemed just another encounter between tourists.

There was one additional order, just before Killian stepped away. "Cut your hair," he said, turning back to his car. Vittorio only smiled.

At dusk Killian returned to his musty room in the pension and slept for several hours. He emerged at midnight and took the road for Vienna, which he reached at dawn. There he took sanctuary in a house that faced the Danube and was run by a brotherhood of worker priests who welcomed him as one of their fraternity. He counted it an extremely productive day.

17

Joyce crossed three frontiers, using as many passports, and took two whole days, which included a tour of the Rhine beyond Cologne. He stopped in Frankfurt where he encountered a balding American car salesman named Delany, who consumed a meal at Joyce's expense while recounting in detail the history of his partnership with Victor in an ill-fated hustle involving the discounting of mutual funds to American servicemen in an already glutted market.

Victor's story, so optimistic until now, took a tragic turn. The threat of a state investigation closed Karl Ecker Associates SA, propelling Victor north in the company of the car salesman's ex-wife, a German girl named Eva.

Victor had been introduced to her in Munich. Photographs presented an unflattering image of a young woman with a hard, almost calculating stare. She was attractive in an obvious sort of way, Joyce thought, but not the woman he would have chosen for Victor.

Eva had been named as a partner in the venture, though she never did more than some occasional office work. Delany supplied the contacts and Victor the capital. Part of the hustle included the participation of some American intelligence officers in a closed base outside Oberusel. And as one could predict, that information was suitably underlined in incriminating red pencil in Stepinak's now famous file.

Victor had been a frequent guest on the base, using one of the officers' quarters as an operations center and the officers as lures for other clientele, for which they received suitable, albeit illegal commissions. But the yield had been disappointing. And when two of the officers were transferred back to the States, the hustle collapsed.

"Sure, he still drove a Mercedes. Hell, Victor always had style," Delany went on. "Of course, the car wasn't as new or as elegant as all that. He and Eva had lived in a small flat in a newly built condo near the Patrick Henry Village. That's housing for military dependents," he explained, a fact Joyce already knew.

"Eva was a girl who liked flash and didn't mind who was buying," Delany went on. "So when sales slowed down, economies had to be made. Only Eva never favored economy as a style of life, I can tell you from experience. That girl liked her luxuries, no mistake. They split up a short time later. She was a smart little cunt, that Eva," Delany finished off wryly. But Joyce detected the pain in his eyes.

"She got pregnant somewhere along the line. She didn't want Vic to know, so I loaned her the money for the abortion. I don't think Vic ever found out about it. They split up about three months later, and that was that."

Victor took off a little while later; Delany never knew where, though he remembered hearing Victor had gotten into some kind of sales promotion for a while.

Joyce returned to his hotel, not much wiser but certainly a bit sadder at the unhappy turn Victor's life had taken. It played well as soap opera; as a cover, it was marginal at best. Victor had skirted arrest and scandal, first with stolen technology, then with military intelligence. Each misadventure contained the threat of prison and exposure. No KGB directive would ever run an agent with such recklessness, especially not one they hoped to resurface at some point and utilize in a major operation. The analysis in Victor's file was idiotic. Victor was not run but running, always from himself.

Joyce felt annoyance and disgust at Stepinak and his breed, who would so distort the facts to achieve any result their masters craved. He felt a mounting impatience and paced the room for half an hour before throwing his belongings into his worn canvas bag and tearing out of the hotel on his way to the Banhoff and a night train to the next oasis on his arid trek.

Therefore Joyce missed the call that came in for him around midnight, a call from the Paris switchboard relaying information from one of his operatives in the field. A sighting of the quarry had been made.

18

Vienna forced Killian to take risks.

But the city was a shoppers' paradise, a place where negotiations for arms were made over Sacher tortes and Schlag during coffee hours at cafés decorated like baroque palaces. His hosts, all of them young worker priests no older than thirty-five, were efficient drones. They subsisted on simple fare and donated their wages to the brotherhood. They welcomed Killian as a martyr in the struggle to uplift the poor and downtrodden, hid him, and followed his directions as if they were papal directives.

In the name of Liberation Theology they had collected a stock of arms and carefully hidden them in ancient foundations beneath medieval churches throughout Graz, a provincial city straddling the Mur River. The arsenal was rich and selective. Assault rifles, antitank weapons, rocket launchers, and machine guns, together with an assortment of vehicles used by the priests to transport the arms to various ports on the continent for shipment to Latin America.

The priests bought discreetly and in small quantities from trusted Catholic contacts who accepted payment at a discount for the good of their souls. Killian supplied the cash collected from his network of divorced nuns, and the priests dutifully filled the requirements of his shopping list. To be sure, a substantial portion of what they bought reached ports in Latin America and were smuggled to various revolutionary movements, but Killian funneled off what he needed for his own operations without having to establish separate lines of supply.

Killian had come to prepare the logistics of his operation. He selected the weapons he needed and the vehicles necessary to transport his unit. Arms were carefully wrapped and secreted in special cocoons welded beneath the chassis of automobiles. Killian had selected two older Mercedes sedans and a van. They were powerful cars with turbocharged engines, to be used as assault vehicles. Three more cars would serve for their escape, delivered to various locations by the priests, who believed they were serving the cause. They were experienced drivers, resourceful, and tested in the field. Killian had supreme confidence in their ability and envied the Jesuit leaders of the past who dispatched their own secret emissaries in an effort to reconquer terrority lost during the Reformation.

He remained in Vienna for the better part of a week, checking inventory, seeing to the careful storing of arms and equipment, working beside the priests in their efficiently stocked shop that had been converted from a large garage. They had everything from drill presses to milling machines and were adept at customizing weapons of all sorts. They did not question why he wanted the body of one of the vehicles stripped from its chassis and the hollows of the chassis filled with packages of a soft, plasticlike material. Special wires were inserted into the material and connected to an electronic device from which sprouted two stubby antennae that protruded from beneath the car. The body was then securely replaced and sent out for repainting. The car selected was his maroon Volvo.

Only when the other cars were safely in storage did Killian make plans for leaving. He was ready; his assault team had been selected. Like a good general, he had seen to their logistics and supply. All he needed now was the blessing of patience.

Kapinski was an impatient man.

He was also a clever man, a man who subsisted on his wits, which had been, over a period of decades, honed like an insect's fine antennae. It was Kapinski who had made the sighting of the Volvo; Kapinski who had divined the route the quarry had taken after leaving Paris.

Kapinski was a small man, an impish, grandfatherly type with a tiny nose and red knobs on his cheeks, wry and humorous. He had no grandchildren but had collected a nice assortment of photographs that he freely displayed wherever he went. They won him the necessary level of sympathy that eased suspicions and caused mouths to blabber. Kapinski was older than he looked and kept his hair dyed the same raven tint as it had been when he was in service in Cracow.

In those years he had built a reputation for doggedness, for sticking with it. He had worked for the British then, and they had fondly code-named him Bulldog. It was a fitting label.

For days he had lived with almost no sleep, pushing on,

circling and backtracking. Questioning every gas station owner and attendant, even those whose shifts had been completed and were home asleep. Those he had awakened, soothing them with a folded bill, probing and wheedling until he pried loose a piece of memory about a maroon Volvo with a French license plate and the dark-haired man driving it, a man with a graven face, an unforgettable face, whose hair had been tinted black, like his own.

He had not been supplied with a picture, only a general description. But it had sufficed. An attendant in Düsseldorf remembered, as did one outside Munich. There was another in Garmisch, pointing him south to Innsbruck. From there he followed the trail to Vienna, scouring each parking lot and garage, each gas station and repair shop. Somewhere, somehow, he would find what he sought.

19

Joyce made a second stop in Mainz, where Voss had reserved a room for him in a comfortable pension. Voss also arranged dinner with a British sales rep named Jacobs, an energetic, white-haired promoter in a neat double-breasted suit who spent an enjoyable half hour recounting his days selling insurance in India before he answered Victor's ad in a Manchester newspaper. Jacobs had returned to England, retired and bored. His children had their own lives, the grandchildren he so looked forward to seeing had been spoiled rotten. "You know the drill," he said wearily, and though he had no experience of such things, Joyce nodded his understanding, pretending a family he did not have.

In any case, Jacobs continued, Victor's ad looked promising. After an exchange of letters and one phone conversation Victor had paid his way over.

"It was a pretty setup. Nice offices, well organized. All legit, mind you. None of your fly-by-night produce. Vick had three teams out doing the hustling. All girls, you see. Quite a circus, it was. Most of 'em lookers. Pommies. Aussies. Couple of frogs. All of 'em nuts about old Vick. He had a way with the ladies, no doubt about it. Kept the whole thing going like a juggler. See, they were there for the gelt, no doubt about that. But they were doin' it for old Vick too. And that's the secret, ain't it? Motivation. Show me a decent salesman without it."

The waiter hovered. Jacobs hesitated, but Voss ordered him a brandy and the bottle.

"Nice girls, like I said. Good manners. Well brought up. The Yanks like that. Intimidates 'em. Most of 'em, anyway. See, we kept away from the officers. Most of 'em are just a waste of time. Too educated. Talkers, you know. Get you inside and chat you up. Bored, that's what they are. Well, who wouldn't be? Cooped up in some godforsaken military housing, miles from nowhere."

Joyce continued to smile and Voss poured another brandy.

"Like I said, we worked the ratings, warrant officers. Spec fives. Once in a while we'd hit the kasernes for the enlisted men. But the family men were our cuppa. Training, that was their weakness and my specialty. See, old Vick, he had each team out with a young German kid who saw they didn't get into jams. Paid for the meals, arranged hotels, etcetera. Me, I switched on and off. One team a week. Took 'em around, showed 'em how to knock a door."

He paused for another refill, which Voss obligingly poured. You could see Voss liked old Jacobs. They were cut from the same uneven bolt.

"Oh, we had a lovely pitch. No obligations, see. We were only conducting a survey, that's all. What kinda products would sell and where. That sort of thing. But once you got 'em on the card, willin' to try it out, free, no obligation, then you hit 'em with the pitch. And it was a lovely pitch. We weren't sellin' a thing, see. Just lettin' 'em use the product as advertising, word of mouth as it were."

Here Jacobs paused and leaned forward, as if letting them in on a secret.

"We let 'em think they were doin' us a favor, see. But to make sure they'd use and not abuse the privilege, we asked 'em for only ten cents a day. That was old Vick's idea. Smart, he was. And once you got 'em on the payment plan—well, do I have to tell ya? You'd keep comin' back, see. We had china, silver, German radios, Belgian lace. You name it, me and old Vick sold it. And the girls, of course. And he was fair with 'em. No mistake. Gave 'em nice presents. Parties. Bought 'em dinners. Carried 'em when they weren't selling. Consoled 'em. A regular father, he was—no mistake. He had a boy, too, you know, back in the East. Handsome little tyke. Sick too. Cancer, it was. Pity. But he did what he could. More than some in the same situation. Made sure the boy had everything. Oh, yes, old Vick pushed us hard for him. Not that anyone but me knew. Oh, he put on a show, all right. Fancy car. Nice digs. Had to under the circumstances. Made the girls feel like we was all gonna be millionaires. But most of what he took as his share went for the boy."

Here he paused, bending to refill their glasses.

"Something, wasn't it? I mean, old Vick, the ruthless lady killer sacrificing himself to save the little lad. See, underneath all the fancy veneer there was something desperate about old

Vick. Something lost and driven. Like he was trying to burn himself up, don't you know."

Here Jacobs smiled, and Joyce and Voss smiled with him.

"Of course, the girls never knew about Vic's boy. Bad enough they got jealous of each other, but that was part of the game, wasn't it? And he had his bit of crumpet whenever he wanted it. Nothing wrong with that, is there?"

No, they agreed. Nothing at all.

"See. He'd recruit 'em here and there. London, mostly. He had a talent for it. Never came back empty-handed. Always with a Sheila or two. Of course, that always shook the rest up. Whenever he brought a new one in. Jealous, you see. But that was the game, wasn't it? Didn't do no one no harm, did he?"

No, Joyce agreed, no one was hurt. There was no harm in it at all. Not until the end, when the military police made it impossible for him to operate. When old Vick's past finally galloped up and the German authorities politely but firmly escorted him to the border and, "Oh, Christ, all the tears and tribulation then, do I have to tell you? Plenty of heartbreak. Poor girls. Hell, poor old Vic . . . let's not forget him."

That, Joyce reassured him, was something they would never do.

Kapinski was a tracker, but he was also a warrior, which those who employed him often forgot. They relegated him to secondary surveillance when he should have been assigned to more important work. Perhaps that was why he delayed reporting his sightings, teasing the Paris switchboard with inconclusive information. Keeping them a step behind, building up his role, until he was counted as indispensable. Keep 'em guessing. He had learned that from the British. The important thing was to be in on the kill.

He found the Volvo on the fifth day.

Found it where he knew it would be found, at a shop that specialized in new paint for old cars. Of course, he had made the rounds, leaving a large bill and a phone number where he could be reached at each paint shop he visited. It had paid off handsomely. The mechanic had called at seven that morning. A maroon Volvo with a French license plate had been driven in the night before and would be picked up at eight-thirty that evening. Kapinski had called Paris with the information that he had sighted the quarry but gave no more details. He had been told to sit tight and continue surveillance; a security team would be flown down immediately.

By seven, Kapinski was parked across from the paint shop waiting as dusk deepened and the streetlights came on. The Volvo was now a sober shade of dark blue. It awaited him inside the courtyard of the building that housed the paint shop, a homing device securely bolted to the underchassis. The device broadcasted an electronic impulse every thirty seconds that would be picked up by the receiver on the dash in front of him. There was no chance of losing his quarry now.

Kapinski checked his watch. It was just eight. The street was silent. The shop was preparing to close. The device was set to broadcast, but nothing showed up on the screen. He waited until five minutes after eight, but there was still no signal.

Kapinski felt a surge of anxiety. What if the fool he had paid off had not fastened the device properly. He would have to double-check.

There were several figures inside the office when Kapinski slipped into the compound. He moved quickly in the uncertain light, weaving between parked vehicles toward the Volvo.

He had instructed the mechanic to locate the device behind the rear fender where it would be safely out of sight, even if the car were put on a lift. Kapinski knelt, and his fingers slid along the uneven metal undersurface, feeling for the small metal box.

Found it.

So far so good. The signal switch was on top. Sliding his palm up, he found the dial and realized it had not been turned on.

Idiot! He cursed and gently eased the dial toward maximum frequency.

He heard it click into position and smiled. Now it was all set.

The explosion came three seconds later. It rocked the building to its foundation. Glass shattered three blocks away. Within minutes the building that housed the paint shop became a conflagration. Nothing remained of the shop—or of the first three floors, for that matter. The shop's owner and bookkeeper, along with a mechanic, were missing and presumably blown to bits. An investigation was launched by the fire authorities. Chemicals used for the painting of automobiles were blamed for the blast, which was deemed an accident.

Joyce met the security team Rosensweig had dispatched from Paris. They remained in Vienna for two days following the fatal occurrence, but there was no trace of his tracker or of the quarry he sought.

20

Six weeks after their return to Paris, Michelle and Victor became lovers.

And that, too, seemed part of some inevitable conspiracy to which Victor felt he was now joined. The attraction he supposed was inevitable. They were far too alike, almost mirror images. To an onlooker, both dark, perfectly formed, part of some lost and beautiful race. Their glances, cool, measuring, almost defiant, seemed to confirm it. Entering a room together, they could stop conversation. There was even a similarity about their movements, a measured grace that seemed unconscious, a way their eyes had of conducting a silent conversation. The magnetic attraction was evident in each glance and their unconscious orchestration of movement. It would have been normal to have taken them for lovers. But Victor continued to resist, to withhold his final submission.

It was not an easy thing for him to struggle against. He liked women. Needed them. In their eyes he saw the purest reflection of himself. The self that existed without taint or sin or entrapment in time. Even ugly women entranced him, for he could always find something to engage him. A mannerism, the lilt of a walk, some unnoticed loveliness in a strand of hair or the way a face formed a smile. Women sensed that quality of admiration in him and were drawn to him for it. They felt he understood some deep, unknowing part of themselves, imagining that in his glance they were truly beautiful and worthy of love.

Still, from Michelle he kept a measured distance, maintaining a cool edge of space in spite of their being thrown together every day. There were others who could satisfy his urges, who could provide a narcotic for his loneliness. He alternated between a pretty young actress with punk hair dyed several shades of blue whose house sat a flat on the Rue Jacob, and a coolly elegant textile designer in her middle thirties, divorced, with a young child he often took to the Bois. The actress was unfaithful and frivolous, but her body was a miracle. The designer knew his moods and provided a nurturing hand. There were others, too, but these were casual liaisons lasting for one or two encounters, then abandoned. But the urge for Michelle persisted and in the following weeks grew stronger and finally, inevitably, triumphed.

They were busy weeks. Their return to Paris did not go without notice. Michelle's performance had been commented upon by a clique of young critics who saw a resemblance between her and the young Jeanne Moreau. She became the lead feature in several magazines, all written in the same pretentious style, all equally enthusiastic. Michelle's performance was found to have universal meaning. Her silence possessed an eloquence that spoke for the inarticulate masses of repressed and enslaved women everywhere.

Michelle's picture, serious and unsmiling, was featured on the covers of half a dozen trendy *cahiers,* all of whom labeled her as a new and fascinating discovery. It was a windfall of sorts, and Victor played it for all it was worth.

He hired an energetic publicity flack, an American named Rosa Levine, with a rasping basso voice and the body of a fireplug, who spoke French with a Brooklyn accent. Her first act was to arrange a press conference.

"She must be seen," Rosa bellowed when she saw Michelle for the first time. "She will simply wipe them out."

But Victor was leery of the maneuver, wanting to preserve the elusive aura of mystery already created. He did not have to worry. Michelle offered her impassioned young inquisitors the same dark elusiveness he had seen on the screen that morning in Cannes. She was clearly in command, deflecting questions that were too personal and articulating her views on the current state of the cinema and her own artistic ambitions with directness and intelligence, offering the kind of sincerity that convinced them she was one actress not afraid of speaking the truth.

Victor was impressed by her performance. In that he was not alone. The interview was a great success. The articles that followed were a press agent's joy, as Rosa gleefully broadcast. Victor was less enthusiastic. He had been through it all before and knew the name that blazed so large one month was completely forgotten the next. He needed something bigger to stitch it to, something with staying power. In the peculiar meaning of his trade that meant a film in production or one about to be released. He felt a sense of urgency, a need not to let the moment escape and with it the precious glittering ephemera that was all they truly possessed. And beyond that, any chance he had of saving his son.

But his desperation remained unshared. Both Roberts and Michelle seemed curiously content with the success of the moment than with the bigger picture he was trying to create. But then Victor was still part of the charade, still playing the part written for him.

Rosa arranged a series of parties and receptions, noisy gatherings at which all those who fed off the current and trendy were present. During one of these Victor discovered Michelle had been a fashion model. He asked Rosa to bring him samples of Michelle's work, and so one chilly afternoon three days later, Rosa trudged up three flights to Victor's office, located in a traffic-clogged street off the Boulevard Montparnasse. A street that hosted cosmeticians and hairdressers, a tanning salon, and two Lesbian bistros. On that occasion Rosa presented him with a portfolio of magazine covers and clipped advertisements, all of them featuring Michelle.

"Feast," she bassoed, spreading the covers across his desk. "Skip lunch. Her you can eat with a spoon."

Victor puzzled over the pictures, absorbing the face of the woman captured in each glossy image. Each of her expressions seemed less a pose than a disguise. He found himself staring at a face that was both familiar and foreign with each turn of the page, her eyes darkly swimming opals in a pool of secrecy.

He found it difficult to get a real fix on either of them.

Of Michelle's past he knew next to nothing. She had apparently grown up in Montreal, moving to Paris, where she attended the Sorbonne. She had earned a degree in economics but never held a job in the field. After graduation she modeled. Did some acting here and there. Traveled. Returned to Quebec and several film roles for the National Film Board. More detailed questions were answered with a smile, a turning of the head. Evasion.

Roberts seemed even more of an enigma, a personality rigged out of mirrors and sleight of hand, eternally smiling. He was casual to the point of madness, a perfect, laid-back California specimen, and Victor half expected him to show up one day, barefoot and in shorts, carrying a surfboard down the Champs Elysées. His speech consisted of a series of nods, *okays, can-dos,* and *will-dos.* His expression a perpetual opaque grin. Even their agreement seemed more a joke than a business maneuver.

The deal had been set even before they left Cannes, the result of a bewildering series of phone calls and two conversations in the gloomy interior of an unfashionable café bar not far from Victor's hotel.

Roberts had scratched the details on a paper napkin and completed them with a pair of telexes. One from a corporation in Bern formalizing their agreement, the other confirming a deposit in Victor's account made on a draft of a Swiss bank. And thereafter the money just flowed.

There was a solid-gold Rolex for Victor—present or incentive, he could never figure out which. It just arrived one morning by messenger. A Jaguar sedan arrived the same way, brought by a leasing company driver. It was prepaid in Victor's name for a period of twelve months. There was an expense allowance in dollars without a corresponding signature. Accounts in several fashionable Right Bank restaurants, along with a suite of rooms complete with gilt mirrors and antique armoires in a small but expensive hotel on the Place Vendôme.

Michelle was housed on the same floor in an adjoining suite behind a connecting door. Victor used the suite for business but preferred returning each night to his own apartment in the Rue Bonaparte, a converted duplex he sublet from a Hungarian antique dealer whose shop occupied the ground floor.

Roberts seemed to exist only to satisfy Victor's weaknesses. Each acceptance was another stitch in the net that drew him tighter, the wet, slick sides of the trap he knew were closing around him. But he had no other choice. The advances enabled him to pay off the avaricious Corsicans who owned a trendy Left Bank disco and had bankrolled his last venture, an outlet for their cocaine profits.

The Corsicans protested his repayment, arguing that he take as long as he wanted to square the debt, offering an unlimited line of credit for an insider's participation in his next venture. Obviously the word had gotten around. Invitations were extended that had not come before; doors opened where he had only known walls.

Bunin, too, sensed the change in the wind with that sixth sense all KGB operatives had for the scent of lucre. He

TO KILL A KING

passed along two pictures of Victor's son at their next meeting, together with a letter from his ex-wife. The Russian even insisted on buying him a dismal lunch at some noisy Arab bistro near the Port Clignancourt before accepting payment.

Victor barely glanced at Bunin, who was greedily ladling greasy spoonfuls of couscous between his wet lips. His attention was fixed on the slightly out-of-focus snapshots of Alexi. They had been taken on the grounds outside the hospital. The boy's spindly legs, lopsided grin, and the tightly drawn lines of pain around his eyes twisted like a fist around his father's heart.

Victor tossed Irena's letter aside when he returned home, or rather, kept it open and unread on the table beside his bed for several days before torching it with a gold cigarette lighter, another present from the grinning American.

Days became an amalgam of activity in a Paris that was bitterly cold, that would not warm toward spring. Scripts poured in, were read and analyzed with the help of a pretty young assistant with shapely legs and a degree from a Polish film school. She offered him her nights and batted long eyelashes at him. But so far he had kept his distance.

Projects were discussed and dissected in long, wearisome meetings. Luncheons were scheduled. Breakfast meetings and evening tête-à-têtes, with a score of producers, agents, writers, and assorted talent-mongers. And so it went.

Nights, he returned to the Rue Bonaparte, sleeping alone, tortured by dreams of Alexi and the failure that had been his marriage. He awoke at odd hours, his head filled with the echoes of arguments he and Irena had battled through years before. Fumbling for cigarettes in the darkness or for the bottles of vodka stacked like soldiers on the kitchen counter. His mind filled with images of his son, dying alone and unaided in some wasteland of his imagination. Lost, as he was lost.

He sat before the mirror staring at his face, repulsed by his good looks. Wondering aloud, *Who are you, Victor . . . what are you? What do you feel? What's happening to your life?*

He became haunted by visions of his father, steely-eyed and impervious, moody, and as cold as the Moscow winters of his boyhood. His father had been an *apparatchik*, an important functionary in the Moscow Party apparatus. Wily and discreet enough to have survived both the purges of the thirties and Stalin's last fit of paranoia. A man to respect but not love.

Only his mother provided the warmth he craved. She was a professor of biology at the university. She had her own ambitions, loftier than playing nursemaid to a healthy son whose banishment to day-care centers was evidence of the progressive nature of his parents and the State.

His parents had become estranged almost from the moment of his birth. Victor never remembered them in the same room together when someone else was not present. His mother flaunted her lovers making them surrogate fathers for the lonely, intelligent boy who excelled at school and sports and so desperately desired the attention of the tall, dark-eyed woman everyone found so vivacious and charming, whose parties were famous throughout Moscow.

His mother always smelled of flowers and exotic colognes. And whenever the boy climbed into her lap, his mother would laughingly allow him to burrow into the special softness between her large, firm breasts. It was the favorite place of his conjuring, a refuge and a castle from which to launch the wild adventures of his inflamed boyhood imagination.

He vividly remembered the chill spring day when she returned from the hospital, pale and weak, the gloss gone from her fine, dark hair, her eyes strangely distracted. And how she would no longer allow him to hold her, nor touch the places where her breasts had been.

His father sent him away to an aunt in Odessa after his mother was buried in a large cemetery outside Moscow that was filled with statues of socialist heroes. His aunt was a kindly but distracted woman who had never gotten over the death of her two young sons, killed in the last year of the war. Victor never saw his father again. Exile was a habit he had acquired early.

Michelle came to him in the end, as if the choice had been hers all along, never his own. The moment long ago selected, the wait a perfunctory part of the stage directions.

There was a strange finality to their lovemaking, a sadness, as if their mating had happened months before and they were old lovers exploring an ancient joy, a path once taken and now revisited. Lovers who were bitter about the intervening years, the opportunities missed and not taken. Like so much else in his life, it happened when he could least prevent it.

When there was nothing left to compromise or exchange. When nothing mattered but keeping his son alive.

He had remained in the hotel suite longer than usual, exhausted after a long day of appointments and conferences. They were coming close to a decision on a project for Michelle. A script had been chosen. Financing was available. A director was interested. All that remained now was to tie up the loose ends.

He ordered a bottle of Scotch and something to eat and was in the middle of a sandwich and a phone call when Michelle entered the room.

"Are you busy?" she said casually.

"No, of course not. Stay." He offered her a smile and wagged his head, indicating his boredom with the conversation.

She took a place on the leather couch opposite his chair. She was dressed in a chaste, wine-colored dress whose long skirt covered her legs almost to the ankles. But it flattered her eyes, accented them. Luminous, they fixed on him with an expression he was unable to read. A look of doubt and expectancy.

He kept his glance locked with hers, making yes-and-no noises into the receiver to punctuate the interminable drone of the director's agent, who wanted certain details ironed out before they attempted an understanding.

He finally hung up, conscious that it was perhaps the first time they had actually been alone together, except for the short intervals when Roberts or Rosa, or someone else, left them for a few moments.

"Did you want anything special?" he asked.

She shook her head. "I just thought you might be alone."

They faced each other in silence, interrupted only by the occasional grumble of traffic from the street below. Their eyes never broke contact.

"We play this little game of avoidance," she said finally. "Why?"

He shrugged. "I didn't know we were doing that."

"Liar."

He smiled. "Agreed. I must be afraid of you."

Her smile matched his. "This is just the kind of fencing I hate."

"What do you want?"

"Something real, I suppose. Instead of this artificial indifference."

He was silent for a moment, watching her.

"What are you thinking?" she asked.

"Not thinking. Weighing the risks."

"You're not afraid of risks."

"Perhaps not."

"Then what is it?"

He did not answer. He could have called upon enough internal discipline to rise and walk out, allowing still another day between himself and the inevitable. But he was weary; resistance seemed pointless. Perhaps she sensed his surrender.

She rose and crossed to him, kneeling in front of him and taking his hands in hers.

"You know what I feel," she whispered. "You've felt it, haven't you?"

Victor nodded. "Yes. I know."

They remained like that, without moving, without speaking, absorbed by the points of contact between them, the warmth and feel of each other's flesh.

"Come," she said simply.

She rose and led him into the bedroom.

She undressed in darkness. He watched her silhouette, now etched against the light from outside; the points of her full breasts and the long, slender curve of her hips.

When he was naked, she knelt beside him on the bed and enclosed him in her hands, warming him the way one warmed a brandy glass, placing him inside her mouth. He closed his eyes as she moved her lips up along his body, slowly, suspensefully, finally touching her soft mouth to his. There was a silent, urgent need to possess her, drown in her.

"Now," she said softly. "I'm ready."

She parted her legs and he entered her without effort, pressing her forcefully into the softness of the bed, as if he wanted to drive her and himself into the earth. To dispel his own separateness and merge with her. Possessing her as she now possessed him.

They lay entwined afterward. He was hers now . . . and the others he could not see. The unknown presence he sensed somewhere in the room with them. A presence that would soon demand what he no longer had a right to refuse.

21

A bloody fucking travesty.

That was how Trager described the scene some hours later when he stood, elbow to jowl, in the crowded bar of the Royale, spieling the tale to the perspiring faces gathered in a knot around him, all of them reporters and members of what he referred to as Her Majesty's Horniest Establishment.

Not only was the afternoon a bloody fucking travesty, but the damnedest irony of all was that he had nudged and cajoled that old woman Kennedy into giving him the fucking assignment in the first place. And not for the money, mind you; forget the bleeding money, he had gone for the gash.

Only instead of the usual bevy of hot young actresses shoving their scrumptious titties at the camera every time he focused to shoot, he got the come-on from a room that was jammed to the aisles with a bleeding lot of poofers. Queens. Pansies. Imagine!

And not just queens, mind you. Bloody giant faggots in elastic pants and rolled-up socks shoved down their bloody knickers! It was enough to blow his bleeding mind!

If Trager expected appreciative roars and fists pounding on the polished wood of the bar, he got that and more. He even gave a prancing imitation that sent the howls up another decibel.

Heads turned from a knot of Yanks standing farther down the bar, smiling in empathy as the laughter grew infectious. It was a damned good story, and Trager spared none of the embellishments. How he had rifled through Kennedy's pile of free-lance photo assignments while the old man was in the loo, urging his sluggish pecker to produce some bloody piss. Another imitation that sent them reeling, turning faces an apoplectic crimson.

Then going on to tell how he had found the press agent's notices and the advert of the producers pre-opening press party and convinced the old bastard to give him the assignment as a personal favor. Knocking off a good twenty percent of his price because of his immense love of the theater.

That really sent up the screams. They were all well aware of the part of the theater Trager loved. "The part that squats over the ladies' loo, you mean," someone ad-libbed, and this produced more squeals.

"A regular little Shakespeare," another voice chimed, grabbing the front of his pants to demonstrate the spear he meant to be shook.

Trager laughed along with the rest, sputtering and grasping his heart, to show how that slayed him. In truth, he had given a fairly accurate description of the do he had attended earlier that evening in a minor banquet room of a Hyde Park hotel belonging to an American chain.

The food had been as plastic as the decor, and the room, in truth, was packed with a fair proportion of the West End's gay establishment, accompanied by the usual auxiliary of overly made-up hags and hangers-on. Trager usually found these assignments lucrative. They were generally attended by a fair number of young actresses, ingenues, who were easily impressed by his press credentials and the lure of suggested contacts within the film world, which, as he name-dropped, grew more impressive as the evening wore on.

There was also a possibility that one of Trager's shots would include one of the young hopefuls, taken as she stood alongside one of another of the more famous names. A coup that would get an agent's heart pounding. That affair was easily arranged, after he had zeroed in on what he considered the more gullible, and therefore more promising, quarry.

Trager had more balls than brains, his cronies liked to remark. But they, the balls not the brains, stood him in good stead, especially when he elbowed his way into a private conversation with the young actress in tow and posed the embarrassed girl beside an annoyed but smiling Mr. Big.

The results of these intrusions were, often as not, deposited in a copy room wastepaper basket, Fleet Street's equivalent of the cutting room floor. But that conclusion occurred long after the girl had been safely bedded, her legs resting on Trager's shoulders as he gave her a bit of the old in-and-out on the electrically warmed water bed housed in his messy Kings Road studio. But what were the poor girls to do? It was only a decent sense of gratitude for what could be their big break, now wasn't it? No harm done.

For all of Trager's exaggeration, there actually had been a prospect at the afternoon's affair, a pretty brunette with dyno legs and a bored expression. She had entered with a convoy of young faggots, all apprentice stage designers. Trager began to operate in the usual manner, until he discovered the bird was a graphic artist whose only interest in the theater was in poster design. Changing tact, he left her and circled the room, nonchalantly snapping away while he racked his brain for the name of some cinema advertising executive he could pretend was a best buddy.

That was when he ran into the Yank.

At first Trager thought he was just another bloody dandy on the make. The looks were too perfect. The clothes just a bit too in style. But that had been a mistake. The American introduced himself three times before Trager bothered to remember his name. But when he said he knew Chinky Pierce, Trager backed up a step.

"Chinky? Christ. It's been an age," Trager commented with surprise. Chinky was a free-lance photographer's agent specializing in fashion layout, a field Trager had once had ambitions for but too few connections to attempt.

"Chinky said you were interested in fashion," the Yank stated, smiling in an enigmatic way. "He said you might be interested in an assignment. We're looking for someone who likes to travel."

"And who might the 'we' be?" Trager requested, one eye trailing after the brunette as she moved toward the buffet.

"I represent a film company located in Paris," the American answered. And that was the last Trager remembered of the girl or her pretty legs.

His name turned out to be Roberts. He made the offer of a card and a drink, which they took in the hotel's bar, hollowing out a place free of the usual white tourist trash. The noisy, twanging chatter of the Midwest had no effect on the American, and he waved away Trager's suggestion that they adjourn to a quieter pub he knew of nearby.

It turned out the American was in town for only a few days and had a rather full schedule, as he put it with a smile. Besides, he had no intention of interrupting Trager's work. In any case, they could continue their conversation when he flew over again, which was, he said, scheduled for the following weekend.

Chinky had shown him samples of Trager's work which he

liked and now wanted to know if Trager was interested in doing an exclusive photo spread on a new actress they were promoting.

Was he interested?

Is the pope bloody Catholic? And here's the kicker, Trager would have said, had he thought it appropriate to include this information at the tail end of his recent hilarity at the Royale, which, of course, he did not. If the session turned out okay, then they were prepared to offer him an exclusive contract for his services. Which meant his work would become part of a million-dollar promotion presently under way, including two films presently in production. That meant Trager's stuff would be seen in every bleeding magazine and tabloid from here to Timbuktu. Imagine. *Stern, Vogue,* you name it.

It sounded too good to be true. It was a break he had been waiting for. The chance to break out of the paparazzo game. No more super scoop, lucrative as that was. Not that he was giving any of that up—not right away, mind you. He wasn't tossing away a bird in the hand. Any bird, the wags at the Royale would have said.

The only problem was they wanted an answer right away, and that was going to be difficult. Trager had a prior commitment to a photo assignment in the Caribbean. A hotel opening in the Bahamas. But Roberts waved that objection away. And then came the weirdest coincidence of all. Believe it or not, his actress had been invited to the same opening. So the thing fit perfectly. Imagine.

So the initial photo spread was set in the Bahamas, where the actress, whose name was Michelle Duran, was doing a piece on swimsuits for a French concern. *Paris Match* had already optioned the spread, but Roberts had insisted on their own photographer. It seemed a perfect coincidence, kismet, as Roberts said with a grin.

Bleeding kismet, and no mistake. Trager had laughed at the idea and had another, which the American insisted on buying before he checked his watch and said he had to be running. Cards were hurriedly exchanged, penciled with several phone numbers where each could be contacted in case they could not be reached at their usual numbers. The American shook his hand and slipped through the crowd, giving Trager a final wave and smile at the door.

Bloody serendipity, that's what it was. Imagine Chinky coming through after all that time, which was how Trager put it to the petite blonde from the Kings Road boutique when they lay side by side together, experiencing the comfortable undulations of his electrically warmed water bed in the seclusion of his studio later that evening. Banging her had been a form of celebration. It would be the first of many, he mentioned as much to the ceiling as to the girl, who was clenching the filter end of a cigarette in her teeth. Luck was running his way, of that you could bloody well be certain. . . .

22

Trager was introduced to Michelle on the terrace of a hotel on Paradise Island at the moment Joyce was heading north toward Frankfurt on an autobahn crowded with early-morning traffic.

Still woozy from the drink he had consumed on the flight over from London, he wanted only to hit the sack. But when he checked, he was informed his party was awaiting his arrival on the terrace. Surprised, he stepped into the brilliant glare of Caribbean sun and was momentarily dazzled. A moment later he heard Robert's familiar voice.

"Hello, Trager. Over here!"

Trager turned in the general direction of his table, and before he could quite focus, the introductions were accomplished.

"Rob Trager, Michelle Duran and our producer, Victor Sorge."

Trager was conscious of Victor rising and of shaking his hand, but he never quite recollected if he had actually taken Michelle's. He remembered recounting some idiotic anecdote about the flight over and hearing Michelle laugh, which both embarrassed and reassured him. He also remembered Roberts droning on about the hotel and the crowd of celebrities there for the opening, and the Bahamian officials zooming around like sharks. There was something else about scheduling the setup for the shoot, but the rest was fuzzy.

Trager slept the sleep of the dead until the following morning. Awakening ravenous, he ordered breakfast from room service and stepped onto the balcony, where he caught sight of a woman running alone on the beach. Bloody gorgeous, she was, perfectly proportioned, with magnificent breasts, shaped just the way he liked them. High, firm, and well spaced in a rib cage that curved to slender hips and impossibly beautiful legs.

He realized he was looking at Michelle.

She disappeared into the hotel without looking up. But he followed her with his eyes, taking in the lines of her taut body as it moved with a runner's grace and the raven sweep of her hair. He had done numerous shoots with models before, but "God, she is bloody fugging magnificent."

He remained in his room unpacking his equipment and awaiting a call from London. The call never came, and when they all met for lunch, he was edgy, smoking too many cigarettes, and letting the others do the talking while he studied the bird beneath lowered brows.

Michelle was conscious of his gaze, meeting his eyes once or twice and darting him a fleeting smile. But she mainly played to the others. Roberts, he had not yet figured out. The American's eyes strayed neither right nor left, were not distracted by the passing of a pretty girl or boy. But Trager suspected something was up between the other two. The Romanian, if that's what he bloody fucking was, kept a special eye on Michelle. Though she smiled at him frequently, it was never long enough or frequent enough for Trager to figure out what kind of footing their relationship rested upon. Anyway, he was there for a different kind of action, wasn't he? This was just a bloody sideshow.

The call he expected came with dessert. The message was brief and exactly what he wanted to hear: "All systems go, chum. Antigua's where the action is. A lawyer named Samuels is the man to see. Have fun in the sun." The voice rang off that quickly. But that loosened him up, relaxed him for the shoot and the rest of the idiocy, which erupted in the late afternoon.

The hotel was loaded with Hollywood types. None he would call major-major, but stars still, from some of the top-rated TV dramas. All of them pulling grand entrances, sweeping out of elevators or onto the terrace, where a buffet had been set up, and flashing professionally for the cameras.

Trager was only one of the usual troupe, all of them jostling for position like a pack of howler monkeys, flashes going off like Chinese fireworks. Michelle was there, too, together with Roberts and the Romanian, but getting less attention, as did the other European actors, one of whom was a pretty well-known Scandinavian sex goddess but a decade past her fame.

He drank his lunch in Bloody Marys and prowled the pool later, getting wiggle shots of starlets who had come down for the bikini show. Michelle did not appear, but she was present for the evening stampede, a black-tie soiree held in the main ballroom, which was decked out in bunting like a prizefight.

The major razzle-dazzle focused on the celebs, who outdid each other in the fashion department. That's where Michelle really put them in the shade. She wore something that gave the illusion you could see her body through the layers of gauze and silk. As Trager would say to his cronies later, "For my rubles she stole the show."

She was largely indifferent, but their eyes did meet once or twice across the room. Once she gave him a fleeting smile, like a goddess deigning to notice one of her subjects. Trager refrained from going over. *Patience, you ignorant sod. She'll be yours bloody soon.*

They set up the shoot on the day following, waiting until late afternoon, when it began cooling off. A small side garden had been set aside for their use, filled with palms and rioting hibiscus. He used one of the desk clerks as an assistant, a bloody big sod, black as your hat, but who turned out to have an innate understanding of what he wanted and some experience of his own with lenses and filters in an amateur sort of a way, of course.

It was Michelle who made all the magic. The superb way she moved. The instantaneous magnetic contact between them. She was no bullshit, either. A total pro, no muss, no fuss. She had an instinctive knowledge about how to show off her body, better than any bird he had ever shot. Bronzed all over she was, not a white line on her, the result of a Parisian tanning salon and a couple of days on the beach before he arrived. And when she came out in a bikini, no more than an artistic web of threads, she absolutely blew his mind. But by that time Roberts and the Romanian sod had left them alone and he had sent the boy away. So it was just the two of them, which was just the way he wanted it.

Never had it worked so smoothly. Her moving. Him shooting. And, oh, how she moved.

"Yes, yes—just like that. Hold it. Now shake it. That's it, baby. You got it! Lovely. Just there. Mine, you are all mine. Oh, what a lovely little bitch. No, I said kick. Right. Right. Lovely. Beautiful. Oh, nasty, nasty, nasty. And how I love it. How I do love, love, love it. Into my eyes, woman. Right here. And lower, lower, lower, like you're hungry for it, bitch. Oh, yes. Divine. Yes, darling, absolutely bloody divine."

He pranced like a pansy and got her to laugh, open up. Giggling like a little girl. Pouting. Putting it on first for an audience. Then just for him. Only for him. Kicking, swirling, inventing a lovely little dance as he snapped and danced with her. Playing tourist with her gorgeous body, caressing her limbs through a soft-focus lens. Breaking to inset a 150mm for a close-up that caught the shadows under the tip of her impossibly gorgeous nose. She was a bloody marvel, moving in perfect sync with each shot, permitting him to change lenses without changing the mood, and by the end of the session he was in love.

23

That night they went black tie. The celebs had gone or were in seclusion somewhere, so they took dinner in a lovely French restaurant facing a lagoon. Trager was flying, off on a nonstop binge. So high, he couldn't stop talking. Focusing all his attention on Michelle, making her laugh. Breaking her out of that solemn sophistication she was bottled up in. He got looks of bemused toleration from the Russian, Romanian, whatever. Ballocks to him. He wanted the girl and didn't care who knew it.

They hit the casino afterward. He shot craps and won, keeping her close for luck, insisting she share the winnings, which she proceeded to throw away at roulette. And while the Romanian played chemin de fer and Roberts watched, they sneaked off to the slots, laughing uproariously every time she hit a combo, holding out her hands like a child to receive the shower of dimes and quarters. It was a joyride, and they were making it last, finally slipping away to some black disco down the beach, where a live band alternated rock and reggae.

"God, it's all so bloomin' lovely, and you are bloomin' lovely, and even I am a bloomin' love," he whispered into her ear. She just laughed and laughed.

He held her close, no matter what the rhythm dictated, knowing the tight, perfect feel of her, the supple delirium moving under his hands, and the magical, instantaneous flashes of mood that made little thunderheads out of her glance. She would not let him kiss her, not then. But even her refusal was a promise, making up for the disappointment of having to meet the others for a nightcap. That was when he realized her suite was next to Victor's, which made four out of two and two and left him knotted with frustration.

"My dear, it has been bloomin' lovely," she said when she left him with a parting giggle. He played the jester and did a little dance down the corridor, sending her into further hysterics. But when she closed the door, he went glum.

He remained at the bar, drinking down a half bottle of

Chivas. It occurred to him to return to the disco. But he went up to his room instead and dreamed of Michelle all night, or so it seemed to his restless imagination. He jumped up early to catch sight of her on the beach. But she never made an appearance. Nor did she appear for breakfast. He called her room but there was no answer, and he discovered when he bumped into Roberts in the lobby that she and Victor had gone sight-seeing, which pissed him off plenty.

He spent the afternoon at the pool, drinking Irish whiskey and eyeing a score of super bodies clad only in string bikinis, but the flesh failed to move him. He resonated with the feel of Michelle against him, still smelled the scent of her perfume, grew so hard that he had to turn over onto his belly on the chaise, and that without her even being there.

In late afternoon they went off on a chartered, two-masted schooner to shoot some candid stuff around the harbor. Trager moved around the boat with Michelle, leaving Victor and Roberts aft with the crew. He posed her against the sea, catching the gradual moods of the sunset. If they touched, her eyes rose to meet his, held, and played a silent dialogue.

"God, you're so bloody, bloody gorgeous," he whispered mockingly in his high-pitched jester's voice. "Disturber of all my dreams; you are, my dear. A bloody blooming rarity. An orchid among all these tiresome weeds."

"Some weeds," she said with a smile, but her eyes held his in spite of the banter.

Kneeling side by side in the bow, they watched the blood-red orb slide into the sea. When he covered her hand with his, it remained soft and unmoving beneath his touch.

She went below to change as the crew barbecued conch for their meal and a sailor came forward to serve drinks. "In a minute, mate. Got to put the little ones to bed," Trager said, patting his cameras.

He caught the Romanian's eye just before he went down the companionway. They were filled with something he could not quite understand. Resignation, perhaps, and a form of sadness. But that was not Trager's lookout.

Michelle was in the act of brushing her vibrant black hair when Trager pushed open the louvered door of the state room.

"Whoops, sorry, luv. Wrong venue, ain't it?" But he did not move.

She lowered her arms and turned to face him. She wore

only a single piece of black lace circling her slender hips. Trager let his eyes capture the luxuriant curve of her belly and the dark, erect tips of her heavy breasts. Then he stepped inside and slid the door shut behind him.

Victor sat on the hotel terrace, dressed in white trousers and a soft white cotton shirt with sleeves rolled to the elbows, protected against the glare by a pair of dark glasses. He sat alone, nursing an iced glass of rum, and watched the two distant figures on the beach below, seated side by side on their chaises, facing away from him toward the sea. One of them was Michelle, the other Trager, whose presence had now become an irritation.

Ostensibly the Englishman was there to do a photo spread; instead he had become an indispensable part of their party, with them at meals and afterward. In the pool with Michelle, on the beach with Michelle, dancing with her, gambling with her, playing the clown but never failing to make her laugh, something Victor had little talent for.

Trager was a jump-up opportunist, coarse, ill-bred and obvious, with a kind of presumptuous vitality that grated on Victor's nerves. Or was he just being intolerant? In truth he was jealous. He acknowledged that to himself. It was a feeling he was unaccustomed to, and it was accompanied now by a burning tightness in his guts that so far he had kept under control.

Trager kept Michelle entertained. Trager was also young, and that injected its own special venom. He had good looks in a rough and ready sort of way, and a muscular, athletic body. Not that Victor was lacking in that department. But it was Trager's enthusiasm, his optimism, that perhaps rankled the most. Certainly, for all of their enjoyment of each other, Victor never had been able to communicate that. He had offered Michelle only his melancholy. Trager was fresh, alive. He could not blame Michelle for being attracted.

Victor ordered another drink and continued to stare at the two figures, leaning together as if they shared some complicity. Earlier he had broken a rule and mentioned it to her as they sat in her suite, preparing to meet the others for a drink.

Their eyes locked. She spoke, and for the first time Victor was witness to something he had not yet experienced. Existing beneath the elusive layers within which she masked herself, he glimpsed a hardness he had imagined but had never seen. She turned to him and, in a tone remarkable for its evenness, said, "I don't remember offering you ownership of me."

Victor smiled and bowed. No, she had not offered herself. Nor had he. Not in words. They were both free. Both professionals. That was the assumption; at least, that was what he told himself, in spite of the burning sensation that left him feeling as if he had just been slapped.

Poor Victor. Had you deluded yourself that there could be more when you know in your belly that what you share is only momentary, part of a plan that is not of your making? And yet . . . is it possible that you could feel more? You? Fool . . . Petrushka. Clown.

Victor signaled the waiter to bring him a phone. The man brought over a receiver and plugged it into the receptacle beneath his table. Victor dialed Roberts, who was paged at poolside. They held a hurried conversation. Then he called the airport and made arrangements to leave for Paris that night, taking with him the illusion of a freedom he no longer possessed.

24

Joyce made his crossing into Belgium from the Ruhr and entered the port city late the following afternoon, speeding over the flatlands of the Kempen and crossing the Scheldt River, sparkling under a glorious sunset. He established himself in a small commercial hotel near the Pelickan Straat, filled with a noisy collection of Zambians and evil-tempered Israelis, all of them dealers in the diamond trade, which was experiencing a market glut.

Joyce wandered the maze of tiny medieval streets arranged around the *straat,* crowded with Namibians in dashikis, speaking Yiddish to South Africans in black skullcaps, until he found a narrow cobbled street housing a restaurant that served kosher food beside the narrow entrance to the floors above.

In a fourth floor workroom, Joyce was escorted past rows of littered tables where Hasidim in fringed shirts and striped aprons sculpted bits of gemstone beneath a flat northern light.

His hosts were waiting in a cluttered rear office, seated around a circular table. They were patient men, long on experience and understanding, who spoke in the hushed accents of Tel Aviv.

It was an informal conference, brief and pointed, a conversation between professionals. Joyce had come to confirm details he already possessed. And this, too, was understood. Files were passed back and forth over cups of tea, cake, and triangles of soft cheese. Dossiers were examined, figures noted and commented upon in crisp, humorless tones. A large window exposed Gothic spires and the harbor beyond, where commercial freighters were endlessly disemboweled.

Later the downstairs restaurant was visited for corned beef and dark Flemish beer. Hands were shaken and his offer to pick up the bill declined. And so Joyce continued on his way, refreshed in his knowledge but saddened in his spirit, feeling a weariness that would not be shaken.

He had undergone a final ritual, dissecting yet another of Victor's attempts to escape his past. Victor had brokered for a syndicate of Corsican drug dealers, turning their profits into diamonds, which were smuggled through the port to destinations in Central America. The Israelis had shown him pictures, the usual candid surveillance. It was pure vintage Victor, looking prime and unbowed. All the old swagger was still present, the custom tailoring and silk shirts. Only his eyes gave the game away. Portrait of a man bent on his own destruction but going at his own pace and with a certain grace. No, you could never fault Victor for lack of grace. Was that all it came to in the end?

Joyce paused in his walk to rest along the river, feeling a sudden weariness, a deep, persistent aching in his bones, and worse, where his arm once had been. A strange itch to manipulate fingers that were no longer there. He fought off the urges and stared out at the gulls swooping and circling over a clanking buoy.

The old man in Paris had found him out. *Are we hunting him or saving him?* Joyce still did not know which. In some mysterious way he had become both hunter and deliverer. The twisting past he had been exploring was somehow also his own, a path darker and more sordid than the one he now pursued.

And what of his own sense of grace? The need he felt for redemption, a need now suddenly grown more pressing.

Perhaps in some mysterious way his search was a final chance to save both his quarry and even himself—or was it too late? Would he become the final enemy? The dark emissary of Victor's eventual destruction . . . and perhaps his own?

25

Trager edged forward slightly, easing the discomfort in his arms. His muscles were tortured. Pain bayoneted through his tendons and corkscrewed each nerve ending. The agony came from trying to balance a heavy camera sheathed in its waterproof casing against razor-sharp edges of a coral reef a hundred yards from shore.

Accompanying the pain was the unpleasant sensation of being roasted alive inside his wet suit. He was bleaching out like a beached turtle.

Patience, boyo . . . patience, and the world will be yours.

He stared through the lens for the hundredth time, scanning the beach for some sign of life, but except for an old man in ill-fitting shorts raking jacaranda leaves, as black and crooked as a briar cane, there was no one.

Patience, darling. Those were McNabb's words. But he was sick to his stomach of being patient, of being stretched out on his belly on a tiny spit of coral since the hours before dawn, waiting for his bloody muckamuck and the blessed Magdalene to appear. He needed some action and he needed it pronto, before he succumbed to heat prostration.

Up until now the entire operation had been a piece of cake. Trager had flown in on a chartered Cessna paid for out of the black magic fund of a major tabloid. He possessed a blank check. Whatever he asked for. He wanted a plane, he got a plane. Order up a boat and it was his. "Go, you sweet little darling," McNabb had uttered, holding his hands over Trager's bowed head in mock benediction. "Go and be blessed, just bring us back the bacon, and make it kosher, if you please." But hadn't he always?

What he resented was the lack of a challenge. Not even a decent security force to outwit. That would have put some fun into the business. The island was overrun by black goats and a handful of hacks from MI5, who thought taking off their ties made for decent cover.

TO KILL A KING

The local cops were falling all over themselves to put on a proper show, all spit, polish, and don't spare the starch. After all, you can't blame them. The minister was important, a keystone of the London government. They never even suspected Trager's presence. To them he was just another tourist. Besides, the cops spent all their time providing motorcycle escorts and stiff-backed parades for the boring hulk who had the foresight to choose the right party in the last election.

Thankfully Trager had the services of a good contact man, a local black solicitor named Samuels who had a finger in some of the local rackets. He had provided the blinds where Trager waited to pick off his game. Not as principal a quarry as the last score, thank you, but then, you couldn't have everything. Still, the minister was somewhere among the top ten, in direct line for the prime minister's throne, should the earth open up and swallow Downing Street and any number of other establishments.

Anyway, for all his pretending, McNabb had been eager when he had outlined the proposal, and when dealing with McNabb, one did well to pretend it was the bloody queen that was in his sights, or the tightwad would bargain you down to taxi fare and a burger sans bun.

The minister was a potbellied lecher who wore a hairpiece and dyed the hair on his chest to match. But the woman he had slipped into his little Caribbean goodwill venture was a dynamite piece of fluff. And that was what got the old Scots ballocks on the boil. He had already designed the headline: CABINET SECRETARY ON CARIBBEAN HOLIDAY.

It was another exclusive. Super scoop strikes again.

Trager spent two days getting some good informal stuff of the politician and his strumpet visiting the delights of the island—informally, of course. What he really wanted was some spice. But that he knew could only be gotten by infiltrating the private resort where the minister was holed up, a guarded sector near Nelson's Harbor. To do that took a little ingenuity, which was how Trager came to be lying among the barbs of a coral postage stamp, flat on his stomach, staring through a 200mm lens off the private beach, as the waves lapped over his legs and tiny sand flies made kamikaze dives at the unprotected skin of his face and hands.

In the end, of course, he was rewarded. His Eminence eventually appeared along the dunes. His mistress came gently after. There were some comical shots of the politico's lumpy posteriors as he bent over to search for sea life among nearby rocks. And a positively embarrassing series of the man sunbathing *au naturel,* his hairy belly flopping over his shriveled little peter, while his mistress remained disappointingly zipped up in her equally disappointing one-piece suit. A shame because she had a truly spectacular bod.

So McNabb had to be content with the scandal and some carefully cropped photos. But in the end everyone got what they wanted. And some even more than they expected, as in the case of The Honorable Mr. Samuels, the solicitor who was so helpful to Trager, even to the point of offering him one of the local professionals as a diversion. A not bad-looking mulatto with an elephantine posterior and incredible tits. This Trager accepted—he never turned down any of the perks. Anyway, a refusal would not have endeared him to the wily advocate. However, his performance on the girl's willing body was interrupted by candid shots of Michelle that went off like a flash in his mind.

However, Samuels—indirectly, if unwittingly—received another form of compensation. It came by way of a telephone call he made to a distant island after seeing Trager off at the airport. The solicitor confirmed to the flat American voice at the other end that Trager had indeed come, seen, and conquered.

Samuels received an out-of-proportion remuneration for the service. The message he delivered was relayed to a phone booth in Paris several hours later. The snare so carefully set was operating smoothly, a cause for satisfaction. Trager would lead them directly to the target they so patiently and painstakingly stalked.

26

The first duties Joyce performed after returning to Paris were purely administrative. He accomplished the organization of a myriad of details in a remarkably short stretch of time. And that, under the circumstances, was a small miracle.

His team was already installed in separate residences, supplied but not financed by his French allies. None of the organization was particularly young, except for the team of followers supplied by his Brussels connections, who drove a collection of motorcycles that had been imported in a spacious carrier.

Collectively both boys looked about nineteen, one dark, curly-haired, and cynical. The other blond, blue-eyed, and always grinning. Each possessed a magically forgettable face. The others, some fifteen in all, had been formed into teams of static watchers, followers, and communications specialists, all mirthless pros with long experience at their tasks.

Except for the boys, David and Zivi, whose talent and enthusiasm he grew to appreciate daily, Joyce had worked with the others before. They were all free-lancers, veterans of various intelligence services—Belgian, Dutch, and French—and included a team of former Parisian police detectives, two full-bellied, sallow-skinned professionals with jaundiced eyes who would facilitate their installation and movements through the quirky and often capricious capital.

Rosensweig had already begun their orientation, providing detailed observations on the movements and habits of their various targets. He had also provided another and even more impressive service, organizing a systematic harassment of the CIA teams already in place. Subtle pressure had already been brought through certain government channels. Inquiries into the CIA operation was beginning to cause some embarrassment to the American embassy staff, which had cause to worry about the delicate nature of Gallic relations.

Joyce cautioned the old Frenchman to go slowly, but his prejudices against anything imported from the other side of the Atlantic were in a violent state of arousal. Naturally a certain duplication of effort could not be avoided. And to the Frenchman was delegated the task of tracking the foreign watchers.

Though it should have been a normal government operation, no additional funds had yet been appropriated by the financing arm of the Intelligence Bureau that oversaw his subdivision. Rosensweig was up in arms over having to absorb it out of his own meager accounts. It formed an even greater source of irritation, further personalizing his sabotage of the American efforts.

There was some squabbling over transport and lines of command, but in the end these, too, were ironed out in a manner mutually satisfying to all concerned. There might have been additional bickering with Joyce's own superiors, if Stepinak had not precluded that by having co-opted Joyce into his own burgeoning jurisdiction.

Joyce's disappearance was bound to be reported and discussed in the Washington circles he inhabited. The question was when and how quickly? He owed little to those with oversight over his own operations. Most were already deserting, casting about for other berths. Those who remained were men like himself, written off as inflexible and expendable, clinging to loyalties that were pitifully outdated, awaiting the next budgetary ax. Stepinak would not hasten the process; of that Joyce was certain. It would add to the atmosphere of unreliability and mutual suspicion between their respective agencies. But that increasingly narrow interval gave Joyce the time he needed, a mercy he could not count on being continued. So time, too, was now edged against him.

27

Victor kept his monthly meeting with Bunin in a crowded café off the Rue Danou. He wore a leather raincoat whose collar was turned up against the chill. It was a morning sodden with drizzle and mist that shrouded the dark facades and spilled droplets from window ledges. Victor scouted the locale twice, passing the café and making a circuit of the block, detouring around puddles left over from an early-morning drenching.

Before leaving his apartment, he had wrapped the envelope containing Bunin's payment in a copy of *France-Soir,* around which he secured two rubber bands, one on either side of the bulging envelope, then slipped the newspaper into his outside pocket.

His tan caused heads to turn, making him feel as conspicuous as the collection of punks with rainbow-dyed hair, sponging up heavy metal rhythms that blasted from a record shop across the narrow street from the café.

Bunin was standing at the bar, lovingly applying pâté to a croissant. Victor entered and eased his way through the crowd. The café reeked with the stale smell of soaked clothing. Victor edged alongside Bunin and tried to catch the barman's eye. "No tables." Bunin shrugged, cramming pâté into his already occupied mouth and shoving his own cup over with a nod for Victor to help himself. But Victor declined, and when the barman turned, he pantomimed his order for a café au lait.

"Nice tan," Bunin said, mixing admiration and not a little envy. They spoke in Russian. It was a place where foreign accents raised few eyebrows.

"I want to see Alexi."

Bunin glanced up at Victor, unsure if he had heard correctly. "Your son. See him? What do you mean, see him? I have shown you pictures."

"I want you to get the boy out," Victor said as a foaming cup was placed in front of him, speckled with cinnamon. "Out of Russia, understand?"

133

Bunin stared at him without speaking, his head cocked back, wet lips slightly agape, a tiny piece of pâté wedged in the corner of his mouth. The pose reminded Victor of the portrayal of a drunk he had once seen danced at the Marinski.

"You m-must be insane," Bunin stuttered. "It's impossible."

"Why impossible?" Victor had intended to speak in a dispassionate tone. Now he heard the desperation in his voice. "Get Vasnikov to certify that Alexi needs treatment in the West."

"The West?" Bunin stared, bewildered. "Where?"

"Vienna. Anywhere. What does it matter? I'm sick of this life. I want my son."

"And your wife? What would Irena say?"

"Forget Irena. I'll take care of her. A new car in exchange for the boy. A Volga. Explain it to her, say it's for his own good. She'll agree. All she ever wanted was the damn car."

Bunin exhaled in exasperation. His breath was sour, his skin tinted a pale Van Gogh yellow under the fluorescents.

"It's not feasible. The difficulties are too great. I couldn't even begin to attempt it."

"Name a figure, Nikki, baby," Victor said evenly, staring at his own face, which was elongated by the swirls of an imitation Art Deco mirror on the other side of the bar.

"No figures. No amount would be enough. Not for the son of a defector. They would smell it a mile away. Subject closed."

Victor raised his cup and took slow sips of its bitterness. "Can you at least arrange for me to talk to him?"

"Impossible."

"On tape, then. So he can get to know my voice. Do you realize my son doesn't even know what I sound like?"

Bunin shook his head firmly. "No tapes." He had gone back to the pâté in a serious way, separating the gelatin with a surgeon's skill.

"Then a letter. Just a few pages."

Bunin tore off a chunk of bread as if he were wringing the neck of a chicken and crammed it into his mouth. "You know the perimeters. No letters. No contact. There's already too much risk. Even Vasnikov has been advised to ship the boy off to a clinic. I prevented it out of personal regard for you. Now be reasonable. Accept reality for what it is. You made the choice. You have to live with it."

Victor stared at Bunin's reflection with a look of disgust. He removed the newspaper from his pocket and casually laid it down on the bar. He picked up his cash stub, threw a note on the wet zinc counter, and turned toward the cashier. In the mirror he could see Bunin's hand caress the newspaper, seeking the envelope's telltale bulge. He drew it affectionately into his possession.

28

Joyce was guided to the first of his static locations by one of the policemen temporarily in his possession. His destination was a fourth-floor sublet, designed, but never used, as an artist's studio. It came complete with slanting skylight, which had been carefully covered with black muslin. The room was bare, except for several pieces of rental furniture, a daybed, a table and chairs, and pieces of optical and electronic equipment of various descriptions, from which a series of aerials of different lengths and shapes protruded.

The narrow floor-to-ceiling windows offered views of mansard roofs above, and the narrow but fashionable Left Bank address where Victor had established residence. The street was dominated at one end by the Ecole des Beaux Arts, a maze of courtyards, gardens, cloisters, and shadowed alleys. There was a bar farther down, called Les Deux Frères, its windows filled with stacked cans of foie gras and pyramids of wine. Another shop specialized in ceramics from Florence. Another sold books, the titles obscured by soot. Beside it was a dealer in Third Empire antiques.

"Come have a peek," one of the watchers offered. He was a portly, unshaven Belgian named Gige, wrapped in an outsize raincoat, whose posture behind the lens of his telescope always reminded Joyce of a tent about to collapse. Gige chain-smoked cheap Turkish cigarettes and continually complained of the cold, in spite of being surrounded by a battery of electric heaters, which gave the room an eerie orange glow. Because of the narrow field of view, most of the watching devices had been rigged with periscope sights. Joyce bent to an eyepiece, and Victor's living room ballooned into his vision. Fireplace with gleaming andirons. Bookcase. Empire desk. Flowered chair. Oriental carpet contrasting with dark wooden floors.

"Cultured, your friend," Gige volunteered. "Likes Debussy. In a Russian that's a miracle. And the woman is enchanting. I have to fight the boys away."

TO KILL A KING 137

Tuning out the street noise made some problems for the listeners. The narrow street was a convenient detour for trucks and taxis trying to avoid traffic near the Boul Miche.

"Get him to move to the suburbs," Gige pleaded. "If the carbon monoxide doesn't kill us, the dog shit will." With disgust Gige pointed out the municipal collector on his yellow scooter.

After congratulating Gige and the others on their ingenuity and sympathizing with their difficulties in having to operate in such a less than favorable environment, Joyce was led down some back stairs, past a dour-faced concierge whose silence had been purchased with Swiss francs. They emerged into a series of winding alleys and from there into the bright bustle of the noontime rush hour.

The rain began again, falling in transparent silver veils. Before returning home, Victor stopped at his office in the cramped street behind the Boulevard Montparnasse. Alone in the static mustiness of the dreary interior, he thumbed through the mail that had collected during his week of absence. There was nothing out of the ordinary. Neglecting the list of phone calls he was obliged to return, he locked up again and left. The temp who free-lanced as his secretary would be notified that he would be back the following day.

Victor stopped for a brandy in a bar along the Quai Voltaire and was welcomed by the barman, who knew him as Mr. Kirov. But he did not stay long, rankled by the false air of familiarity and the barman's inane chatter. He fought traffic back to his street, which surprisingly yielded a place to park without his having to pray for it. He unlocked the door and saw her valises before he smelled the acrid smoke, and knew she was inside.

Michelle was still in her coat, seated on the edge of the couch, leaning forward, elbows on knees, smoking and facing the unlit fireplace in the stillness of the darkened interior. She held a glass in her hand but had not bothered with a light or the heater. The room was cold, collecting shadow like folds of dark velvet.

Victor closed the door behind him and took off his leather coat, methodically shaking off the droplets that filmed the surface. He hung it over the door in the hall closet and stepped into the living room, which had once been a library before the house was subdivided into luxury flats.

He crossed in front of her to get a glass and another brandy from the inlaid buffet, employed as a bar.

"Do you want a drink?"

She shook her head in the negative.

He poured himself a Fundador and took up a position on an armchair across from the couch. Their eyes met for an instant before she drew her gaze away.

She was wearing a rust-colored dress that revealed the shape of her breasts and her jutting nipples beneath the soft jersey. Her legs were crossed, encasing the convex hollow of shadow between her thighs.

He raised the glass and took a short slug of the acrid liquid.

"How was the flight?" he asked quietly.

She shrugged and inhaled, then stubbed out the cigarette, brushing her dark hair away from her face in the same practiced motion.

"Why did you leave without saying anything?"

"Why bother asking? We're both free. Isn't that the way it is?"

Her eyes probed his for some hint of feeling. But he was impassive.

"Would you like me to go?"

Victor felt a sudden weariness. He let a moment pass before responding.

"Do what you want."

Her eyes fixed on him pointedly, but their expression was unreadable.

He was on his feet, surprising her by the suddenness of his movement. The glass in his hand was hurled against the tiles of the fireplace.

Glass shattered and bits flew past her. She winced but did not take her gaze from him, her eyes shimmering like a wary animal.

"Do you think I enjoy watching you fuck another man?"

"He's nothing."

Victor stared at her. His eyes were dark points of anguish.

"Don't let me keep you."

She stared at him for a moment, then rose and went into the bedroom. She kicked off both shoes, unzipped her dress, and tossed it over a chair. Naked, she turned to face him, one knee turned in to guard the soft triangle of her sex. Her arms were held against her sides with the awkwardness of a child. Her eyes were dark and unfathomable.

She lay down on the bed, her legs tucked beneath her, one arm crossed in front of her breasts.

He took a sip of the brandy and stared at the dull maroon sheen of her expensive leather bags, ranged side by side on the polished wooden floor of the entryway. He felt rage, as intense as the dull striking edge of an ax.

He rested the curved glass against his mouth.

Anger was no longer possible. He had sold that, along with the rest of himself. He would play any role they chose. He no longer had a choice. The only irony, of course, was that he loved her, and that knowledge was as bitter as the liquor he slowly poured between his open lips.

He rose and went inside.

He stood at the window, staring into the darkness outside, listening to the grunt of shifting gears as an occasional car made a midnight foray into the silence of the deserted street.

Michelle lay curled on the bed behind him, breathing softly, one hand stretched across her belly, fingers curling toward the dark patch below. The other was outstretched, grasping for something in her sleep. Her hair formed a fan of shadow on the pillow, contrasting against the glazed highlights of her face.

He watched her in the darkness, aware of her beauty and the double reality within which they existed.

He heard her stir and returned to bed.

Her arms reached for him even in her sleep. She embraced him, feeling along his leg until she held him in her fingers, freeing his flesh from the fly of his pajamas.

Her mouth closed over him, sucking like an infant, curled tightly against his thighs.

He closed his eyes and allowed himself to flow with the sensation, trying to lose himself, as she now lost herself in him.

She turned and wriggled across him, hunching in order to insert his hardness within her.

She began a slow, writhing motion above him, twisting on his thickness, emitting short, harsh cries until she brought on her orgasm. Then she rested on both arms, breathing hard and darting her tongue to caress his face.

"More," she whispered urgently. "Again."

He pushed up into her, and she fitted herself to his rhythm, forcing him more deeply inside her.

"I want you . . . I want you. Want you." She moaned, forcing him to turn over on top of her as she spread her slender legs obscenely, her fists against his lower back. Urging him to seek deeper until he was rubbing the clenched opening of her womb.

"Don't stop . . . please, don't stop." She was shaking, crying out for him to hurt her, to tear her, shuddering uncontrollably as she convulsed again and again, her face wet with perspiration and tears.

He held her against him afterward, trying to ease her tension, to rock her back into sleep. But she moved back and forth, her hand buried between their legs, trying frantically to make him come, but he resisted, pushing her hands away.

She lay across him, her breathing slowing, becoming more regular. He rested against the pillows and closed his eyes, forcing himself to affect a sleep that would not come. To evade a torment that would not disappear.

29

Joyce continued on the tour of his domain, visiting a recently vacated boutique on a crooked street behind the Boulevard Montparnasse whose front was coated with an opaque glaze. Here were located the static listeners, ears tapped into the phones in Victor's office. There was another such outpost, lonely and forlorn, in the musty wine cellar of a restaurant located beside the foundation of Michelle's hotel, manned by a team of dour Belgians.

Later he went to observe the lovers, protected from observation like some Libyan diplomat behind the smoked glass of a rented Mercedes. The expensive car cruised slowly, tailing Victor and Michelle along the boulevards where they strolled arm in arm, like any of the anonymous couples around them. But no, not like the others. There was something that marked them apart. A sadness perhaps, and the intensity with which they looked at each other, or was Joyce projecting, playing at melodrama.

They were a handsome couple, one could not deny that. And so obviously in love. Yet it was both a fiction and a tragedy, but so brilliantly acted, that in spite of himself, even an old rhino like Joyce was moved.

In the end, the major portion of their effort went into tracking Roberts.

It was an accomplishment of no small difficulty, due to the American teams already in place. It was also a bit of a comedy, as the Israeli boys loved relating over glasses at La Deviniers, a wine bar specializing in vintages from the Touraine. They enjoyed the daily games of hide-and-seek with the unsuspecting Yanks, whose efforts were clumsy and obvious and not up to their critical standards.

In their little drama Michelle was the bait, Victor the foil, and the American was their Mercury, the messenger who provided communication both ways from his mysterious source.

So it was to Mercury that Joyce assigned the bulk of his resources. His teams of surveillance specialists who improvised out of a series of transports. One always in use, the other in reserve, a third on standby, ready to switch locations as soon as their quarry came to roost.

In this way they came to terms with his habits, understood the motives for his sudden cab rides, tracked him to the hairdresser, the boutique on the Rue Margaritte where he purchased his shirts, a tailor on the Rue de Longchamps where he was being measured for several expensive suits of clothing.

Lives well, this boy, was the consensus. Likes his little indulgences, his afternoon forays into Fouchons for mousse. The glass of Taittingers or a Veuve Cliqot or two before dinner at any one of several expensive cafés on the Champs Elysées. His apparent love of gadgets, for which he hunted through the *grand magasins* and none of which he could seem to resist purchasing. And, of course, his bank, which gave them the greatest trouble of all, as the deposits he made were on a Swiss numbered account, a dead end in their present state of resources.

But Trager was the wild card.

They had been taken off-balance by their trio's little jaunt to the Caribbean, so they drew breath and waited. But when the excursion developed into little more than a continuation of Victor's film venture, Joyce eased up a notch.

He had been tempted into putting in a team, but the knowledge that Stepinak had already swamped the island with personnel caused him to reconsider. Instead, he contented himself with secondary intelligence, gathered after the fact by a free-lance operator he had called in from Miami, a former detective on the Boston Police with absolutely reliable antecedents.

At first Trager seemed merely another member of the legion of production people Victor employed. His credentials checked, though Joyce wondered why, with all the photographic talent that abounded in Paris, they had gone so far afield to employ a photographer who was not even known for that type of work. It suggested an economy not yet in evidence in Victor's well-heeled operation. Was there some other reason Trager had been used? They were puzzled for an angle.

"He's a pretty boy, this Trager," Rosensweig observed, and Joyce had to nod in agreement. A good-looking, well-set-up young Brit, a trifle brash, even arrogant. But attractive.

TO KILL A KING

Pursuing that line of thought, the question was, to whom? Roberts, perhaps. The American's preferences in that arena were still uncertain. Victor and Michelle were lovers, which ruled them out, and yet Victor had flown back to Paris a day or two ahead of the others. Trager had remained on for a day or so, then chartered a plane and gone island-hopping.

That gave either Roberts or Michelle an opportunity, providing one was taken. It was an interesting conjecture but one that seemed to go nowhere. And nowhere was indeed where it was relegated in the scheme of thinking of those early days, only to reappear when Joyce received a follow-up call from Miami from his operative, who spoke with the rapid inflection of South Boston.

"Here's the thing. The English kid's checked in, but he hasn't slept in his room for three nights. The bed wasn't touched. Both maids remembered it because they thought he was cute and joked around about whose bed he was shackin' up in. Now here's the thing. The American guy, Roberts, he's neat, see; the maids remembered that, too, because in the bathroom everything's perfectly lined up. So neat, they're afraid to touch the stuff. Slippers, too, under the bed, toe to toe. Robes folded over the other bed. Only one pillow's been used the whole time."

"Not the case with the French girl. They won't swear to it, but these are two healthy black ladies, you understand? They get a kick sniffin' the sheets to see what the tourists have been up to, *comprends?* And this is no ordinary tourist. This is a beautiful actress. From France, no less. A celebrity. So these ladies took a keen interest, if you read my meanin'. They even unfolded the tissues to see what kind of makeup she used. They swear both beds in the room were used—and they mean used, and I mean by two people, not one. They think our French girlfriend was up to something, or something was up her. And I mean right up to the morning she left."

The information was as intriguing as it was distasteful. It pointed to the fact that Michelle had been unfaithful to Victor, either out of resentment or out of some sudden passion. Naturally there could have been other motives more appropriate to the case. Victor, or someone else, could have put her up to it. But that assumption, if unspoken, was still not proven. If the reasons were elusive, the fact of her unfaithfulness was not. It became the cause of some distress, and in ordering surveillance on Trager, Joyce felt a sense of guilt and no little remorse. In a very real way, Michelle's betrayal of Victor was also one of his own.

30

Michelle made her confession in a small church wedged between the crumbling walls of a convent school, in a tiny street just off the Madeleine.

It was not the first time she stepped into a church to light a candle and kneel in prayer for a few moments. This impulse extended to an occasional Mass and even the confessional. It was accepted as a normal aspect of her behavior. Her followers used these moments to snatch a cigarette, call a girlfriend, or down a brandy.

They had no inkling that her confessor was Roger Killian.

It was not the first confessional Killian had visited that week. He provided this service for a series of working-class arrondissements, where Algerian or Moroccan populations displaced once prospering parishes. Churches that once employed a dozen priests were now reduced to one or two. These overworked *curés* were occasionally aided by substitute clerics dispatched by the archdiocese. Killian arrived at these rectories with credentials identifying him as a Breton priest from the maritime provinces of Canada, which accounted for his fluent, but heavily accented, French.

Killian made his circuit every few weeks, arousing neither suspicion nor comment, except for the thankful exclamations of the prelates he came to relieve. He offered Mass, heard confessions, and made himself available during the hours when the other churchmen were gone on various errands.

During these times he was alone. Visitors would slip inside the darkened interiors then, sometimes to say confession when the pews were filled with the usual assortment of widows and pensioners bowed in prayer before various aspects of the Virgin or a particular patron saint. One of these was a young student type who spoke with a Croatian accent. The other a handsome Milanese who wore black motorcycle leathers.

At other times Killian would exchange quiet words with his visitors in the sanctum of the vestry, surrounded by embroidered albs, gleaming chalices, and polished censers. Ironically these temples became his safe houses, providing a form of sanctuary in an age when the notion itself seemed a ludicrous impossibility.

The church in the Madeleine was not on Killian's usual itinerary. Entering it that morning was not without some risk. Embraced by fashionable precincts, the church was used as a place of momentary refuge by scores of weary shoppers who paused to discharge various religious obligations.

One of the younger priests, who usually heard confession during the hours when many of the shops closed for the midday break, had suffered a minor accident when he was sideswiped on his moped the evening before. The incident was not accidental. Killian appeared at the rectory early the next morning with the explanation that he had been sent as a substitute while the young priest was mending. His presence was accepted with relief and without question. Killian was dispatched to the confessional, where he heard the usual litany of venial sins and prescribed the appropriate penances.

Michelle entered through a side door a little after one o'clock. She came along the transept to the nave, genuflected before the altar, then made her way to one of the side chapels, where she knelt and lit a candle. Then she joined the dwindling group of penitents seated on the dully gleaming pews, awaiting her turn at confession.

Michelle entered and closed the carved and ornamented door, murmuring the usual plea for forgiveness. Killian returned his part of the formula and bent toward the grating as she began to speak.

He had recruited her in Paris, four years before. Like the others in his group, she fit the psychological pattern he found most effective. Someone with a personal involvement in the world's injustice. A brother in prison, a sister murdered by some act of imperialist aggression. Michelle's father had gone to his martyrdom a few weeks before his twenty-sixth birthday, attempting to run a police blockade in Derry with a van loaded with galignite.

Michelle's mother was a dark, diminutive woman with a degree from Trinity College, Dublin. After her husband's funeral and the attendant publicity, which she found repugnant, she took her infant daughter to New York. There she found an apartment in a Chelsea brownstone and supported herself and her child by teaching evening courses in contemporary English literature to polyglot classes of Puerto Ricans and black dropouts in a community college in Brooklyn.

It was arduous but challenging and provided enough of a living for herself and her growing daughter. Michelle was in nursery school two years later when her mother was approached by IRA militants who attempted to recruit her as a courier. When she refused, their persistence turned into harassment. She escaped to Montreal where she found another job, teaching in a Catholic girl's college.

Michelle spent her childhood in a French-speaking neighborhood, and she grew into a sturdy young woman, intense about the world and its injustices and fond of dramatics and political essay-writing. She became the editor of her school newspaper, the leader of a group of young Gaulois-smoking Quebec separatists. Identifying more with the French than with the Irish, it was natural for the brilliant young student to choose the Sorbonne when it came time for college.

Michelle's indoctrination had not been without a certain agony. Her mother had shielded her from any knowledge of her father's revolutionary past. Michelle believed he died in a car accident. In her third year Michelle fell desperately in love with a handsome young Moroccan with a taste for revolutionary literature. He introduced Michelle to Guevara and Fanon, Sartre and Marcuse.

During their school holidays Michelle and her lover toured the Mediterranean. Her lover had student friends in working-class slums across the region. Instead of hostels, they slept in tiny, crowded flats, crawling with roaches and the stench of unwashed bodies and spoiling food. These experiences expanded her education.

In Tehran she received advanced indoctrination firsthand, when the Savak kidnapped, tortured, and mutilated their student-activist host.

Michelle refused to leave the country until the kidnapped boy was found. She maintained an embarrassing vigil at her own embassy. But before she could create more severe disturbances, she and her lover were hurried to the airport, the same day the boy's mutilated body was found in a refuse dump outside the city.

They had warned her it would be bad, but she had insisted on going. She did not understand how bad, not until she saw his empty, staring sockets and open mouth, gorged with his own severed genitals.

It was to be a turning point, for it molded Michelle, toughened her, and started the transcendent fire with which she wished to ignite the entire world.

After they returned to Paris her lover confessed his own involvement in the Khomeini underground. He belonged to a group responsible for blowing up the European facilities of companies dealing with the Shah. Michelle was profoundly affected by the disclosure. She wanted to join her lover's organization but found herself blocked by their insistence on a fundamentalist religious devotion that came in direct conflict with her own views on equality for women.

In her burned the need to find a cause, a personal god to whom she could sacrifice herself. It was provided purely by chance, or so it seemed at the time. Michelle regularly attended meetings of radical organizations. At one of them she had a conversation with a young IRA activist. He was an extremely handsome boy with black Irish looks and blue eyes. His name was Sean, and she found herself drawn to his cause. She joined a secret student cell and became acquainted with the past that had been so carefully concealed from her.

She could not have known then, though she came to suspect it later, that Killian was behind the incident. But it both exhilarated and liberated her. Her father's death confirmed her own connection with the oppressed everywhere. She and her new lover agonized over their existence and the direction of their lives. They found others to confide in and act with. First in public marches and protests for a whole slew of causes, then in more serious actions directed against the imperialist establishment.

In all these actions Michelle showed dedication, devotion, and exceptional courage. She never suspected that this was her proving ground. Fortunately Killian stepped in before Michelle became further enmeshed in amateur revolutionary theatrics and their little group was infiltrated by the police.

Killian's cadres were made up of people like Michelle, all unknown to the international intelligence services. Most were young, fanatically devoted, and battle-hardened. They accepted the roles he assigned without question, though he was careful to sound out their feelings before he attempted a particular operation.

He was more than a leader. He had become a surrogate father who understood their hearts, and the confessor of their most intimate secrets. Killian knew the anger existing within

TO KILL A KING

Michelle, her strength and vulnerability. The depth of her passion both stirred and frightened him. So he was not surprised when he surveyed her agonized expression through the grating.

"You've got to get me out of this," she whispered. "It's impossible. He knows he's being used. He's aware that he's being set up as some kind of sacrificial pawn."

"He told you that?"

"No. I can sense it. I know."

"Are you sure he actually knows anything? He's made no attempts to protect himself."

"I think he loves me. I think he believes he can save me."

Killian allowed a moment of silence, his eyebrows raised quizzically, scanning her expression for some sign of inner emotion.

"And what are your feelings?" Killian asked flatly.

"I know I'm not supposed to feel anything," she began in a whisper. "I didn't before, not with anyone else. But this time it's different. I can't explain."

"Have you fallen in love with him? I have to know."

Michelle did not answer, not for several moments. "I don't know."

"Has he reproached you for what happened in the islands?"

She paused, trying to make contact with Killian's eyes, but saw only a dark profile edged in a harsh yellow light.

"He started to, but no. He knows everything. He can read it in my pores. But he doesn't say a word. No reproach. Nothing. And that's worse than if he cursed me and called me a whore. Because that's what I am."

"You're not a whore. We are not amateurs," Killian commented in a flat tone. "I warned you about the emotional preparation you would have to make."

"It worked for a while. It doesn't anymore."

Killian let a pause lengthen before he spoke, his whispered words gentle but spoken with resolve. "You've performed brilliantly. No one could ask for more. You're the best I have. That's why I gave you this role. But I have to ask you to go on. We're almost there. Trager is the key, and he's in your hands now. Preparations have been made. We go into action very soon. Then all this will be over. You've been through an ordeal, I know. But it's coming to an end. Just hold on for a little longer. It's only a matter of days."

"Will you have to kill him?"

"No. Not unless he forces that decision. His death is not necessary."

He watched her eyes seek for his own in the darkness, her glance expressing an agony only he could relieve. He wanted to reach out and draw her to him but restrained even the impulse to open the wrought-iron grating and reach for her hand.

She rose and stepped into the stillness outside. He heard the staccato tapping of her heels long after she had left the sanctuary tormented by a purgatory he had created but from which he could not release her.

31

It was going to be a siege.

The pattern had been established, the theme and variations were all apparent, but there were no breakthroughs. No sudden insights. No changes in rhythm or routine.

Victor's existence had become a humdrum string of meetings with various cinema types, all of whom were valid and certifiable, as Rosensweig and his police team swore and attested to.

So Joyce encouraged them to take pictures, filling up a lovely album, mementos of every man or woman who stood beside Roberts at a counter that sold the gadgets he adored, rubbed elbows with him when he was gripped by his chocolate cravings, and shared the surrounding tables when he had his little glass of bubbly.

The snaps were flown out to Joyce's special friends in Brussels—by messenger, no less, as Rosensweig commented acidly. They became an additional expense to grumble about. But it was essential to continue the sense of drama without which the team might slacken and lose interest, falling into patterns of boredom that might cause weary eyes to blink at the very moment they should have been open.

They were now in the trying time, the testing time. Many of Joyce's varied and complex resources were called upon and taxed to their limit. But it was the morale of his little family that concerned him most.

To the Belgian boys he played an indulgent father, tolerant of their little tricks and improvisations, treating them to tasty meals in a score of little *boîtes* where they might feast their eyes on the dark and pretty side of Paris, whetting their appetites for what would be, but could not be at present.

To the listeners in their cramped little holes he was a generous uncle, spoiling them with unexpected presents. He knew each man's special weakness and indulged it generously.

For the watchers, doing their special kind of time, he

became the longed-for visitor. Offering a touch of home and concrete evidence that they had not been forgotten.

He sat longer with them than with the others, huddled in his raincoat, absorbing chill and discomfort, sometimes sharing their meals or taking a turn at the periscope, indulging with them in their special vice of conjecture as they speculated on the psychology of their targets and the eventual outcome of their destinies.

From them he received the news that Victor and Michelle had resumed housekeeping, that they seemed affectionate, even passionate, which provided his watchers' boring existence with a much-needed lift.

The lovers were very domestic these days and spent a good many evenings in. Michelle seemed quite content to play the hausfrau, read, prepared meals, cut and pasted fashions from various magazines. Victor seemed moodier than before, drinking quite a bit. Prone to spending longer periods alone and in silence, without his beloved Debussy, mind you, which they had gotten used to hearing and now so achingly missed.

All was noted and stored. Encouragement given to relate even the smallest detail. To leave nothing unstated. In that way Joyce was given his own daily quota of confessions.

He did not neglect his other duties. He dined with Rosensweig in mournful little restaurants frequented by expatriates from Eastern Europe who spoke with angry gestures and melancholy accents. Joyce sipped Armagnac while lending an attentive ear to the Frenchman's many complaints.

Afterward they returned to the safe house in the Neuilly-sur-Seine suburbs, where they went over the reports that periodically came in from Brussels. Much of the material was negative—all of it, really. If Roberts communicated or was communicated with, the method remained a mystery. Yet they knew it must be accomplished. Killian was either somewhere in Paris or would return to it soon. The very complacency of the moment was their greatest cause for alarm. It was a lull that could not last.

It was the other possibilities that frightened them. Victor's little circus could be moved elsewhere. The film was in pre-production. The location could be anywhere. So they undertook a little field exercise, a little adventure to break up the routine.

It was made to resemble a conventional burglary. Victor's production manager lived in a housing block in Passy, which turned out to be a piece of cake for his professionals. A copy of the script was removed and reproduced. The information was reassuring. All of the film's locations were inside Paris and no farther than a few miles from its environs. That put them right back on square one, guarding their petty conjectures and minor assumptions, like the crew of a warship that has no idea of its destination but must nevertheless prepare itself for battle against an enemy it has never seen.

Again they waited, returning to the small comforts of their routines.

The message, when it finally came, arrived like an unexpected gift in the form of a telex, messengered from a London exchange: "Dig successful. On verge of major find. Your presence urgently needed."

And so Joyce returned to England, where his enemy lay burrowed deep and waiting.

32

In those first weeks after his return from Nassau, Trager went from supreme euphoria to black depression. Success could not lift the dark shroud that continually enveloped him. Only a few weeks earlier, stepping off the British Airways jet that carried him back to London, he had been flushed with victory. Invincible. There even had been an unexpected conquest on the plane, a pretty young flight attendant who had found his charm irresistible.

They continued the magic through dinner in a posh West End dining spot. Getting her to his apartment and into the sack had been accomplished with similar sleight of hand. Yet when she lay beneath him, her soft, slender thighs wrapped around his, impassioned fingers clawing along his back, the sorcery suddenly vanished and was replaced by a dark, self-conscious awareness, a hatred for the mechanicalness of the performance. The girl was desirable, ripe, hungry, even adulating. Everything that should have turned him on. Instead he grew soft, lifeless, the heat replaced by an emptiness, an icy feeling that gripped his guts. He wanted Michelle, not this stranger, wanted her so badly that it almost amounted to pain.

The days that followed brought no abatement. His little triumphs had soured. He made a stab at calling the hot little bird in the Kings Road boutique, who was now his, palpitating and accessible. But he never got past the first few numbers before replacing the receiver with a feeling almost of despair.

He had the pictures, of course, waiting in an agony until they were developed, irritated when a hitch at the Battersea lab caused a few hours' delay. He screamed bloody murder at the technicians with whom he had always shared a professional camaraderie. He went about his other assignments in a kind of morbid lethargy, lacking even the energy to arrive on schedule and even blowing one or two plums, which cost him a pretty penny when he had to beg other photographers for their discards.

TO KILL A KING

Christ, what the hell's the matter with you, Trager? Snap out of it!

But that was impossible. He was caught.

The pictures finally arrived by special messenger, but he was almost afraid to look at them. A thing that had never happened before. Not to Mrs. Trager's little boy. He felt a strange shiver before tearing open the envelope, smoking a cigarette while they lay on the table before him, his face covered with a sheen of perspiration. But they were good, better than good, jolting him with the realization that he had actually taken them.

He danced around the room with the contact sheets in his hand, whooping once or twice before the dark feelings crashed down again: the desperation of wanting her so badly, together with the knowledge that she was so distant, so impossibly out of reach.

He lay on the daybed, smoking, reliving the moments when he had touched her, been inside her, exploring her with his hands and tongue. The very easiness of his conquest seemed a cheat, the product of some momentary heat and the artificial intimacy of their situation. He knew the routine too well. Had played that game too often himself to be deceived by it. And yet he had been deceived, conned into believing it could be more.

He suffered this remorse, haunted by the flimsiness of his own position and lack of status within the profession that magnetized them both. The door that still remained closed. And worse, the frightening implications of her relationship with Victor. She seemed part of another galaxy, a distant plane impossible for him to attain.

Flyte's call took him unawares. Before he could summon the gumption to refuse, a meeting had been arranged. That, too, caused his stomach to knot. Flyte's voice had lost the supplicating edge that previously offered Trager mastery over their little situation. There had been several messages from Flyte on the answering machine when he returned, pitched in the usual coded references. Specifying a place and time. But he had ignored them. When he did answer, Flyte's tone had been downright demanding.

"I must see you. Understand? *Must.*"

Must. Bullshit. But in the end Trager yielded and kept the appointment. He drove out to Regents Park unshaven, parking his Datsun a few blocks from the discreetly fashionable little pied-à-terre that Flyte kept tidied for their private interviews, as he enjoyed terming them.

"You look a sight, darling," Flyte said, opening the door after Trager rang. Not once but half a dozen times. Flyte's tone was arch, condescending.

"Fuck you," Trager replied, shunting past and sprawling on the leather couch, legs spread arrogantly.

"We live in hope," Flyte responded, unruffled. He handed Trager an outsize crystal goblet filled with whiskey, into which he had deposited several cubes of ice.

"And did we have a lovely trip?" Flyte continued in the same order of bitchiness, seating himself opposite on the diagonal formed by the meeting of both settees.

Flyte had the usual Dry Sack standing at attention on the coffee table. He had already downed two or three, unless he had changed his habits, which Trager knew was not bloody likely.

"It sucked."

"Really?" Flyte's eyebrows made quizzical arches. "From what one saw in the newspaper, one would have thought you'd have been in seventh heaven."

Trager glared at him. As usual, Flyte was uniformed in a wine-colored one-piece velvet jumpsuit. His at-home togs, as he liked to call them, as opposed to the regalia of civil-service black. He wore soft leather slippers, and one wrist was circled with a heavy gold bracelet.

He posed with one leg across the other, leaning back so that his razor-thin body formed an elegant question against the beige leather of the couch. He surveyed Trager with a sardonic smile, one arm cocked back, wrist bent, the delicate crystal dangling from his long, tapered fingers.

"The tan is simply perfection. All over, one prays."

Trager stared at him with irritation gulping down his whiskey, shooting the glass out for more. Flyte smiled and rose to pour another from the Queen Anne sideboard, the single piece of antique furniture among all the contemporary plastic, chrome, and glass trash with which the rest of the one-bedroom flat was decorated.

Trager took the tumbler without looking up, and Flyte returned to his seat, toying with the liquid in his own glass.

"Are we going to have a scene, darling?" he asked in a gentle voice, but Trager did not see fit to respond.

A pale sun filtered through the half-closed blinds but was

unable to warm the atmosphere inside the room. They sat in silence, coupled by past intimacy, distanced from each other by more than the few feet of carpet separating them. One adoring, the other adored. A connection made more intense for not being spoken, suspended like a living tissue between them.

They had encountered each other in one of the Prince's innumerable receptions. Trager had been one of the usual annoyances but brasher than most, seeking Flyte out and offering him a bribe for some kind of exclusive, a sneak picture of Lady Di in the loo, or some such vulgarity.

Instead of anger, Flyte had actually been amused by his impudence and, of course, the charming, boyish smile. So innocently seductive. The older man did not deceive himself. Trager was a perfect little tart. And so it began. First with a drink to clarify the air and put the little upstart in his place. Then dinner and a play. All innocent at first, both pretending it was fun and games in the city. Hands across the gulf of class and all that rubbish.

Flyte was caught even before he knew it, though he certainly felt himself slipping. Was it love or punishment? he liked to ask himself. Trager had made no bones about his price. Nor had Flyte. It remained an unspoken assumption in those first few weeks, when nothing more than a touch had been attempted. A testing of the waters, so to speak. A casual brush with the back of the hand against the front of the trousers. Then Flyte had dropped a casual remark about the location of one of the Prince's weekend hideaways. He also mentioned one of his own. And so it began.

"Wasn't the money enough?" the older man said at last, breaking the uncomfortable silence.

"Christ, it's not the bloody fucking money," Trager spat. "I'm not a fucking whore."

Flyte smiled, sardonic again. "Don't be silly, darling. No one would ever accuse you of that. Are you in love?"

Trager glanced up, and the look that passed between them caused the older man to grin.

"I don't mind that, darling. It makes you more endearing—human, even."

"You are a bastard," Trager said, but without force.

"But why? We all have our little sufferings. Join the club."

"Not your bloody fucking club. No thanks."

Flyte merely raised his eyebrows. "Don't give it a thought, darling. We don't want you. It's not having joined that makes you so charming and our friendship so special."

"You can kiss that off, sweetheart," Trager said jauntily, taking a gulp of the liquor.

The older man looked at him without changing expression and shrugged. "I might live, but it would make me very unhappy. I've grown very attached to you, darling. Perverse as my nature is, I find our meetings have become quite an important part of my existence. Yours, too, I imagine. As they say, we have a good thing going. Why chuck it?"

Trager sat upright and slapped the glass down on the table. "I'm chucking it and pronto. I have a new line, bucko. So you and this town can both fuck off."

"Really?" Flyte said patiently. "Do tell."

"I did a fashion spread for a producer while I was down there. A star, or soon to be one. And so, ducks, it's a whole new ball game."

The older man absorbed that and nodded. "Yes, it might well be. You do have a talent; never have I denied that. But one swallow doesn't make a summer, as dear old mother used to say. One contact doesn't make a career. And one may add, I have never been content with one swallow, have I, darling? If you will forgive a small indulgence."

"It's a start, and a bloody fine one," Trager retorted.

"True as that may be, you're going to need more than one photo spread to launch you, especially the way you go through money. By the by, in case you've been too busy to notice, I made a small deposit with your tailor."

"I told you once," Trager announced emphatically, "I'm not you're bleeding tart."

"Don't be a fool," Flyte said firmly. "The only thing that distinguishes you between that pack of scandal-mongers from the gutter press has been the information I supply you with. Think where you would be without it. Now you think, because of one photo session, you can just toss all that aside. Look around you, darling. The Kings Road is chock a block with photographers who've had more spreads to their credit than a Chelsea tart. To survive in the world you're describing takes contacts and something you have yet to acquire—class, my dear. Class with a capital *C*. It could happen, perhaps. But it's going to take more than your hot little buns to accomplish. And that is my mission to fulfill." Flyte paused

TO KILL A KING

and smiled wickedly. "Ah, I've hurt your feelings. So you rise, cross stage left, and utter a pleasant 'Fuck you' before exiting."

Trager, who the instant before was about to utter those very words, clamped his mouth shut and jumped to his feet. He began moving toward the door.

"Before you go, darling, there's a bit of gossip I think you might be interested in." Flyte raised his voice slightly to accompany Trager on his march.

"It's a charming tale about a prince and a princess and a certain secret, one might add: a top-secret trip planned by the happy couple at a certain vacation spot known only to the elect. They will be alone, far from the hoi polloi, and the usual restless vagabondage you generally run with. And, one might add, very scanty security arrangements. In other words, an exclusive opportunity to photograph the royal couple at play. And with total candor while they believe that are safe and unobserved. Who knows what outrageous little indiscretion they might perform for your benefit. And the rights would be yours, dear boy. Worldwide. Interested?"

Trager cursed, one hand on the knob, his limbs trembling, unable to open the door.

"Yes, I know. Fuck and double fuck," Flyte continued in the same sardonic tone. "But it's a cruel, hard world, darling. And it don't get any easier. So why not come back inside. I'll pour you another drink and we can discuss the future of our charming situation."

Trager turned to face the older man's mocking expression of false concern.

"Oh, come now, darling. Don't pout. It could still turn out to be a lovely afternoon."

Trager was mildly drunk when he drove away from Regents Park sometime later that same afternoon. Dusk had turned central London into a quagmire of glowing headlights. He avoided Baker Street and navigated the serpentine south to Knightsbridge. He found a noisy pub along the Kings Road and settled into a booth to sort things out, a thing he did best when surrounded by gabble.

He had been handed gold on a plate. That knowledge, along with the other tidbits he had been granted over the year and half he had known Flyte, always eased whatever feelings of shame he felt when leaving the rumpled sheets of Regents

Park. But this was by far the winner. The grand prize. And it was his, wrapped up in a pink ribbon. The question was how best to use his blessing.

His first impulse had been to contact old McNabb and arrange a prior payment in exchange for an exclusive. But that quickly gave way to an even better proposition. It would be madness to offer the deal to McNabb without knowing what his competition would pay. Only once the word was out, it would be anybody's game. So that course was abandoned.

No, he had a better way. He would do the job alone and afterward offer the pictures to the highest bidder. That way he ran no risk of a leak. The only chance he took was of information seeping from the palace itself. But Flyte had reassured him. The trip was top-secret, known only to a handful of the elect. So when you balanced it out, a seepage from that source seemed remote. It was a risk, sure. But it was damned worth taking.

That decided, Trager quit the pub in spite of a handful of greetings from the far end of the bar and dodged his way back home along a street crowded with the usual punk riffraff and goggle-eyed shop girls.

Once inside his flat, he scooped up the glossy contact sheets and dealt them out across the table. Taking a red grease pencil, he began the process of elimination. By nine-thirty he had finished. Satisfied, he gave them a once-over and placed the receiver on the table in front of him.

His heart was trip-hammering like a bloody schoolboy about to ask his first Sheila for a walk home.

Shit. Here goes.

He picked up the receiver and dialed, getting blips and static before he heard the phone pronounce a double ring. He counted eight of them before it was finally picked up.

"Michelle Duran, please. I'm calling from London."

A voice told him to please hold. There were more beeps before the phone was finally answered.

"Michelle? It's Robin. Robin Trager . . ."

Later, when he would replay the conversation in his mind, she would seem cool, almost distant. She only began to warm up as the conversation continued.

He was nervous, for openers. Shit, who wouldn't be? But he steadied pretty quickly, keeping it casual at the beginning, making conversation about her flight back to Paris and rejoindering with a joke when she questioned him about his mysterious island-hopping adventure. When he mentioned the pictures, her interest level rose.

"God, they're terrific," he reassured her. "But I wanted you to see them before we do the final retouching and create background effects."

There was a pause. He sensed reluctance and held his breath.

"Yes, certainly that would be very nice," she said cagily. "Exactly what did you have in mind?"

"I'd say this weekend in Paris, only I couldn't count on having your undivided attention, could I?" Without waiting for an answer he plunged ahead. "Look, I'll be frank. These pictures are important to me. I want to spend the right kind of time on them, not rush the job. I want to be alone with you, that's the selfish part."

Her laugh was warm and intimate. He felt his guts ease back into place.

"There's a town in Brittany, La Boule. A friend recommended the place. There's a hotel called L'Espedon. Did I mangle the name?"

"No." She laughed again. "I know the hotel. But I have never been there. It sounds charming."

"Then I'm on course. Is it a date?"

There was a pause. He sensed a moment of uncertainty.

"Can I call you back?"

"Sure. I'll be in for another hour."

"All right. Good-bye."

Trager drank more whiskey, smoked, went over the contact sheet again, rubbed out one red circle and replaced it with another. It was forty minutes before she called back. He waited three rings before he picked up.

"Yes," she said. "I'd love to go. But I could not be there before ten on Friday. Is that all right?"

"No problem. See you Friday, about ten."

Trager hung up and whooped. He was grinning just like a kid. Good Jesus, he was home free.

33

Joyce entered England as inconspicuously as he had left it, flying in on a corporate messenger service that landed him in a private airfield near Coventry. It had been a long day since leaving Paris that morning. He faced the promise of an even longer night.

He entered London on a vacationer's special into Victoria, took the underground to Russel Square, crossed Euston Road, and headed toward St. Pancrass where he was picked up by a black Cortina opposite Kings Cross Station. They headed north, but the driver made several abrupt changes of direction, that took them through streets walled by monotonous brick villas, that were trimmed in white. Flowers were set out in boxes, struggling for survival amid the grime. There were red mailboxes and latticed telephone booths and a kind of moldering exhaustion, the settled domains of the middle class.

The house was a half-timbered builder's fancy, located in the western reaches of the city, part of an innocuous suburb blanketed by drizzle. The interior smelled of mildew and disuse and was lit by cheap low-intensity bulbs.

Joyce was ushered into an upstairs parlor that was bathed in a jaundiced light from a yellow cluster, an Edwardian conceit of painted metal curlicues sprouting from the ceiling. The rest of the furniture was springless, vinyl and dusty.

Blake was in profile when Joyce entered, bent above a walnut table where he fussed over setting up a small bar from ingredients he was removing from a large paper bag.

"Gin. Whiskey—Irish if you please. Swans lager and some Guinness," Blake said with forced heartiness, and Joyce was touched that Blake had remembered his fondness for concocting black-and-tans out of Guinness and lager. But he ordered a whiskey instead, which Blake served neat and in a glass whose cleanliness Joyce did not wish to investigate.

Blake poured gin for himself, then went to the stairs to shout down to the driver about a six-pack he had deposited in the kitchen for the man's use. He shut the door after that, which Joyce knew was double-thick and soundproofed. The room's comfortable surroundings were deceptive. It was also used for interrogations.

Blake settled himself in an armchair, facing Joyce with the nod and smile of an old acquaintance who offers no concessions to intervening time and picks up a conversation begun years before, as though it had been dropped only yesterday. He eyed Joyce over the rim of his glass, taking several rapid sips of fortification with the intensity of a worker about to return to his shovel.

Like the house, Blake, too, was swiftly going to seed. His big face was perspiring. His blue eyes were bloodshot and watery. Rashes of broken capillaries sprouted across his cheeks and neck like a garden grown to weeds. He supported a paunch and carried the rest of his weight poorly, thick in the legs and upper arms, which stretched the shiny synthetic of his wrinkled suit, making it resemble a badly used mattress.

"Been busy little scouts, haven't we?" Blake commented, putting down his glass on the end table beside him, a spindly affair supporting an unlit chromium lamp.

Joyce smiled and nodded, his fingers wrapped around the glass, which he kept cradled in his lap. Blake's large, perspiring face became suddenly animated, the muscles around his lips and eyes moving like the deployment of troops before a battle.

"Hell, you stuck my foot in it this time, didn't you?" Blake announced, not without a certain relish. "Old Blake and company is in the shit, deep like, as they say where you hail Mary from."

Joyce pantomimed a genuflection, waiting for Blake to continue.

"Well, here's poor old Blake and company, practically semiretired, ready for his pension in Costa Rica. I mean, do you comprehend, *amigo*, just how reduced old Blake has become? Lear on the moors, ranting and in rags. A half-staffed, half-funded relic. The remnant of what was once an action service—I repeat, an action service."

Joyce now realized Blake was fairly tight, a state of exultation he wished to attain himself.

"Okay, you got the picture," Blake continued. "Beached and in despair we were, until along comes Father Joyce, who lights the lamps of obligation. Drops a little holy water and saves the day, he does. And so old Blake rouses himself off the toilet he's been squatting on for the last decade or so and trots himself off to see what he can see.

"Right off, he spies the blessed Reverend Stepinak, only he's Cardinal Stepinak, and we lesser mortals are careful to address him as Your Eminence. He's landed on our sceptered isle with an operation that makes D Day look like a company picnic somewhere in the primitive wilds of New Jersey."

Blake took another gulp and settled himself.

"And what an operation. Mainframe computers and hundreds of bleeding terminals lined up in rows like he's launching a blooming satellite. And who does he report to, and who's his liaison? Here's the rub, dearie. There isn't one. No higher British authority to oversee his operation. And as for liaison with any of our security services, you can laugh up your own bleeding asshole until you find it. His bleeding Eminence is a law unto his obnoxious self."

Blake heaved himself up and, edging backward as he spoke, found the table and refilled his glass. He made an offering jut of his chin in Joyce's direction but received a negative shake of the head.

"That's right my child, you heard correctly. There is no linkage between His Eminence and Her Majesty's government. No linkage at all. Our good cardinal owns his own piece of the rock, as your adverts put it. Great Britain is his by right of abdication."

Blake paused to quench his outrage with a good belt of gin, then hunched his meaty shoulders and gripped one arm of the chair.

"All right, so we suit up. My whole bleeding contingent, or what's left of it, and we settle in, squatting in the duck blinds, clutching Thermos to chest. We wait and we watch. And we see things among the holy that make us blush, and our tiny hearts trip like hammers, for the synod is gathering. Oh, yes, there are other cardinals, my child. Intelligence lords from distant realms, from lands far and foreign. We glimpse their comings and goings. The question is, why are they here? A lesser man might have let it go at that. I mean, after all, he would have no authority other than his yellowing, out-of-date directives and only the whisper of an old friend to guide him. An old friend who himself is drifting alone at sea. So the glimpse might have been enough for him. But for old Blake—*never!*"

The last word was pure imitation Churchill. Blake grinned,

showing some discolored bridgework. Joyce raised his glass in a mock toast.

"So what does old Blake do, you ask? This rotting, rum-soaked dreg that never was. He performs a little surgery. That's what he does. He makes a snatch. Oh, don't be alarmed. Nothing of importance taken, I assure you. Nothing that will be missed."

Blake smiled an evil smile, then continued.

"You see, His Eminence was not master of his domain all at once. Oh, no, he had to take command in easy stages, so he was forced to use some leftover staff. Old English housekeeping staff. Perfectly darling figures, they are—if a little too effete for His Eminence's taste. A bit prancy, you see."

Here Blake waved a palm in imitation and batted his eyes coquettishly.

"And that must have been annoying, I'm sure, considering all the gorgeous young things in three buttons His Eminence surrounds himself with these days. But things move in a gentler fashion this side of the water, and His Eminence, as always, is in a tempestuous hurry. And hurry, as we know, makes for careless oversights which we are permitted to take quick advantage of under the dirty rules of the game."

Blake grinned like a well-fed cat.

"Actually it was too good to pass up. The target was a temp, you see. On housekeeping loan from a bureau I shall not dignify by naming. He was only waiting for his Yank replacement before he was to go on holiday."

Blake paused to relieve himself of some gas, belching at the same time with an apologetic grimace, then resumed in the same arch tone.

"Imagine the scene. My thugs burst in the exact second the poor ponce is standing in front of a mirror, modeling the scantiest of bikinis, which he had purchased for his sojourn on the island of Mykonos. His sexual preferences being his own affair, my darlings wrap him up in a tarp and remove him to a place of grace, where he proceeds to bitch and moan and hold little protest demonstrations. But to no avail, since we have the edge over him in bitchiness. So little by little the beans begin to spill. And we get some names and some places and some dates. And even more important, and get this, old queen . . ." Here Blake paused, leaning forward for emphasis.

"Not one of these high lords was here with the knowledge and permission of Her Majesty. Not a single one. And NATO men are they all. Careful of protocol and meticulous about leaving their cards whenever they go calling. But not this time, old duck. Imagine, such lofty strata, and all here on the sly, like boys slipping out of school for the day. Beguiles the mind, does it not?"

Joyce's brow furrowed. It did indeed. But he knew there was more and allowed Blake to continue.

"Oh, and here's another little tidbit for your gossip column. While our friendly housekeeper is busily identifying their photos in my album, with part of his eager little brain still fixated on the carpet of buttocks to be vacuumed on those glorious Greek beaches, we find even more interesting information. It seems Holy Father Stepinak has granted a special audience. A very special audience, mind you. Only the most trusted in attendance awaiting his visitor in the deepest, darkest hours of the night. But who was favored, my darling? Who is this visitor who leaves no calling card? And for whom there is no picture to match any of the rogues in my entire portrait gallery, extensive as it is?"

Blake paused to pull on his glass.

"Of this secret visitor we have the barest of glimpses. Tall, he is. Imposing, he is. This much we get but no more. My thugs are for plucking a few more petals off the pansy, you'll forgive me for that one. But I decline. Question him gently, lads. Go over the terrain yet again. Treat him like an archaeologist would a delicate shard. And so they do. They can be such nice boys when they want to be. But after all is said and done, we have only the scantiest profile, or rather, a fast-fading memory in the not terribly reliable mind of our good fairy. And *das es alles.*"

Blake hoisted himself to his feet and made another visit to the walnut table, this time not only refilling his own glass but also carrying the bottle back for Joyce, who submitted to a refill.

He was silent, too, as his glass was replenished. Not looking at Blake but off in the distance somewhere, as though he caught the glimmer of something moving too quickly to perceive. Joyce sighed and brought the glass to rest on his lap. His eyes drifted into meditation.

So Stepinak had brought his operation to England without the official knowledge of the intelligence establishment. Other highly placed NATO officials, all of them barons of their own intelligence services, had visited him without making it official, slipping in and out of the country in secret. Now Blake had snatched a housekeeper who had seen a mysterious visitor, to which no identity could be affixed. Its meaning truly beguiled the mind.

"Is there more?" Joyce queried when Blake was again seated. Joyce prayed there wasn't. He was fatigued to his joints.

"But of course," Blake answered with a smirk. "A little bedtime story. The Three Little Queens and how they grew."

Joyce winced, but Blake was too far gone for restraint. He leaned forward, holding up three fingers and counting off as he spoke.

"The first little queen is a queer little queen. Him, I snatched. The second little queen is an inquisitive little queen. Poking his camera where it doesn't belong. Him, you want. And the third little queen, well, he's a curious little queen. His name is Flyte and he works for a prince in a palace. . . ."

And just like that, Joyce was suddenly wide-awake.

34

It turned out to be a splendid weekend.

For a shaky moment Trager was not sure Michelle would arrive, and he spent a nervous half hour soaking up three cognacs and keeping an eye cocked on the clock. But at ten-thirty on the dot, Michelle entered the lobby, looking stunning and furtive and just a little unsure of herself. A way she had that made you want to put your arms around her and forever protect her from the world.

Trager waited a long moment, watching her glance around for him before he stepped out of the lounge and made his appearance.

"Hullo," he said, smiling.

"Hello," she responded softly. Her liquid gaze absorbed him totally, and he was lost forever.

He had taken two adjoining rooms so as not to push it if she had other ideas.

"Like it?"

She stepped to the window with its view of the aquamarine ocean spilling away toward an infinite horizon. "It's beautiful. I love it."

"Where's your room?" She turned toward him.

"Just next door, actually."

"How convenient," she said slyly. "So no one will disturb our concentration?"

"That's right," he said, moving toward her.

"I'd like a drink." And she turned away with a demure smile.

They went down to the bar again, first exploring the elegant lobby of the huge hotel, which had set him back a pound or two, no joke. But this was one weekend when considerations of gelt did not apply. He was doing it up like a bloody Rothschild.

They held hands in the lounge and exchanged shy, almost virginal glances, while her delicate fingers did a graceful dance over his own. God, she was so bloody gorgeous. He

TO KILL A KING

couldn't take his eyes off her. Later, when they went upstairs, it was she who came to him, kissing him shyly in the elevator. He felt the soft, clinging touch of her lips and went weak in the knees. Imagine. Him, Trager, whom no bird had ever affected.

Inside the room, it was she who went to the adjoining door and turned the key. He waited until she came out of the bathroom dressed in a black lace peignoir before he entered her room, wearing white silk Sulka pajamas, of all things, and feeling like a prince. He took her in his arms, and it went like a dream, no rough spots, no apologies for a gesture or word unintended. Indeed it was one of those rare moments when life gave him exactly that. A dream turned into a fairy-tale reality.

They rose late on Saturday and breakfasted in the formal dining room high above the sea, waited upon by a staff that treated him like a ruddy lord. He had rented a Mercedes coupe the day before, and they toured the coast as far as Saint-Malo, stopping so he could photograph the pink-granite cliffs and the emerald-green Riviera. Everything he said seemed to make her laugh, and he lost himself in the sorcery of her glance and the delicious way she had of pronouncing things. It was the way he had always imagined Bardot in the erotic fantasies of his childhood. They returned late, made love, and slept, waking when it was already dark and dining in the hotel's sumptuous restaurant.

Michelle wore a stunning black evening dress, high at the neck and made of embroidered Oriental silk, and it sheathed her magnificent body like a surgeon's latex glove. He wore the new tux he had purchased from Flyte's Saville Row tailor earlier in the week, paying a premium for it to be ready in time. The rest of the night was spent wedded to her suppleness as they danced to a small orchestra. They were the prettiest people on the floor, and curious eyes followed them wherever they went.

After a nightcap they returned to her room. He couldn't keep his hands off her. Slower now, they moved to a sinuous ballet, twisting around each other in a kind of endless dance, seeking with their mouths and fingers. Opening to each other without restriction.

"Yes, now . . . take me . . ." she whispered, and he shivered to its poetry.

Afterward it was he who opened up, spilling his guts as he recounted the early days of struggle in a block of Manchester flats.

"Two up and two down. Loo in the yard. Bloody horror show. I got out of it on a fluke. Won a contest given by a photography school. I got a bloody scholarship. My mum figured I'd spend the rest of my life taking bridal and baby pictures. Fat chance. I was on the train for London six months after graduation. And the rest, my dear, is history."

The miracle was how avidly she listened, focusing on him completely, like some simple Sheila he'd picked up in a pub on the Brompton Road.

It was truth he offered her. The raw, unvarnished truth. Oh, well, he embellished somewhat, which was only natural. It was the truth as he wanted her to know it. His struggle to break into fashion. How he'd gone to work on a weekend rag that serviced a London suburb, how he got a break assisting a hot free-lancer.

"How hot?" she said with a furtive smile. And he took her again. Christ, it was Allah's paradise.

Sunday morning was gray and windy, but they bundled up and walked along the beach, hand in hand in a profound but delicious silence that seemed to him almost holy. They spent the afternoon going over the contact sheets and several enlargements he had made of his own favorites. She would have to show them to Roberts, of course, and to Victor.

"Yes, your bleeding Romanian," he said aggressively. "Just what is he, some kind of bloody Svengali?"

She smiled and placed a quieting finger against his lips.

It was before dinner, after they had enjoyed the indoor pool and sauna and returned to his room this time, that he mentioned the trip.

"See, I've got this important assignment. We could make a weekend out of it. Do it up in style."

"You've spent too much on me already. I couldn't."

"The money's nothing," he insisted. "Look, this assignment is special. I need you there with me."

She shook her head. "It's impossible. Don't you see? Not at this stage of my career."

"I'm not important enough, is that it?"

She faced him with a level gaze. "It's not you. It's the publicity. All those photographers."

"Hell, it's not like that. This one is all mine. Exclusive. No one else even knows about it. I swear it."

She placed her hand over his. "This weekend was wonderful. But it's been stolen, and you know it. We can't do it again."

"You won't come, then?"

"I want to, really. I know it's important, but you have to understand."

"No, I want *you* to understand."

He made his first mistake then, more significant than he could possibly foresee. But he could not help himself. He was not the hustler she thought he was, scrounging after crumbs off the table. He was desperate to tell her the power he possessed, a power beyond her estimation.

"Did you ever hear of someone the press calls Super Scoop? I know the name sounds stupid, but did you?"

She looked at him quizzically. "The British press?"

He nodded.

"Yes, I think so. There was something about it in *Paris Match*. Something about a mysterious reporter who manages to get inside the British government establishment. Is that it?"

"That's it. I'm it. I'm the reporter."

"You?" she said, staring at him wonderingly.

"Where did you think I took off to that time in Nassau? I island-hopped and caught a major politician in flagrante delicto." Trager grinned mischievously.

She listened avidly as the words poured out of him, revealing to her what he had told no one else. And as he spoke, the power of words invaded him. He felt ownership of that power and the mastery it conferred upon him.

"Without me, people like Murdock are nothing, nothing without what I feed 'em. Have any idea what I get for each of those Super Scoops?" He named a sum and watched her eyes widen.

"Don't you see, there isn't a journalist in the world who wouldn't cut off his right arm for a scoop like this. Imagine what the networks will pay for the footage!"

She glanced down and smiled. He had grown hard at the telling. She placed her hand on him and drew him to her, cradling him within her open thighs, murmuring as he filled her, her eyes open, fixed on his adoringly.

"Then you'll come?"

Her arms came around his neck, her voice was a whisper in his ear. "If you still want me." It didn't seem possible, but her answer brought him more pleasure than the fullest possession of her gorgeous body.

35

They snatched old McNabb, Trager's crusty editor, in a quiet street near the Uxbridge Road. It was a textbook operation, enacted with more than the usual enthusiasm by its participants, who were whipped into their roles by Blake with the fervor of a provincial director whose company suddenly receives a command performance.

Fortunately it needed little advance planning. McNabb led a solitary existence, played out between his office in the Strand, his pub in the Haymarket, and the bachelor digs he shared with a huge spayed Siamese, whose existence no one suspected until the massive animal hurled itself onto Blake's team of burglars, who broke in to check out the old Scot's digs. The animal's loyalty was rewarded by a chloroformed sleep, while the burglars roamed through his master's effects. Unfortunately they found nothing to delight their overlord, and that made the snatch inevitable.

"What about the old man's heart?" Joyce said with genuine concern, but he accepted reassurance from Blake after a look-see at the editor's medical records. "Sound as a horse," Blake pronounced with relish.

There was also concern about the amount of alcohol they could allow him to consume and how it would react with the assortment of drugs at their disposal. But that was expertly resolved by the intelligent young man with lively eyes who happened to stand beside McNabb on the evening of a depressing Monday, when the pub was filled with a boisterous, shouting multitude. "A motley to the view, who wouldn't let you get two words across," the old grizzled Scotsman shouted above the din. "C'mon. Let's find us a stealthy corner."

So McNabb and his newfound friend battled their way over to the door, taking their drinks with them. The attentive young man avidly listened to the stories McNabb had been regaling his pubmates with for the better part of two decades. Anecdotes of outrage about his trade and its injustices. Somehow the old Scotsman assumed the young man was an integral part of his establishment and vented his boiling spleen about this piss-up of a universe while downing two double-malt whiskeys.

"My advice, young man: Stand clear of the fan. Shit hits, every hour on the hour." And upon raising his glass, he said, "To the cellulite on Her Majesty's pimply ass—bottoms up."

The strange thing was why McNabb felt so woozy after barely a snort. He generally needed more like two flagons' worth to even get a buzz going. He barely remembered blanking out and finding himself outside and halfway down the tiny mews behind the pub, pointed toward his car with an arm over the shoulder of the decent young fellow who expressed concern over his being able to drive but was reassured that it would take more than a couple to put old McNabb under. "Plenty of piss in the old boiler."

McNabb stabbed the key into the slot with amazing accuracy, switched on the motor, and kicked hard into first, skidding rubber along the curb. He cut hard over, weaving toward the intersection.

McNabb never saw the truck, not until it was too late. It seemed to float toward him from around the corner like the disembodied part of a dream. Before he could jam on the brakes, he heard the sound of crumpling metal, and a sickening fear carried him into oblivion.

He flashed in and out of darkness after that, remembering the ambulance that had gotten there with such incredible speed, and the attendants who hurried him inside in spite of his protests that he was okay.

Things went a bit queer after that. He had the distinct feeling someone was jabbing him with a needle, someone with less than a talent for the task. But he could not be sure, only that the sick feeling returned and he felt as if he were floating along on a continuous elastic belt that rose and dipped like an endless roller coaster. He remembered a hospital room and some kind of Indian in whites with a stethoscope that felt cold against his flushed skin. He remembered trying to speak but feeling as if his mouth were filled with cork that melted away in whispers of cotton candy.

Voices came and went for a while, like words lost in a wind tunnel. Then he felt the soft sensation of floating just beneath the surface, if he were dreaming and drowning at the same time. There was a lopsided room containing a lopsided man. White-haired, he was, with a warming kindness in his eyes, his face as seamed and lined as roadside erosion. He wore a black suit and white shirt and spoke to him of the rottenness and deceit of the world.

"Right you are," the old Scot agreed. "Blackest asshole of the whole bloody universe."

McNabb was never actually aware when the questioning began. He could not discern the predators in the sea of words that came swimming toward him. His own speech seemed trapped in the skeins of a net. He struggled not to speak. But in a little while, he felt embraced by a warming current that eased secrets he had buried deep. But the white-haired man seemed to understand, smiled, and gave him dispensation to speak.

Release felt like the easing of a burden he had carried too long. His words flowed forth, filled with the gentle effusion of a child given permission to confess. Before he blanked out, which happened somewhere in the middle of his epic, he remembered having the notion that death would come as gently. And he almost welcomed the son of a bitch.

36

It came shortly before noon. Two rings, followed by two more, then four after that. The code Victor and Bunin had agreed would signal an emergency.

Victor moved quickly, taking a taxi rather than his car and driving across the Seine past Notre Dame onto the Right Bank and the Boulevard Sebastopol. Paris wore gray mascara beneath dense and looming clouds, marching in closed ranks toward the English Channel.

Victor was bundled in a worn but indestructible Harris tweed sport coat with leather patches on the elbows. He forced himself to concentrate on the eddies and whorls of traffic through which the vehicle buffeted its way. He did not want to think about, nor establish any weight to, the cryptic signal he had received half an hour before.

Bunin had always been prompt. Now Victor was running late. He checked his watch repeatedly to make sure he had allowed enough time. The ground rules provided only five minutes of grace, should one or the other fail to appear. Fallback would occur an agonizing twenty-four hours after that. For Victor those hours would be a limbo of not knowing. A torment of anticipation. Expecting the worst: the dreaded information that his son had taken a serious downturn or that some disaster had occurred to imperil the child.

By some miracle, the bus sailed into clear seas and moored safely across from the circular island that dominated the center of the Place de la République. Victor stepped off and was absorbed into the bustle of surrounding streets.

The bistro he sought was on a side street and embraced him with its noise and the garlic pungency of provincial cooking. At a glance, the ornate clock over the entrance placed him within the perimeters of allotted time, and he breathed easier as he elbowed past the bar and was guided to the rear where the closely packed tables were already crowded with lunchtime diners.

It was Bunin who was late, as the clock edged toward its outer limits.

Victor felt a screw of sour anticipation. He would have to continue the charade, order something and consume it alone, to maintain the appearance of a casual customer. He craned a look at the blackboard that served as a menu, but the words were a blur.

Then, miraculously, Bunin materialized.

Victor heard the chair opposite being scraped into use and turned expectedly. It was not Bunin who took the place across the white tablecloth.

"Hello, Victor," Joyce said quietly, settling both elbows on the table.

Only later would Victor be able to sort out what he felt at that moment. Surprise, certainly, followed by the impulse to run, prevaricate, invent, dissemble. Despair, finally, as the implications of Joyce's presence flooded through him. And the knowledge that his lies, no matter how skillfully assembled, would not form an adequate defense. There a mingled sense of relief at seeing the familiar, careworn face. Anxiety battled with the feeling, lasting but a moment, that something dark and oppressive had been suddenly lifted.

"Bunin won't be joining us," Joyce added in the same casual tone. "He's had an accident. Nothing major, but someone collided with his car and the police were summoned. It's become a tangle, but it will give us some time to talk, if that's all right with you."

A waiter appeared, and they went through the charade of ordering a meal, appearing to any onlooker as two friends meeting for lunch, their gestures relaxed, familiar, their conversation inaudible within the general hubbub.

"How bad?" Victor questioned when the waiter stepped away. He brought both hands together in front of him, extending his fingers to bayonet the salt shaker, his eyes fixed steadily on the older man.

"About as bad as it could be," Joyce answered, meeting Victor's gaze and allowing the weight of a pause to emphasize his meaning. After a moment Victor nodded deliberately, as if confirming some inner conviction.

"So. My luck is still holding," Victor said wryly.

"First, tell who's running you," Joyce said pointedly. "I've got to know how involved you are."

Victor smiled, but Joyce saw the flicker of some inner

pain. "No one. I'm still free-lance, completely on my own," Victor said quietly. "How could you believe otherwise?"

"And Bunin's involvement?"

"Bunin?" Victor shook his head, a quick, negative gesture. "He's a courier, that's all. He carries payments for my son. The doctors are quite charitable. They're only demanding everything I have."

"You're sure that's all it is?"

Victor shrugged. "How can someone like me be sure of anything?"

Joyce exhaled slowly. "Do you understand the position you're in?"

"Vaguely. I imagine I am to be used as something sacrificial." Victor's smile had a sardonic edge. "The lamb, is it not? Or is it a goat? I should have studied more of your Bible."

The look Joyce fixed upon him was suddenly harsh. "The belief has been advanced that you're a link to Moscow Center and that Bunin is your conduit."

Victor raised his eyebrows. "A link? Of course. Yes, certainly. It's obvious they would think that. But a link to whom?"

"To Roger Killian."

Joyce scanned the Russian's face, searching for a reaction. Evasion, perhaps; even astonishment or disbelief. But Victor's eyes only narrowed, his brow knitting as he burrowed deep into memory, probing for recognition. It came with the shrug of someone for whom everything is preordained. Another insult for one already condemned, which must be borne as part of some continuing penance. When he spoke, it was with weariness.

"Ah, yes. A fanatic for hire, is he not?"

Joyce darted a glance across the table. He had no patience with any of Victor's games.

"That's a mild way of describing him."

Victor smiled and shrugged.

"Current knowledge is that Victor Kirov runs Roger Killian. That you're involved in something big. Something important. They think Killian's carrying out some sort of program for a score of terrorist organizations. Major assassinations. And that the KGB is behind it."

"And who created this fantasy, Disney or Spielberg?"

TO KILL A KING

"It's become high-level knowledge on my end, I'm afraid. Very high-level. Do you understand?"

Victor bowed playfully. "Of course. I accept your reading. You see, these days I accept everything."

Joyce realized he was facing a sardonic mask, the expression of a man without hope. A man for whom little mattered any longer. With that realization Joyce felt his ground sliding to darkness beneath him.

"Who is Roberts?"

"I have asked myself that question every evening before I say my prayers. So far He has not seen fit to enlighten me."

"And the woman, Duran?"

"She is an actress."

Joyce darted a glance across the table. "Are you in love with her?"

"That is a possibility."

"There's still time," Joyce said, hearing his own schoolboy tone, earnest, exhorting, strangely intact after all the intervening decades. "We don't know where Killian plans to strike next or when. But it's imminent, that's certain. It will be very high-level. Someone in the British government. Cabinet-level. Perhaps even the PM."

Victor raised his eyebrows. "The PM? Very impressive. But for what purpose?"

"If there's an IRA involvement, and we know they've used Killian before, it would be an eye for an eye. Any other motive is a little murky at the moment. I don't know enough. Not yet. Only that we've got to move quickly if we're going to stop him.

"There's been a general security blackout in London," Joyce continued. "It could just be routine, or it could be important. I no longer have that kind of access. But someone important is about to leave England. We don't know where or for what purpose. But I have every reason to believe that Killian does."

"Why can't you warn them?"

"I don't think they would listen. What I have is purely circumstantial, and I no longer have the kind of power base I once had."

"So then, what do you want from me?" Victor said with sudden impatience. "Some kind of miracle?"

Joyce leaned forward intensely. "Victor, listen to me. Killian's found a way inside the British security setup. A way to hit them when they're most vulnerable. And more important, a way to get out after it's done. I'm ahead of my side with that bit of information. But I don't know for how much longer. I'm operating alone, and I'm not exactly welcome to the powers that presently be. They believe your defection was staged. That I was taken in. That you're being run as a conduit to Killian. I need your help, Victor. You could still save yourself."

"You were always a fool about such things, dear old friend. If what you say is true, then that is no longer possible. All that remains is to select the color of the blindfold. Or is that too old-fashioned? A needle in the vein, then. Painless and silent."

Victor tilted the salt shaker back and forth against the tips of his fingers. His heart was somewhere else, lost in some dark unfathomable region, distant and inaccessible.

Joyce dropped the smooth accents of his actor's tone, making Victor's survival an act of pure will.

"Stop feeling sorry for yourself. Think of your son. Think of him now. At least save the boy."

If Joyce expected a reaction, he was disappointed. He thought he detected a glimmer in Victor's eyes when he mentioned the boy, but he could not be certain. Victor's face was impassive.

"I can do nothing," Victor insisted.

"We've got to know where the strike will come. You've got to supply that for us, before it's too late."

Victor's lips tightened. "You overestimate my position. How do you suggest I find this out?"

Joyce edged forward intently.

"You've got to use the woman," he said quietly. "She's the link between Killian and Trager."

"Trager?" Victor's eyebrows rose quizzically. "Why Trager? He's a fool."

"We think he is the key to all of this. That somehow he has gained access to top-secret information and that Killian somehow found this out and is using it. Trager is the only chance we've got. The only chance you have of salvaging anything. Michelle has been with him. Both in the Bahamas and in France. She knows what Trager is up to. You're close to her. Use her, Victor. Before it's too late."

Victor's laugh took Joyce by surprise. "Don't you understand, it's me who's being used, old friend. I am the gear they shift."

The hum of the room filled Joyce's ears. He glanced at his watch.

"I'll be back in London tonight. Use the old transmission code to reach me."

Victor's eyes locked with his a moment before he stood, but whether they were filled with anguish or self-mockery, Joyce could not explain.

Joyce moved away, squeezing past customers waiting for a table, a blunt, square figure whose features formed an unreadable icon. Only when he was outside and had ducked into the rear of a waiting car did he realize it was not laughter that had passed through Victor's lips but a message of despair.

37

In the end, method won out over inspiration. Joyce returned to London as quietly as he had left it, arousing not a ripple on the vast sweep of Stepinak's impressive radar screen. But it was a harried Joyce who now appeared, hiding his desperation behind a stoic facade, impelled with a sense of foreboding. The witness to events he could predict but not prevent.

The single spark of inspiration concerned the poor housekeeper snatched by Blake, whose Greek vacation grew more remote with each passing day. Joyce had not seen fit to visit the man, who was housed in a collection of wretched surroundings. Houses, theoretically safe but rarely used, leftovers from the days of Blake's plenty, and so decrepit as to be refused by the overlords who succeeded to his authority, when much of his domain was taken away.

Something had lodged itself in Joyce's imagination that would not be dislodged. Not an idea, certainly. But a kind of irritant that demanded attention. It prompted Joyce to make a trip to the general post office, where he sent off an express letter to an address in Washington, having included a prepaid and specially addressed envelope for the reply.

So much for inspiration. For method, Flyte's handsome little house in Regents Park remained the object of rapt attention for teams of Blake's watchers who soon came to know, if not love, each lintel and windowpane. Nor was its owner overlooked. Like the rich filling of some gossipy confection, his comings and goings became the subject of each morning's conversation, a conversation shared by Blake and Joyce over bitter coffee and rolls in the dingy Hampstead villa Blake had set aside for the use of his American counterpart.

Naturally there was far more in the Flyte bag, as Blake termed the reports, than either of them really wanted to know. But they sifted and stirred, filtering what was significant from what was not, discovering the byways and patterns of the functionary's day.

Flyte spent much of his time traveling between Whitehall and various government departments, organizing transport and special security for various members of the government.

Each day Joyce scoured the single-spaced typescript that traced each security route on the stained and punctured maps Blake's housekeepers provided each morning, along with the overcooked bacon and tasteless oatmeal he never touched. There were also pictures of Flyte to digest.

Flyte in various poses, relaxed yet vigilant. Standing at a discreet distance from the prime minister, dressed in morning coat and striped trousers, maintaining a casual but alert composure should a VIP finger be raised in his direction. If the security was for politicians, Blake merely grumbled. For the Royals he howled.

"Will you look at this bloody army!" Blake chortled. "More security than Churchill had during the whole fucking war. Is it any wonder this country's stone broke with half the civil service standing sentinel for a collection of useless, bloody parasites?"

In truth, the precautions were commensurate with the prevailing sense of fear. Special units scoured every inch of ground. Helicopters scanned overhead. Squads of police infiltrated the crowds. Ceilings, walls, and floors were X-rayed with electronic devices before a VIP arrived. Others established watching posts, screening the routes of travel.

To Blake's comments Joyce merely smiled and nodded, concealing his own fear of the moment slipping past and his advantage along with it, listening instead as Blake ran and reran his familiar tapes. But no matter. They could do nothing but watch and wait, as neatly skewered as butterflies on a pin. And so Joyce lent a sympathetic ear to the other's tirades, knowing it was better to let the poison ooze than the bile fester.

Of course, it was Trager they were waiting on, Trager and the missive from Washington that might provide a key. But Trager was tangible, and so it was on him that they spent their devotion. "Our golden lad," as Blake loved terming him. And how well they knew him. Seated side by side in Blake's vintage Jaguar, a scrupulously maintained relic of the fifties, Joyce and Blake swept the familiar locations, taking in the sights of Trager's world like a pair of old soldiers revisiting the scene of some long-healed carnage.

Blake kept up the abuse as they glided past the hairdresser

on New Cavendish Road. The health spa in St. Albans. The Lion in Spats. And the Marble Crown, Trager's favorite pub and eating spot. Finally the shop that housed the gorgeously put together vendeuse in Knightsbridge with whom the photographer indulged in lunch-hour orgasms, taken in the cramped rear seat of his car, a form of sex that was active on her part, passive on his.

Then it was on to other pubs along Fleet Street, where the professionals hailed him as a "luv" to his face and a regular little shit behind his back, in what was to become a pattern, almost a melanoma, of jealousy.

So they waited, as patient as Mandarins. Their attention focused on Trager and Flyte, two poles of consuming attraction, waiting for them to come together as Joyce knew they must. The gilded boy and the golden retriever, in Blake's acidy parlance. Inevitably destined to mate. A law of nature. Preordained. Yet when it finally occurred, there was something of an anticlimax about the whole operation that both disappointed the watchers and equally baffled them.

It was a morning of surprises, occurring oddly enough on a rainy Monday, the dreariest segment of the week, and at the equally obscene hour of eight A.M., when commuters were struggling to survive the peak of the incoming flood.

First to arrive was the missive from Washington in its crushed but unopened envelope. Joyce did not open it, since he was well aware of what it contained. Instead he offered it to Blake with the instruction that it be shown to the kidnapped housekeeper by someone trusted. No one else was to witness the transaction. Blake promised compliance, but it would be several hours before he could spare the man or the time.

Trager surprised them next. He was nattily dressed that morning, in shirt, tie, and a dark suit, an uncharacteristic costume, for he seldom got out of bed before ten, except, of course, when he was on assignment and generally dressed with California casualness.

Flyte supplied the third little jolt, appearing in jeans and a sweatshirt instead of his usual striped suit and immaculate appearance. He drove over from Mayfair in his own car, parking it in a reserved place in the mews behind the house in Regents Park, and let himself in some forty minutes before Trager arrived in a taxi.

The house had been wired and spiked, a mike discreetly hammered into the mortar along one alleyway. And if that didn't work, a borrowed laser device that scoured the windows for vibrations of speech that might decode into words. If anything, the morning was to establish a new respect for Flyte's sophistication. His eavesdroppers were treated to ear-fracturing renditions of Joan Sutherland, which did not quite mask the conversation inside but turned it into aural mush.

Deciphered and run through filters, it turned out to be no conversation at all but a disconnected series of references, none of which had any apparent meaning. They picked up nothing of importance beyond that, other than the normal sweat and grunt of males mating.

The interview lasted two hours. Trager left by the front door and found a cab at the Hampstead Road. Flyte remained inside an additional half hour. He made two phone calls. One to his boot maker concerning the payment of an overdue bill. The other was to his club, confirming a luncheon reservation. Blake cursed throughout the playback, which was filtered through several devices but produced almost nothing they had not already heard.

"So where do we go from here?" Blake shouted at no one in particular. Joyce made no answer. Only time would tell, and they had blessed little of it to spare. How little was made apparent that evening.

At six o'clock the watchers phoned in their hourly report. Flyte kept his luncheon appointment. He went to his club afterward and failed to emerge.

Trager occupied his afternoon with a series of errands, then took a cab to Knightsbridge, stepping out of the vehicle when it was stalled at a light. He dodged past the team of followers. Before they could regain their balance, Trager was sponged up by an excited group of overdressed Japanese who disappeared into Harrod's. He never returned to his apartment, nor could he be traced to any of his usual haunts.

By noon the following day, they realized Trager had eluded their net and completely disappeared.

They now waited in a limbo of uncertainty. They had only their listening posts, manned by Blake's regulars, who were stationed at various points of observation, watching the PM and certain key government ministries. There had to be a reason for the security blackout. Some arrival or departure. "Your president, perhaps?" Blake suggested. But this highly unlikely suggestion was greeted by silence. But the security blackout was still on. Something had to break somewhere.

The call arrived at ten. And from the least likely place of origin. An observer making a routine check of the palace observed several cars emerging through a rear gate onto Grosvenor Place. In the lead were two chauffeured limousines, followed by three black security sedans, a police car, and a van.

The observer alerted his backup and they followed. Blake screamed for his regulars to abandon their posts and converge. The convoy passed through Knightsbridge, then split into three sections.

"Target car and decoys," Blake spat excitedly, as each report was broadcast.

The limousines, each followed by a security sedan, sped through central London, then returned to the Buckingham garages. The contingent vehicle roared its way toward the A5 and Windsor. The innocuous tail, consisting of the police vehicle and van, meandered through central London and arrived at Heathrow airport thirty minutes later and drove to a special departure area where a Vulcan transport waited in a secured hangar. Already cleared for takeoff, the aircraft taxied to a runway and roared into the sky, destination unknown.

Joyce received each bulletin with a sense of quiet satisfaction, as though each piece of news were part of a plan he alone had set in motion. He was surprised at nothing. There was only one more piece of evidence to gather, and that arrived just before midnight.

It was Blake who broke the piece of news, entering the room where Joyce was sitting with a face pale and contorted with amazement. The man he had trusted with the pack of photos Joyce had received from Washington had just called in. The housekeeper had identified the man in the picture as the same man he had seen being welcomed into the confines of Stepinak's comfortable safe house.

The man in the picture was Roger Killian.

His targets would one day be the king and queen.

38

Trager landed at a private field outside Roissy, where a car and driver were waiting to transport him into Paris. He had phoned Michelle from London the previous morning. Her voice had been warm and reassuring, reviving the still vivid sensations of their last encounter and making him nervous with anticipation.

Arrangements for the pilot, aircraft, and even the small field outside London had been made at Flyte's direction and were totally foolproof. They would guarantee Trager complete secrecy. So far it was working.

Trager appreciated the favor. He had made a good show of keeping his Super Scoop identity a secret so far. But knowing the predilection of his colleagues for uncovering secrets, he had grown edgy about the information remaining that way. McNabb drank too much for his own good. In fact, he had absented himself from the newspaper for the last several days. When Trager inquired, it was hinted, with the usual smirks, that the old Scot was on one of his annual benders.

Maybe he was getting paranoid in his old age, but lately Trager had the feeling he was being watched. It was nothing he could put his finger on, but his phone had developed an unusual overtone, and once or twice he had noticed the same blue car following his cab. In any case, it did not hurt to take precautions, especially on a run as special as this.

Michelle was waiting on the Quai d'Orsay. She had instructed him to signal her from an outside phone and leave a message at the number she had given him. She had her own reasons, he supposed, connected with evading her Romanian producer.

She wore a leather outfit that clung to her body and made it difficult to resist touching her. He started to speak but she touched a finger to his lips. She kissed him in the rear of the car as it sped along the Seine, and frankly he was dazzled.

"Where are we going?" she asked when she released him.

"Can't tell. Surprise."

"Don't be foolish, darling. I need to know what to pack, don't I?"

"We'll be doing some skiing," he said with a mischievous grin.

"Yes, but where?" she asked pointedly. "Gstaad? Chamonix? I've got to know how to dress. I haven't got a thing."

He clammed up after that, and she couldn't get a thing out of him.

The afternoon was spent making the circuit of fashionable Right Bank boutiques, where she purchased an assortment of outfits. They took afternoon tea at the Crillon. While she sipped champagne he pretended a certain reluctance but let slip the information about the private plane he had chartered and the chalet he had rented after outbidding a famous Hollywood director. It was worth it. Her expression was a delight.

She insisted on taking a cab back to her apartment. He wanted to go with her, but she held him off. They would meet in two hours, back on the same quai where he had picked her up. Reluctantly he allowed himself to be persuaded.

She drew him to a quiet corner just as they were leaving the hotel. Her eyes were sparkling with excitement. Her lips were millimeters from his own, but she refused to let them touch. Suspending his hand just above her breast, she twisted his fingers to prevent contact.

"Tell me first," she said playfully. "I want to know where you're taking me."

"Curiosity killed the cat."

"It's going to kill you if you don't tell me just this once. I'll never ask again."

He could not help himself. He said the word quickly and without regret, for she was bliss—pure, bloody bliss. The first he had ever really known.

39

Michelle realized she was not alone. He was there with her in the darkened apartment, shadowed by the flat light of late afternoon.

The moment before, she had rushed inside, tossing her packages next to her open bags beside the bed. Then she went inside to pack and, with a start, realized he was there.

"Victor!"

He stood in the open doorway of their bedroom, watching as she assembled her things beside the leather case she had placed on the bed.

"What are you doing here?" she asked. "Weren't you supposed to be scouting locations?"

He should have been miles from Paris, accompanying a young director. Roberts should have kept him out of the way. Something obviously had gone wrong. Michelle realized she should have checked the answering machine. Now he was there, staring at her with an expression that should have warned her of what was to come.

"So you're going away," he said, making it a statement rather than a question, and that, too, should have alerted her.

"Just for a few days," she volunteered, regaining her composure.

He took a step toward the bed, glancing down at the outfits carefully folded in a neat pile beside her luggage.

"Skiing?"

She felt a sudden panic and struggled against it.

"Perhaps," she answered calmly, continuing to move between her bureau and the bed. Calculating each gesture. Folding her lingerie and methodically placing it in one of the fabric panels.

"Don't you want to tell me where?" he asked softly.

"Does it matter?" she responded, purposely avoiding his gaze.

"I thought so once."

She kept herself from responding, continuing her mechanical actions. But he stepped in front of her, forcing her to face him.

"Isn't there anything you want to tell me?"

She glanced up. His eyes were dark and glittering. Some inner sense told her that he knew, perhaps had known all along. She felt a sudden chill.

"It's no good, Michelle. I know about Killian. And Roberts. I also know about Trager. There's nowhere you can go. They'll hunt for you. If they catch you alive, they'll force you to tell them everything you know. Then they'll kill you. Roberts, Killian, all of you."

She sat slowly, feeling for the side of the bed. Her eyes were fixed straight ahead, her fingers twisted around the piece of silk she had taken out of her drawer. She was aware of him looking down at her, faceless against the light that came from the window behind him.

"I've got to know what you're going to do. There's no other way I can help you."

She became aware of him at her side. His hands held hers. He turned her chin, forcing her to look at him.

"I can get you out of this. But you've got to tell me."

Her head was shaking. His words had become a blur of meaningless sound. She no longer heard him. She would not allow the words to register. She half expected the doors to suddenly bang open, for Roberts, somebody, to rush in and drag him out. Allowing her to continue her packing and what she must do afterward. The carefully planned steps of what was to come flowed toward her like a dream. He was no longer there in front of her, no longer imprisoning her hands. She hated the sound of his voice suddenly, hated him and herself and everything that had formed her life.

"Michelle, listen to me. I'm offering you our lives. We can walk out of here together. We could make another life somewhere. Anywhere. It doesn't have to end like this. There's only death with Killian, regardless of what he's taught you to believe. Death and more murder. Don't throw this away. Don't destroy us both."

The phone was ringing. She counted four, then five rings, but it went on like the tolling of a church bell she remembered from her childhood.

"Let it ring. Don't answer."

But she knew he would not prevent her. She freed her hand and reached for the receiver.

Roberts's voice came over the line, urgent and precise. "Michelle, Victor skipped. We don't know where he is. If he's with you, hang up and keep him there. I'll be right over."

She wordlessly replaced the receiver. The phone line on Roberts's end went dead.

"Let go of me," she said harshly.

Victor released her hand and rose, staring down at her. "How soon will they be here?"

She remained without moving, as if a shell had formed and hardened with the quickness of a plaster cast over what the moment before had been confusion and turmoil. She rose and returned to the bureau. When she turned to face him, she held a small Belgian automatic in her hand.

His mouth drew into a tight line. Their eyes met and held. "Do you really want to kill me?"

He could no longer read her expression. She had withdrawn from him and from herself. Her actions were mechanical. Frozen. She faced him with the mask of a stranger, placing the weapon on the bed beside her.

The closing of the door registered on her consciousness like a sudden gust of wind. His image remained for a moment, a ghostlike filament dissolving into darkness.

Victor closed the door of the apartment behind him, forcing himself to move, struggling against the in-rushing sensation of loss. He stood facing the darkness of the elevator shaft, listening to his own breathing in the stillness.

Survive, you must survive. For Alexi. For your son . . .

He heard the crash of the street door and the movement of feet on the tiles of the vestibule. There was a buzz, and the elevator shifted into descent. Victor was suddenly alert, the old instincts ablaze with a startling momentum.

He reached for the automatic in his pocket. He had picked up the weapon almost without thinking, an instant before he quit the room; afraid, perhaps, that she would use it to do something to herself. But he realized almost instantly that such a fear was groundless. Michelle was one of the survivors. She had proven that.

The elevator passed the second floor before he started moving. There was another way out. A back stairway led to the rear and the center court,, used as a work area for a decorative sculptor. Once across the courtyard, he could find his way through the maze of back alleys to the river.

Victor started down the narrow stairs quickly. Unlike the walnut veneer of the corridors on his floor, the walls of the stairwell were a dirty, unpainted plaster. The stairwells had been used by maids when the building was the residence of an aristocrat before the French Revolution. Now they provided access for workmen, whose ladders and buckets crowded the landings.

Nearing the bottom, he slowed and glanced through the dirty, almost opaque glass of the door. But he could see almost nothing. He would have to chance it. He turned the knob and eased open the door.

Baroque nymphs and huge, muscular torsos suitable for public fountains faced him. Half-finished figures struggled to emerge from the rough stone imprisoning them. One after the other, they twisted and danced their way across the yard. Victor sucked in breath and ran through the doorway, right into the embrace of two horn-blowing Neptunes.

His movement was followed by the explosion of automatic gunfire. Chips of stone flew overhead as he dodged around the figures. He raised his arm to protect his eyes, keeping low as he moved, the pistol clutched in his hand.

Another burst caused him to drop. A head was decapitated, bounced and chipped, nose and ears bursting as it struck the flagstones. Victor threw himself forward, reaching the center of the courtyard where he skidded to a stop beneath the protective eaves of a marble fountain. He glanced up.

A dark figure was silhouetted against the gray sky, holding a weapon and moving laterally along the roof. Victor raised his arm and fired. The figure ducked and drew back, away from the edge.

Windows were flung open. An alarmed voice shouted something.

Victor flung himself toward a protective centaur. Automatic weapon fire amputated the creature's limbs, sending them crashing on either side of the horse's belly, beneath which Victor paused before he raised his arm and fired again.

Roof tiles shattered, then came sliding and crashing to the stones below. The figure on the roof was flung backward—whether hit or to avoid his fire, Victor never discovered.

He hurtled toward the door opposite, striking the inset panes of glass and shattering them. The knob turned, but the door was locked. Victor sent the butt of his automatic crashing through the glass. He reached through and opened it from inside. In an instant he was plunging through an oily darkness and into the corridor ahead.

Roberts burst into the apartment moments later, a submachine gun in his hand. There were others, outside on the landing and farther down the stairs.

"He's gone. Christ, why didn't you keep him here? Why didn't you kill him?"

Michelle mumbled something, but Roberts ducked past her. She heard the clatter of footsteps on the stairs, then several shouted words. The words echoed in her ears. Victor was gone, escaping into the same darkness she must now enter.

40

The house was located along a back lane, somewhere beyond the streetlights that illuminated a nondescript outer suburb. It was shabby little place, set behind a low stone wall and a shielding grove of plane trees. Grass sprouted in dank clumps amid bare spots of ground, while the garden was embraced by a scrubby ring of overgrown and untended hedge. There was a garage detached from the main building, its doors gaping as they approached. They made out the twin shapes of two housed vehicles as their headlamps flared past.

Two of Blake's outriders were already inside, standing glumly in the lifeless interior that exhaled an indecent, musty odor. The lights came from two lamps whose shades had been turned to illuminate the shape of both bodies. They had been left where they fell, with legs drawn up under them as if they had been shot while kneeling. Their hands were bound behind them with a piece of twine from a roll carelessly tossed aside on the threadbare rug. Both corpses belonged to Blake. There was no sign of the housekeeper, for whose exclusive use the residence had been so recently reopened.

An electronic device blinked harmlessly in one corner of the room, an ironic indication that the area was free of intruders. The device was mother to a flock of sensors nesting in various hidden niches around the establishment, none of which had been tampered with.

"Cozy little job," Blake remarked bitterly, after drawing Joyce into the brambles at the rear. They trudged around the perimeter through damp weeds, guided by the light from a pale moon and Blake's flashlight. "I'll tell you what. A bloody fucking traitor, that's what. Sold us out."

Joyce said nothing. The statement was moot. Blake's mole must have led Stepinak directly here. In any case, taking the housekeeper had provided Joyce with the answer. He did not want to burden Blake with the implications or the danger.

Blake paused, suddenly short of breath. Even in the darkness Joyce could see the slack return to his features, his eyes ringed with dark circles of defeat.

"Got my man on the cheap, I suppose. And who could blame him? Tied to a dying limb, he saw his chance. Get out while the going's good. No fool, he. I'd have done the same, should have long ago. The position, as they say, sucks ducks. There's no point in going back. Not to any of my installations. No telling how deep the rot goes. Question: Who will they be gunning for next? You or me or both of us?"

Joyce took a breath and exhaled slowly, leaving the question dangling. The answer he expected would not be long in coming.

They stopped at a small commercial hotel in Camden. This time Joyce indulged in a Guinness and lager, forming a thick froth over his black-and-tans, while Blake spent a harried half hour on the telephone.

Joyce did not waste the time. Instead he played with the pieces, arranging them in patterns that produced the same errors in logic each time he performed the addition.

Blake returned to the booth Joyce inhabited in a distant corner of the hotel's nondescript restaurant, unattended by either customers or help, and plopped down on the worn Leatherette banquette with the glass of whiskey he had purchased at the bar. Joyce could see it was bad. Blake seemed shriveled, his skin jaundiced and pale, his hands torturing the glass in small, nervous circles.

"Christ!" he spat. "Fucking bloody hell!"

Joyce allowed himself to be absorbed by Blake's agonized glance but said nothing.

Blake took a pull at the glass. When he spoke, his voice was a hoarse whisper.

"Well, it's clam up all round. I was damn lucky to get a word out of anybody. There's some kind of hush-hush on. Anyway, I had to play stupid, but it's evident you're being inquired after. Gently, mind you. No one's insisting, but the assumption is that we've been in contact. So I figure the sellout is fairly recent, or they'd have pressured me to give you up before now."

Joyce nodded calmly. "Understood. How is it being put?"

"Oh, damned politely. The usual sort of thing. Some question as to your whereabouts. The innuendo that you're carrying some heavy inside dope that could be dangerous if you were apprehended by the wrong parties. And that your disappearance is unauthorized and damned awkward, which puts your reliability in the crapper. Everyone is uptight and looking to distance themselves from any and all relationships with the disaffected non-person you have now become."

Joyce bent his head slightly to show the news was expected, but he did not change expression as Blake continued.

"The order of the day is apprehension for your own good and the welfare of all concerned. Everyone is scrambling to be the first one on the queue nosing up to friend Stepinak's flabby nether cheeks."

Blake took another pull on the whiskey, then rubbed his hand across his forehead.

"Question is: Where does that leave me? Already bloody suspect as having harbored you, which compromises any chance I might have had at worming my way back into grace with the powers that be. Question two. What do I do with our interesting little work-up on friends Flyte and Trager? There's a total security blackout at the Palace. Couldn't get a peep out of anyone, and don't worry, I was *mucho* discreet. Merely tried to offer my unit for the general welfare in these trying times and was firmly but politely refused. So I'm damned if I do and damned if I don't. But if the prince and princess are off on a little jaunt, taking friend Trager along as a stowaway, and knowing what we do of his relationship with the Red Queen, our darling Señor Flyte, I'm duty-bound to file my report, aren't I, and let the geniuses at the SIS merry-go-round piece it all together?"

Joyce read the desperation in Blake's eyes and withheld comment for a moment. He did not wish to destroy the delusion, nor the hope.

"Not with the SIS," Joyce said firmly. "Find a disaffected cabinet secretary. That shouldn't be too difficult."

Blake nodded, his eyes brightening. "Yes. Good. That's good. I know just the sod. Pure bloody slime, but fits the bill."

"Make no calls. Do it tonight. If you get an audience, it would be important. It would give us an ally. He could keep you out of sight for the duration, anyway."

"And you?" Blake asked.

"I have a stop or two to make."

They exchanged glances, and for all the seriousness in his eyes, Blake tried a smile.

"I can't offer you much," Blake said finally. "Transport if you want it. I can pretty much guarantee they haven't tailed us here. But I wouldn't take more than a used car salesman's word for it."

"I can make my own way from here."

Joyce smiled and offered his hand. Blake's palm wore a film of cold sweat.

Of course, it was far worse than Blake let on, poor Blake now clutching at razor blades. The net was closing fast. For Joyce there were no odds at all.

In London, Blake found his undersecretary. Their phone call was brief, made in a noisy after-hours saloon in Soho. The secretary agreed to see him just after midnight. Now he had a hope.

Blake cruised the dark, respectable streets of Belgravia, marking time that moved with turgid slowness. At eleven-thirty he drifted toward Mayfair. The undersecretary was staying at his club, a regency building wrapped in quiet dignity at the end of the deserted street. He parked a block from the place and walked toward it slowly, timing his movements so as not to be unduly early. Bad form would do him no good in the undersecretary's jaundiced eyes.

He was thirty yards from the club's ornate metal doors when he noticed the car. It moved into the periphery of his vision and pulled alongside.

Blake reached into his coat for his Colt automatic, but the car continued past without stopping. Breath eased in his throat. He increased his pace. Home free in ten seconds, safe inside the club.

The pain staggered him, a dart of blinding white agony that struck below his shoulder blades and nearly threw him off his feet. He grasped for the iron railing of the club's regal gate and hung there as the shock passed through his body. He tried to move, but his legs were numb. Paralysis gripped his body.

Christ! Help me! The world exploded in his mind. Speech was already beyond possibility.

He reached out, pulling himself along the railings, one hand after the other, but felt the numbness rising toward his arms. His eyes bulged with terror. He tried to call out, but there was no sound in his larynx, only a harsh, dry rasp. He forced his arm up, fingers outstretched, willing them to make contact with the iron railing only inches away.

He fell with a terrifying slowness, watching the railing bend, his fingers warp, as if the world had suddenly turned into dripping, visual jelly. He was unaware of striking the sidewalk. He saw only the black, starless sky and the reaching talons of branches before he was lifted into the car. Then a hand gently closed his eyelids and he saw nothing.

And thus poor Blake permanently and mysteriously disappeared from the face of the earth within the next twenty-four hours, disappearing before he could keep a hurried and confidential appointment with a senior cabinet undersecretary presently at war with the inner circle of his own government.

The undersecretary would make persistent but unavailing inquiries into Blake's whereabouts, and eventually leak a story to the media concerning the mysterious disappearance of a senior intelligence official. In its time, this would lead to several embarrassing questions in the House, which the home secretary would promise to investigate under the provisions of the Official Secrets Act, thereby foreclosing all further public inquiries.

But this result was expected. Joyce was concerned with what was not.

His first business after leaving Blake was to transmit a long-awaited call to a Paris computer from a telephone booth in Hampstead, using prearranged codes. He waited two hours for the reply, which he received on a phone bolted to the graffitied wall of a lavatory in a Nottingham restaurant specializing in West Indian cuisine and noisy with Jamaican dialect.

Rosensweig's heavily accented voice came over the line, distant and disembodied, counterpointed by the grumble of Parisian traffic.

"My God, where have you been?"

"It doesn't matter. What's happened on your end?"

"Everything. Disaster. This came over the wire this morning."

The message he read was cryptic. A high-priority transmission had been received from London, to a special branch of the SDECE in Paris, whose jurisdiction was counterespionage within France. The message named Victor as a high-level agent of the KGB, to be apprehended on sight.

A bulletin also had been issued concerning Joyce's whereabouts.

It was a subtle request for information. But the indication

was clear. It signaled that Joyce was no longer reliable and carrying information most secret.

"They won't state or admit anything," Rosensweig continued. "But the message implies that you are a double agent whose extremely senior status threatens to compromise important areas of Western intelligence."

"Understood," Joyce said. *A deadly menace to us all,* poor Blake would have slyly added.

"But what's happened?" the Frenchman asked in a bewildered tone. "Why are they hunting you?"

"I don't know exactly who's involved or how deep it goes. Not yet. But the next cycle of killings must be prevented. That may still be possible."

"Are you doing this for yourself or Victor?"

"Does that matter? Take care of yourself."

"Don't you know any old Jew who lives this long has twenty-nine lives?"

"Have you seen to the others?"

"Need you ask? In my old age I have become as protective as a Jewish mother."

With characteristic efficiency Rosensweig had already aborted the Paris operation, sending Joyce's agents scattering in all directions, eradicating their trail behind them.

It was just as well. Contact with Victor had been lost. "As if the ground opened and took him," Rosensweig commented wryly. But then, Joyce fully expected that. Victor would have plotted his own lines of escape long before.

Michelle and Roberts had offered their followers a final dervish dance around central Paris, accomplished with several changes of conveyance and some professional sleight of hand, before they, too, vanished in the confusion of retreat. Poor Rosensweig was torn between keeping them in sight and saving their people. Now he was mortified. All their time and effort for nothing. A waste. But what could he do? Paris was blanketed with a CIA net. Hands had been shaken at a higher level. Accommodations with the Americans that seemed impossible only six months before were now solidly cemented.

The cardinals had cast their ballots. Stepinak now wore the white surplice. It was his ring their lips now suckled. Rosensweig was in exile once more, his unit questioned, his facilities under twenty-four-hour surveillance.

The maneuvers were now academic. The case against Joyce was in the polishing stage. It need only a single act of terror to complete the indictment. Killian would supply that. But Joyce was still at large, and that was a source of some embarrassment. A situation that would soon be rectified.

A web was being spun in all directions. Each known or suspected contact was being pressured; all the goodwill Joyce had so carefully nurtured over so many decades was being systematically traced and destroyed.

In a strange way Joyce's disappearance conferred a benefit on his hunters. It provided the needed drama. A measure of deep concern suffused the highest levels. The necessary temperature of fear had been created, especially among the more vulnerable, for whom another intelligence scandal would bring down the blade that, in a very real sense, hung suspended above all their heads.

And so the tables had been neatly reversed. Joyce was the hunted now, with time and terror pitched against him. Carrying with him a deadly secret that must be protected no matter what the cost. Heading into a night he had predicted but could not prevent. Alone, without aid or charity.

41

Dazzling. That was the word for it.

Glinting pink and white beneath a brilliant sun, the ice-tipped peaks thrust up toward the belly of the aircraft like the spears of some ancient army on a southward march toward Rome.

Trager was awed.

He leaned forward in his seat, his mouth slightly open, breath frosting the narrow window directly behind the pilot. The small craft, too, seemed affected, shivering nervously on the erratic updrafts. The flight had taken them across France and over southern Germany before venturing toward the Bavarian Alps, partially obscured by a sulfurous layer of clouds. Only when they crossed over the border into Italy had the mists been torn away revealing the Dolomite range in its pristine magnificence.

"That's Cortina," the pilot called over his shoulder, jerking his chin to indicate the geometry of rooftops two thousand feet below.

In the seat beside him, Michelle remained silent, shielding her eyes against the blinding light. They were losing altitude quickly, which allowed bits of road and habitation to appear through fibers of torn cloud. First the ski lifts on the upper slopes, casting shadows like a line of gallows, then, lower down, the steeply pitched roofs of barns and patchworks of meadow, and finally clusters of houses and a road weaving between steep crests surmounted by picturesque chalets. The ground tilted up to embrace them, and the wheels came down. Two hard bounces and they were rolling toward concrete hangars and the main structure of the airport.

They took a taxi into Cortina and had lunch at a restaurant with panoramic views of the ice-blue peaks. Michelle was enthralled by the scenery and charmed by the attentive waiters who bustled around them. Trager was buoyant. They were off to a running start.

He left Michelle sipping a brandy on the restaurant's terrace and scouted out a rental agency. He wanted a Mercedes but returned with an expensive white Fiat with leather seats.

They drove out to Orsolina along a breathtaking stretch of road that offered them views of the Cristallo, its apex shrouded in torn bits of cloud. Trager finally located the chalet after making several wrong turns beyond the village, a tiny hamlet that looked as if it had been borrowed from an Austrian toy shop.

The house was an upscale villa, pleasantly secluded on a private road due east from the center of Cortina on the eastern hump of the Sorapiss range, which rose in rugged cathedrals of limestone almost from their back door.

It was a white stucco affair, outfitted with green shutters and three tiers of ornately carved wooden balconies permitting soaring views of the mountains from almost any angle. There were three bedrooms and a master suite with a skylight, Jacuzzi, and separate dressing rooms. Privacy was insured by a thick stand of pine that fought its way up along the rocky slope behind the house.

Trager unpacked his gear, laying out his cameras in one of the unused bedrooms. He stripped and slipped on a dark blue one-piece ski outfit with thin red stripes running along his body on both sides. He slid the Polaroid into his shoulder bag along with a light meter, his Nikon, and a telephoto lens.

Michelle was in the Jacuzzi, soaking in the bubbling foam, her head back against the curved neck rest, absorbing a view of ice-capped peaks through the skylight, purple and white crests against a sky of pure cobalt.

"It's wonderful," she said, smiling invitingly. But Trager knew the light was already beginning to fail. He wanted to scout the slopes before dusk.

"I'll be back in two hours," he said, bending to press his lips to her naked shoulder.

The map Flyte had provided was extraordinarily accurate. The main road took him around the Sorapiss to Auronza, then continued in a circle past Lozzo, and would have brought him back to Cortina if he had not left the main road at San Vito.

Here the route lifted him along the Valle d'Oten to traverse the "groin" that was inset between two steep ranges. Within minutes he was past the stone-walled hamlet of Vallesella and climbing. Walls of alpen fir, and aspen screened sleeping meadows blanketed with frost. Snow clumped against fence posts, and Trager could feel the temperature dropping as he climbed. He rolled up the window but did not turn on the heater. He did not want the windows to fog when he stopped the car.

The Royals would be staying at a private estate that nestled between the conjunction of three ranges. The estate was private and inaccessible. It belonged to an Italian contessa who had turned the place over for their personal use. Flyte's briefing had been precise. Beside the prince and princess, there would be only a small personal staff and several of the couple's friends. No more than a dozen people in all. Security consisted of a half dozen CID specialists. Too few to secure such a large area. But they were obviously counting on the inaccessibility of the locale to provide adequate protection.

In actuality the estate was immense. Trager could only guess at its actual size from indications on the map. It blanketed several ranges, sweeping from San Marco to Vitolina in the north, clear over to the peak of Mt. Bastioni and beyond into the *valle* itself. The main housing complex was reached along a narrow road bordered by thick forest winding up from San Vito toward the peak of San Marco. Along one of the hairpins, Trager glimpsed the black turrets of a stone chalet built in the last century. That would be the Royals' residence, and outbuildings housing the contessa's professional staff.

Around the chalet the land was wild and thickly wooded. Narrow trails led toward a series of slopes, tiered one above the other in a gradual arc. Two of them had bar lifts, accommodating two people at a time. Rope lifts served the lower slopes.

Trager sped past grim faces in ski parkas standing between stone entrance gates, scanning the road as he went by.

Security.

Italian or British, he couldn't tell.

Trager intended to climb well above to gain access to the grounds. Checking the map, he sped around a tight curve as the road narrowed, rising in a series of hairpins as it approached the summit.

After navigating the last series of curves, he slowed down. Red pencil outlined a tiny logging road almost invisible between a tall stand of aspen.

Trager cut hard, and the car nosed between the trunks, leaving the roadway and bouncing along on a rutted surface partially encrusted by a layer of hard-packed snow that crunched beneath his tire treads. When the road became a hairpin between a magnificent stand of pine, he braked. An *X* had been marked on the map.

"Lovely," he muttered sarcastically, adjusting the parking brake against the steep angle. He got out gingerly, stepping into ankle-deep snow, and started along the trail, which became even steeper as he began his ascent.

The trees formed a natural shield from any possible observer. He could see how they projected in daggerlike formations, jutting onto the slopes and forcing skiers coming from above to zigzag back and forth around them. The snow was now calf-deep. Perfect skiing stuff, he thought, though it was a sport that had never interested him. Only the image of meeting leggy birds at the bar afterward and fucking before a raging fire, stuff he had acquired from magazine ads. He unlimbered the polaroid and slipped off his gloves, feeling nips of frost assail his fingertips.

Trager moved quickly, breathing hard as he continued upslope between the trees. He dropped to one knee to steady the camera, shooting whenever he found a natural vantage point. It was wonderful country. A man could remain hidden for hours—days, actually—and not be spotted.

He focused on the spot where the skiers would be most vulnerable, where they would have to slow down to cut around the curves, and where the spills would be most likely. Those would be worth their weight, he could tell you. At each stop he made a small notation on the map, careful to turn back the plastic overlay where Flyte had marked the security positions in black grease pencil.

The terrain had been carefully mapped out beforehand by a special team sent down from London. Because of the wide area, they had recommended a force of thirty men and a helicopter to scout the ridges. That, of course, was out of the question. A security force of that kind would have only increased the danger of being observed. Getting in and out of the area quickly with the smallest possible number was the surest guarantee of cover.

Informing the Italian authorities posed another danger. Contact was at the highest level of State, made on the eve of the trip to guarantee the fewest possible leaks. The royal couple had performed for the Itals on a State visit only a short time before, an incredible success by any standard. Security arrangements had been most impressive. These days, when it

TO KILL A KING

came to counterintelligence, you could rely on Rome, or so the assumption went.

Trager held his light meter to the sky. Light was quickly fading. Not so much on the upper slopes but lower down where the timber was thickest. The light failed early in winter. He would have to shoot in the middle of the day and take his chances. Besides, if the sun was warm enough, there was always the possibility that one or another of the women in the party would decide to sunbathe. That alone would be worth the risk. The princess in a halter top was too tempting a trophy to ignore.

Before he left, he turned to survey the mountain. He had been too absorbed in shooting the slopes before the light failed to really take the measure of his surroundings. Above, the line of trees thinned toward the summit. The peak was truly awesome. Not a single peak, actually, but a series of jagged levels resembling a broken pitchfork. The center prong was the highest, reaching in a kind of bent angle toward quickly scudding clouds.

Trager could not resist a final shot, though he knew it would probably be a total loss. But he wanted to show it to Michelle. The thought of her in the Jacuzzi, naked and waiting, drove him quickly downslope. When he reached the car, he was sweating.

He backed into the main road, deeply shadowed now as darkness shrouded the landscape.

He wheeled the Fiat back around the Sorapiss toward the chalet. He took the short way this time, passing through Cortina. But he had failed to realize that the roads would be clogged with traffic at this hour.

Fuck! And double fuck.

He grumbled and cursed until the line of cars eased and he was able to continue along the main road beyond, his mind filled with the image of Michelle in the Jacuzzi, and the desire to make love to her in front of the enormous fieldstone fireplace.

It was dark when he arrived; this time he managed it without losing his way.

He pulled into the drive and could see Michelle silhouetted in the large living room window, her body softly outlined against the dim light from inside. He ran up the outside steps two at a time.

He came through the doorway, sending it slamming shut

behind him, and started for the soft glow of the fire, ready to gather her up in his arms.

He never made it.

Trager's legs were jerked out from under him. He crashed down hard against the wooden floor.

Knees slammed into his back, jarring the wind out of him. Hands that felt like steel talons gripped his wrists and pulled them back behind him, where they were fastened together by clips of cold metal. Fingers pressed down on his lids, and tape was peeled across his eyes. Another strip sealed his mouth. He was lifted across the floor.

The last thing he remembered before the needle was jammed into his flesh and he lost consciousness was the image of Michelle turning away from the fireplace to welcome him with the gentle warmth of her smile.

42

Joyce was aware of his hunters the way a wounded gazelle senses a pack of jackals. But unlike the wounded animal, Joyce knew the habits of the pack. He had hunted with them too often not to appreciate their special strengths and weaknesses.

It was a combing search they mounted now, trying to deny him refuge or sanctuary. They were relying on their own self-professed efficiency and the fear of those who might accord Joyce a respite. Naturally they overestimated their own talents and the level of fear they inspired.

There was fear, of course, a great deal of it. Joyce could not discount that. It walked with most bureaucrats like a second shadow. Increased, it sent them scurrying into burrows shutting the entrances behind them.

Joyce had been around a long time. There were few in the inner circles of NATO governments he had not dealt with, or who had not dealt with him. Those who had not were far too junior to bother about. Only senior men could provide the evidence Joyce needed to prepare his case. But they were now buried deep and inaccessible.

So he turned elsewhere. To the unexpected first, and later to those held in private reserve, the way a gambler holds back a special sum, waiting for a perfect, unbeatable hand.

He moved quickly, picking his way carefully around central London, which was being drenched by an unrelenting downpour. He spent an hour or two in dark railway stations, opening a locker here and there, until he had assembled his traveling gear. It included a reserve of dollars and several passports, along with other items he kept tucked away in various places on his person.

His missing arm created a problem. It was an easily identified characteristic that he knew would absorb even experienced watchers, who would focus on it above all else. So he created his own special effects, eliminating the problem in a respectable travelers' hotel just off the Brompton Road, by first removing his jacket and shirt, then opening the battered valise he had rescued from a pit of unclaimed parcels in the cellars of St. Pancrass Station.

He struggled into the shoulder harness of an artificial limb with a retractable elbow and a marvelously realistic hand made of a soft plastic, whose fingers bent like a pianist's and whose perfect nails he dirtied with shoe polish.

The plastic hand curved around the handle of a worn but serviceable attaché case. A ball joint made the arm swing at the shoulder, offering even the most hawk-eyed observer a perfect image of reality.

The genius who had designed the limb was presently retired somewhere in New Mexico. He had outfitted the arm with two screw-off compartments above and below the elbow. They enabled Joyce to carry material in and out of places where men with both limbs would have been searched. One compartment now held his cache of documents and cash, the other a small Belgian automatic with two reserve clips. A lead sheath made it undetectable to even the most efficient machinery.

On the last of his little journeys Joyce had been amused by a murky, out-of-date photograph of himself that appeared in several London papers the day after Blake had been abducted.

DIPLOMAT DISAPPEARS, read the headline. Or rather, the bold type above the photo, since it appeared far below the major stories, along with the comment that the authorities feared Joyce had been kidnapped by IRA terrorists.

Joyce tested his new celebrity in front of a news kiosk in Piccadilly. He bought nothing and made himself an obstacle to business, browsing through a series of tabloids that featured his picture.

The two annoyed Parsi who ran the kiosk finally snatched the newspapers out of his hands and refolded them with ill-concealed glances of disgust.

Joyce took public transport out of London, riding the suburban bus lines as far as they would take him before transferring to a local train. He progressed toward Cornwall beneath a forbidding sky pregnant with rain. From the depot in Plymouth he made a single phone call, remaining on the platform only long enough to make a change of trains.

He arrived in Truro after several hours on a clattering local, emerging from the toilet with only one arm, just as the train pulled into the station.

TO KILL A KING

Joyce made his way to the harbor along winding streets between Victorian brick warehouses on slippery cobbled streets. He was entitled to a missed turn here and there after so long a time.

He allowed himself a single warming whiskey in the local pub, then loitered along the quay until it became dark, casting an eye at the fishing boats and pleasure cruisers, bobbing at anchor on the murky green slick.

When the street lamps came on, he turned and headed for a small office tucked part of the way up a narrow street, filled with ship's chandlers and ancient warehouses, now remodeled and dispensing sets of expensive racing sails.

A pretty girl with model's legs stepped onto a brick platform outside a ship's chandlers and waved a farewell to those still inside. Joyce waited until she turned the corner before he crossed the wet paving stones and climbed the stairs the girl had just come down.

There was only one person inside when Joyce entered. A young man of thirty or so who had tucked the phone receiver beneath his chin as he slipped into his raincoat.

"We're closed," the young man said, a look of irritation on his face as he fought to retain the receiver.

"I have an appointment," Joyce answered with a smile, putting down his valise and turning to make sure the young man noticed that he had only a single arm.

An imposing man of sixty or so, dressed in a three-piece tweed suit, stepped out from an inner office and measured Joyce with a glance of disapproval. Then he made a sign that the young man could go.

"I'll be there in ten minutes," was spoken into the receiver before it was slammed down. The young man shouldered his way past Joyce with barely a glance, and slammed the door just as jarringly behind him.

"Inside," the older man said brusquely, and Joyce trailed after him into an inner office whose beveled-glass windows looked onto the harbor, now black with rain and the blistered glow of boat lamps.

"It's been an age," Joyce said with the same benign and irritating smile.

They huddled across a desk, Joyce and the older man, who had considerately placed a bottle of twelve-year-old Scotch on the blotter between them. They went through a kind of haggling, mostly for form's sake, but it was not an especially happy conversation.

Joyce was forced to remind the scowling countenance of the shipments that traveled all the way from Colombia in clear plastic bags before they found their way to the gentleman's doorstep.

Joyce laid out these and other equally unpleasant facts for the gentleman's consideration. But he also added the sweetener of dollars to counter the argument that there was too much heat at the moment for the gentleman to undertake the risk Joyce required.

In the end, Joyce closed the sale. But he was more than certain that he had also sold himself.

It was a journey to the Hook of Holland undertaken on choppy and disturbing seas. Joyce was a good sailor, but near the end even he began to get queasy.

He forced himself to devour about half a small loaf of dark bread and some strawberry jam, washed down with whiskey to ballast his stomach.

He remained below for most of the way, out of the constant, chilling drizzle. He was the only passenger on the converted fishing trawler, now an expensive charter for hire, complete with powerful engines and all the amenities. It was piloted by the same young man who had slammed down the phone, obviously annoyed at having been summoned out of some pleasure or other not more than half an hour after leaving the office. He said barely two words during the entire voyage, another blessing Joyce was grateful for.

Dawn embraced the Dutch coast and a tiny fishing village, where the natives still wore rustic costumes and wooden shoes to delight the scores of tourists that descended from glass-roofed buses twice a day. Joyce was put ashore at the end of a stone quay, guarding a score of bobbing fishing boats.

He waited until the trawler drew away from the quay before he made his way toward a tiny church, whose doors were opened by a rector in an ankle-length cassock.

Inside, Joyce found the door to the bell tower unlocked. He climbed to the first landing on solid, wooden stairs. Through the slit in the masonry he could view the harbor and the trawler, now inching seaward, part of an assembly of fishing boats heading into a lowering mist.

Joyce slipped off his coat and jacket and opened his valise. He had few illusions. The man he had dealt with in Truro could have sold him already, or could be selling him now from the trawler's ship-to-shore phone. It would happen shortly, of that he was certain. He had only one advantage. Those selling him would have to allow a respectable interval. They would not compromise the illusion of reliability and trust that brought them future trade. So he had eight hours at the most.

Joyce emerged from the church ambidexterous once more, a minor testimonial to the power of faith.

He had two cups of muddy coffee before the first tourist buses growled along the narrow cobbled streets, now filled with smiling women in starched caps and long dresses.

After four hours and several changes of transportation, he arrived in Rotterdam, seated among a tribe of vacationing workers from a factory in Cologne.

Joyce spent the afternoon in one of the old markets, filling a carefully purchased backpack with an assortment of canned and preserved foods. He did not neglect the chocolate vendors.

Seven-thirty that same evening, Joyce became part of a cargo of Canadian machinery and American cigarettes that would never be accounted for on any Euro-market manifest. He was enthroned on an air mattress, behind a false wall, among a shelter of cartons, a tiny product of Japanese ingenuity to keep him company.

The individual who arranged this travel service remained with Joyce until the rear doors of the van were sealed. He was a solid-looking Dutchman with a sour expression, who had run an important North Sea operation back in the mid-sixties. Over the years there had been mutual understanding and some profitable exchanges. Now there would have to be trust.

The hunt would be forming behind him. He had a day, perhaps two. No more. He would go on the block in less than half of that. But the day would be his, if only for appearances. Unless, of course, the price for him made even a public betrayal worthwhile. How fast had Stepinak upped the ante? Joyce wondered. The answer would come in the uncertainty of the next few hours.

The Vulcan touched down at the small military airfield outside Bolzano two hours before dusk. It taxied to a special area in a remote corner of the field, cordoned off by an elite squad of Italian special forces.

A ramp was lowered from the underbelly of the cargo plane, and three vehicles drove out, one behind the other. They were all civilian automobiles, two medium-priced Mercedes. The third a four-wheel Land-Rover.

The passengers in each vehicle were protected from view by black glare-proof glass. The vehicles picked up an escort of civilian transport and sped quickly and with surprisingly little notice through the town.

Once past the outskirts, the convoy changed direction and took the Autostrada north. The cars loosened their formation to blend with the evening traffic, winding between the mountains, now tinted shades of purple and gold as the sun gave up its hold.

They increased or decreased speed according to the pattern of traffic around them, remaining inconspicuous among the other vehicles transporting skiers for the weekend.

The drive to Cortina was winding and stunningly beautiful, ranked by the guidebooks as among the most scenic in Europe. It ran for a distance of sixty-eight miles through breathtaking mountain scenery. The vehicles of the convoy changed position every fifteen minutes according to plan, so it would have been impossible to guess which car transported the royal couple, if they were traveling together at all, which was unlikely.

They crossed the pass at Falzarego, then the Pordori at 7350 feet, which offered its unique spectacle. So far it had been a walk, but tension increased as they approached Cortina.

Traffic slowed. *Carbinieri* fought to direct the weekend flow through the picturesque streets of the town. It had been decided not to alert the local police. But Italian security men had been stationed along the route wearing plain clothes, their responsibility to make sure nothing interfered with the passage of the three specially designated cars whose passengers' identities were top-secret.

There was a single anxious moment when the lead car was stalled in the crosswalk of the town's center. A swarm of young Austrians surrounded the Mercedes, pounding on the fenders and hood and taunting the driver. Stomachs tightened. Hands reached into inside pockets where pistols were concealed in warm covers of goose down.

Laughing and taunting, the group crossed to the other side. The light turned green. The cars filed through the narrow streets and sped on toward the mountains beyond.

By some miracle there were no cameras. No mobs of press snarling and jostling. No pounding, shouting horde of cameramen. No gawking, gaping crowds.

By some miracle they had at last eluded the barbarians of the media. For once it promised to be a delightfully private weekend. No one in the world outside their sanctum of security had the slightest hint that they were even there.

Not a single, solitary soul.

43

Victor came over the border on a train packed with skiers down from Munich for the weekend. Corridors quickly became obstacle courses, filled with rucksacks and skis clumped like tiny stands of forest. The skiers were already aglow with schnappes and goodwill, linking arms and bursting into impromptu songs and good-natured rowdiness. Victor let himself blend, flirting with several women as he made his way from car to car, joining with the usual conversation about lifts and powder. And prayers that the weather would hold.

He had reached the Italian border by way of the Rhine, refusing sleep, driving part of the way, doing the rest by bus and rail. Deep inner feelings of desperation had combined with a strange exhilaration. The indecision and lethargy that had clung to him for so long in Paris had disappeared. For better or worse, he was going into action. The old feelings were returning. Conditioning and training took over, reviving long-buried instincts.

The automobiles he used belonged to a string of old acquaintances who handed over their keys without asking questions. Some offered money. Others offered a different kind of help. He refused their kindnesses, phoning them at the end of each leg of his journey to report where their cars were stored, so they could arrange for the return of the vehicles.

Victor became aware that he was wanted when he entered Cologne. The word came to him from a stoop-shouldered truck dispatcher named Lobell, who had once run a network of couriers out of Leipzig for a now obsolete British disinformation service.

The service had offered Lobell and his network to the East Germans in exchange for the detritus of a failed operation. Through some miracle of bad timing Lobell had managed to escape. Victor used Lobell in one of his own operations, setting him up as a phony middleman in a one-shot buy-and-sell to an Eastern bloc research secretariat hungry for satellite technology.

TO KILL A KING

Word on Victor came down to the dispatcher from a contact man in the OPC, the West German counterespionage service, now busily spreading the word to all of Victor's former contacts throughout the Federal Republic.

"You're as hot as a bowl of boiling kasha," Lobell said with a crooked smile. Warning Victor was an act of revenge against the same system that had once betrayed him. He had long ago substituted malice for hope.

Lobell treated Victor to a second-class ticket obtained from an avaricious travel agent trying to complete a package. Victor rode the ticket all the way into Italy, making a single stop in Munich during the two-hour layover during which the train was loaded. He used the time to exchange his city clothes for a dark blue parka, fleece-lined boots, goggles, and a woolen cap, along with two pairs of gloves and a rucksack into which he slipped the plastic envelope containing a West German passport and a Walther PPK, along with a small store of ammunition. A parting gift from Lobell, along with the distasteful image of his vicious smile and evil breath.

It was night when they pulled into Merano and encountered the first skirmish line of security circulating among the hordes of weekenders disembarking for waiting buses or changes of train to Cortina.

Victor attached himself to a group from Stuttgart, the one German city he knew best. They were already a single happy family, drunkenly shouting and singing as they moved toward the buses.

Victor shouldered the skis of an unattached fräulein with whom he had exchanged several words and a good many meaningful glances. She was in her middle thirties, a blonde with thin lips and a good figure, attractive in an outdoorsy sort of way. Victor became part of her nucleus, casually slipping his arm over her shoulders as they headed for their transport.

"*Liebchen* . . ." she whispered, snuggling close and passing an eager hand across the geography of his groin before clasping both possessively around his waist. He raised the goggles over the woolen cap and shot direct glances at each probing set of eyes, none of which so much as blinked in recognition. The crowd provided cover. But he could not count on being as lucky in the openness of the slopes.

He squeezed into a bus with the rest of the tour, which jammed the aisles and made a proper count impossible. The driver didn't even try. When everyone who wanted to got on, he slammed the doors and took off.

Victor found himself shoved into a corner seat, with the blonde on his lap, nibbling his ear and teasing his zipper, as they jolted their way out of town. Victor became part of the shouting and singing, imitating a joyous abandon that had never been his to own.

44

For hours they had been going over every detail of Trager's maps in turn. Killian insisted each of them memorize both terrain and security points.

Now there were five of them in the large living room. Killian and Roberts huddled over the charts scattered on the massive coffee table, littered with cups and plates of cheese and biscuits. Helga and Dietrik watched from the couch. Helga was tense and watchful. Dietrik sat back, casting appreciative glances at Michelle's legs, his face wearing a perennial smile of self-confidence.

The other two were outside: Vittorio watching the front; Stepan, Killian's pet Croat, as Roberts had dubbed him, taking the upslope position at the rear, from which he could watch the road in both directions.

Michelle sat across from Roberts, watching from the deep pocket of a leather chair.

At first there was some debate on how to position themselves along the slope. Dietrik was for hitting the security guards right after the royal party started down. But Killian overruled him.

"The guards are completely out of position once the party leaves the lift. By the time they react to our fire, we'll already be off the slope and moving toward the road."

The group voted to accept Killian's plan. It was just after midnight when they finally chose the killing ground.

"Here," Killian said, pointing to the overlay, "where both slopes meet."

The point formed a perfect *X* where the forests came together. At the center of the *X* was a slot through which the skiers would have to pass single-file before they emerged onto the lower slopes. It was where Trager planned to catch the party on their final schuss. In the Polaroids the slot showed up as a steep run between the trees, a dozen yards of open ground. It was a perfect blind, the one place they would be hidden from security both above and below.

The plan itself was simple.

"The Mercedes stays hidden on the logging road," Killian stated in his action voice. Each of them knew its intonations: low, precise, almost mechanical.

"Michelle continues along the main road and turns around at this curve just below where the hairpins begin and the road heads back down to San Vito.

"Michelle will perform two functions. The first is to warn Roberts by radio of any security approaching from below. The second is to set the timer on the explosives in the van as soon as we have completed our operation and returned through the woods to the car.

"Vittorio will pick up Michelle in the Mercedes, as it comes down the logging road afterward. The van is set to blow five minutes after that, closing off the road to the upper slopes and eliminating the possibility of pursuit."

Killian sent Helga to call the others inside. When they had gathered, Killian went over the plan again in a low, terse voice. Then he glanced around the circle, searching each face for a response. The Italian was mute. Stepan also nodded his acceptance, Helga and Dietrik theirs. Killian fastened his gaze on Michelle.

"Then there is Trager to dispose of."

Michelle felt their eyes on her. She would be going up last. The responsibility for Trager was hers.

Michelle nodded slowly, indicating her acceptance of the task and the inherent cruelty Killian had intended as her punishment for allowing Victor to escape. She would have to kill this man who had possessed her body.

"Then we're all agreed," Killian said solemnly. This was his priest's voice now. "It's decided, then. We go at dawn."

He reached out his hand and closed it into a fist. One by one each placed his own hand over the others, until all of them were bonded by the living tissue of each other's flesh.

45

Sleep was out of the question. The ski lodge was a tumult. Packs of half-drunk revelers roved from room to room, banging on doors to rouse anyone inside. Victor remained with his blonde and her group in one corner of the restaurant, drinking brandy and exchanging stories. Victor fabricated information about himself, which the blonde greedily and possessively absorbed. But other eyes sought his across the crowded room as the largely single crowd reconnoitered for romantic opportunities.

He fought exhaustion, counting the hours until dawn when he would be able to reconnoiter on his own. He secured a map of the area, leaning across the counter at the desk while the blonde caressed his back and asked innocuous questions about the location of the lifts and the best slopes, the types of roads and clusters of housing. There had to be some way he could narrow the areas of search. But that seemed impossible. The area was packed with hotels and private lodges.

He had only one possible edge. Michelle would either be in one of the most expensive hotels or a luxurious private chalet in one of the exclusive areas. Trager would have seen to that. But where? There were dozens of likely places. He would have to chance renting a car, using the passport Lobell had given him. But he would not do it here. The lodge would serve as a fallback. He had made enough acquaintances to blend with one of several familiar clusters, should that become necessary. He weighed sleeping with the blonde. It would provide sanctuary if he needed it. The area would be crawling with security. But a glance around the room revealed the women outnumbered men by a substantial margin. There was no need to push it with the blonde. He would find plenty of replacements.

By three the noise showed some signs of abating. People were falling asleep in their chairs. He whispered something to the blonde, and they made their way to her room. She caressed him anxiously, seeking to complete her possession.

But he deflected her inquiring fingers, pretending exhaustion, stroking her breasts and belly, gentling her into slumber. When he was sure of her breathing, he closed his own eyes and let go.

Somewhere just before dawn, the blonde turned to reach for him, but Victor had already slipped away.

They moved before dawn.

Six dark figures with Killian at their head, all of them outfitted in white-quilted coveralls, not identical but sufficient to provide effective camouflage, equipped like a group of climbers out to catch the first light.

Michelle stepped out last, clothed in a dark blue ski suit. She had been assigned to drive the metallic-gray van with Austrian markings Killian had driven down from Innsbruck. It contained packages of galignite wrapped in plastic and sealed in hollows between the frame and chassis.

There was no speech between them, only the driving sense of urgency. Each was aware of operating within the confines of his or her own timetable and specific assignment.

Roberts drove the white Mercedes that would transport them to the killing ground. Killian rode in front beside him. Stepan and Vittorio rode in back. Helga was in charge of setting the explosives in the van and rode beside Michelle. Dietrik would handle the HK-91 assault rifle and squatted between the van's bucket seats.

Killian communicated with Michelle through a walkie-talkie at ten-minute intervals. They spoke in German, using a code devised from tour directors' jargon. It would arouse no suspicions.

They avoided Cortina and took the long way around, on the 48 heading northeast toward Auronzo, then south and west on the 51 past Lozzo, and finally swinging back north toward San Vito. It was identical to the trip Trager had taken the day before.

It took two hours to circle past Auronzo. Another hour before they reached San Vito and left the main road, passing through the alpine hamlet of Vallesella, which was still shrouded in mist, before they began their climb along the steeply curving hairpin turns along the flank of the Sorapis range.

The van followed thirty yards behind the Mercedes. Silence now, except for the swishing of the windshield wipers. They ascended in low gear, radials squealing as they accelerated around the spine of each serpentine.

Twenty minutes.

They reached the logging road, exactly marked on Trager's map. The Mercedes turned into the track and proceeded a quarter of a mile until Killian signaled a halt.

In silence they jumped down and slung the climbing equipment over their shoulders. Then, with Roberts in the lead, one by one, they stepped off the road and into the trees.

By seven, they were in position.

Embraced by stands of aspen and fir, the slot between the slopes formed the apex of an almost perfect X, just as Killian described. It was a perfect killing ground, and each nodded to the other before spreading out, forcing a grin and making the thumbs-up sign.

Each unlimbered a Uzi model-B from his or her rucksack.

Vittorio and Stepan slogged into deep snow to cross the slot, then fanned out in the blackness between the trees beyond. Helga and Killian would form the other wall of fire. Dietrik covered the lower slopes with his assault rifle.

Roberts took cover thirty yards above Killian with the other assault rifle, positioned to cover the upper slopes. He also carried a walkie-talkie, tuned into Michelle's frequency, and was ready to provide covering fire if they were surprised from the road or to come forward and spray the slopes if security moved from above.

The security teams would be easy to handle. They were lightly armed with 9mm machine pistols and mounted on snowmobiles, on which they were expected to make general sweeps of the area, communicating with each other by walkie-talkie.

But as Trager had observed, the narrow break between the upper and lower slopes was too steep for the snowmobiles. Security would have to dismount and make their way on foot into the slot, either from above or below. Since the ground was steep and deeply covered with soft snow, Killian was gambling no one would.

For the next two hours they huddled in position, spread out like the spokes of a wheel, hidden by formations of rock and the dark stand of forest that flanked either side of the pincer. Once the skiers entered the break from above, they would be invisible from both slopes for approximately fifteen seconds. That's all it would take to finish them.

The Uzis were equipped with boxlike silencers. The sound of firing would be muffled by the trees. By the time security realized what was occurring and advanced onto the killing ground, Killian and his men would be tearing open the doors to the Mercedes and barreling down toward Michelle and the waiting van.

They would split up into three teams at a point just beyond Calazo, leave the Mercedes, and pick up three cars parked in an auxiliary outdoor lot of the ski lodge. Michelle and Roberts would head south toward Belluno. Vittorio and Stepan would head due east. Killian would follow south and west toward Trento, with Helga and Dietrik. From there it was only a matter of a few hours to Milan and safety.

The plan was perfect, or as nearly that as he had been able to make it. His people were veterans. All he had to do now was wait.

By nine o'clock, they knew something was wrong.

Faces and fingers provided the evidence. In spite of the double set of gloves and woolen ski masks, each extremity was almost numb.

Killian realized the temperature must have fallen fifteen degrees in the last hour. Killian moved away from his hiding place and inched down toward the stand of trunks fringing the lower slopes.

Visibility had fallen. A thick gray cloud covered the slopes, making the red-tiled roofs of the hamlets below completely invisible.

At nine-fifteen two dark spots forged their way upslope: security men on snowmobiles. But they halted about halfway, their drivers indecisive about continuing. One behind the other, the skis of each vehicle drew the arc of a compass against the soft white background as they performed their return downslope.

Killian struggled upslope between trunks of fir, clutching brush to gain a footing, trying to find a vantage point from which he could see the ski lift surmounting the horizon of the upper slopes.

There was no movement. The cables were still. Snowmobiles were parked outside a hut at the crest of the slope. But the wall of blue mountain beyond was almost invisible behind a descending wall of drifting cloud.

A hand grasped his shoulder. Killian turned to follow Roberts's pointing arm. Farther up, two more snowmobiles were moving back to the cover of the lifts.

Killian's brow darkened. He felt a pull in his stomach. If the weather turned bad, there would be nothing to hold his prey. Nothing to keep them at the resort. Unless . . .

Killian clenched his fists. The weather reports had been perfect. This couldn't be happening. Not without warning. But reason told him otherwise. Of any of them, he knew the mountains best. In South America they had protected him. Their uncertain weather had covered his movements and sheltered his escapes. How many times had a sudden, unpredictable downpour dispersed a well-coordinated government offensive and saved him?

Killian hunkered down against a tree trunk. Waiting. Oblivious to the cold.

The upper slopes were hidden. Only when the mist drifted between the trunks around him did he rise and give the signal to return to the car.

They moved back along the rutted track in single file. Ghostly shapes shrouded in cloud, apparitions from another cosmos.

They spent a half hour listening to weather reports on the local radio. The mist had settled without warning. Most slopes were closed, at least for the time being. But most forecasters were predicting the cloud cover would vanish as quickly and unexpectedly as it had descended.

So there was still hope. Killian closed his eyes and began to pray.

46

The weather bought him time.

Victor slipped out of the lodge under a cold gray sky, shouldering a pair of skis taken from a pile of unclaimed luggage in the foyer.

Hiking down to a local café, he took up a position at a corner table, nursing two espressos produced by a hissing copper monstrosity that resembled a Verdi opera house. Two hard rolls completed breakfast made palatable by coating them with a sugary marmalade, while he waited for a frizzy blonde in a tight-fitting leather jacket to open the car-rental agency across the street.

It took another half hour for two customers to enter and drive off with identical powder-blue Fiats before he paid his bill and strode across the street.

The blonde was preoccupied with paperwork and gave him less than a casual glance, irritated by the unusual upturn in business in what should have been a slow day.

"Momento, prego," she said with annoyance.

Victor used Lobell's passport and a French credit card, which produced a dirty white Fiat without an apology. The car coughed and grumbled in the yard behind the office.

Victor nodded politely at her rendition of the conditions of the contract. He dumped the skis in back and took the road toward Cortina.

Dark smudges of gray filled in the places between the blue peaks, which were barely visible on either side. He parked in a quiet street near a collection of ornate chalets that should have housed cuckoos, shouldered his stolen skis, and sauntered toward the town center and the intersection of the main shopping streets.

There were over a half dozen car-rental agencies, all busy servicing tourists making impromptu journeys now that the slopes had to be abandoned for the day.

It went badly at first. Victor's questions were greeted with annoyance by the harried clerks. No, they did not remember anyone who vaguely resembled Victor's friend, down for the weekend with his beautiful, dark-haired French girlfriend.

"Mi dispiace, signiori. No ho ancora."

It was at the fourth stop that the clerk behind the desk paused to recall the young Englishman, only because it was off-season for the Brits and because he had a fine memory for accents and remembered thinking that Trager's accent was Australian.

"Si. An Australian. *No, signorina.* And in a great hurry."

The car Trager rented was a four-door white Fiat sedan in the high price category. There was a license plate. But Trager had not given a local address. The clerk assumed he would drop off the car in Milan or somewhere else.

Victor smiled through the pain and departed with the man's goodwill and the Fiat's plate number. A license plate but no address. Shit! He cursed in three languages.

Any momentary lift he felt at locating the car-rental agency was quickly dispelled. The weather, which had given him a momentary respite, was now turning against him. A cold rain began falling, thinning traffic on the roads. People would be staying in to wait out the passage of the front, which the radio assured was only fragmentary and would disappear momentarily.

Victor had gambled that Trager had settled close to his target. But that hope was now illusory. The Royals would have chosen a private slope protected from the public. The question was where. He needed a location, someplace to begin.

He found the tourist-information office across from American Express. After asking several questions he was referred to a pompous assistant manager with a waxed mustache and permanently upraised eyebrows.

Victor explained that he was a scout for a French motion picture company looking for a slope for action sequences, someplace secluded and private. The man bustled with self-importance and efficiency, rattling off a whole series of films that had used locations around Cortina.

Victor nodded patiently but insisted on something special, somewhere away from the public, with its own lifts. A private chalet, perhaps. The man pondered, then shook his head. There were several. But all of them were out of the question. Their owners would never rent.

Victor pushed this line of inquiry, which produced a gush

of description. The assistant manager turned out to be a snob. He ran on and on about the aristocrats who lived in the region. The finest of their estates belonged to the Countess Faranese. It came complete with a converted chalet that had once been a castle, gorgeous slopes protected by private timber reserves, and its own lifts. The countess often hosted some of the world's leading celebrities, even royalty, but she was not presently in residence.

"Sounds fabulous," Victor gushed. "Could you at least show me where it's located?"

The man eagerly drew a diagram of the location on a glossy tourist map but doubted if Victor would be admitted by the security staff. Victor insisted on taking the manager's name for further discussion—should something develop, his name might even appear in the titles. The man fairly glowed.

Victor returned to his car and pulled away from the town. He drove with cold desperation. He was clutching at the improbable, trying to discover the chalet Trager would have rented, the kind of place he would have wanted to take Michelle to. Thoughts that brought their own inner agony.

He followed the glossy map out to San Vito, then up along a series of hairpin turns until he arrived at the entrance of the estate the manager had described. The gates were closed, but a four-wheeled vehicle was stationed a little ways along the drive beyond the ornate iron grillwork. Security. Assumption proven. He had located the Royals.

He turned around and returned to the main road, continuing east and then south along the lower slopes, gaining and losing altitude as the road ran and dipped, curving tightly around the towering formations. He kept track of his movements with a red pencil, marking off each section traversed.

The freezing rain kept the roads clear of traffic. Some cars were parked outside chalets, but most were inside garages; Germans would have kept them housed. He was gambling on Trager's natural carelessness, praying that he would spot the Fiat resting on a driveway just around the next bend.

But there was none, nor around the next.

By midday, that hope failed to materialize. Reason told him the car could be anywhere. With the slopes closed, they could have driven to Bolzano for lunch. Any of the local hotels, for that matter. Anywhere.

He cruised past the Palace and the Poste hotels, both piles of medieval masonry standing in the center of Cortina. But neither hotel's parking garage housed the Fiat. Nor did the valets remember seeing an Englishman with his French girlfriend. The Park Victoria was next, then the Ancora. The Gambrinus and the Da Sello, two of the better restaurants they would be likely to frequent. But the message was the same everywhere. *"Dispiace, signore."* Sorry. No Englishman and his French girlfriend.

It had become a dead end.

By four o'clock, the sky suddenly shattered. The rain blew off. Streaks of cerulean speared through the batter of gray. Sunday would be perfect skiing weather. The radio predicted a day of delightful skiing before the possibility of an oncoming winter storm.

47

They were moving south in heavy rain, part of a lumbering convoy of double-hitched trailers that had fallen into line as the weather dirtied and turned the autobahn into a nasty slick of ice.

In his compartment Joyce grew worried and calm in turns, absorbed by the shriek and whine of the big diesels, listening to the static of news that burst from the radio inside the cab through a tiny door that provided whiffs of cheap Turkish cigarettes chain-smoked by the driver, a bulky Silesian who also provided a running commentary that damned both the weather and all the world's current infamies, which were being reported over the radio in the smooth vocalization of six languages.

The worst of his curses were reserved for the road, the other drivers, and the schedule they were falling behind, a deadline set by his masters in Rotterdam who would lacerate him unmercifully if he failed to meet their unreasonable and clearly insane demands.

Joyce found his situation not entirely without humor. He was the man in the plywood booth, condensed and isolated in a cell of rattling wood. A cell with all the amenities, including tiny flickering images on the Sony that offered all the banality of daytime television, endless reruns of American soaps dubbed in Westphalian dialects.

The continuous jolting made him nauseous, leaving him in a state of uncertainty, not knowing if the weather would hold or break and what that would mean on the slopes to the south.

Killian had his targets in sight. He would not allow them to escape, even if it meant a frontal assault on the chalet. Surprise would be on his side. Security was minimal. Joyce could do nothing but gamble on possibilities he could no longer predict.

They had crossed three borders without being stopped. That luck could not last. There was a mountain pass to traverse that could jam with traffic and cause impossible

TO KILL A KING

delays. He was the prisoner of circumstances he could no longer control. But the belief in controlling anything had long since forsaken him.

He drank from his thermos, generously refilled with bitter coffee at each truck stop, and huddled against the cold. Austrian scenery slipped past now, glimpsed when he stood to relieve the cramping in his legs. Onion-domed steeples and the frescoed faces of angels on half-timbered chalets screened by sheets of sleet. He watched the kilometers click by on the odometer, excercising patience that had long ago turned into despair. He no longer had the currency to purchase time—or anything else, for that matter. He was owned by the freezing temperature and the agonizing rack of his desperation.

They slipped past Innsbruck, part of a procession of ghostly lights in the darkness, and rolled toward the Brenner Pass, gaining elevation and even denser sleet, which encrusted the windshield and drew inventive curses from the exasperated driver. A silence and then the shrieking of gears as the vehicle fought for way, shimmying on the uncertain tarmac, hemmed in by darkness as they rode a wake of mud and frozen spray. And as suddenly, their luck ran out.

"Grus gott!"

The driver fought with the wheel, performing a frenzy of maneuvers between the brake and gears as the lights picked out the shapes darting ahead. A searchlight split the murk. Through bullhorns voices shouted a mountain dialect, shrill and piercing.

"Fermasi! Presto . . . Fermasi!"

The police materialized like specters, slipping into the haloed light from out of nowhere, demons in heavy-weather gear, waving them down with giant hands thrust into clown-white gloves.

Gears downshifted painfully as the van whined and bucked, rumbling onto the shoulder and jerking to an abrupt halt at an obtuse angle. Icy air sliced past the open window, clearing the stale reek within.

An enormous white mitten jerked open the door of the cab. In seconds they were swarming everywhere, shouting orders and counter-orders, pulling the driver out of his seat, ignoring his sputtering protests.

Joyce waited and crouched, barely breathing, as voices echoed around him.

Metal crashed as the rear doors were thrown open. An icy draft licked toward him beneath the bulkhead. Footsteps along the steel flooring. A moment of hesitation and the hush of voices. Silence.

The explosion resounded directly above his head. The bulkhead splintered around him. Light blazed, blinding him. Faces peered inside. Hands reached in to pull him out with surprising gentleness.

The police were businesslike and professional. Joyce was bundled inside a green sedan with a blinking light and monitored by two young officers with pink faces who smelled of basil and treated him like an errant uncle. The substation they drove to was in Vipiteno. It was a mountain town, ancient and rugged with rough stone facades and streets that inclined steeply. It had been Austrian once and remained so still, in its little Germanic efficiencies.

He was given coffee from a thermos and Strega from a flask, which he accepted, nurturing its warmth in the overheated vehicle. They did not see fit to take him inside.

It took some time to locate an interpreter, though one or two of the officers tried out their English. But when it became clear that one could not be found at that hour, arrangements were made to transport Joyce directly to Area Command without interrogating him at the substation.

And so he was bundled off to Merano an hour later, accompanied by the same polite young officers who opened doors for him and were otherwise solicitous of the white-haired foreigner, who was most likely a major crime figure with deep and abiding political connections. It could do their careers no harm to become his captors, before bigger fish came to claim what was rightfully theirs.

So they drove with a sense of assurance, wishing in every way to make their honored guest as comfortable as possible, giving him the entire rear seat to stretch out on while they rode in front. They even assisted him off with his coat, which he slipped over himself like a blanket, offering them a nodding thanks as he nodded off to sleep.

They heard him shifting on the seat a few times as he settled down for the long, tedious ride, and they smiled at each other with bemused tolerance. Half an hour later they heard him stirring.

"Toilette, prego."

There were no places to stop until they reached Merano.

The young officers looked at each other and shrugged. It was against regulations, but what harm could it do? After all, the prisoner was an old man, and they were on a steep mountain road.

The van pulled over to the side. The prisoner's door was unlocked. Both officers stood on either side when he stepped out. The prisoner had drawn his coat over his shoulders like a cape against the cold. The prisoner stepped away and turned his back, fumbling with his zipper. The officers stamped their feet against the frost and huddled together, shuffling out smokes from a crumpled pack and lighting up. They exhaled in frozen clouds.

It was then that the strangest thing happened. The old man turned toward them, and his coat slipped off his shoulders, revealing the interesting fact that their prisoner had only one arm.

The officers gaped at the empty sleeve, flapping helplessly in the wind. But it was the other arm that was by far the more fascinating. It held an automatic pistol aimed in their direction.

The report from Area Command in Merano went through routine channels, so it was not until some hours later that it found its way through the various capillaries of Interpol bureaucracy and arrived in the form of an inquiry into the possible identity of a suspect in his early sixties, male, Caucasian, carrying a valid Canadian passport.

Thus it was not until it passed through an assortment of hands that it finally wound up on the desk of a hastily assigned liaison in the Paris Sûreté, whose responsibility it was to report such descriptions to a special bureau of the SDECE. But the message was not acted upon, not for several hours, since there was no mention of the suspect having one missing limb. And that was the tickler, the identifying characteristic the duty officer had securely imbedded in his memory.

It was only after the officer on the next tour of duty had picked through the pile and run them through his analyzer that a special telephone with an open line to a headquarters halfway across Paris was picked up. Within minutes it was walked through a series of well-lit corridors to a command chamber where Stepinak sat before a battery of communication monitors.

"What the hell is this?" he spat, after glancing at the

communiqué. "This asshole has two arms. Joyce has one. Tell those fucking guineas, one arm *capish!*"

His message, lacking most of its color and charm, took another sixty minutes before a response was rushed back inside by a red-faced duty officer who slapped the computer printout in front of Stepinak.

"The son of a bitch was wearing an artificial limb."

48

The weather was now his enemy.

Killian stared at the mountain, observing changes in its light and color. Shafts of sunlight sliced through the cloud cover, blanketing one slope a bright pink while those flanking it remained the chill color of pewter.

Dusk brought blasts of Arctic wind, sweeping and howling across the valley. The windows shook, causing them to close the shutters. It would be a long and anxious night.

There was the question of whether their targets would remain, or quit and return to London. If the latter were true, it would mean an attack in darkness across unknown terrain. They would have to make an assault on the chalet whose layout and interior security setup were sketchy at best. Even if they surmounted those obstacles and succeeded in killing their targets, the possibility of escape was negligible. Not unless they were able to completely isolate the grounds. But the chances of that were almost impossible.

Just before darkness, Killian sent Roberts out to make a general reconnaissance of the area. The team waited for his return in an anxious silence, tense and expectant, each weighing the various possibilities Killian had outlined. Killian spent the time going over each option open to them. But each rendition only reconfirmed what they all knew.

They heard the car pulling in. But no one moved from his position. Roberts entered and went directly to where Killian was waiting, threw himself across the couch, and spoke in a terse, excited voice.

"I cruised by twice. There's absolutely no sign of movement. No transport. Nothing. I think they've decided to stay and chance the weather."

Killian said nothing. He rose and went to the window, staring up at the darkening sky. Everything now depended on tomorrow.

* * *

Dawn brought a slanting chaff of light snow.

Seven o'clock and it was still falling, coating the slopes with fine powder and masking the dense patches of ice that had formed on the roads. The sky remained a steely gray, but visibility was good. Snow was falling in the Palatinate, and farther east, along the Rhine, blanketing the northern passes of the Alps. But the sky above Bolzano was clear. The weather reports predicted the possibility of a winter storm, but there was an equal possibility it would climb the western side of the Alps and skirt the Tyrol entirely.

By eight, the lifts were moving.

Half an hour later, tiny dots could be seen from the restaurant of the Cristallo Palace, schussing in tight little serpentines along the lower ranges.

Roberts was on the road before dawn, making a general sweep past San Vito, trying to ascertain if morning had brought any renewed activity. It had not.

The chalet was closed up like a tightly wrapped present. The gates were still locked. Security had not yet made its appearance at the mouth of the private road. Sloppy, he thought, his mind filled with reserves of contempt for the British and their attempts at security. Only the relative unimportance of their current position in the world and the second-rate nature of their enemies had kept them from greater harm.

The little town was just rousing itself when he stopped for a warming cup of coffee, parking across from the café, which had a perfect view of the local police station. There was no indication of anything out of the ordinary. Patrol vehicles were lined up in their places when he slipped by ten minutes later. There were none of the extra vehicles one would expect, had there been any special operation going forward. But he had to make certain.

Roberts returned to his car. He had taken the Fiat Trager rented. To remain as inconspicuous as possible he had changed cars for each of his tours. First the Mercedes, then the van, and finally Trager's Fiat. With so many sporty vehicles in the area the simple white four-door sedan drew little attention.

He drove away from the town, slowing cautiously to navigate bits of white, which he knew covered patches of ice. He circled around behind San Vito, taking the secondary road at Resinego. It had not been completely plowed, and he had to maneuver in second gear, plowing through the powder until he regained the main road at Vallesella, a point some six kilometers below the chalet.

The Fiat sprayed slush as it ascended along the ribbon that looped back and forth and rose along the flank of the Sorapiss. There was no one on the road.

Roberts slowed as he rounded the curve toward the logging road. He changed gears and hesitated. The road was almost invisible beneath several inches of drift. His tire tracks would be seen. He pulled over, but instead of entering the narrow defile between the trees, he jerked to a stop just beyond and angled sharply on the shoulder.

After opening the hood Roberts leaned inside and carefully readjusted the wires leading from the starter. He left the hood open and began striding downhill along the shoulder, planting the tracks of someone intent on heading back to the village.

When he reached the apex of the curve, he edged off the shoulder onto the roadway, meshing his track to blend with the chain marks of other vehicles. Falling snow would shortly obscure the tracks completely. But anyone stopping to investigate within the next thirty minutes would believe the illusion of a distressed motorist. Then he backtracked to the logging trail and, careful to avoid marking the narrow track with his footprints, headed off into the trees that ran toward the private slopes beyond.

Thirty minutes later he emerged through the stand of aspen a quarter of a mile farther up. He was breathing hard, his eyes glittering with anticipation. He started down the road toward the curve below, beyond which he had parked the car. He rounded the curve and came to a sudden halt.

The car was gone.

49

The road to San Vito was blocked.

Victor sat locked in a single crawling line of traffic that stretched almost all the way back to Cortina. Three cars had collided on the slick surface. Police flares were on the road. Ahead the red light on the top of a police vehicle kept up its mad blinking.

Victor clenched and reclenched his fists on the wheel, craning his neck to watch for any sign of movement. But there was none. The lane opposite was almost as bad or he would have made a U-turn and reentered the town. Skiers were coming out in force as the falling snow was reduced to a whisper. The wind, too, had slackened. The new powder made conditions ideal, in spite of the grimy sheet of gunmetal gray that stretched away above them and made the peaks almost invisible. No one wanted to waste the day, in spite of the chancy weather reports that came over the car radio.

Victor had been on the road since well before daylight. He had pulled into the parking lot of a hotel and eased into a fitful hour or two of sleep, lying on the front seat, which he had levered to an almost prone position. He had been awakened by the cold and the whine of a garbage truck that had lumbered into the bay behind the hotel.

He doused his face with water from the tap in the bathroom of a nearby café before grabbing a quick espresso and a hard, crusty roll at the bar. Then he was out on the roads again, making one complete circuit of S.P. 51. There was no sign of life at either of the two private estates he had marked on his map and where he still believed the Royals to be. But none of the chalets along the route had yielded a clue. They were all sealed up for the night. Shutters closed. Garage doors shut. And in his repeated sweep of the roads he had seen dozens of white Fiats like the one Trager had rented.

A horn blasted behind him. The cars ahead were inching forward. Victor eased out the clutch and rolled a few feet before braking again. He squinted behind the dark lenses of his ski goggles. Highway police in white gloves and helmets were waving traffic around the accident. But it would still be minutes before he would be rolling again. He felt the bitter acid of desperation again filling his guts. The weather was right for the slopes. There was every reason to believe the royal couple would take advantage of the favorable conditions before the weather changed for the worse.

There was an equal possibility that the storm would push off in another direction. Anything could happen in the mountains. Even if by some miracle he found where Michelle was located, he would be too late. Killian would have already left on his mission.

The horn beeped again. Annoyed, Victor turned his head to shoot a nasty glance at the driver behind him, a young Austrian in a sports car, skis sticking up behind him like an insect's antennae. The Austrian made repeated gestures for him to move. Victor sighed. There was no point in fighting this fool and the rest of nature. He returned his gaze to the crawl ahead and eased the clutch forward to roll another six feet.

He pressed his head back against the leather rest and closed his eyes, knowing it was over. He was finished. There was no point in going on. Not for Michelle, nor for Alexi. It would only be a matter of time before they picked him up. He had no illusions about what would happen after that. An endless interrogation, followed by a bullet behind the ear, unless they had some use for him he could not yet fathom. In that case, he would prefer pulling the trigger himself.

The horn again. *Merde!*

Victor clenched his fingers into a fist around the wheel, opened his eyes, and saw Trager's car.

Startled, he glimpsed the square black license plate and confirmed it. Trager's Fiat was being towed past, behind a van painted with the green-and-black markings of the highway police.

In the front seat of the van, between two leather-jacketed, white-helmeted policemen, was Vincent Roberts.

50

Killian watched the clock inch past the hour. The time Roberts was scheduled to call in.

He remained seated in the chalet's kitchen, nursing a cup of coffee and turning the cup around and around in his fingers as the second hand swept in a monotonous, never-ending orbit around the face of a handsome walnut clock.

The clock complemented the decor of the kitchen, executed in white tile and blond wood that represented spotless Tyrolese efficiency that was somewhat incongruous beside the hanging strands of garlic and ripening tomatoes set out in baskets, a present left to them by the previous occupant.

Michelle watched Killian's long, blunt fingers, which seemed to curl into knots around the thick porcelain cup. But his face had not changed expression. Members of the team moved in silently from the other room. Gear packed and ready. Grim-faced and waiting.

Michelle stared at Killian, waiting for him to speak, to mention what had not been spoken between them since the previous night. What none of them said, but the accusation was there each time they looked at her.

"You left him alive. Why?" Killian asked.

Michelle was silent.

"Have you no answer? You disobeyed orders. The group has the right to take your life; you do understand that? I can have you executed."

Michelle said nothing. Her glance rose to meet his harsh gaze.

"You led us here, knowing what Victor told me. That the operation had been compromised. That they knew."

Killian shook his head. "Not compromised. I have seen to that. No one will interfere."

"How can you be certain?"

"I have reason to be certain."

"What reasons?" she demanded.

The muscles of his face tightened. "You have no right to

question me, only to follow my orders. Will you follow them now?"

Michelle faced him for an instant, then she nodded.

"You will execute Trager. Is that understood?"

"She should not be trusted," Dietrik blurted. But a glance from Killian silenced him.

"Those are my orders."

Michelle rose and went inside. The rest of the group dispersed silently to wait in silent agitation.

Thirty minutes later the phone finally rang.

Helga picked up the receiver, but Killian snatched it from her. Roberts was on the other end.

"Where are you?" Killian asked in a controlled voice.

Roberts spoke in a hushed tone. "The car was towed by the highway police. They picked me up just as I got to Vallesella. I'm at a garage in Cortina."

"Are they holding you on any kind of charge?"

"No," Roberts stated. "They're having the car checked out, that's all."

"Did you check the slopes?"

"Conditions are perfect. The lift is in full operation."

"And the patrols?"

"Never even got off their snowmobiles."

"Do you want us to pick you up?"

"Not necessary. As soon as the car's ready, I'll take in a little sight-seeing and find my way back."

Killian turned to face Michelle and the others, who had filtered into the room when the phone sounded.

Killian let his eyes move first from one to the other before he spoke.

"We go into action."

51

Verona was as placid as Joyce remembered. Unhurried and evenly breathing in spite of some scooter traffic and the bellow of a diesel or two from the periphery. There was even a statue of Dante to contemplate quietly before Joyce sauntered toward the post office, which squatted like a pious window in the center of a tiny square planted with parking spaces.

He entered through the double doors and went businesslike to a side table from which he scanned the room. Airless, it contained small, impatient clusters of people before each of the two windows opening for business after the long afternoon break.

Joyce entered one of the telephone booths and pulled the door shut behind him. He was equipped with a supply of telephone tokens. He inserted one and juggled the receiver as he waited for the requisite number of beeps. Then he dialed, hearing his transmission echo off into the ether. It was a Milan exchange and it was busy. Joyce decided to remain where he was before dialing again.

He eased back against the wall, keeping the receiver under his chin to forestall interruption. But no one outside approached the area. He breathed deeply and closed his eyes.

It had been an eventful morning.

He had not really slept, except for the few minutes when he had been able to close his eyes on the train between Trento and Venice. He had boarded in Bolzano, leaving the car he had stolen in Merano in the cobbled street beside one of the bridges across the Passerio.

The train had pulled in after midnight, filled with skiers. Joyce had boarded with a second-class ticket, changing it to a first-class one after they left the station. He had been lucky and found a seat in a first-class compartment where he had been able to doze until the train slowed down outside Mestre. He had stepped off into a noxious cloud of polluted vapor and entered the industrial flats bordering the lagoon, where the nine-o'clock bus carried him through the flat farm country of the Veneto and into Verona.

Joyce glanced at his watch. It was almost ten. The two policemen would have been discovered by now. He had left them in a wooded culvert outside Rifiano, handcuffed together in the backseat. He had disconnected the horn and taken the distributor cap. But they were young and vigorous and would have discovered a way to attract attention.

A smile forced itself to his lips at the memory of their surprised faces when he pulled out the Beretta instead of his prick. They never suspected the weapon had been concealed in a hollow compartment in his artificial arm, along with two Canadian passports, matching driver's licenses, credit cards, and a small cache of U.S. dollars.

After hiding them and the car, Joyce walked two miles into town before selecting the BMW parked outside a luxury villa. The car took him all the way to Bolzano, where he abandoned it. The oval markings on the rear too easily placed the car's origins, especially in daylight. So he took the train instead.

He glanced at his watch again, then deposited the token. There were more blips before it rang. A businesslike female voice answered. Joyce asked for a special exchange in a number code and was promptly transferred to the office of General Bruno.

No, the general was not in. Yes, Joyce would leave a message. He named the Trattoria Bagutta. Two o'clock. A table in the name of Señor Regio. The general would understand.

Joyce hung up and stepped out of the booth. He smiled at the scowling woman waiting to take his place and moved toward the exit in an unhurried manner.

It was snowing outside, a delicate tracery of lace filtering slowly and heavily to the wet cobblestones. Joyce turned up his collar and headed back toward the piazza, pausing to pay homage to Dante with a line he could not quite remember. He passed the handsome *loggia* with its quintet of statues and disappeared beneath the Arche Scaligere heading toward the Adige and its hundred bridges, one of which would conduct him to the terminal where a train would shortly transport him to Milan.

Forty minutes after Joyce's phone call, General Bruno bustled into his office where two aides waited to offer the English-style breakfast the general favored, along with the pick of the evening's reports, which had been compiled by the duty officer.

Bruno's massive jaws masticated forkfuls of bacon and overdone eggs as he perused the single-spaced flimsies. He paused when he came to the report of two missing policemen from Vipiteno who were conducting a suspect to Area Command in Merano. The general's forehead folded into accordion pleats when he read the description of the suspect. He was about to reach for the phone when his eye scanned his appointment book and he saw the strange note: "Bagutta. Two P.M. Señor Regio. He says you will understand."

The general put down the receiver and pushed away his plate. He did in fact understand. He had just been placed in charge of the manhunt assigned to find Joyce and bring him in.

52

The house was almost invisible from the road, screened by a plantation of firs and set back on its own drive. The shutters were closed when Victor drove past, and the garage door was shut. Victor turned around and drove back, passing it at twice the speed, which should have convinced anyone watching that his business did not concern them.

He parked half a mile lower down and went the rest of the the way on foot. He had used an old fence post as a marker. Once past it, he would be visible from the house.

He slipped inside the marker and stepped off the road, edging along the border of brush separating the house from the property alongside. Snow had begun falling again, offering him its protection.

He threaded his way through slender uprights of pine and toward the rear of the chalet. The shutters were closed, which became his next real worry.

Killian would have posted people to watch both the rear of the house and the road, so the closed shutters made no real sense, unless they had already gone and he was too late. The thought made him move more rapidly.

Ice crunched beneath his heavy shoes as he slipped toward the rear. He dodged across the narrow border of snow separating the house from the trees and flattened against the siding. Unzipping the outside pocket of his parka, he closed his hand over the Walther when he heard the squeal of the garage door sliding open.

Victor drew the weapon and headed toward the front, reaching it just as the large red door swung all the way up. A van stood within. He crouched and scrambled inside, with the barrel of his weapon level.

But the garage was empty. Victor realized the door must have been opened from inside the house. He backed against the cinder-block wall. He heard a step, then a handle turn.

Michelle stepped into the garage.

She was dressed in a blue cold-weather jumpsuit. Her

dark hair had been tucked beneath a brimless ski cap on which were a pair of tinted goggles. She carried a heavy blue zippered bag. She stepped toward the van and reached for the handle on the driver's side.

Victor's hand came across her mouth. His other hand clamped over her wrist and drew her hand away from the door. He felt her start, then twist, her leg seeking to hook beneath his, her elbow jutting back for a blow to the solar plexus. He was just a beat ahead, moving with her as he neutralized her motion and turned her wrist back painfully while still cupping her jaw shut.

He pinned her sharply against the wall, jarring her breathless. Her eyes stabbed toward his, widening with the shock of recognition.

"How many inside?" he whispered. "Nod your head. One? Two? Three . . . ?"

But she made no movement.

"They've gone, then?"

She nodded.

"And Trager? Where is he?"

Michelle jerked her head, indicating he was still inside.

"Alive?"

She nodded, her eyes still locked with his.

"We're going back in. Don't open your mouth."

He eased her ahead of him, still pinning her arm back, which he knew was causing her pain. But he had no choice. She was not his yet. She still belonged to Killian.

The house was silent, dark. Victor edged them through the musty rooms, one after the other. The rooms were empty, sterile, without evidence that anyone had been there. Even the ashtrays had been boiled free of fingerprints.

They found Trager in a back bedroom. His hands and feet were bound. Tape had been shoved across his mouth and over his eyes.

Victor released Michelle.

She sprang away from him, her eyes fixed on the door, but Victor stepped in the way.

"Still alive? I'm surprised."

"It wouldn't have mattered. He won't say anything. He's too implicated to say anything."

Victor smiled. "Which means you still have a use for him. Why not? Through him you get all his valuable contacts. I admire your friend. He has learned not to waste anything."

"Let me go," she said, trying to hide the urgency.

"You know I can't," he said quietly.

"You can't keep me here." She was desperate now. "You can't stop it. Get out now. Before—"

"Before what? They come for you?"

Her movement took him off-guard. She bolted toward the door, then sidestepped when he tried to prevent it, leapfrogging the bed and tearing open the door on the other side of the room.

She expected Victor to follow. Instead he charged back through the bedroom door, intercepting her when she raced into the hallway from the adjoining room.

He caught her around the waist, and they hit the floor together, knocking the wind out of her. Victor lifted her limp form and carried her back inside, laying her down alongside Trager.

There was a towel in the bathroom that he quickly tore into strips, binding her wrists behind her, and her ankles together.

Finished, he knelt beside Trager and gently stripped the tape from his eyes, watching the pupils dilate in the dim light, then blink as he sought to focus. He drew the tape away from Trager's lips.

"Christ," Trager whispered hoarsely. "What the fuck is going on?"

Victor placed his hand on Trager's head and turned it gently toward Michelle.

"What did they do to her?"

"Nothing. It's what she did to you."

Trager's eyes filled with confusion. "Did to me? Are you fucking crazy? I walked in and somebody jumped on top of me. I've been blacked out. They must have put me on something."

"Listen," Victor said sharply, "I know why you're here. You've been set up. Michelle is part of a group that came here for the same reason you did. For a shoot. Only, her friends don't use cameras. Do you understand?"

Trager looked at him blankly before his features contorted. "Oh, Jesus. You mean she set me up? Oh, Christ."

"We don't have much time. We already may be too late, but you've got to tell me where you planned to shoot from. Can you do that?"

Trager nodded.

Victor cut his bonds and helped him into the other room.

There was a bottle of whiskey in one of the cupboards, and Victor half filled a glass. Trager drank the whiskey in two gulps. He was slumped forward, staring into space with glazed eyes. Victor gave him another minute while he searched for a pencil and paper, which he found inside one of the kitchen cabinets, then placed his own chair opposite. When he spoke, his voice was low-pitched and deliberate.

"Trager, listen. Concentrate. You're a dead man if I don't reach those slopes in time. Now, where were you going to set up? Draw me a map."

Trager turned to face him. His face was slack, pale. His eyes were watery. He began haltingly, but within five minutes he had outlined what he knew of the terrain and what he had noted on his maps.

"I'm going to have to trust you. I'm going to leave Michelle here, with you. You can't let her out, not for any reason. Not if you want to see her again, understand?"

Trager nodded deliberately.

Victor rose and stared down at the photographer. "One more thing. Stay away from the van. It's wired to explode."

Trager again nodded, trying to clear his eyes. But when he opened them, Victor was already gone.

Brunch was exceptional. The chef had simply outdone himself. The princess even insisted on asking him up and congratulating him. The prince raised a glass and said something flattering in Italian, to which everyone laughed.

The party lounged around for a half hour, drinking some quite excellent local brandy and watching the light snow fall through the large plate-glass windows that offered stunning views of the delle Marmarole and the extraordinary configurations of jagged limestone that continually beguiled the eye.

At eleven the snowmobiles were called. The party collected in the hall, then went outside when the snow tracks appeared. They loaded the skis aboard and headed upslope. The prince took the wheel of the first track, guiding it over the uneven terrain, causing some shrieks when he accelerated and jumped a low hummock.

They reached the lifts and loaded aboard, two to a chair. They began their ascent, cheeks glowing red against the wind. As they rose, the wind increased, forming ragged banners of cloud against the flat, gray sky.

The peak appeared suddenly, rising above them, a twisting

TO KILL A KING

knifelike projection, ominous and chilling. There was a hush in the party as they were suddenly swept by the realization of their smallness and fragility against the immensity of the mountain. They swayed immobile for a moment, rocked by a gust. Someone laughed, and the cables creaked, drawing them toward what awaited.

53

It took fifteen minutes to climb the ribbon of road carved into the limestone flank of the Sorapiss. Victor kept his foot down, trying to avoid the patches of ice that sent the wheels planing.

In the distance he could make out the glint of sunlight on the aluminum casing of a cable car swimming the distance between two peaks like a determined insect. The sky was a burnished metal, bright and severe. Flakes had begun to fall, faster and more energetically than before. But there was still plenty of visibility.

He eased around the curve and almost ran past the logging road before he remembered Trager's landmark, an old tree trunk almost buried in snow. He pulled off the road and backtracked toward the spot.

The logging road turned out to be a narrow track between a towering stand of fir. Victor stepped off to one side and followed the trail through the woods.

The snow was deep in places, and he sank to his ankles, then almost to the knee in spots. The trail curved. A quarter of a mile from the main road he came across the car, a white Mercedes, almost invisible within the trees and covered with shovelfuls of snow. But that was no longer necessary. The snowfall had already blurred its outline, providing perfect camouflage.

Victor continued past. The wind was picking up, blowing a fine silt of powder into his eyes. He lowered his goggles, which helped only until they frosted over. He was breathing hard, searching for Trager's second landmark: a blazed trunk. But the trees around him all looked the same. He continued for a few more yards before he realized the track was no longer visible. He plunged off deep snow on either side, searching. He followed his own footprints back, but the snow had already obscured them.

Panic churned through him. It wasn't possible, but he had completely lost his way.

* * *

Trager clutched the glass in his hand, absentmindedly taking another slug of whiskey. He was sick, mired in a huddled mass of self-pity. He felt empty, lost, crushed. So it had been a setup all along, and he had been the patsy they had suckered in. Michelle was part of a frigging group of terrorists. Killers.

A shudder ran through him, along with the ebb of disbelief. It could not be . . . could not be happening to him! Anger was stirring in his bowels, mixed with a sickening feeling of nausea. He wanted to punch someone and vomit at the same time. Bloody fucking Christ!

He rose and started for the bedrooms, suddenly overwhelmed with the need to see her, hold her, have her tell him it was not true. That she was innocent. That she had come because she loved him, not for any other reason. That what that son of a bitch Romanian had said was only jealous swill. Yet how could he account for the men who had grabbed him? And the flitting dream in which he had heard the soft tone of her voice in conversation with others? Not a tone of distress but one of intimacy, friendship.

His guts were grinding, painful bits of shattered glass. He felt like passing out but held on. Fought the intense surge of feeling that flowed over him, powerful as a wave, that sought to knock him to his feet.

He gripped both sides of the toilet and heaved.

Water helped. Then he returned to the kitchen and grabbed a cigarette and inhaled, puffing hard. The smell and feel of the smoke actually revived him, making him feel better. He went to the window and stared through the chinks of the shutters. The sky looked bitter. The wind was up. He abhorred the cold but could not stay indoors. Something was forcing him out, away, anyplace but here.

He seized his parka, shoving cigarettes and lighter into an outside pocket, then grabbed his gloves and slipped into his snow boots, parked one beside the other in the hall closet.

He went to the door, then remembered he no longer had a car. He remembered the Romanian saying something about a van, but he did not have the keys. Michelle would have them, unless the Romanian had taken them. Fuck her and the van, he would get his own car.

Going to the phone, Trager stopped to search through his pockets, looking for the rental agreement. It was folded neatly within a zippered breast pocket. He shook it open and picked up the receiver, dialing the number beneath the name of the agency, which was written in a bold Gothic type. Fucking Itals up here, think they're bloody Germans, he thought as the phone beeped seven or eight times. Come on . . . come on . . .

Someone finally picked up.

"*Prego . . .*"

Bugger you and your *prego*, was what he wanted to say. Instead he asked for a car. A bloody fucking car. Instead of the delay he anticipated, the voice assured him a car could be arranged on the same terms if he preferred. Yes, fine. But could they get it to him now?

"*Signore, momento, prego.*" There was a pause, then the same voice came on again, reassuring him that the car could indeed be delivered and without charge. A man would be sent up with the car immediately. But they did not have his address.

Trager recited it into the phone. The voice on the other end issued a reassurance that the car would be there within the quarter hour, then hung up.

He smoked another cigarette, feeling a wave of exhaustion, followed by the realization that he had acted on an impulse he no longer felt. What did he want a car for? He had nowhere to go except back to London. He would return empty-handed, without Michelle and without what he'd come for. Unless . . .

The thought struck him like a bolt of loose current. Christ, the story of the century and he was sitting here feeling sorry for himself.

Flushed suddenly, heart pounding, Trager rushed back into the bedroom.

He ignored her, lying there, legs drawn up, tape still over her mouth. Her eyes were on him as he opened the closet and pulled out his equipment.

He took the Nikon with its continuous-load, machine-driven magazine, started to grab the Hasslebad but thought better of it. Better to keep it light.

He started out of the room, passing her with a feeling of disgust. Then he remembered he had to wait for the car. So he turned and stared at her, filled suddenly with an uncontrollable anger. Slut . . . the filthy, fucking slut . . .

He bent over the bed, watching as her gaze meshed with his.

"Bitch," he whispered. "Fucking little pussy."

His hand closed over her throat. She squirmed, brought her knee up behind him, and jarred him off the bed.

"Fucking cunt."

He leapt, avoiding her knee as she tried to wriggle off the bed. He drew back. Holding her against him, her back up against his belly, his hands cupped her breasts, squeezing as hard as he could, feeling her struggle against the pain.

He realized he had a hard-on. Suddenly wanted her, wanted to tear into her, wound her. Brand her. Humiliate her.

He reached higher and found her zipper, drawing it down beneath her locked elbows. Then lower, until he found the snap securing the two parts of the suit. He shoved her forward, pushing her face into the pillow until he could pull the quilted pants partway down her thighs.

He tore her panties at the seam and drew down his zipper. His cock felt enormous. He shoved it against her, feeling her buck. She writhed against him, struggling. He was excited by her softness, her helplessness, and pushed harder; felt his hardness tearing into her, knew he was giving her pain.

"Cunt . . . fucking bitch . . ."

She was no longer resisting. He was no longer excited but continued to push back and forth mechanically. He became aware that the growl of passion in his throat had become something else. He could not explain why his own eyes were filled with tears.

From a distance they resembled an assembly of tiny moving dots, shuffling in the awkward movements skiers have on a flat surface, resembling skaters somehow stuck to a frozen pond. Snow had begun falling again. The wind was constant now, hard against their backs, urging them on.

The prince had organized the party into teams of four, strong skiers beside the weaker ones. He pushed off first. The princess would follow with the next batch. Goggles were pulled down. Gloves tugged on. Poles grasped. Then, one by one, they were gone.

The phone in the hut at the bottom of the lift began ringing. But the security men standing nearby ignored it, field glasses sweeping back and forth between the royal party and the slopes beyond.

The area below was still, the powder virgin and uncut. It needed only the sun to make conditions perfect, and as if by a miracle, the skies suddenly parted and a shaft of brilliant sunlight enveloped the slopes.

The phone persisted, irritating the men in front of the hut.

One of them finally turned and trudged inside, grasped the receiver in one gloved hand, and brought it to his ear.

An altogether unexpected voice almost blasted his ear off.

"Red alert. Repeat. Red alert. Stop the party. Repeat. Keep them at the lift!"

The startled security man dropped the receiver and charged outside, mouth open to repeat the command. But it was too late. Those he sought to protect were brilliant bits of blue and red against the waves of powder, following precise geometric angles as they raced gravity down the perfect slope. Down to where Killian, and death, waited.

54

Michelle heard the horn outside, followed by the slam of the outside door. Trager had left her sprawled on the bed, her legs exposed, her groin alternating between pain and numbness. She could feel his ejaculation oozing down between her thighs. She ignored it, focusing instead on the sound of the car ignition and the squeal of tires on ice, then the growl of shifting gears and the receding sound of the engine.

Michelle twisted onto her back. Her legs were free. Trager had released one strip of toweling that held her tied to the bed frame. A single strand still remained fastened to her bound wrists. She wriggled until her knees were tight against her chest, straining to exert as much leverage as she could.

She closed her eyes against the pain, flexed, and felt the towel rip. It took several thrusts, which left her breathless and sweating, before the strip of material burst, freeing her from the bed.

Standing brought a feeling of giddiness, but that passed within moments. She hopped out of the room and into the corridor, moving as quickly as she could toward the kitchen. There was an instant when she almost fell, but she managed to regain her balance by supporting herself against the wall.

She reached the kitchen, pulled open a drawer, and found a knife. Sliding it into the open space, she slid the drawer closed until the knife was securely wedged. Seconds later she had cut enough strips of toweling to pull the rest apart. She freed her ankles and rushed back into the bathroom where she wrapped toilet paper into a wad and cleaned between her legs. Then she pulled her quilted pants back on.

The van started instantly. The bag containing her pistol and walkie-talkie was missing. Victor must have taken them. She had nothing to fight with but the explosives in the van. She had to warn Killian.

She felt a wave of panic but bit down against it, waiting until the engine was warm enough before starting off and peeling out onto the road.

Snow was blowing in fine grains that quickly coated the windshield. She turned on the wipers and increased her pressure on the accelerator. She had to maintain control. Too fast and she increased the possibility of skidding. Killian had drilled that into her, along with the other details of her task. She had been assigned the backup position. She had to drive the van to the checkpoint and set the detonators. The explosives would destroy the mountain road, making pursuit impossible. But Victor's appearance made that impossible. She had to warn Killian before it was too late. Prevent Victor from reaching him. Killian would have to abort. It was the only way to save them all.

She reached down and pulled off the gear housing. The detonator controls were just beneath. Two yellow dials. One for the timer and one to set the charge.

She had less than five minutes to reach the logging road. She pushed the pedal harder.

They came downslope like a formation of fighter planes, each group separated by an equal interval, fanning out in a perfect V behind the leader.

Killian would let the first group ski well into the pass before opening fire. The last group would be caught in the open in a cross fire from the trees.

Killian had watched them come down from the lifts, moving in leisurely arcs of motion, each following in the wake of the one ahead. A perfect game of Follow the Leader. No. The Pied Piper was a better image.

At this distance there was no way to see their faces. It was better that way. There were no residual images to disturb the sleep or ripple the conscience.

Killian braced himself, drawing back the bolt on his Uzi. He sensed rather than saw each of his people doing the same. They were spread out on either side of the double V formed by the encroaching border of trees that framed the narrow pass leading to the lower slopes.

He would let the prince and his group through before he opened fire. His burst would be a signal to the others.

Killian sucked icy air into his lungs. They were close now, turning to begin the long, slow loop across the final ridge that would bring them directly into his line of sight.

His insides were roller coastering exactly as they had done the very first time he had gone into action. It was always the same, the superb instinct his species had for taking its prey. The desire and joy of destroying a target. Thou shalt not kill. . . .

He wiped the thought away. The leader was making his turn, a perfect sweeping motion that set up a curling wave of white. The man's face was masked by goggles and a dark band of blue across his forehead, that much he could make out. He did not want to see more of the face. He drew the stock to his shoulder, focusing on the center of the chest, then raising his sight to the leader of the group beyond. His target.

It took a moment more for him to realize it was a woman. The princess, unmistakable.

They were coming on now, fanning out single-file to follow the prince as he turned into his final curve. He was approaching the bush Killian had set as a marker to signal when they would be within range.

Killian sighted along the humped curve of his weapon. His brows narrowed. The brilliant sheen of the prince's sky-blue parka filled his line of sight.

Glare danced on the lens of the prince's goggles. White-gloved fists rose and fell in a swimmer's rhythm as the ski poles moved up and down.

Bits of snow spit past Killian's lens. He drew a sharp intake of air and gentled his gloved finger around the trigger. Counting. One . . .

Two . . .

Three . . .

55

The curve appeared dead ahead.

Michelle gunned the engine and reached for the detonator. The nearest setting read one minute. She reached down, feeling for the dial. Turning gently.

The van flew into thin air, skidding broadside to the road.

The wheel kicked away. She grasped it with both hands, turning instinctively toward the mountain an instant before she realized she must turn into the skid. Turn in the opposite direction—who had taught her that?

She fought the wheel as the wipers banged back and forth. The mountain blurred across the windshield, like the humped back of a surfacing whale. Then road and empty sky, and she became aware in the most ridiculous way of the glimmer of light on a distant cable car crawling its way across the pale, gunmetal-gray sky.

The retainer came crashing toward her like a wave of stone. Instantly she realized that there was not enough room for the van to complete its circular motion. Realized that in some crazy way the wall was going to strike her. She felt a rebellious sense of unfairness just before it hit. She had never been in an accident before.

The explosion gorged on the silence, swallowing it whole, engulfing the slope in a quaking tremor that bounced light off the low sheet of sky in a pale orange flash.

Blue blurred for an instant and flew out of the eyepiece.

Killian lowered the weapon.

The prince was no longer in his line of vision. He was sliding off somewhere. Moving laterally along the ridge instead of continuing his motion downslope.

Behind him the formation had lost its beautiful symmetrical coherence. Two skiers had actually fallen, disappearing in creamy puffs. Others were darting sideways in startled, erratic motion. All of them were stalled in a kind of slow-motion charade, just upslope of the bush. Just a few yards out of range.

Something had gone wrong. At first it sounded like someone bombing the slopes. But Killian realized that was impossible. The sound had come from farther off, in the direction of the road. He visualized the van and Michelle inside it, blown to pieces. He cleared his head quickly, refusing to accept the image, not without the evidence of his own eyes.

There was movement beside him. Roberts was dodging upslope through the trees, scrambling to reach him.

Killian raised his arm, signaling Roberts to follow. If they headed upslope, they could still set up a cross fire without moving the rest of the group out of position. To risk that would leave them without covering fire on either slope.

Killian started moving, using the trees as cover. He continued upslope and, as he ran, glimpsed the skiers starting to clump together. That would make his job easier.

He dodged from trunk to trunk, afraid of being seen, of panicking the skiers before he could fully position himself within range.

He was beginning to struggle: breathing hard and having to draw himself along with one hand. The ground was deceptive, even steeper than he thought. The snow had drifted, making it knee-deep along the tree line, hiding escarpments of slippery limestone, boulders, and clumps of piled rock.

He turned, looking for Roberts among the trees behind him. He saw movement and paused, realizing Roberts could not have covered the ground so quickly. Dietrik was standing back up. He must have broken position. Killian stifled his irritation, realizing that Dietrik was armed with a heavy-caliber assault weapon. It could easily cover the slope from where he was. He waited for the other man to show himself, but nothing stirred. He must have imagined it. Killian pushed on through deeper snow.

Ahead, ground broke toward the ridge. The trees fell away in an irregular line. He had reached the limit of his cover.

Killian reached the last tree and leaned against it, breathless. Beyond, he could see the skiers moving toward the prince. They were within range, but he would have to leave cover to get them all. He prayed Roberts was behind him. He would shoot those farthest upslope first. That would force the others down toward Roberts. He slid back the bolt and stepped forward.

Something caused him to turn.

A dark shape moved behind him in the trees. He glimpsed the blue of a parka and the glimmer of light on burnished steel.

Killian wheeled and fired.

56

Trager pulled onto the shoulder well past the logging road and cut directly into the woods from there. He planned a trajectory that would intersect the slope some three hundred yards above the cut leading down to the lower slopes. He had been clever. Starting above the road gave him the advantage of a downhill trek. He practically flew, his heart in his mouth, waiting for the burst of gunfire that signaled he would be too late. No matter, pictures of the bodies alone would still be worth a fortune. He would not be greedy, just get in quick, before anyone reached the scene, run a roll, and get out of there fast, before the area was blanketed with security.

The devil would take care of him afterward. He would send the pictures—wire them, rather—in from somewhere on the Continent. He could decide that later. Of course, the photographer would remain completely anonymous. Even he didn't want that kind of notoriety.

Strange how things turned out. He had lost Michelle, true, but she had provided him with a photo spread that was beyond any of his wildest imaginings. A fortune, it was worth too. Bloody priceless.

Luck was running with him. He could sense it. Especially when he made it to the tree line and saw the royal party still on the slopes. Of course, he was too far out of range—and without a 200mm telephoto. But he had decided against such a large piece of equipment in the woods.

Remaining well within the trees, he inched his way downslope. He had the advantage of having picked the very spot for the terrorists' ambush. He didn't want to get too close. He could get shots of the bodies later, once the killers had quit the area. It was a cinch they wouldn't be hanging around. Not bloody likely. Not on this day. Mrs. Trager's little boy was making hay while the sun shone.

He unlimbered the camera. He was using a 120mm on the Nikon. He sighted through the lens and watched. It would not be long. The skiers were moving toward the pass to the lower slopes.

The explosion took him off-balance. But he recovered quickly. Only when he looked through the lens again did he realize the skiers had veered off. That meant getting closer or losing the whole spread. No one would pay for dots of color on the snow. He had to have detail. Faces.

Trager moved cautiously, inching downslope over the rough ground. Ahead, the trees made a kind of irregular hitch, bulging out onto the slope. That promised the best vantage point. He made for it as quickly as he could, readying the camera, preparing to shoot when—Christ!

Losing his footing, Trager slid several feet into calf-deep snow.

He had only a glimpse of the man, but his instinct was perfect. He raised the pistol grip and pulled.

Killian's burst caught Trager full in the abdomen. The Uzi was on automatic. Full burst. Six hundred rounds a minute. Bullets riddled Trager's spine and chewed his intestines into pulp.

Bloody fucking Christ.

He sat splat down in the snow, hands still on the camera, his finger jammed on the trigger, running out the entire roll.

Trager's face held the most amazing portrait of surprise Killian had ever encountered.

The burst echoed across the slope.

The prince was no stranger to gunfire. He dropped to one knee, signaling those around him to do the same.

The faces around him wore looks of shock. His wife's expression was more perplexed, disbelief etched onto her features. Her eyes had locked with his, expressing the very thing they most feared.

Strangely enough, he was quite calm. The explosion had surprised and shaken all of them. But in the moments that followed, he felt a sense of inner relaxation, almost of peace. In a sense this was what he knew best. It was like being at sea again, on the bridge, his hearing torn by the shriek of the klaxons signaling some emergency. The rush of adrenaline was familiar, too, as was the increased beating of his heart. There was no panic. *All right, I can handle this.* That was when the gunfire started and he realized they were under attack.

TO KILL A KING

Of course, he was not totally unprepared. Nor was the princess. They lived with the threat of it every day. The dread that some maniac, some fanatic, was out there, poised and ready. But the reality had the most peculiar feel to it. It had come, not in the crowds as they had expected but here, when they were least prepared. So this was it, then. This was actually happening.

Then his thoughts resumed their normal speed, and the prince realized how exposed they were and knew then that they had no chance at all. Not unless those shooting had somehow been surprised by his security force. In any event, they could not chance continuing downslope. They had only one route of escape, and that was back upslope toward the lifts.

He skied toward his wife, shouting to those around him to move laterally, toward the tree line opposite. "Low. Try to keep low," he shouted, but his voice was snatched away by the wind.

Someone was pointing, and the prince turned. A figure had left the cover of trees and was fighting his way toward them in deep snow, his weapon raised high at the level of his head.

The man was wearing a white one-piece ski outfit, making him difficult to see. He had not yet fired because he was still not entirely within range.

The man lunged through the thick snow, his movements almost comical if they had not been tinged with horror. He shifted sideways. Lost his balance, righted. Lost his balance again. But doggedly kept on.

When he was within a hundred yards, he stopped and seemed to collect himself. He raised the weapon slowly, methodically, and brought it to his shoulder.

They never really heard the shot. Nor did the man in the snow. But a shudder went through him, as if he had touched an electrical wire. He wheeled in annoyance before he fell facedown in the powder, which rose in a kind of sugary cloud around his shape, and he was immediately sucked into the glimmering waste.

Killian did not hear the shot. But he saw Roberts fall.

The wind must have carried the sound away from them, which meant the man who fired it was between Roberts and himself.

Killian drew back, hesitating. He glanced upslope. So far

security had not appeared. Even if they were moving, it would take some time for them to traverse the slopes on their slow-moving snow vehicles.

After hearing the shooting, his own men would be moving. Killian debated remaining where he was or moving onto the slope. But the prince decided for him. He was leading the skiers in a cross-country transverse along the ridge. They were heading right for him.

Killian backed into the trees, slipping higher up along the ridge. Two of his men emerged from the tree line, fanning out behind the skiers to close the pincer. The one on the left to cover the lower slopes, the other to cover the higher.

Killian knelt and waited.

One or two of the skiers had become aware of their pursuers. Word spread along the line. Heads turned. The pace increased. They were coming faster now. Poles flashing, digging hard into the loosely packed snow. He raised his binoculars, watching the strained faces of the royal party, the looks of fear and desperation. Yet there was no panic. He gave them something for that.

They were narrowing the gap. One hundred yards and closing. His weapon was made for short-range effectiveness. He did not want to chance a burst that would send them scattering. His men were armed with the same type of weapons. They had expected to cut down their prey in the narrow confines of the pass. But Vittorio and Stepan kept on, slogging their way through the drifts. They were on a tangent and closing. Killian realized they would be in range before him.

This time he heard the shot. A loud, cracking whine.

Stepan spun and fell, clutching his face.

Vittorio turned and fired at the trees, moving back toward them instead of toward the skiers.

The first shot caught him in the belly, the second in the chest. He fell backward, one arm flung out, his weapon falling harmlessly into the snow.

Killian estimated the distance between himself and the skiers. Less than fifty yards. Another minute and he would open fire. He knelt and raised his weapon.

The prince raised his arm and changed course.

Killian drew his eye from the sight. Instead of continuing straight ahead as they had been doing, the prince was leading the party in a zigzag back up the slope, tacking like a sailboat in the opposite direction, taking them farther out of range.

TO KILL A KING

Killian cursed. He would have to move. His only chance was to push on and meet the party when they zigzagged back in the other direction.

He scrambled through the brush, fighting his way between the rocks but remaining hidden within the tree line.

He moved quickly, watching the skiers as they approached the forest opposite. His vision filled with the rise and fall of their poles, the rhythmic, back-and-forth extension of their legs. The pace was killing.

When they were within fifty yards, they turned and came back toward him, faces gleaming with sweat, chests rising and falling as they fought for breath. One or two of the men were holding their arms around the women's waists, skiing in tandem. The prince still led the way. The princess was directly behind him, doggedly keeping pace with her husband.

Killian pushed toward a little island of pines that impinged upon the slope. He kept low, balancing himself with one hand as he scraped through the snow, fighting for footing on the slippery stone beneath.

He was out of breath when he reached the pines, ducking almost on his stomach, creeping toward the farthest trunk and stretching out prone, the barrel still close to his body.

They were only fifty yards away now and coming on hard. Killian edged the weapon forward, waiting until the prince raised his hand to signal his party to go in the other direction. Killian pressed the scope to his eye.

The prince was squarely within the cross hairs, a sky-blue blur of motion, fighting his way toward Killian with infinite slowness, his jaw moving, counting the beats. Glancing behind to measure their progress, eyes scanning the trees ahead for what he knew must be there.

Killian slid his finger onto the trigger and took a deep breath. Squeezed.

The report exploded in his ear. The shock of the bullet entering Killian's body momentarily stunned him.

He felt a blade of extreme cold, as if someone had plunged a jagged piece of ice down through his shoulder blades. His eyes refused to focus. He tried to grasp the weapon, but his hands would not react. He felt his mouth fill with a warm flow of blood. Then he slid sideways into an oily darkness.

57

Victor lowered the assault rifle.

Killian lay motionless beside the trunk. Framed between the trees, Victor watched the prince drop to one knee, one arm reaching back to pull his wife down into the pillow of deep snow. He shouted something, and the skiers behind him slipped to their bellies, scraping for cover in the piled drifts.

Sounds of automatic weapons fire erupted from two directions almost simultaneously, echoing up and down the slope. An instant later that was answered by the higher-pitched whine of the Uzis. Security must have been ambushed by Killian's people hidden in the trees.

Victor moved back into the shelter of timber. Crouching for cover, he slipped back toward the road, following the spines of limestone protruding through the thin snow cover. He ducked and ran, using the trees as cover, pacing himself between the bursts of gunfire, keeping distance between himself and the shooting. Desperation etched his features. He had to reach the road and find Michelle.

Earlier he had backtracked until he found the trail again, following it toward the slopes where he knew Killian would be waiting. He had not expected the explosion. At first he believed Trager had ignored his warning and accidentally set it off. But he had stumbled over the photographer's body farther downslope. Only then did he realize that Michelle must have set off the detonation. Whether as an accident or as a warning, it would draw security. When he heard firing, fear for her burned like a brand in his chest.

Only when he reached the logging trail was he aware that the gunfire was not coming from the road but from the slope. He pushed harder, forcing his legs to move, fighting the exhaustion that rode over him in thick, pulsing waves.

He never made it to the point Trager indicated. The explosion altered that, forcing Killian to shift position. That was when Roberts materialized, scrambling upslope over the jutting rock, piled in layers like a collapsed stone staircase.

Only when Victor reached the fringe of wood and witnessed the confusion on the slope did he realize why Roberts had left his cover. Victor had taken an assault rifle from the canvas bag Michelle had been carrying when he surprised her. It gave him the range he needed to bring Roberts down. Killian's men must have thought the shot came from farther downslope. They left cover, trying to force the skiers toward the place where Killian lay waiting. It was an effective maneuver, only Victor had gotten there first.

Breath burned in his throat. The trees thinned ahead. Victor glimpsed the road now, slick with ice. Snow was falling; in fact, it had been falling since the moment he entered the woods. But he had been cloaked by the thick fir cover. Now it swept toward him in overlapping curtains of lace, whipped by a tormenting wind that bit into the flesh of his face and glazed his eyebrows and hair.

He saw what was left of the van before he found her: a tire, blown into the trees and lying sideways across the track, separated from its rim like a snake shedding its skin; part of the axle was dug into the earth, leaning at an impossible angle like a spent javelin. The van lay on its side, a burned husk, split open like a ripped foil wrapping.

A large tree leaned sideways, roots exposed, blocking the road. Piled against it was a rubble of rock and detritus that once had been the retaining wall. Glass carpeted the tarmac, glittering in the silvery light like smashed Christmas ornaments.

He did not see her. Not until he left the cover of the trees and crossed the road, slipping once on the glimmering surface. Then he rounded the blackened hulk and found her.

Michelle lay on the tarmac, arms outstretched like a discarded doll.

He knew even before he reached her, knew with a logical finality, that she had not survived. A bloody ooze seeped through the charred quilting of what had been her ski outfit. It formed a scarlet outline, greedily sucked by the absorbing sleet.

But she was not dead.

Impossible. Yet somewhere in the depths of flesh beneath his touch there was a pulse, a flutter almost beyond feeling. But she was alive.

His car was there, where he had left it, disappearing beneath a glaze of ice; but it started almost at once. Victor eased it off the shoulder and inched cautiously around the curve, feeling the tires struggle for purchase on the glazed sheet the road had become.

He brought the vehicle as close as he could, easing it around the rear of the trashed van, and pulled to a halt six or seven feet from where she lay.

Lifting her was a terror he almost could not accomplish. Her hair was caked with frost, stiff and unyielding around her face. It fell back, away from his gaze, as he carried her carefully, the way he would an infant, placing one foot in front of the other, terrified of stumbling.

He angled back the front seat, forming a cradle for her limp form. He slid her into it, carefully bringing the safety belt down over her burned skin and across the char of flesh on her breasts.

He released the brake and eased the accelerator, heading them back around in a tight arc of motion before straightening the wheel and heading back down the mountain.

But where could he take her? Where would she be safe? Somehow that no longer mattered. She had to live. Beyond that he would not think.

He followed the warping of the road, downshifting at the curves, descending the twisting ribbon, both hands on the wheel. Not steering but guiding the vehicle in its glide as tires growled and clattered on the icy incline.

Victor failed to hear the helicopter until it was almost overhead.

It passed low, compressing the air, enveloping them in its thundering *whoosh* of movement. A Cobra the color of mustard, bearing Italian Army chevrons.

Victor watched as it swooped away. Changing course, it flew straight out from the mountain, wheeled on its axis, turning nose first, the double barrels of its machine guns aimed toward them.

Victor had the sense it was going to fire an instant before the helicoptor's belly erupted. He chopped down on the pedal, hurtling them down the incline. Chips of limestone were eaten out of the wall behind them.

The Fiat swung out of control, sliding into a skid as the aircraft gained altitude and swung around for another pass.

The wheels locked, barreling them into a half circle of blurred motion. He let the wheel spin, then clamped onto it with both hands. The front straightened only inches from the

TO KILL A KING

retaining wall, and they half slid, half drove, around the next curve.

The Cobra made a lazy maneuver and paused to hover, bringing both barrels to bear.

A tunnel beckoned ahead.

Victor raced the bullets into the darkness, a beat ahead of the shattering barrage.

He was out of the tunnel almost as quickly as he entered it, weaving across both lanes, creating erratic patterns, zigzagging back and forth.

He was conscious of the chugging of machine guns but could no longer keep track of the trajectories.

Ahead was the second curve, and beyond, another tunnel.

Swerving, he rode the shoulder, hugging the tree side for protection. Branches were lopped off as the stream of bullets probed for him.

He cut hard over, sending the Fiat into a long, graceful, sidelong skid, interrupted by the wall of stone, which neatly dented both fenders. His wheels found some grit and pushed off just ahead of the chain-sawing flurry of shells that dropped more fir onto the tarmac.

They were through and heading for the longest tunnel. Beyond that, the mountain closed in on itself with clamping jaws of rock. They would have to climb into the closing gray fury, now showering them with clouds of flying ice. He could lose the Cobra on the other side, lose it just long enough to give her back her life.

But that was a prayer, not a probability.

He had been too lucky when he should have known better. It took his stomach to discover the wheels were no longer on the road.

There was a sickening feeling, like the last few seconds on a roller coaster. He glimpsed the blurred insect shape in the rearview mirrors, dropping toward the road behind them, then disappearing in a whirling maelstrom of grit and rock.

The final burst was short, a gutsy pilot's toss of the dice before the skids rose and disappeared, climbing for altitude in a vector of sideways motion.

He felt the impact and heard the tires burst. A sudden jet of imprisoned air jolting the chassis sideways. He watched the rear move faster than he could control it, tried to turn into the arc of the skid. But the maneuver lacked the necessary traction—was not quite fast enough, in any case.

A wall of mountain stepped out to embrace him. He threw his arm back to shield her, knew it would be bad when they hit.

He felt the impact an instant before he heard the sound: the crying sound of dying metal. He went down struggling, fighting the blackness like a swimmer battling the tide.

58

Bruno took command almost at once.

There could be no doubt of his authority. It came directly from Rome. The force at his command was impressive. Two units of antiterrorist specialists from the EMI. Grim service regulars in camouflage fatigues and black berets, armed with assault rifles. One unit dropped onto the slopes from Cheyenne attack helicopters, the second swarming through the woods from below.

The Royals were safe and unharmed. For that he thanked the gods, pagan and otherwise. They were now his first responsibility and greatest worry. He wanted them out of the area and as far away from Italian soil as they could go.

Unfortunately for the general, nature was not cooperating. The storm that had been predicted, but not necessarily expected, arrived in full panoply, making a mockery of all the radar devices installed in all the airports from Munich to Milan. It threatened to make the roads impassable, if not for days then for at least the next twenty-four hours.

That meant the royal party were now the guests of the Italian security forces. In bureaucratic parlance that translated to mean the general was to be responsible if any disaster occurred.

So far he had avoided answering the barrage of phone calls that came from Military Command in Rome. Of course, there would be questions. They would probe his knowledge of the terrorist operation, and that would prove embarrassing, since he had been informed of the operation by a fugitive who at that moment was being sought by every intelligence agency in the West. But all that would come later.

Bruno introduced himself to the prince and princess, who were acting the part with perfect British aplomb. Jolly good, but Bruno was not taking any chances. He made it fully understood that they were not to leave the chalet for any reason, not until he considered the area fully secured.

That caused an exchange of smiles between his aides. The

269

general was famous for never believing in the security of anything. It was often joked that Bruno would have demanded a gynecological examination of the Virgin before he accepted proof of Christ's paternity.

In any case, he had stationed a double ring of troops around the chalet, closed off the roads both above and below to any and all traffic, and ordered reinforcements from a famous mountain regiment that wore plumed kepis and measured double time everywhere—including, it was rumored, the toilet and the brothel. He had given orders to sweep the towns and villages for a distance of ten miles. And that was just the beginning.

Bruno went to look at the bodies, almost as an afterthought.

They lay sprawled on the slopes not far from where they had been shot, staining the crisp, granular surface a bright whore's scarlet. Tracks cut across the slope now where the snow tractor had laid down imprints. Farther up, Bruno could see the imprint of skis crisscrossing in their desperate zigzags as the party tried to elude death.

The five bodies were being photographed and fingerprinted, the records flown to Rome, if ever the skies cleared. One of them was a woman. Of course, there was no identification, only their piled equipment. Expensive and well cared for, he observed professionally.

Bruno stood over the bodies and muttered to himself, for he had a bad feeling in his stomach. And that meant he had a decision to make. One that would perhaps decide his career.

If he dispatched the Royals now, they would be exposed to not only the weather but also to the possibility of further attempts on their lives. The wisest course was for them to remain here, until the weather permitted a flight out. But by no stretch of the imagination could it be said that the area was safe.

Five bodies. And the place where a sixth had been, and the ragged trough from where it had been dragged back into the woods. The terrorists had been shot on the slope before Bruno and his men arrived, killed by some mysterious hand. Surprisingly enough, the fourth was a woman. She had been killed by his own security after ambushing three fools who rode to glory on a snowmobile.

But where was their leader?

The slopes had been scoured. They had found blood beside a tree where the prince claimed another shot had been fired.

But so far there was no trace of the man from whom it had come. The blizzard made his helicopters useless. They could not mount a ground search until the weather cleared, which meant the terrorists might still be at large. That meant they might yet return to attempt to finish their operation.

Of course, logic told him that was clearly impossible.

The chalet was on the opposite side of the mountain from the ski slopes. There was no way to approach it except from the direction of the valley below, an area he had saturated with security personnel. He had drawn his men in a tight, protective semicircle, the mountain at their backs. Defensively it was all but medieval. But Bruno was an old hand at fanaticism. He was also a man of few illusions. Killian was a creature with many more than nine lives. Bruno was sure he was still breathing.

Bruno knew Killian was out there. He had to be found.

59

The weather had now become his ally.

Killian maneuvered the car slowly in the blinding sleet that made the wipers worthless. It was Roberts who had discovered the trail on one of his sweeps, an ancient quarry track twisting steeply around a spur of jagged stone like a Chinese dagger.

It was not part of the map Trager brought. Roberts discovered it when he went off to observe the chalet on that final morning and returned to find the car had been towed.

Roberts had started back to Vallesella on foot. He kept off the road, pushing through thick brush alongside. He had stumbled on the trail by accident, thinking it was a shortcut. But it petered out finally beside a disused quarry, and he had been forced to climb all the way back to the main road.

Experience had long ago taught Killian the value of such accidents. He had made them stop on the way up so Roberts could point it out. Now it would serve to bury him.

The Mercedes lurched forward, rocking and twisting on the uneven roadbed. Steering was difficult. Blood was soaking through his sleeve and onto his hands, making it impossible to grip the wheel.

Fortunately the wound was not serious. The bullet had entered high on his shoulder, grazing the clavicle and passing neatly through the hollow beneath. The force had knocked him unconscious, but he had fought against the blackness, struggling to his knees to find that his quarry was escaping downslope, out of range, escorted by a phalanx of security.

Killian watched as the prince raised his arm, pointing to the place where he was hidden. But the security men had ignored his warning in their zeal to protect the royal party. Dietrik managed to ambush two of them before he was killed. Helga took care of another group who rode toward her on a snowmobile.

Killian had just enough time to force his way through the drifts to where Roberts had fallen. He managed to drag him back into cover just as the gunships swooped over the trees.

The Italians became preoccupied with Dietrik and Helga. Dietrik was cut down as he tried to escape toward the upper slopes. Helga tried to reach him along the tree line but was caught in cross fire from both ships. They held out long enough to enable Killian to half carry, half drag Roberts back to the car. There was nothing left of the van. He would not let his mind piece together what had happened to Michelle. He had learned to preserve his agonies within a private chapel.

Roberts was dying, bleeding to death on the rear seat. There was nothing he could do for him. He had to attend to the possible.

The road petered out, ending abruptly in a pile of stone. He gave no thought to hiding the car. The storm made aerial reconnaissance impossible. He went around to the trunk and carried the first-aid kit back to the front seat. The radio was military-issue, set to Italian Army frequencies. It was equipped with a twenty-foot directional antenna.

He tuned in on the static blip of local transmission. He had enough experience with standard military operations to know that patrols would be out scouring the area until the storm made the roads impassable. He twisted the antenna and made a quick calculation using the compass on the dash. It confirmed his instinct. They were using the chalet as a headquarters, calling in at regular fifteen-minute intervals.

A work party was trying to clear the rubble around the van and make the road passable. From their chatter he estimated the job would have to be abandoned without heavy equipment. But that could not be brought up until the weather cleared.

Killian opened the back door. Roberts lay sprawled, arms and legs akimbo, his head arched back, his eyes open and staring. Lifeless.

Killian closed the door and returned to the front seat. He unzipped his jumpsuit and stripped to the waist. He no longer felt the cold. From the first-aid kit he extracted a small hypodermic syringe and injected himself with morphine. He sat back and listened to the transmissions, waiting for the drug to take effect. When his shoulder felt sufficiently numb, he bathed the wound with antiseptic, wadding a bandage between his lips to bite against the pain. Then he improvised a bandage and secured it around the shoulder with gauze and tape. The worst pain would come later. For that he had plenty of morphine and a supply of penicillin. He had lost some blood, but he had a supply of plasma. He had long ago learned how to sustain his existence, a lesson taught by pain and the bitterness of watching comrades die.

He drew the suit back over his shoulders and unzipped the sleeve. He drew out the needle and quickly pierced a vein, leaning back against the seat as the IV trickled into him. He closed his eyes, let the weariness absorb him, and allowed his mind to float, listening to the fluctuating melodies of soldiers' voices coming from the radio.

His course of action had already been decided. But he went over the score like a conductor before a performance. The transmissions only confirmed what he had already pieced together. The security force was drawing back into defensive perimeters around the chalet. His quarry was still in place. They would not risk moving them until the storm subsided. Fate had provided him with a second opportunity.

The next few hours would be a struggle. He had to move while there was still enough light. He carefully filled a knapsack with rations and the medical supplies he would need. He would not need crampons yet—not until he reached the upper slopes. He took out the rest of his gear and laid each piece beside the trunk, deciding what he would carry and what he must leave behind.

Methodically he replaced the discards, then tied the rest to various fastenings on the knapsack. It was a Bergman pack, secured to an aluminum frame that fastened over his arms but distributed the weight evenly across his entire back.

Weapons were slid into a waterproof canvas bag, tied crossways to the frame. They provided the greatest weight. His last and most crucial act was to set the timers on the detonators. For this he made a systematic calculation based on the distance he had to travel and the time he would allow himself.

Then he locked the car and struggled into the harness. He lowered his goggles and turned toward the mountain.

60

They were dancing together in the large sunlit house. His concern was to keep her in his arms, keep her moving, for then she would be safe from the others who stepped into the room from time to time, staring at them with forbidding expressions before going out again.

His mother was there, too, nodding approval and passing close to them. Her large breasts were bare, and she displayed them proudly. He commented on how wonderfully firm they were and invited Michelle to rest her head against his mother's swelling, heaving bosom. For then she truly would be safe. But she only smiled at his concern, turning in his arms to execute a difficult dance step. That was when he lost her to the soldiers in white coveralls who rushed in from the next room and tore her out of his grasp.

Waking brought another kind of pain.

First brightness against a filigree of dark lace. Then a face very like his mother's, resonating with the same comforting smile. For an instant he slipped back into the dream, until he realized the face belonged to Joyce.

Then he remembered.

Words began to form in the dryness of his throat, until Joyce held up a hand to quiet him. Joyce was using his distinct actor's tones, reassuring him that there was nothing to worry about. Victor was safe and under the protection of General Bruno.

Victor had been knocked unconscious and had a mild concussion. Moving would cause dizziness and nausea. It was better if Victor remained where he was, which was in the master bedroom of the villa Trager had rented.

"Michelle—is she alive?" Victor said, forcing the words from his throat. The effort caused a vise to clamp over his frontal lobes. A rush of villainous bile contaminated his stomach.

Joyce reached toward the nightstand and handed Victor a glass of clear water he could sip through an angled straw.

Victor sucked on the liquid, which made him feel worse. But his head cleared quickly, and he faced Joyce with the same question filling his gaze.

"Yes, she's alive," Joyce responded quietly. "But we musn't expect too much. She's been pretty badly burned."

"Where have they taken her?" Victor mouthed silently.

"There's a hospital here in Cortina. The general assures me it's a fine facility. He's got a burn specialist coming up from Milan. At the moment she's on life support. If she lives, she'll be pretty badly scarred, I'm afraid. That much is already apparent."

The sound came from somewhere inside Victor. A kind of stifled agony that made Joyce wince and turn away.

When he spoke again, he was not sure Victor was listening, but he spoke, anyway. Telling Victor of his travels and how he had avoided the manhunt so vigorously mounted by their friend Stepinak. How he had made his way into Milan, hitching a ride on a tractor-trailer filled with wine from the Veneto. How he had his meeting with Bruno in the Trattoria Bagutta, a restaurant famous for its walls filled with caricatures.

Bruno was being watched, of course. Just like all of Joyce's old contacts. But the Bagutta was crowded, noisy. Men rubbed elbows over the buffet, selecting delicacies with precise concentration. It was not easy to get a table at the Bagutta, not unless you had the general's status. His watchers undeniably lacked that. And the maître d' was a terrible snob who defended the door against all but his regulars and those influential enough to win a reservation.

Bruno was cordial, but he warned Joyce immediately that he was now one of the hunters. It was an obvious ploy of Stepinak's—using Joyce's own contacts against him. But an old friend from Paris had warned the general that their mutual acquaintance might show up. So Bruno had not been completely surprised by Joyce's call, fortunately made in a code so ancient that none of his eavesdroppers were able to decipher it.

Bruno lunched on an extravagant scalloppini, followed by one of the Bagutta's specialties, tongue and mashed potatoes. Joyce ate more modestly. The wine was strong and red; it put a floor under his stomach. It was a long tale he had to relate, a tale about Paris and Frankfurt and various excursions to Brussels and London.

During its telling, Bruno made noncommittal grunts, his

chin hardly above his napkin, his polished pate reflecting beads of light, accompanying the telling with a series of sympathetic gestures. To his credit his impassive features never expressed astonishment, not even when Joyce mentioned a certain loving couple and their trip to a private chalet outside Cortina.

If Joyce expected a reaction, he was disappointed. Bruno's eyelid barely flickered, even though Joyce had uttered a State secret, known only to the general and a handful of the inner elite. Bruno raised his plump hand and summoned the waiter for two cups of cappuccino and a marvelous Sicilian Cassata, which Joyce declined to share.

Bruno insisted on signing the check, after which he escorted Joyce through the kitchen to a private exit that led them through several narrow turnings to a side alley, where a black Ferrari sedan waited. Bruno never returned to his office, nor to where those observing expected him. He organized the operation by radio from the backseat of the moving car, transferring from there to a helicopter in a military airfield outside the city, where elements of his antiterrorist commando force were being loaded into two monstrous Chinooks.

They spent an anxious hour and a half listening to the weather reports before landing in Bolzano, where the attack force transferred to assault ships. At top speed they skimmed the ice-covered peaks toward the slopes.

Bruno had dropped the operation into a dark box of secrecy, banning all outside transmissions. He was no friend of Stepinak or his ilk and was willing to ignore the directives he had received until Joyce and Victor were well outside his jurisdiction.

Joyce leaned back in his chair and changed expression, his brow notched with irregular furrows like a badly plowed field.

"The KGB will be implicated, of course. There will be that harvest. You're the link. That much is too damn obvious. So we've got to find somewhere to deposit you safely."

Joyce lit a cigarette and stared into the darkness. Victor was no longer in the room with him. The Russian's face was immobile, his eyes focused on some distance Joyce could not penetrate.

Joyce rose and went to the window. It was no longer light. Snow fell in a blinding curtain, obscuring the dark green military vehicles parked below. Joyce had omitted telling Victor of the sentinels Bruno had posted. The general's protection could become something quite different if the situation altered. Joyce had no illusions. In the last analysis, survival was all that mattered. Bruno would have to sacrifice them to save himself. So, in the end, they were all terrorists, even if it was only to their own petty self-interests.

He stared into the tapestry of falling snowflakes. Killian was out there somewhere, a dark force that had to be dealt with. Killian had to be found, alive or dead. Their own survival, both his and Victor's, now depended upon what he would do next.

61

Killian reached three thousand feet just as the sky turned black. Below, darkness had already painted the hollows and was brushing shadow into the fringe of aspen that thinned toward the summit, two thousand feet above.

The weather worsened as he climbed. The trees provided some protection, but once through the last of the timber, the wind clawed around him with incessant fury. He had tied on crampons earlier, when the drifts gave way to bare surfaces of slippery rock. The ice ax provided leverage, but he had to fight the mountain for every foot. The weight of the pack was crippling. He fought the urge to discard some of its contents, but there was nothing he could drop that was not essential.

His arms were numb. He had lost feeling in his hands and feet, but the ball of concentrated fire in his shoulder was increasing. Throbbing, tearing, biting, the pattern of pain varied its attack. Morphine would have relieved the spasm, but it would have aided the voices crying for him to rest. To sleep. To enter the warmth of a dream. So he continued, fighting his body's instinct to survive, driven by his will and the discipline that had long ago formed the core of his existence.

Total darkness now. He began feeling his way, probing with his ax and fingers, inching straight up the limestone face, fighting the rock for balance and leverage. He hoisted his weight against the tearing tendons in his arms and the grinding agony in his shoulder. His mind was fixed on a single thought. A thousand feet more and he could rest. Only a thousand feet more. An eternity.

Sleet froze to stone instantly, in spite of the driving wind. His ax cracked its grip, dug into the porous stone, permitting him to gain another precious meter.

The mountain was unforgiving, spiked with jagged, saw-toothed escarpments that dropped away to nothing on either side. He reached into air, balanced himself, and found frontage, traversing a sheer face until his fingers searched out an ascending ridge. He was a blind man picking out the features of his enemy with frostbitten fingers.

The wind ground its jaws and moaned, crying out like an injured child, ripping along his body, seeking to tear him from the wall and spin him out into the void.

His fingers slid along the slippery surface. He could not find a crevice. The wall beyond was sheer, a sheet of glass. He hammered in a piton, penetrating the mountain like a dentist drilling enamel. He snapped on a carabiner that carried the safety line, tested its hold, and let his weight hang from the steel spike. Raising his knees, he crouched against the stone face, crampons digging against polished rock like jagged teeth. Breathing hard, he drove in another piton and reached out to nibble at the sheer rock face.

He fell—a long, breathless scrape along the wall.

He was jarred to a stop fifteen feet below, suspended by the belay, the rope twisting and swinging like a demented pendulum. His legs scrambled for footing as he fought the terror and the ax of pain that threatened to sever his shoulder. The rope groaned, but the piton held. He forced breath in and out, measuring beats against his panic. Then will replaced instinct, and he drew down on the line and rose, using his body as a counterweight.

When he reached the piton, he eased up on the line, dropping slightly, legs extended. The weight on his back drew him out and down, but he arched against it and reached out, leaning toward his searching fingers. He found a hold and pulled toward it. Hand first, then boot. Then body.

He was on a ridge that widened as it rose. Freeing the carabiner, Killian flattened onto the ascending ledge, which became a stepless ladder reaching upward. The ax bit, and he drew himself higher, one foot at a time. Then meters.

Thirty yards farther on, the rock broke into a shelf that flattened, then angled, to form a long, undulating spine. He was on his feet, bent against the wind and the sandpapering sleet. Facedown and moving, battling the velocity and the agony jutting from his shoulder like a splintered harpoon.

Ten minutes later he found the chain, following it link by link to the climber's hut half buried in a granular drift. It took an endless age to dig his way to the door, on his knees in the snow, tears freezing to his burning cheeks.

There was a gasoline stove inside, rations, water, and blankets. Lighting the stove with frozen hands was another odyssey. Finally it burst into flame, a pinkish glow illuminating rugged, hand-hewn stone, reminding him of the comforting walls of a monastery.

Killian curled into a ball beside the fire, knees drawn to his chin, huddled in blankets, unable to control his shivering. He closed his eyes and sought the sculpted darkness of oblivion.

62

Michelle was barely breathing. Her face was cupped by a transparent mask that fed her sips of oxygen. Only the dial on the meter of the heart-lung machine indicated the actual intake of air.

Victor stood in an outer cubicle that was separated from Michelle by an inch-thick sheet of Plexiglas. An oscilloscope recorded her existence in pulsing waves of light across an opaque green monitor. So little of her was visible amid the metal armatures, the brackets that held the IV, and the plastic tubes leading to and from the overshadowing life-support systems that were housed in gleaming aluminum casings.

Her hair was hidden by a circling bandage that folded across her cheeks and over the bridge of her nose, leaving only nostrils and eyes free. The lids occasionally fluttered, as if the spirit inside somehow sought an exit. The rest of her face was obscured by the oxygen mask. Her body was hidden beneath a tent of sheeting. Only her hand was visible, curled into a tight fist by her side, the skin black and mottled, slick with unguents.

A screen closed off the area, which was visited occasionally by nurses dressed in surgical green, their faces covered by masks. Otherwise there was only the two of them, part of one space they could not share.

It was Joyce who had arranged it or, rather, insisted that Victor be allowed to be at her side. The doctors had done their work. There could be little harm in Victor remaining with her until the end. The general grumbled a little, but in the end, he gave in. What could it matter now?

They went under full escort, three jeeps slogging through slush and mire on the nearly impassable roads. Joyce left Victor in the hospital entrance, waiting until Victor and his guard stepped into an elevator before he returned to the military convoy outside.

Victor remained on his feet as the night ebbed toward dawn, mesmerized by the line of life that beat across the glass screen. Fatigue clawed through him, but he refused to step away from the window. Soldiers entered from time to time, offering coffee or cigarettes, which he gratefully accepted. Their voices penetrated occasionally as they conversed or joked. But he was barely aware of their presence.

Her eyes must have opened minutes before he became aware of them. He was transfixed in a waking reverie, a dream that would never become reality. He brought his gaze to hers and tried to smile, unsure at first if in fact she could actually see him. There was no movement of recognition, but that would have been impossible, considering the mask and the bandages covering her face. Yet he was sure she knew he was there, knew she recognized him.

It lasted no more than a minute, perhaps less, before her lids closed. In the interval, he offered her his dream and felt her reach out to enter it.

Morning revealed the full extent of the storm but did bring them its end. Roads were blocked throughout the valley. The Bolzano converse was impassable. Snow vehicles were out answering a series of emergencies. Hotels were without electricity, whole hillsides without phone service. Only the weather forecast held any promise of relief. It was to come late the same afternoon.

Bruno now had his reinforcements. Contingents from the mountain regiment fought their way into the valley throughout the night and were in position by mid-morning. It freed the general's own force to begin conducting a house-to-house search of the entire valley. Roadblocks were in place at each point of entry, from Mt. Paina in the north, to Lozzo and Auronzo in the east. Anyone entering or leaving without his knowledge would have to scale the peaks, which in this weather would be an impossible feat, inspired by lunacy. If there was one thing Killian was not, it was a lunatic. Whatever Killian was doing had been calculated long before.

The general had drawn a double ring of security around the Royals' chalet, blocking the road to all but military traffic as far as Perarola. The military airfield at Bolzano was on standby alert. As soon as the weather cleared, he would convoy the royal party by helicopter. It was a sixty-eight-mile journey over peaks famous for their dangerous down drafts, but he was unwilling to risk a journey over land, especially over a route that would take them through a series of narrow mountain passes where a single man could remain hidden long enough to launch an attack.

The possibilities clicked through the intricate circuitry of the general's intelligence. Killian had either eluded his net during the storm and escaped on one of the roads leading south and east, or he had somehow found shelter and was therefore close by and capable of anything.

A gut instinct warned him against considering any but the worst-case scenario. But as the morning progressed and reports came in from his units, the possibility that Killian or any of his men were still in the area began to diminish reasonably.

Bruno remained at his post in the gate house of the Royals' chalet, sipping innumerable cups of cappuccino from a hastily commandeered café, which also supplied boxes of succulent Viennese pastries. His eyes never left the huge wall map collected from the city hall in Cortina, upon which every road and habitation in the area was depicted, along with elevations, slopes, lifts, forests, and mountain trails.

Starting with those closest to the chalet, each habitation was circled in blue after having been scoured by his search teams. By mid-morning, the area around the chalet from the tiny hamlet of Chiapuza, to a distance of five miles toward Vallesina, had been secured. Military vehicles were making regular sweeps of the roadway he had directed to be cleared, creating a web of movement around the security area extending in a horseshoe whose ends reached up along the Sorapiss and deep into the Valle d'Oran. It was a reassuring display of efficiency, and the general was beginning to feel optimistic that Killian had not survived the night. It was a feeling that quickly and dangerously infected his staff.

Only Joyce was doubtful.

He had joined the general an hour after midnight, after dropping Victor off at the hospital. He remained a dark specter, haunting the command post with his hawklike glance, which caught what had been missed with an annoying precision. But Bruno tolerated his presence, even if it was driving his aides to distraction. He urged patience. They would not have to concern themselves with his presence very much longer. Discreetly he sent one of his staff to make arrangements for an Army helicopter that would ferry Joyce and the Russian to Trieste. As soon as the Royals were safely free of

Italian soil, the general would have Joyce and Victor moved as far out of his jurisdiction as possible.

Shortly before dawn, a call came from Rome warning him that Stepinak's hunters were collecting around Milan.

Bruno had done some hard bargaining with his superiors, getting them to agree to a head start of twenty-four hours. He owed Joyce that much, at least. He would soon owe him a great deal more.

63

Killian jerked painfully awake, his eyes blinded with the brilliant glare of morning.

Pain etched itself into his back, down through his legs and stabbed deep into the flesh of his shoulder. He groaned aloud, turning onto his side and fighting to gain his feet. The fire was out. Chill air was cutting through the stone chamber. His body made its usual demands.

Killian staggered toward the door and pulled it open, jerking hard against the blocking snow. Light streamed through the crack, a shimmering band just clearing the peaks. Darkness still filled the long distance below. He cleared a space and pissed into the blinding waste. No longer sleet, the snow was the texture of yielding fur.

He spent an hour of housekeeping, emptying the knapsack of the tent and its tackle and reducing the medical kit to the barest essentials after rebandaging his wound and giving himself a shot of morphine. He would discard the weight of pitons and carabiners as he went down.

A meaty broth boiled in a plastic pouch revived and warmed him. He dozed afterward, nested within the scrawl of blankets. He loaded the radio after picking up a weather transmission through the squeal of static. Heavy as it was, he would need it later. It would become the lifeline to his target and his escape afterward, though that possibility might no longer be a reality.

By eight, he was out and moving.

The descent was easier, at least in the initial stages, because of the series of chains fixed into the stone to guide mountaineers over the more dangerous traverses. Ironically the gentler slopes now became his problem. Blanketed by snow and mist, he could not be sure of what they hid, whether there was solid footing beneath or a bridge over space through which he would fall to certain death.

He went along at a crawl, using the ice ax as a probe, the way a surgeon hunts for shrapnel buried deep in flesh. He descended a hundred yards, then another hundred, carefully pacing himself and resting where he could, with his back to the driving wind, crouched in a tight human ball.

A thousand meters. Two. He expected to meet the treeline, but he traveled another two hundred meters before he realized he was lost. He must have strayed somehow, thought he was descending when in fact he was moving in a diagonal that could take him miles toward the other side of the mountain.

Exhausted, he struggled toward an outcrop and hollowed out a space on the far side, away from the wind. The snow formed an embracing warmth, and he closed his eyes. He could die here as easily as anywhere else, safely pocketed within the womb of yielding matter, white as a surplice.

He was serving Mass. His mother's face beamed up at him from the pews. Proud, she was, though he had tried to wean her from that sin. But he felt as radiant, as proud, holding his arms aloft, hands filled with the gleaming gold chalice. He joined his voice with the others, chanting its beauty to the heavens. Kyrie eleison . . . Kyrie eleison . . . Kyrie—

"*Attenzione . . . attenzione . . .*"

Perhaps he would have died there on that cold pinnacle of unyielding stone that pointed toward a blank, unspeaking heaven. But a voice he did not recognize, an alien voice in an alien tongue that spitefully sought his death, somehow saved him.

"*Attenzione . . . tutto Carabiniere . . .*"

It came over the radio, left on purposely to pick up a frequency. And now, his head lowered almost to his chest, he heard a voice. Distant, almost inaudible, but drawing him back to life on a fine thread of language.

He fought off a final urge to sink beneath the wave and rose, still groggy. Dazed, he staggered a few feet before the cold air slapped him into full consciousness. Pausing, he withdrew the radio and listened. They were broadcasting at regular intervals. Army patrols, he realized. Conducting a house-to-house search. Sweeping the roads and calling in their checkpoints and map coordinates.

Killian held the radio outstretched, aiming it where the signal was strongest. That would be his guide. Homing in on the signal, he followed it down the mountain toward his unwitting targets, ensconced in comfort and safety two thousand feet below.

64

Joyce came for Victor at noon.

He found the Russian maintaining his vigil alone in the glass-walled chamber beyond which Michelle struggled with existence, still connected to the complex array of machinery charged with the duty of keeping her alive.

Victor's face was sallow and unshaven, deeply pocketed with shadow, looking older than the date stamped on his passport, the gray in his hair more evident.

Joyce took a place opposite on one of the tubular steel chairs that adorned the bare cell. Victor slumped into the other, accepting a cigarette from the crumpled package Joyce held out to him.

They lit up and smoked in silence. Joyce watched the continuous line of light, streaming in a wave of monotonous motion across the small screen suspended above Michelle's gurney.

"Bruno's going to fly them out in about three hours, or as soon as the weather lifts," Joyce commented in a monotone. Lines of fatigue had etched themselves into his face. But his eyes remained alert, filled with their usual expression of watchfulness and sympathy.

"And what happens to her?" Victor asked, his eyebrows raised.

It took Joyce a moment to answer. "I could try to arrange something."

"You mean, if she lives? Or will they inject a bubble into her veins as soon as we leave?"

"*If* she lives"—and Joyce stressed the first word—"I may be able to have her disappear. Bruno would rather there were no complications. She would become an embarrassment. There would have to be a trial. But I can't promise anything. We're not in a position to bargain. Not just yet. The party's not over."

"What happens to you when it is?" Victor asked.

"You mean to us, don't you?"

Victor shrugged, forcing the same weary smile Joyce remembered from their conversation in the Paris café. It was the expression of a man who no longer cared.

"All right, to us," Victor said finally, reaching over to stub out his cigarette.

"We'll be flown out of here. To Trieste, I think. At the moment we're still insurance. Afterward we'll become a liability. He'll give us his good offices and a head start. We might get a day, but that's all. There's a great deal of pressure coming down just now."

"And we go where?"

Joyce shrugged. "There are places."

Victor shook his head. "For you, perhaps. Not for me. It is no longer feasible for me here."

"And Alexi? Is he no longer feasible?"

Victor stared at Joyce, but his expression was unfathomable. "I don't know what you're talking about."

"I'm talking about you and your son. About trying to save him."

"And just how do you expect me to accomplish that?"

"There is a way. A place where you would be safe. Where even they could not penetrate."

Victor laughed, a short, harsh sound. "Certainly. I could sneak back into Moscow and give the KGB the pleasure of slitting my throat."

"Perhaps," Joyce said softly. "Perhaps we could arrange just that."

Victor's reaction was to blink in stupefied amazement. Incredibly, Joyce was dead serious.

65

The descent was perfect.

By noon, Killian had made his way to the treeline, where he discarded the pitons and his ice ax and freed his boots of the heavy crampons. He unzipped the weapon bag, drew out the pair of short skis, and extended the collapsible poles.

He was a shadow on the slope, undetectable in his white coveralls, a breath of streamlined motion cutting his way downslope between clumps of aspen and standing plantations of fir and pine. The wind was dying off. The snowfall was not as dense now, making for increased visibility.

At a thousand feet the slopes gave way to dense stands of heavy forest. The terrain was chopped with granite spines, making further skiing impossible. He halted in a cul-de-sac of towering fir and hid the skis and poles within the copse of brush, then thrashed his way downslope, thigh-deep in powder.

The going was an ordeal. He fought his way across the hollows between rough plinths of slippery rock. He was breathing harder. Sliding sometimes, propelled into drifts out of which he struggled like an exhausted swimmer.

Another five feet and the forest thinned again. He should have been in sight of the chalet, but he could not be seen for the drifting cloud of mingled snow and mist. The storm was falling off. But visibility was almost zero. The cover stubbornly refused to lift. Killian continued down, the radio turned to the central frequency.

Another five hundred feet. He was sliding rapidly over an undulating slope, his own weight and gravity taking him down. A stone marker stood dead ahead. Killian ducked, checking his speed. The pillar held a coat of arms, frosted white, like the decoration on a wedding cake. He had reached the border of the estate.

Kneeling, he shut off the radio. He slung the weapon's bag off his shoulder and pulled out his assault rifle, turning on the infrared sight. He slung the bag over his shoulder again and skirted the marker.

TO KILL A KING

He was entering the grounds.

His shoulder began throbbing, or had it been throbbing for some time? He could no longer tell. The nerve endings were on fire. But he dared not take any more painkillers. Exhaustion fed on his strength, nibbling deep into the fiber of his tendons. But he kept on.

Another hundred yards. He heard the sound of movement in the trees to his right. He raised the sight and detected the ghostly shapes of three soldiers patrolling on foot.

Killian slipped into the trees opposite, following the patrol in his sight, until they disappeared between the timber. Then he moved. The ground was leveling. He zigzagged between the trunks, heard another patrol, and held them in his sights. But they slipped away in the opposite direction and never even reached him.

He started forward and slipped, cascading headfirst into snow that gave way to smooth stone beneath him. He slid several feet until he reached bottom. Sitting up, he realized he was in a drainage culvert, a deep, V-shaped trough of smooth stone leading directly into the heart of the estate.

Killian scrambled along the bottom of the snow-filled culvert, his head well below the level of sight from the ground above.

Another hundred yards and the culvert was joined by another reaching branch of smooth stone. He made a rapid calculation and followed it toward a sluice gate that impeded his way.

Crawling on his belly, he scraped his way along the embankment, peering over the edge. Through the mist he could see the rough outline of a building. In a moment he made out the silhouette of a stone barn.

He was out of the culvert and scrambling toward the whitewashed stucco wall dead ahead. Reaching it, he paused, rifle ready, breathing hard and waiting. But there was no movement, no sound, except the slow sawing of the wind.

Killian inched along the wall. At the corner he dropped to one knee and peered around it.

A stone wall faced him twenty yards distant. Beside it, firewood had been neatly piled beneath a tarp. A four-wheeled farm wagon stood alongside. Then a narrow door.

Killian moved, skirting the wagon and dropping to one knee beside the door. It was latched but unlocked. He slipped inside.

The interior was unlit. It smelled of dry pine and wet straw. A tractor faced double doors at the far end, through which glimmers of gray light splintered. Implements of various kinds were neatly stacked in bins. There were two windows, both shuttered. A narrow wooden staircase led to the floor above.

Killian crossed the wooden floor, which was laid over with a fine covering of straw. Pointing the weapon ahead of him, he began to climb.

Above was a loft, bare except for more straw and bits of discarded metal. There was a window at the far end, also shuttered.

Killian crossed the floor. Against the far wall, almost unseen in the darkness, was a series of wooden slats nailed into the wall. Killian glanced up. It took a few moments to detect the carefully fitted door that had been cut into the wooden ceiling.

Killian mounted the slats and raised the butt of the rifle. It took a grunting effort, but it gave. Killian climbed into the crawl space beneath the slanting roof. It was not high enough to stand in, but there was a tiny vent at the far end.

Killian slouched toward the vent, his backpack scraping across the ceiling beams. He crouched down and peered out.

Through the horizontal slats he could just make out the towers of the chalet two hundred yards distant. Two military-green armored cars mounted with machine guns played sentry at either end of the house. Dark shapes broke through the curtain of blowing sleet, moving back and forth before the shuttered windows.

Killian's eye was caught by the bulldozer parked beside a half-track.

He had almost failed to notice it in the mist, but the bulldozer had smoothed a place in the snow, a landing pad for a helicopter.

Killian's pulse began hammering. Excitedly he raised the sight to his eye and measured off the distance. The center of the pad was less than one hundred yards from his perch, directly in his line of fire.

Killian slipped the pack from his shoulders, inching back to the opening and refitting the heavy wooden slab back into the square. He returned to the vent and began feeling around the frame. It was secured by screws spaced two inches apart.

He found the tool kit in the side compartment of his

knapsack. Within minutes he had worked the screws halfway off. It would take less than a minute to remove the vent, leaving a perfect gun port, a perfect zone of fire.

Killian unzipped the weapon's bag and brought out the firing tube, then the nozzle, and finally the mount and sight. He had trained himself to assemble the rocket launcher in the dark. Each piece clicked perfectly into place.

He lay the launcher on the bag, removed the six shells, and stood them on their ends beside the vent. Then he hunkered down to wait for the snow to stop falling.

66

It was the general who arranged the call to Moscow.

Bruno had resisted at first, but that was before Joyce applied his considerable powers of persuasion. In the end, the general was convinced that it was a wise course of action that would alleviate responsibility and remove any danger to himself.

Of course, there was risk.

The call might be traced, involving the general in even worse embarrassment. But as he said finally, "You can't make an omelet unless you break eggs."

So the call was put through, relayed through a special switchboard in Vienna and from there to Moscow Central, using a code that would make no sense to a cryptographer but would be understood nevertheless.

It took several minutes to locate Major-General Vanova, a few more before General Bruno designed to come to the phone. Joyce imagined the expression of perplexity that must have flooded Vanova's pudgy features, an expression that would be quickly replaced with one of suspicion and cold calculation. But the message also held a meaning that General Bruno would find irresistible and which would cause him to assume an equal risk and pick up the receiver.

Joyce did not bother with greeting. What he said was short and cryptic. General Bruno merely listened. He answered with a pause at the end of which he uttered a single word. *Yes*.

Thus it was that Major-General Vanova of the KBG canceled all his appointments for the next two days and ordered a special flight whose destination was to remain open until he was on board.

Successfully concluded, the phone call sent certain members of Bruno's staff scurrying. Vehicles were hastily readied. The roads were passable enough. Besides, arrangements to fly the royal party to Bolzano would take all of Bruno's airborne resources. After all, one could never be too careful.

Joyce smiled and bid the general farewell. But it was not to

TO KILL A KING

be. He had just settled himself into the seat beside the driver when an aide rushed out of the house through whirpools of falling snow.

Killian had been located.

67

The Mercedes was a festering hulk.

Twisted hunks of metal had been strewn through the trees, along with bits of shattered glass, glinting like a field of diamonds in the dirty snow.

A row of military and police vehicles lined the shoulder of the narrow road, which was more a trail than an actual byway. An orange bulldozer was stalled farther up after butting its way along the twisting, shattered ribbon of asphalt.

Bruno and Joyce were guided along by several officers in full battlegear. One hurriedly explained that the trail was not on their maps and led to an unused quarry. Snow had been trampled into a kind of path that wound between sleet-laden pines toward daggers of spiny granite that humped through the drifts like a school of migrating whales.

The area was being picked through by security officers carrying clipboards and large plastic bags into which they dropped bits of the charred fallout. They were met at the bottom of the trail by a plump major in a black beret who saluted smartly, then presented his back. The beret trailed two long ribbons that descended halfway down his back, which they followed directly to the body.

The remains were covered with a camouflage poncho, which looked somewhat incongruous against the snow. The major bent and treated them to the sight of a human body, burned beyond recognition.

The blast had seared the flesh of the hands into a single mass of black flesh and exposed bone. The face was nonexistent. The view produced a professional silence, broken when Bruno waved his hand and the major considerately replaced the covering.

Bruno started off on a circuit of the wreckage with Joyce alongside and the major pumping a step behind. The major obligingly detailed his belief that the terrorists had discovered the road and used it for shelter during the storm, probably planning to make a getaway when the weather broke. The tail pipe must have become choked with snow, so that starting the car somehow ignited the explosives contained in the trunk or in a compartment beneath the trunk and therefore in dangerous proximity to the gas tank. Killian had been incinerated instantly.

Bruno nodded at the telling, making little daggers at the sides of his mouth. He straightened perceptibly, the strain of the last twenty-four hours visibly easing. He completed his tour and paused again at the body, staring down at the poncho for a few moments. He glanced up at the sky, now visibly clearing, and strode away briskly to where a soldier stood beside a field radio.

The general snapped out a command and was handed the receiver. Bruno shouted several orders, dropped the phone, and strode back to where Joyce was kneeling beside the body, examining the corpse beneath one edge of the poncho.

"Transport is on its way. Bolzano is being alerted. The weather is clearing. They can be cleared for takeoff in less than an hour."

Bruno turned and headed back to his transport.

Joyce dropped the poncho, rose, but did not follow.

Bruno halted at the door to his car, facing Joyce with a look of annoyance. "What's the matter?"

"Roger Killian is six feet three inches tall."

Bruno glanced down at the exposed corpse. His expression was quizzical. "What are you saying?"

"That this is not him. Roberts is still unaccounted for. Victor claims he put a bullet in him. His body is missing."

"You want us to measure the body?"

"Why not?"

They faced each other. Bruno's expression was transfixed by a scowl. For an instant it looked as if he were going to duck through the open door of the car, but the scowl gave way to annoyance, and he shouted to the major, who trotted back to the body, signaling to a team of officers standing nearby. A tape measure was brought. As Joyce and the general watched, the body was carefully measured.

The major stood up. "Six feet. One inch."

Bruno and Joyce exchanged glances.

"Is it possible for the body to be reduced in size due to the incineration?" Bruno snapped at the major.

The officer considered a moment. "Possible," he said,

but without much conviction. It was obvious the general wanted this body to be the man he sought.

"Roberts was about six, six-one," Joyce commented.

"What are you saying?" Bruno cried. "We've conducted a house-to-house search. How could he have survived without shelter?"

"I don't know. But add it up. Roberts was shot. How could he have survived? Where's his body?"

"Your Russian claimed to have shot Killian as well. If that is Roberts," he declared, pointing to the corpse, "then where is Killian?"

Joyce did not respond for a moment. "Consider this: Victor is a trained agent. We must believe he shot Killian. But, by his own admission, he did not stop to check if Killian was actually dead. Victor was interested in only one thing. Finding Michelle and rescuing her. Suppose Killian was hit by a bullet and knocked unconscious. Suppose it was only a flesh wound. He could have dragged Roberts back down here."

"But why?" Bruno added impatiently.

"I don't know. It's possible Roberts was still alive. Perhaps Killian thought he could save him. Get out when the weather broke . . ." Joyce paused, letting his voice trail off.

"What are you thinking?" Bruno questioned.

"If Killian had a radio, he would have known the storm was predicted to end today. He would have heard your patrols transmitting. He knew he was being hunted. All the roads out of the valley were blocked. Escape was impossible. But it was also impossible for his targets. The royal party never would have chanced a flight out in that storm."

Bruno stared at him skeptically. "So what are you implying?"

"That Killian could have set the detonator to go off at approximately the time the storm was predicted to end, hoping to draw your men here in the belief that they had found him. Security would have been relaxed, giving him a second chance."

"Fine," Bruno stated with annoyance; "So where does he hide when the temperature drops to twenty, no, thirty below? He bandages his wound and goes off to climb the mountain."

Joyce shrugged. "Why not? He spent six years in the Andes making war against three separate countries. And not one of them ever found him."

The look Bruno flashed at Joyce was one he would remember the rest of his life.

68

Ragged wisps of cloud hung directly above the black slate towers of the chalet, like medieval banners torn in battle. Below and farther on, the entire valley was spread in an undulating ocean of white, broken only by spires of frozen stone.

Shafts of platinum and silver speared through the cloud bank that rose like a bedraggled curtain, exposing spears and ridges of ice capped in shimmering alloys of color.

Soaring above them came three droning dots of concentrated motion.

Helicopters.

Two gunships and a monstrous Chinook with double sets of windows and twin sixty-foot rotors.

Killian dropped his field glasses and snapped into action. He eased off the safety on the Kalashnikov and leaned it against a beam beside the vent, setting two dull pewter clips alongside the stock.

He raised the rocket launcher, sliding it forward to on load an armor-piercing shell designed to incinerate the crew inside a tank.

The copters came in quickly, sweeping toward him over the glistening snowfields like a fast-stepping troika and climbing hard toward the chalet.

Killian picked up the orange-handled screwdriver. He had four Phillips heads to loosen. It took less than a minute to slip the vent out of its frame and place it on the floor beside him. Then he edged backward to the trapdoor and drew it open. Once the rocket was fired, he would have perhaps three or four minutes to drop to the floor below and try for the drainage culverts before the security forces could organize.

He returned to the vent opening. The two gunships hovered in the distance as the big khaki-colored Chinook came in over the towers and dropped belly-first toward the circle of hard-packed snow upon which security men in black berets waved their arms to guide the landing. The roar obliterated all other sound. Killian narrowed his eyes as the updraft swept over him, transporting bits of ice crystal and sleet.

The Chinook came down in a slow-rolling thunder, scattering clouds of ice and powder.

Killian cursed softly. Blowing snow obscured his view of the chalet. He lifted the rocket launcher and made a slight adjustment in the sight, then brought the cup of metal that acted as a stock to his shoulder and sighted through the cross hairs.

Troops in battle gear rushed through an arched doorway facing the helicopter pad.

The Chinook's wheels crunched into the snowfield. Two crewmen in green coveralls and helmets jumped down from the main hatch. A ladder snapped into place. Each crewman grasped the angle of rungs, bent against the powerful wash of air from the enormous rotors.

A pair of black-bereted officers came first, followed by the royal party. They came in a scramble, civilian coats over the women's parkas, heads lowered, shielding their faces against the propeller wash and the biting cloud of surface sleet. First the brilliant robin's-egg blue of the prince's ski parka, then the princess's red ski suit.

Killian let his finger slide over the curving guard and onto the trigger.

Motion blurred across the scope.

Killian jerked his eye away. One of the armored vehicles rumbled to a halt, shielding the helicopter and partially obliterating the boarding party.

Killian could hear his pulse throbbing in his temples. He could not risk a shot. Not with snow flying and the track in the way. He would have to wait until the copter left the ground.

Gloved hands reached through the skelter of white, stretching through the hatch from inside. The princess first, then, one by one, the other women. The men next, the prince holding back but being nudged inside ahead of the others. Black berets after them.

Crewmen came last of all, legs scrambling up into the opening. The ladder was raised, the hatch slammed shut. Soldiers scattered. The rotors revved furiously. The Chinook rose, flouncing powder like a dowager shaking her skirts, wheels shaking free of the deep powder of the snowfield.

Killian raised his weapon, tearing off his glove and clenching his fist in three quick squeezes. He brought the stock against his shoulder and aimed through the sight, inhaling sharply.

He counted.

One.

Both wheels were off the ground. The Chinook arched back, belly toward him, ascending past the windows of the second story.

Two.

Climbing quickly, the Chinook rose in a tight arc, passing the medieval tower pointed like a bishop's miter against the mottled blue-and-gray sky.

Killian aimed right between the two huge white numbers painted across the underbelly. It was a child's shot.

Three.

He squeezed, and the backwash on the rocket jarred him off-balance.

They tore inside the grounds in a squeal of rubber, skidding sharply on the ice-sheathed driveway.

Joyce bent to watch the huge Chinook as it mounted the decorative filigree of iron surmounting the slate roof of the chalet.

The helicopter rose, dragonlike, soaring above the dignity of medieval towers, then froze in midair, struck by the shock of the explosion. It burst into a flaming orange ball and dropped, weightless, and out of sight beyond the slate roof.

The sound of the crash came an instant later, making them sick and deaf in the same instant.

The car was headed in a direct line toward the front of the chalet. Security troops poured outside, racing toward the rear of the house. The driver cut sharply, following the racing rush of motion, rounding the side of the house just as the Chinook tanks exploded in a swirling ball of fire.

The car skidded to a stop. Bruno and the others piled out, rushing toward the crashing metal hulk. Only Joyce held back.

He stared at the mountain rising behind the chalet, mantled in impenetrable mist.

Joyce turned and raced away from the wreckage, and from the rush of desperate men tearing toward the holocaust of flame. He ran in the opposite direction around toward the mountain Killian had scaled in a blinding storm and to which he would return to make his escape.

69

He did not wait for the tanks to go up. Killian had the assault rifle in his hand and was through the trapdoor while the sound of the exploding Chinook resounded in his ears.

He half slid, half jumped down the ladder to the main floor, avoiding the door he had come through, racing instead to the shuttered window in the rear.

He unbolted the latch and swung the shutters back.

The window faced away from the carnage, toward the woods and the culverts beyond.

Killian went through headfirst, landing on cushioning layers of snow outside. He rolled to his feet, the barrel facing forward, both hands on the rifle.

But there was no movement. It was a winter landscape, painted a hundred years before.

He moved into the stillness, across the straw-filled yard, dodging between hillocks of piled firewood and ancient two-wheeled wains, protecting him from view.

He skidded toward the stone wall just as the tanks went up, flaming the sky with a flash of incandescence.

He pulled himself over the wall, using both arms, feeling a jolt of pain as he slid to the other side. He ignored the jarring agony as his boots hit a pile of stones. Falling facedown into the snow, he pushed himself to his feet, sprinting between the narrow aspen trunks toward the culverts beyond.

He had not counted on this chance or the possibility of escape. It came now as a gift.

He could retrace his way back upslope, hiding in the thick timber until nightfall. Then he could retrieve his ice ax and other climbing gear and rescale the peak.

He had cold-weather gear and enough food and medicine. If he could just keep on going . . . if his body did not betray him. He had done it before, avoided capture when it seemed impossible.

TO KILL A KING

Ahead was an open patch of white. The culverts were just beyond. He made out the dark edge of stone against the snow.

He could avoid it and slip around, using the trees as cover. But that meant time—each second—was precious, while the security force was still off-balance, confused, and trying to figure out where the rocket had come from.

He headed into the open without breaking stride.

The crunch of his boots echoed in his ears. Only ten yards more and he would be at the culverts.

The wind rose. His vision blurred as the freezing air hit his eyes.

A dog was racing toward him . . . black as death, a dead infant clutched within its slavering jaws.

"Killian!"

He wheeled without stopping, swinging the assault rifle toward the sound in a blur of motion.

Joyce raised his weapon and fired.

Killian saw his killer an instant before he fell, a dark shape silhouetted between the trees against the glare of white snow. A man with only one arm.

He splashed facedown into the drift, through the surface crust, and into the soft powder beneath.

Joyce started toward him at a walk, the gun held straight out and down at a slight angle to the ground, so that if he had to shoot again, it could be done quickly. Killian's legs were bent, pushing his body against the snow. The Kalashnikov was several feet in front of him, lying sideways in deeper snow. But it was not the gun Killian was trying to reach.

He turned onto his back almost as Joyce reached him. One hand was raised; the other was pressed into his chest, as if trying to hold back the bright flow of blood that seeped onto the white of his coveralls.

Joyce stood over him, legs planted, weapon poised, watching as Killian raised his arm toward his face, then pointed at the center of his chest before it froze in midair and fell lifeless across his body.

Joyce knelt and lay the automatic beside him. He slipped his hand under his armpit to remove his glove. He took Killian's limp hand in his, moving it to complete the genuflection, before he placed it back across his chest.

Joyce got to his feet and started back across the sunlit clearing, back into the darkness between the trees.

70

Bruno decided to take the Royals out by car, after all.

Joyce could not blame him, not after what had happened to the Chinook. Felzarego was already open. The road to Bolzano was clear. They would travel in a convoy, shadowed by the attack helicopters.

Joyce remained in a distant room when the prince went down to pay his respect to the men killed in the Chinook. Most could not be recognized. They lay in a row behind the house, covered by green canvas tarpaulins.

The prince appeared, flanked by British security officers toting automatic weapons. There had been some objection to the prince coming out at all, but he had insisted.

They were met by Bruno and several officers, including the plump major from the quarry. The prince went first, leading the others around the row of bodies, walking solemnly a step ahead of Bruno, while the rest of the party continued behind him.

Five minutes later the prince and princess were safely inside an armored troop carrier.

Joyce stood at a second-story window and watched the convoy set out.

Bruno was at the head of the column in a dark green staff car. The royal party had been distributed among several vehicles, spaced between security troops packed into armored trucks and two-ton lorries. The plump major blew a whistle, and the convoy set out, rolling down the drive, away from the chalet, and disappeared, one after the other, behind the stone fence that bordered the Great Dolomite Highway.

When the last vehicle rumbled past, Joyce stepped away from the window and slumped into a leather armchair. He pulled out a pack of cigarettes and lit one, extending his legs and feeling the weariness assault bone and muscle.

Poor Bruno. He felt guilty that Joyce was unable to meet the royal party and be thanked appropriately, for it was Joyce who had seen through Killian's elaborate charade involving

Roberts and the white Mercedes. It was Joyce who had suggested the last-minute switch that substituted security personnel for the royal party in an effort to flush Killian out.

Joyce must not blame himself that so many brave young men had perished, Bruno insisted. After all, who could have predicted that Killian would be armed with such devastating armor-piercing rockets? They had only expected automatic weapons fire. In any case, they died heroes' deaths and would be appropriately decorated and buried with full military honors.

No, Joyce neither expected nor wanted thanks. Just as he neither expected nor wanted forgiveness. That decision was for a God who had long ago given up his existence.

They rode into Trieste just before dawn, driving down from the mountains in time to catch the shimmer of morning incandescence across a brooding Adriatic, before Bruno had them sealed up in a two-star hotel on a gloomy street behind the piazza.

Joyce made no argument over the accommodations. He and Victor had been given adjoining rooms sporting steel shutters behind heavy velvet portieres. The beds were good, and room service brought anything you ordered.

Joyce had a full breakfast and a large pot of hot coffee. Victor remained alone in his room.

Joyce permitted himself two hours of sleep before his meeting with the major-general. He dropped into a dreamless void almost instantly and was awakened by a call reminding him of the time.

Vanova was waiting on the terrace of a cheap roadside café just over the Yugoslav border. He sat alone at an indoor table alongside the removable glass doors reserved for better weather. The terrace was above the road, commanding a view of dirty, glass-topped tour buses and double-teamed diesels fouling the air as they made their single-file run for Belgrade.

The major-general was big-shouldered and bearish, a perfect Kremlin caricature of the old school, complete with bushy brows and a long upper lip. He wore an ill-fitting topcoat and a fedora that needed reblocking. Joyce imagined he was never out of uniform.

Joyce took the seat opposite at the marble-topped table, which had an awkward way of becoming unbalanced on the irregular tiles of the terrace. A waiter danced over without being called, and Joyce ordered a Strega.

"And so," Vanova uttered ominously, "you've gotten me down here for a change."

"And change always brings new possibilities," Joyce added with a smile. "Such is our world."

"Perhaps." The Russian grunted. "Some changes are for the better. Others for the worse. Time will tell."

"For those who manage to survive."

The major-general raised the heavy eyebrow above his watery blue eyes. "You wanted a conversation."

And so he did. But Joyce waited until the glass with its pale yellow syrup was placed before him and the waiter was safely out of earshot before he did his own little song and shuffle.

This was not the Joyce of the sympathetic nod and understanding gaze. This Joyce spoke in crystal phrases, clear and translucent. Nothing vague, nothing ambiguous. Blunt and precise. The Joyce of the famous brick wall.

As he listened, the major-general twisted the glass in his thick peasant's hands. His nails had been carefully manicured, which contrasted sharply with the unruly matting of dark hair sprouting from each knuckle. Occasionally he took a sip of the powerful liquor in his tumbler, but his face remained impassive. He was a good poker player, the major-general. But then, Joyce knew that quite well. He and the major-general had played their long-distance games over a space of decades. What Joyce offered now substantially increased the possibilities.

Of course, Joyce offered only sketches, outlines that would have to be filled in later, when trust had been mutually established. But Joyce dropped a name here and one there, all of them rivals in the major-general's Moscow directive. All of them jockeying for position in the fluidity of the new situation, maneuvering for the plums bound to come the KGB's way with a new man in the saddle—a man who had been dependent on the patronage of Andropov and the KGB. A man with a reputation for repaying his debts.

Yes, Joyce remarked, it must be a fascinating time for the major-general. So filled with new horizons, so fraught with dangers. And it was to that theme that Joyce continually returned.

For they were old investigators of each other's motivations. Each knew the other's weaknesses and forgivable ambitions. There was no shame between them. Joyce spoke frankly

—more frankly than he should have, perhaps. But he wanted assurances. He wanted a deal.

By the end of the second glass, they got down to the quid, as Blake might have said. There was a good bit of haggling. Joyce had to promise dossiers, a fuller treatment than he normally would have provided. It meant compromising several important sources. But those fences could be mended. The major-general, on the other hand, had to prepare a dossier of his own, proving beyond a shadow of a doubt that Victor Kirov was not a defector to the West but an important double agent. The dossier would prove that Victor's defection had been arranged by the KGB in order to mislead a highly placed American agent.

"Highly placed?" the major-general said with a malicious grin, inclining his head in Joyce's direction.

Joyce answered with a smile of his own. It was not much of a price when you came down to it. Only a matter of reputation. A reputation he no longer owned.

71

Victor was in his room when Joyce returned, a half-empty bottle of vodka at his elbow. Cigarettes filled a large copper ashtray. A meal had been ordered but not eaten, resting on a wheeled table in the corner. If he were drunk, he was holding it pretty damned well.

Joyce took a seat in the armchair beside a mahogany writing table. He reached over and picked up a glass from the room service table and held it out to Victor, who tipped the bottle and poured.

"There is the barest possibility that I have saved your ass," Joyce said, raising his glass to toast himself before he swallowed.

Victor's face framed a sardonic smile.

"You have a serious problem, my friend. A delusion, the headshrinkers would call it. You seriously believe there is still something about me that is worth saving. I find that more than self-delusion. I find that positively pitiful."

Joyce leaned back and stared at Victor. "I'm beginning to believe you're right. Fuck you, anyway. I'm doing it for your son. For Alexi. This is for him." Joyce made another gesture with the glass. But Victor did not respond. His eyes had lost their brilliance.

"Ah, Alexi. Of course, Alexi. Who does not even know his father's voice. Who would pass me on the street and not turn his head."

"Until you arrive and become a father to him," Joyce said pointedly.

Victor grinned, tilting his head devilishly. "So you think, my believing friend. So you have given up reality and finally become a priest, after all."

"We're flying out of here at six. Be ready."

"Sorry, but you'll have to manage alone, old friend."

Joyce put down his glass and stood. His eyes had lost their tolerance.

"There's absolutely no chance for her, Victor. You know

that. You can't go back, even if there was a possibility she'd survive. Not unless you want to sacrifice the boy. And I don't see the point in that, do you?''

Joyce waited for an answer, but he received none. Victor was no longer drunk. He never had been drunk, Joyce realized. Victor must have fought hard for oblivion in the hours Joyce had been away but had been unable to find it. He never would be able to find it, Joyce now realized. That, too, was part of his curse.

Joyce went into his own chamber and closed the door. There was nothing more he could do for Victor. What he needed to accomplish now could only be for himself. He no longer had a right to dream for others.

72

It ended as it began, in the dark stillness of a Finnish forest.

There was no wind, only an intense, numbing cold that bit into the exposed flesh of their faces. They stood within a dark shelter of forest, between trunks as slender as pencils, both silent, enclosed within separate capsules of thought.

From where they stood, both Joyce and Victor could see the border beyond, marked by a double row of wire-mesh fencing and plowed earth bisecting a long, rolling meadow covered with a frozen layer of ice. There was a watchtower in the distance on the other side of the meadow, beyond the fencing, rising from the thick stand of aspen on the other side.

A narrow hem of discolored earth, impacted with the cast of tire treads, separated trees and meadow. It curved around the edge of the standing timber and disappeared out of sight. Another bit of trail branched off from the first, cutting directly across the meadow and toward a break in the double fence. It was a kind of maze, only wide enough to permit a single-file, zigzagging entry to the other side.

The flight from Trieste provided its own kind of agony. Victor remained sheathed within an unapproachable silence, nodding each time Joyce explained some details of the journey, accepting cups of steaming black coffee and occasionally smoking, but eating nothing, staring beyond the window into a private anguish.

They changed planes in Denmark and boarded a flight for Helsinki without leaving the airport. When they touched down forty minutes later, a package from Paris was waiting for Joyce, along with transportation standing by to convey them to the border.

It was still light when they arrived, jolting along a narrow track that pierced the snow cover between the trees. There were hushed bits of worried conversation between Joyce and the security men who conveyed them, details that had not been worked out by the series of transmissions Joyce had made on the plane. There was always a worry that the affair would not go quite according to plan. That the other side would not respect the rules of the exchange. They wanted no incident or blemish, but that was something Joyce could not guarantee.

Joyce went alone, except for the driver, who stopped several meters from the wire, allowing Joyce to walk the remainder of the distance on foot.

He went toward the opening along a plowed groove carved into the ice, his breath forming balloons of suspended vapor, like a cartoon without words.

He halted just short of the mesh, facing the tower whose window was an opaque shimmer of pale yellow light.

Joyce turned and signaled his driver. The lights of his vehicle flashed on and off, answered an instant later by the amber lights of another vehicle hidden in the forest darkness opposite. The vehicle pulled toward them quickly, trailing a thick cloud of white vapor.

Vanova was silhouetted in back, alone except for his driver, who leaned across the front seat and swung open the rear door.

Joyce went through the narrow, mazelike turning between the two fences and stepped into the car, shivering as the hothouse warmth enveloped him. He placed the file folder on the seat between them.

Vanova jerked off the strings and drew out the handful of dossiers, thumbing through them like a teller counting out a stack of new bills. He wet his finger to skim the photocopied pages and grunted occasionally, but his face remained impassive.

Joyce stared through the windshield at his own vehicle, waiting on the other side and emitting its own cloud of vapor.

Vanova stuffed the files back into the folder and turned to face Joyce.

"I could take you and these," he said solemnly.

Joyce performed an indifferent shrug.

Vanova laughed and extended his hand. Joyce took it and smiled, reflecting the other man's expansive grin.

"And we meet again?" Vanova asked, showing two gold incisors.

"In six months."

"Good."

Then Joyce was outside, head down as he trudged toward his vehicle. The temperature had dropped ten degrees.

They were waiting just inside the border of trees. Joyce could see them as they drew closer: two security men getting out first, then Victor, and then two more security men from a second vehicle that had been positioned discreetly, as if they expected Victor to suddenly bolt beyond them into the woods.

The driver wheeled the vehicle around in a wide circle to face the fence again. Joyce could see the anxiety in the security men's faces as he stepped down.

Victor was staring straight ahead, his face pale, blank of expression.

Before Joyce could reach him, a security man stepped toward him, blocking the way, whispering that a transmission had been received and offering a printed note.

Joyce glanced down at the piece of paper in his gloved hand and absorbed its meaning.

One of the security men had hold of Victor's arm, guiding him toward the vehicle Joyce had just vacated. But Joyce stepped forward and halted their motion, locking eyes with Victor.

"Michelle will live," he said softly.

Victor stared at him, not fully comprehending. But Joyce nodded and shoved the paper toward him.

"She's going to make it."

Victor bent his head, forcing his eyes to scan the paper Joyce had given him. He looked up at Joyce and his lips trembled, but he could not speak.

Joyce tucked his glove under his arm and extended his hand.

Victor drew off his glove and took it, clasping the other hand with a special force.

Their eyes met this time, Victor's darkly luminous in the descending twilight.

"Good luck," Joyce said, forcing a smile, but the words were garbled somewhere deep in his throat.

Then Victor was moving along with the others toward the waiting vehicle, which growled against the frozen ground before it pulled away, heading for the double line of wire fencing.

Joyce was left with the image of twin red taillights and a single dark silhouette moving steadily toward the amber headlights of the General's vehicle.

Then Victor was gone.

73

The angels were clothed in a light covering of frost.

Joyce strolled among them, accepting the upraised benedictions and inhaling the sharp scent of salt and the fainter odor of shellfish. It was a boyhood smell, invoking memories he had had little reason to welcome.

He threaded his way through the cemetery, taking a long, meandering route past massive granite tombstones and Edwardian mausoleums faced with dignified iron gratings.

It was one of the less fashionable cities—suburbs, really—that radiated from Boston like a series of spokes. It was a place of shabby houses sided with asbestos, one beside the other on narrow streets whose sidewalks were formed from the uneven slate of another time.

Only the cemetery had a sense of style. Was, in fact, almost palatial. And the churches, of course. Grand Gothic piles they were, each bearing the stamp of local pride. Church. Parochial school. Football played with bone-jarring intensity in the practice field across from the cemetery's pointed iron gates, providing an occasional shout that reverberated between the heads of grieving Madonnas.

It was a good day for a funeral. The sky was a flat metallic blue, spotted with narrow winter clouds that were hustled along by the chilling wind.

The mourners were in proper black. There were five in all, each stamped by a family resemblance, Joyce and the priest being the only strangers. None were young. There were no children. Imprinted into each mourner's expression was a kind of resignation, as if the one being buried had been grieved long before his actual death.

There had been a Mass for Killian two hours before, as sparsely attended as the funeral. A black Cadillac hearse transported his body. The hearse was not new, nor was the limousine that carried the family to the grave site. But both vehicles were handsome and well cared for, and that, too, was something Joyce remembered.

But there were no flowers.

The body had arrived at Logan Airport twenty-four hours before and been collected by Killian's younger brother, Kevin, a graying tax accountant who lived in Milton with his wife and three college-age children.

Joyce had exchanged several phone calls with the accountant to complete the arrangements, making it firmly understood that the coffin was to remain closed. A funeral director's van was allowed to pick up the coffin only after Kevin went through the airport formalities.

The coffin was transported back to a Gothic-fronted funeral parlor located diagonally opposite the church where Mass was said at nine the following morning. There was no real wake. The coffin remained in a closed room off the softly carpeted entrance, which Joyce visited just before eleven, when the funeral parlor closed.

Joyce observed the street from the vantage point of a second-story pool hall, looking for a telltale van housing a hidden camera. But there was none. No watchers were in place—not any that he could detect, anyway. He was alone in his interest in the remains. The intelligence community believed Killian perished in a white Mercedes that exploded in an abandoned quarry six kilometers from Cortina, his body burned beyond recognition.

Bruno had arranged for the shipment of the coffin, concocting a false identity for the corpse, based on a forged passport. Joyce only informed Killian's brother of his loss when they touched down at Logan. But he had accompanied the body across the Atlantic, traveling under another identity.

The airport authorities had no reason to suspect anything out of the ordinary. Killian was just another expatriate coming home for burial. It had worked so far, giving Joyce a beat, a full measure to operate within, before the pursuit sniffed out his trail and moved in for the kill. He had eluded his pursuers once. It was a luxury that would not be repeated.

The invocation was delivered by a muscular, red-faced priest with an astonishing spread of shoulders, whose reedy voice rose and fell in a monotonous tempo. "We commend the soul of the departed . . ."

Freed of the embroidered cloth, the dark walnut of the coffin gleamed with polish. A motor whirred, and the coffin began its automatic descent. As it sank into blackness the

TO KILL A KING

family shrank back together. Whether resigned or relieved, it was difficult to perceive from where Joyce stood. But emotion was less than evident. Killian had been their blessing and their torment, in ways he could only dimly imagine.

The priest raised his head, glancing over at the boys scrimmaging in the distance. Remembering his duty, he bowed his thick athlete's neck. When Joyce looked over again, Killian was gone.

Joyce found his way back between the headstones and exited through a side gate. He took the car he had rented at the airport on a tour of the town's older precincts, eating up time while the family gathered for a meal and said their farewells.

He cruised the windswept streets, scenting a feeling of home about the place, in spite of its wear. Joyce no longer had the same feeling about the old city. These days it was a glory of contemporary architecture and fashionable shops, complete with tourists crowding the old brick lanes now slickly refurbished.

Fancy eateries stood where the old markets once spilled out noise and produce. He became nostalgic for the homey seediness he remembered. But there was precious little left of that.

Joyce arrived at the house in Milton shortly before one. It was a large home, built in another time. White sideboard and black trim, WASP colors now flown by the upstart Irish. He realized how neatly those old prejudices dated him. But prejudice of that kind died hard in the old city, in spite of its gentrification.

Kevin Killian was solid, annuity-wise, and fast becoming a pillar of the establishment, advertised by the expensive BMW riding at anchor in the driveway for all to admire. He greeted Joyce with a smile and a firm handshake, still dressed in a tie and jacket. Joyce had been expected.

There had been a phone conversation the previous evening. Joyce had introduced himself as the consular official responsible for the arrival of his brother's body. Unfortunately he had been delayed by an urgent matter and could not be at the airport when the body arrived. He hoped Kevin understood. Indeed Kevin assured him that he did, but there was an edge of apprehension in his voice that Joyce did not rush to allay. It was clear that the brother expected such a call and was, in fact, more than a little appreciative that things were being handled with such uncommon discretion.

Joyce was ushered into a dignified library, filled with a set of the Encyclopaedia Britannica and the Harvard Classics, all bound in leather and stamped with the owner's initials. None of the books looked as if they had ever been opened, nor did the almost surgical neatness of the room hint that it was ever used. Joyce was conducted to a handsome leather Chesterfield and offered a glass of whiskey in a heavy Waterford goblet.

Joyce settled himself against the firm cushions and let the whiskey percolate a little as he exchanged some observations on the way the old city had changed, after admitting he had grown to manhood in an area that was now a black ghetto.

The other man nodded his sympathy, forcing more small talk and gamefully trying to hide his anxiety. Knowing that what would come would not be particularly pleasant to Kevin Killian, Joyce did not disappoint him.

"I'm afraid I misled you when I informed you I was with the consular service," Joyce began. He reached into the breast pocket of his suit jacket and took out a Leatherette ID.

Kevin studied the ID, glancing back and forth several times before it was clear in his mind that the man in the picture and the man seated across from him were one in the same.

Kevin handed back the ID. His features were composed, formed into a kind of terrified acceptance, prepared for the worst.

"You see, I didn't want to alarm you," Joyce said with his actor's warmth. "But I wonder if you had any idea of just what kind of activities your brother has been engaged in over the last few years?"

It turned out that the brother had a pretty good idea. He had been visited by other government agents from time to time. They hinted but never explained. In any case, Kevin knew it was going to be bad.

"There's no point in trying to smooth it over. For the last six months or so your brother has been the most wanted terrorist in Western Europe."

Joyce said this softly, watching the effect on the other man, who blinked several times as the words penetrated, then brought the glass to his lips but did not drink.

"I didn't know."

"I hope, for your sake, that's true."

He watched the accountant's eyes narrow.

"What do you mean?"

"We know he communicated with you. That you were the one person in the world he trusted."

The accountant's face lost its firmness. His eyes calculated. He hunched forward and placed his glass on the elaborately carved table separating them.

"I don't know what you mean," he said finally.

"I mean that he sent you things from time to time. Special things to put away in a safe place for him. Isn't that so?"

"I don't think this conversation should continue without my attorney," Kevin said, rising with exaggerated stiffness.

"Of course," Joyce said, all smiles and cordiality. But he made no move to get up. "We understand your need to protect yourself. But we have to consider the people he terrorized. We have to consider his victims, don't we?"

The accountant was silent.

"We want everything. I don't imagine you opened or examined any of it. That would mitigate, of course."

"Mitigate?"

"Mr. Killian, your brother was a very dangerous man. No one outside the Western intelligence community was remotely aware of his activities or his identity. Without your cooperation I cannot guarantee that that state of affairs will continue. Think about the media. They'd be pretty hungry for a story like this. You have a family, a successful business. Do I make myself clear?"

"I still think I should be represented by my lawyer," he said stubbornly. But then, Joyce expected he would be fashioned from the same briar as his brother.

"Of course. Call him."

Joyce consumed his whiskey and accepted another just to demonstrate his goodwill while he waited for the accountant to phone his attorney. It took twenty stubborn minutes for the phone to ring.

74

The attorney turned out to be both cautious and cooperative. He declined any details of the case other than the barest outline of the situation. He insisted on receipts for everything, but neither he nor the accountant had the least desire to inquire into the contents of the material Kevin had stored in a special safe-deposit box in a Quincy savings bank.

The attorney wanted nothing, other than to record that Joyce had received one unopened package containing material unknown to them. The package had a London postmark, dated within the year. There was nothing else.

Joyce left them and drove back to his hotel in Copley Square. He opened the package and carefully examined its contents.

There was an audio tape and a videocassette. There was also an envelope containing a black, leather-bound notebook.

Joyce slipped down to the drugstore in the lobby and purchased a small tape recorder. He returned to his room and slipped the cassette into the slot and snapped the button marked "play."

Killian's voice filled the room, speaking in a hoarse smoker's whisper. It was the first time Joyce had heard him speak. It was a low voice, precise in its diction, the Boston intonation still very much evident.

"Kevin, as you can see, the videocassette shows me at one of their London safe houses. But, of course, we had picked up the location weeks before. Actually we didn't know if they were going to use this place or another they had out in Kew, so we stationed cameras at both, just in case.

"I insisted on the meeting. I wanted it recorded, as a kind of insurance policy, which may make you laugh, since if you're listening to this, I'm already dead.

"In any case, we had a meeting to confirm our little arrangement. They would supply me with the targets and all the inside details on security, as much as they could pick up,

TO KILL A KING

which was considerable. Then one of my crews would finish the job.

"They were all high-level targets. They wanted to create a machine-gun effect. Kill as many of the leading political and social figures they could in the shortest possible time. Create as much political instability, disruption, and chaos as possible. The objective was to stand Europe on its ear. Then they were going to pin it on the Russians. That's why we needed Kirov. He was our link to the KGB. A real connection. Irrefutable. Not like that Bulgarian fiasco over the pope's assassination attempt."

Killian broke into a coughing fit, cleared his throat, and went on in the same low, even, compelling tone.

"The idea was to make Kirov's defection look rigged. To make it seem that he was really a plant, a double agent, who only defected so he could prepare the ground for the biggest hit of all. The Royals were my idea. The Americans weren't sure about them. They only wanted to hit political figures. But I wanted to hit them in the guts, right where they lived. Make them pay for all those centuries of oppression and what they did to our people. So that I worked out on my own."

Killian paused, a match was struck, and he inhaled.

"They expected an instant backlash against the Soviet Union. All of that fine public relations played by their new man in the Kremlin would have backfired. The Greens and their allies, all the antinuclear parties and organizations would be left flat-footed. In desperation the public would turn to the extreme right. Politically reactionary governments would come into power. Europe would be safe for the American nuclear presence. They wanted a new chapter of the Cold War. It was simple, neat, and untraceable.

"Of course, I knew when they reached their objective, I would be the first one they hunted. I want to save my people. That's why I had the pictures taken. And the other evidence you'll find in the notebook.

"Sounds insane, doesn't it, Kevin? Me doing their work for them? Them, my worst enemies. Six years they tried to hunt me down all over Latin America. I was public enemy *numero uno*. Another Che Guevara. What a laugh."

There was some coughing before he continued.

"They contacted me through an intermediary, some bigwig in the IRA. They would call off their hunt. Supply me with leads. As much cash as I wanted. All they wanted were results. And, of course, Kirov. I had to involve him. I had to make it look legit. They were willing to supply the money for that. Enough to get the Russian interested. I had to risk some of my operatives. But essentially that is the story. The rest of the stuff is in the envelope. It registers names, dates, and places. Use it if you have to. You were always a good brother. I'm sorry. Good luck."

The tape ended.

Half an hour later Joyce phoned the airport and reserved a seat on the evening flight to Washington. It was exactly where his hunters expected him to go. It was the only place he might still be safe.

75

It was state of the art. The monitor offered, a full-color, three-dimensional display of computer graphics. The subject: a detailed map of Washington, D.C. In a few moments it would diagram Joyce's movements.

Stepinak sat before the monitor, facing the image projected on the huge television screen facing him beneath the subdued lights of his underground headquarters outside London. Joyce had slipped through the net once. But it was only a matter of securely closing each option. He would not slip through again.

The first call had come from a Boston attorney to a contact in the FBI asking to confirm Joyce's identity. Tracing Joyce to a New York airport, where he had boarded a flight to Washington, D.C., had been almost academic. There was nowhere else he could go. Every other avenue of escape or refuge had been sealed, leaving only one place for his quarry to return.

Stepinak had created an enormous funnel into which his prey had fallen like a fleeing rodent, scratching his way along the metal walls in a series of futile circles that permitted the illusion of escape while inevitably drawing him to the only possible exit.

Stepinak checked the digital image at the bottom of the screen. Nine o'clock. Joyce's flight would be arriving shortly.

He allowed himself a tiny smile of satisfaction. Joyce had led him a merry chase. But now it was finished. Tomorrow's newspapers would report the car accident in which Joyce would perish.

"Touchdown," a voice transmitted over the audio.

The plane was down and taxiing to the terminal. Stepinak had considered an intercept on the field but decided against it. He would allow Joyce enough time to get through the terminal and into the streets outside before his men closed in.

"Passengers deplaning," the voice commented dryly.

Stepinak eased back to give the appearance of relaxation, but he could not repress the excitement churning through him, a kind of blood lust that accelerated through him before each capture.

"Passengers are entering the terminal."

There was a momentary pause. Stepinak heard a muffled confusion of some kind and snapped on the transmission button.

"What's happening? What's going on?"

"The quarry does not seem to be aboard the plane, sir," the voice said incredulously.

"What do you mean?" Stepinak snapped. "Your men saw him board in New York."

"I know that. I don't understand."

The screen in front of him flickered. The street grid of Washington disappeared, replaced by a familiar street in a London suburb. The camera angled toward the doorway of one of the row houses, set back slightly behind a brick fence sporting a wooden box filled with roses.

Stepinak picked up the mike in front of him and jabbed a finger at the transmit button.

"What the hell is going on? I didn't tell you to switch to this."

There was no answer.

Instead the lens zoomed back from the doorway of the house, past the roses, past the brick fence, and held on a car drawing to the curb in front of the house. A bulky man in a blue raincoat stepped out and nervously scanned the street. Another rose from beside the driver to hold open the rear door for a tall man who started for the house then, as if he had rehearsed the motion, stopped suddenly, and turned directly toward the camera, pausing before the other two stepped to his side, encouraging him toward the door, which opened to admit them.

Stepinak sat back; his eyes were hard, oily dots. The man on the screen was Roger Killian.

The lights brightened.

The national security adviser and the deputy director of the CIA entered the room. And a step behind them came Joyce.

Stepinak felt a wave of black and lost focus for a moment. His ears filled with the irregular hammering of his pulse. He struggled against the feeling of nausea and closed his grip over the back of the swivel chair in front of him.

"We have the housekeeper," the deputy said curtly. "The meeting between you and Killian has been confirmed."

The deputy took a seat behind the bank of terminals and

hunched his shoulders, folding his hands in front of him and eyeing Stepinak from beneath the dark rims of his glasses. "You are relieved of your authority, as of this moment. You have no options. I suggest you inform us of just how deep this goes."

Stepinak considered his answer, shuffling the deck to offer those who were most expendable. His eyes, calculating, shifted from the adviser's narrow form to the stocky bulk of the deputy.

"I want immunity."

The deputy turned to the adviser, who shook his head.

"The president has been informed. He wants indictments on everyone involved."

"Christ," the deputy uttered. "Didn't you stop to figure out the consequences for the agency?"

Stepinak leaned back in his chair, his gaze fixed on Joyce, a gaze filled with contempt. "It was the one sure way to accomplish what he wanted. Doesn't the president realize that? We've provided the means."

The adviser remained mute. The deputy leaned forward. "You know the game. It could get rough."

Stepinak returned his look. His expression suddenly hardened. If there was one thing he had learned, it was never to let them know your fear. "For sure." He grinned. "For everyone, when the shit hits the fan. We're talking instantaneous media. Film, tapes. The works."

"Do you think that will protect you?"

Stepinak shrugged. "I've played this game a lot longer than your boss has. You figure it out. I'm a senior intelligence official. I can document a plot to assassinate Western political leaders, creating an anti-Soviet backlash that would insure the continuation and expansion of an American nuclear presence in Europe. Think of the damage here and at home. He's vulnerable and you know it."

Both officials stared at each other, as if they expected the worst.

"What are your terms?" the adviser asked evenly.

"Full pension. Full immunity. I fade out of the picture. And no reprisals."

The deputy stared at the advisers, whose face remained a mask, blank of expression.

"I want names. The whole fucking schematic."

Stepinak smiled and tilted his head crookedly. "Tell the president he can have anything he wants."

It was dawn when Stepinak was driven away from the Hampstead estate. He felt weary. He had been hard at it for the better part of nine hours, but in the end he had given them what they wanted. It shouldn't have turned out the way it did, but he had been in the game long enough to know that nothing ever turned out quite as predicted. He had gambled and he had lost. Those were the conditions under which he existed.

He settled back against the cushions of the limousine and racked his weary brain. Several possibilities presented themselves. An arms dealership with a Brussels firm, salivating for his contacts. He could do that, or he could just coast for a while on the money he had salted away. It was a considerable sum, far more than even the most calculating suspected. He did not know exactly what he would do. Sleep on it first. He had his wife and family to consider. He would consult them sometime tomorrow.

He edged back in the seat, resting his head on the comfortable cushions. The Silver Cloud slid forward to stop for a light in the gray emptiness of morning. He half closed his eyes and noticed a slender, almost graceful, presence in a tan raincoat and banker's derby who strode toward them swinging a rolled umbrella, a rolled newspaper tucked beneath his arm.

Stepinak almost smiled at the man's total nonchalance. It was to keep assholes like that safe in their smug little shells of comfort and class that he had grubbed and sweated. Fuck them. Fuck them all.

He shut out the image, closing his eyes as a terrible wave of weariness settled over him. He did not notice the driver's release of the security catch on the door beside him. Nor did he notice the deft motion made by the man with the umbrella, who took a dancer's step toward the curb and pulled the door beside Stepinak open.

Only then did he sense danger and open his eyes.

The newspaper flapped toward him, then was drawn away, revealing a highly polished cylinder attached to the short barrel of the KG-9.

He never actually saw the face of his executioner. Turning, he propelled himself toward the door opposite, one hand gripping the handle while the other tore inside his jacket for the blunt handle of the automatic pistol that was secured in a leather holster within the thick roll of fat beneath his armpit.

The 9mm machine pistol spat its cargo of ammunition in hisses of muffled sound. It was obvious the man firing them had a great appreciation for the automobile. Not a single shell tore into the expensive fabric of the Silver Cloud's interior or marred the finish of the specially selected and matched wood trim.

The weapon was dropped onto the carpeted floor. The door swung closed, and the Rolls-Royce drew away from the curb, emitting wisps of white exhaust. The man with the rolled umbrella and derby hat continued along the silent streets, heading toward the city now waking to another day of trade and toil.

76

He should have been charmed. After all, it was less a city than a magnificent outdoor theater, a perfect stage setting. But too much knowledge of its recent history had poisoned the effect. Far too much blood and anguish for him to be taken in by the performance completely. No, Joyce was not really charmed. Comforted, perhaps, for it was a survivor's city where gray-haired men like himself, also missing various bits of their anatomies, sipped dark coffee and savored creamy pastries, dreaming alone in the dark recesses of a baroque *Kaffeehaus*.

He made the usual little trips, to the Belvedere for the baroque collections and the regal Kunstshistorishes to see the Brueghels, touring the museums and several handsome churches he usually returned to. But he was just marking time between appointments. His real purpose lay in a different direction.

Each day he found them walking along the same stretch of esplanade beside the darkly flowing river. He was careful to arrive a little early, instructing the driver to keep a discreet distance while he remained unseen behind tinted windows.

A stranger would have noticed the man first, tall and imposing with an actor's presence. His hair was streaked with silver, worn long over the nape of his neck. He was pushing a woman in a wheelchair. Her hair was tucked beneath a kerchief, dark glasses protecting her eyes, her hands clothed in leather gloves. But it wasn't until you were close that you noticed the skin of her face and neck and realized just how badly she had been burned.

Then you noticed the boy, or rather, the good-looking young man of fifteen or so, pale and slender enough to be taken for several years younger than he actually was. He walked a slight distance ahead of the other two, so that at first glance he did not seem to belong to them. But in a little while an exchange of a word or a glance made it apparent that he and the man were somehow connected. And then you noticed the resemblance and realized they were father and son.

TO KILL A KING

What confused you at first was the color of the child's hair. It was the color of pale straw. The child's skin was also pale, as if he had been ill for some time and was just now beginning to recover. The woman had the same appearance of delicate frailty. Both she and the boy took a kind of sustenance from the man, who was careful not to keep them out too long.

Joyce would turn the car around and follow Victor back to the apartment house near the Ringstrasse where the three lived and where Victor spent part of each day translating for an institute that specialized in analysis of various East European trade and technical operations. The apartment was comfortable, as well as convenient to both hospitals where Michelle and Alexi continued their treatments.

It was Joyce who had actually found the apartment, just as he had arranged for Victor and Alexi's emigration and the boy's program of chemotherapy. He had also arranged for Victor and Michelle's first encounter, though he had not been present when that occurred.

The treatments were now in their third year. Joyce received summaries of both patients' progress from time to time, as well as the usual routine surveillance on Victor. Otherwise he did not interfere. He generally avoided the city unless important business drew him there. This trip was an exception. His schedule had been changed to include a series of meetings in Rome that allowed him an extra forty-eight hours, so he had decided to come.

He toyed with the idea of picking up the phone, of calling Victor and arranging a meeting, but in the end he decided against it, contenting himself with observation from a distance. He would continue to play his role from afar, seeing to it that their needs were met, keeping his part of the arrangement made long ago in the stillness of a forest in Finland.

He watched the trio cross the wide, tree-lined boulevard. The boy leading the way, watching for traffic as Victor carefully navigated the woman's wheelchair. When they reached the entrance of the apartment house, Alexi opened the door and Victor wheeled the chair around to draw it in backward. Alexi reached out to help, taking Michelle's hand in his own.

Victor smiled at the boy, who looked up at his father with an expression that mingled awe and love. Then the three disappeared inside.

Joyce waited a moment, his gaze framing the place where

Victor and his family had been the instant before, allowing their final image to register its imprint on the deepest part of his consciousness. Then he tapped the driver's shoulder.

Joyce settled back against the cushions as the car started, watching as it entered the stream of traffic that would carry him around the Ringstrasse and back into the world beyond.